Lady Avely's Guide to LIES and Charms

MATRONLY MISADVENTURES
BOOK 2

ROSALIE OAKS

eBook ISBN 978-0-6453005-7-4
Print ISBN 978-0-6453005-6-7

Contents

Prologue

The Duke of Sargen stumbled slightly as he meandered down the gravel path towards the hedge maze, stones crunching under his boots. The night was growing cold but his blood was warmed with whisky. Rather a lot of whisky, truth be told. This cursed house party would drive any man to drink.

Damn Lord Garvey, inviting them all, and then flirting with Judith right in front of him. Judith was a widow, for God's sake, with Nicholas dead less than a year ago. Besides, if anyone was going to flirt with her, it was going to be Dacian. He had waited long enough. Damn Garvey for being a cursed lecher.

Even apart from the lascivious Lord Garvey, it was bloody torture, being so close to Judith and yet so far, after all these years. Seeing her day and night, yet knowing he couldn't rush her. She was angry with him - again. They had fought yesterday in the greenhouse. Dacian smiled a little to himself, remembering how her hazel eyes had flashed with fury, and her pale cheeks had coloured. It was good to see some spirit enliven her. She'd seemed so lost after Nick's death.

And Dacian couldn't even blame her for being angry.

She was furious at both of them. For Dacian had helped keep

"""

Nick's secret - how could he not? It was up to Nick to tell Judith about his bastard child. Dacian couldn't whisper it in her ear. He had long ago resolved not to interfere in their marriage, even if it meant sleepless, agonising nights and too much whisky on too many occasions.

He heaved a sigh. The moon hung high above the gardens, round and full, and he slowed his steps as he entered the maze. The yew walls loomed around him, still and thick. Perhaps his time had finally come. Could it have been Judith who had written the note, directing him to the maze? He doubted it, but allowed himself a moment's hope. She had said her piece yesterday; maybe now she would forgive him, and allow some closeness between them again. Maybe she would apologise for pushing him in the chest yesterday. He could tease her about it, and ask her to do it again, and capture her hands and draw her close...

No. It was much more likely Isobel who had written the note. If so, now was the perfect time to puncture any expectations that Lady Vosse might have formed. God knows he had already told her that it was over between them, last year, when Nick died and a secret, wretched hope had been born in his heart. Yet Isobel seemed determined to take this blasted house party as an opportunity to renew their intimacies.

Lord Garvey's suggestive comments had not helped matters. It was almost as if he expected his guests to be debauched. He had set up this accursed maze like a satyric pleasure garden, with coloured oil lamps at intervals and dark corners in others. There were nude statues throughout, and various ribald displays. The Apollo alcove, where Dacian was headed now, was one of them: the stone figure of the god held his bow over his shoulder casually enough, but the quiver at his thigh was thrust at a suggestive angle. At certain hours of the day or night, its shadow cast an obscene silhouette. It was just the sort of thing that amused Lord Garvey's vulgar tastes.

Unfortunately, it also meant that it was highly unlikely Judith had chosen the spot for a rendezvous. Unless she hadn't noticed the erotic, shadowy double entendre? Dacian somehow doubted it. Judith might pretend to be calmly aloof from life, sedately retreating into matronhood, but he knew those ludicrous mobcaps hid a passionate nature. He could prove it to her, if she liked... He could think of several ways to do so, and they all ended with Judith naked and completely undone beneath him.

His blood heated at the thought of it but his footsteps were now quiet on the grassy path. A creature rustled through the hedge, but Dacian ignored it. He was almost upon the Apollo statue. Could Judith possibly be waiting for him, in the black gown trimmed with gold that she had been wearing earlier in the evening? Would she smile at him - wryly, warmly - and put her hand out to him? Forgive him? Maybe she would finally forget Nick. Could Dacian even ask it of her?

He didn't care. He was goddamn tired of playing second fiddle.

And Dacian knew exactly how to make her smile, how to bring light to her eyes. That, in truth, was why he had stayed away. One didn't bring light to the eyes of another man's wife. Especially when that man was your best friend since childhood.

Stealthily, his heart beating fast, Dacian rounded the corner of the hedge. Then he came to a halt, startled.

Lord Garvey was in the Apollo clearing. His profile was to Dacian: his blond hair bare in the moonlight, his stocky, muscular legs planted wide, his hands on his hips. His expression was one of appreciation and ownership.

For an infinitesimal moment, Dacian thought the man was simply admiring the Apollo statute, or the obscene proportions of its shadow. Then he saw a woman leaning back upon Apollo's stone calf, on the other side of the stone quiver.

Her gown was undone to her waist, the curve of her breasts

exposed to the moonlight. Her neck was arched back, her face turned away to expose the delicate line of her jaw. Her hands were splayed on the plinth. She was opening her body to Lord Garvey's gaze.

Dacian's first thought was, of course, that it was Isobel. Then he saw that the woman's hair glinted blonde, without the curl of Isobel's russet red, and the woman's curves were lusher than the viscountess's slender form.

And the gown was black with intricate gold trimmings.

Lord Garvey said something, which Dacian could not make out. Something proprietary in tone, as he took a step forward, brushing a hand down his pale yellow waistcoat. He leaned the same hand on Apollo's thigh. The woman lifted her head and looked at Garvey, her eyelashes fluttering open.

It was unmistakably Judith.

Dacian froze in place, his head swimming. Rage coursed through him, bewildering and painful. He could feel his power thicken in the air, volatile and eager. Then Garvey lifted a hand and placed it on Judith's breast, leaning forward to kiss her neck.

Dacian leapt forward. "UNHAND HER."

Lord Garvey pulled back sharply. He turned his head, but - insolently - he did not step away. Judith's eyes widened in horror as they fell upon Dacian.

"Sargen." Garvey's voice was uneasy yet belligerent. "What are you doing here?"

"Do not touch her again." Dacian bit out the words.

A faint swallow marked Garvey's throat, but still he sneered. His hand stayed resting against the stone next to Judith, as if marking ownership.

"Back off, Sargen. She is mine now."

Dacian lashed out with his Gift.

It was a violent, satisfying surge of power. The Impact

grabbed Garvey and spun him round like a doll, flinging him aside. The quiver cracked off Apollo and shattered to the ground.

Garvey's head hit the corner of the stone plinth with a thud.

A deathly silence followed. Judith was pale in the moonlight, her eyes darting from Garvey to Dacian. She fumbled with her gown, pulling it up. Dacian glared at her, betrayed and furious. How could she dally with that posturing ape, instead of him?

She turned and ran, into a corridor of the maze.

"Wait." His voice was loud, but she did not stop. As she was about to disappear past the hedge, she turned briefly, casting one more terrified look back.

At the same time, Dacian thought he heard footsteps closer at hand. He spun round but saw no one in the clearing. When he looked again, Judith was gone.

He returned his gaze reluctantly to Garvey and strode forward. Yet at his brusque command to name his seconds, Garvey did not move. He was lifeless on the grass, face-down. Dacian leant in and shook him roughly.

"You damn scoundrel. Get up!"

The body was limp. Garvey's head rolled back, his eyes open.

Dacian stared down. An awful sense of inevitability came over him. He looked round again, with the impression of being watched. Had someone witnessed his uncontrollable rage, other than Judith?

He knelt and put his fingers to Garvey's wrist. The flesh was warm, yet no pulse beat through the veins.

"God damn it." Dacian withdrew his hand, filled with hatred. "You damn well deserved it."

Even as he said it, guilt surged through him. He hadn't meant to kill the bastard. He had tried to temper the Impact, just enough to throw the lecher aside. It was confounded ill luck that Garvey's head had met stone with such force.

Not ill luck. Ill judgment. And his own lack of control, let loose by his rage and jealousy, and the sight of Judith in Garvey's arms.

Dacian cursed long and vividly, barely noticing the cold damp under his knees. Then he stood, feeling shaky and suddenly almost afraid, staring at the corpse at his feet. His mind was a little unbalanced from the exertion of his Gift, mixed with whisky, and his head was spinning. What the devil was he to do now? He already had two deaths to his name. They were long ago, it was true, but a third might be enough to hang him. Even if he was a duke. Especially because he was a duke. And if the law of the land didn't fall upon his head, the Musor Custos might well do so.

He had misused his power. Again. This time, they might very well take it away from him.

For a moment, he considered going quietly. Then he scowled down at Garvey. The devil take it, he wasn't going to let that cur's death neuter him. He'd rather flee England and make his own way abroad for a while. What was left for him here, after all?

He turned to look at the place where Judith had disappeared, golden hair flying out behind her, and remembered her last glance of horror. He swallowed. The taste of spirits was now bitter at the back of his throat.

He should leave now, and quickly.

HE LEFT GARVEY LYING THERE, and went to find Biscuit.

Otherwise known as Lord Anthony Triskett, Biscuit was an old friend of Dacian's from their school days. They had helped each other out of trouble before. Furthermore, Biscuit was one of the few who knew about Dacian's Gift.

Although Biscuit himself didn't have any Musing to speak of, his family tended to produce Travellors. It was hard to hide magic from a boy when his younger brothers would vanish and reappear right in front of him. So Biscuit had become accustomed to covering up his brothers' misdeeds, and then, when he became Dacian's friend, the duke's.

Biscuit could help now, if only Dacian could find him.

He crept out of the maze, looking round warily. The gardens were deserted, the trees and shrubs flattened by moonlight. Despite the late hour, candlelight glowed from the drawing rooms and bedrooms. A cold breeze pulled at his cravat, which was already loosened by the night's events. Biscuit was probably drinking and gambling with Lord Vosse and Kenneth. Dacian gnawed on his lip. Kenneth was Lord Garvey's brother. How was he to pull Biscuit aside without alerting Kenneth to his brother's death?

Luck was with him, however. As he trod up the terrace steps, Dacian saw a dark figure sitting on the ground, leaning against a pillar, smoking a cigar. The gleam of moonlight and embers showed the aristocratic features and slender wrist of Lord Triskett.

"Sargen." Biscuit nodded amiably. "Join me? These French rolls are damn good." He took a long draw of smoke.

Dacian's shoulders dropped with relief at the familiar sight. "I can't. I need your help. I've killed Charles Garvey."

Biscuit's eyes widened and he coughed violently. "You've *what?*"

"By accident - I swear." Dacian hesitated. "Well, I did mean him harm, but I didn't mean to kill him. I flung him aside and he hit his head on a stone plinth."

Biscuit stared fixedly. "Good God. You sure he's dead?"

"Fairly sure."

"*Dead* dead?"

"Yes! I checked for his pulse. Snuffed out like a candle, from a paltry blow to the head, damn him." Dacian sighed. "Now I have to leave the goddamn country."

Biscuit's mouth was agape, but he shut it at this. "You think you'll hang? Good Lord, man. Surely not, if it was an accident." He scrambled to his feet, grinding the cigar on the pillar, orange sparks spluttering to the ground. "I guess they won't see it like that, will they?"

"No," said Dacian bleakly. "Third time unlucky. Worse, the Musor Custos might hear of it."

Biscuit grimaced. "Lord. What do you want me to do?"

Dacian jerked his head. "I can ride for Exeter and catch a boat, but I need your help to set the scene first. Do you still travel with your duelling pistols?"

Biscuit wasn't one for violence, but he liked shooting wagers. He could be counted on to have his guns on hand for a gamble or a game. Yet his face fell. "Not this time, I'm afraid." Then his expression lightened. "Garvey has a nice pair in his gun room. I could fetch them instead?"

Dacian grimaced but nodded. It seemed worse to shoot the man with his own pistols, but if there had been a duel, they might very well have used Garvey's guns.

Biscuit vanished into the house while Dacian waited in the cold night. There was no sign of anyone about, not even the footsteps he had heard in the maze. A bird-bath gleamed, flat with the faint iridescence of moonlight, like an eye of judgment.

After a while, Biscuit returned, and Dacian led him into the hedges. Once they were out of sight of the house, Biscuit stopped and pulled a gun from within his coat and handed it to Dacian.

The steel landed heavy in his hands, weighted with what he about to do. The hedge maze loomed over him, suffocating. Yet it was far better that Garvey was found dead by duelling than flung by some mysterious power. Dacian had to fool the Musor Custos, and by doing so, sentence himself to exile.

Selfishly, Dacian knew he was also thinking of Judith. She might guess he had killed Garvey with his unfettered Gift, but she couldn't know for sure. She had fled before Dacian had realised it himself. If he and Biscuit staged a duel, she might still think he had fought Garvey honourably after his slip of temper. Like a gentleman. God knew, she also disapproved of duelling, but at least it gave the other fellow a fighting chance. Not so if you simply pounded him to death with a magical, unseen Impact.

And then Dacian would leave to save her name. For if he was hauled before the courts, Judith's reputation would be blackened by the scandal. He couldn't do that to her, even if some part of him felt that she deserved it.

He always had been a fool for her. Even now.

Curse Judith to hell and back. This wasn't the first time she had devastated his life. A black sense of despair swept through him.

Grimly, he made his way back to the Apollo alcove. Biscuit trailed behind, still muttering muted protests. Then the sight of Garvey's crumpled figure silenced his friend. Dacian turned to face Biscuit, the statue of Apollo behind him, the stone quiver now truncated. Dacian curled his lip at the irony of the God of the Sun overseeing this wretched deed of darkness.

"Twenty paces away," he rapped out. "Fire on the count of three."

Biscuit frowned. "Shouldn't we make it appear like suicide? We can leave your name out of it."

"Someone was here. Two people, in fact. And I did kill him, Anthony. It is only right that people know it. I can't consign him to a pauper's grave, and his family to that kind of shame. He has a daughter, for God's sake."

Biscuit heaved a sigh, but obediently pulled the second duelling pistol out. "You always were a damned honourable sort."

He pointed the gun in the air, then lowered it again. "Will you use your Travelling charm to make it to Falmouth?"

Dacian glanced down at his topaz ring, the unusual blue appearing black in the night: a gift from Biscuit's family. "There's no point wasting it, when I can ride Gallant. I doubt anyone will give chase. I'll be long gone by the time anyone makes it down here."

"Very well," said Biscuit. "Don't stay away for too long. I'm sure it will all blow over soon enough." He waved his gun casually, his thin shoulders hunched against the cold.

Gritting his teeth, Dacian wrenched Garvey's body around so they had a clear shot. Grim horror spun through him, looking down at that lax face, ugly in death.

A short time later, the sound of two pistol shots rang out, shattering the quiet of the night, leaving Garvey with a convincing bullet wound through the heart.

Hands steady, Dacian worked his own gun in Garvey's grip, then let it fall.

"Time for me to go."

HOURS LATER, his hands still stank of the old metal. The boat lurched in the pitiless emptiness before dawn, black waters churning around him. He was headed to France, where he would travel across land to Spain.

He wouldn't return to England for another nine years.

In which a lady is affronted

Nine Years Later

A Truth Discernor is just as susceptible as anyone else to charms and Illusions.

  - from *Lady Avely's Guide to Lies and Charms*

"You saw *an Illusion*? Of me *half-naked*?"

Judith stared at Duke of Sargen, aghast, amid the roses at the Sargenet estate.

A private arbour encircled them, the archways thick with small red flowers. A sweet fragrance hung in the autumn air, and a fountain bubbled in a round pool. It was late morning, and the sun warmed the stone and threw a soft glow through the blooms. Judith, sitting on the bench by the pool, had no thought to spare for the beauty around her, for her mind was grappling with the duke's revelations.

He claimed he had seen her *half-clothed* with Lord Charles Garvey, at the fatal house party nine years ago. He had described her gown - black with gold trimmings - and said that it had *fallen down to her waist*. This was right before the duke had killed the said (and wretched) Lord Garvey.

There was one problem with this account, in that it could not possibly be true.

Yes, Judith had been at the house party, and yes, she had conversed with Lord Garvey on several occasions. Perhaps she had, regrettably, even allowed some flirtatious remarks. However, she had certainly not been *half-clothed* or with her gown *down to her waist*. She was a respectable matron and widow, then and now! Clearly his grace was under several misapprehensions.

The duke had begun to realise it too. "Someone set me up," he said grimly, his scar whitening on his forehead. "And used your image to provoke me."

His anger became palpable, making the roses quiver. He stalked out of the private rose arbour, too furious to stay still, his tall figure striding under arches that were laden with cream and yellow flowers. The tender passion that had bespelled them moments earlier had completely vanished.

Judith hurried after him, her brow creased, trying to make sense of it all.

"Aren't you rather leaping to conclusions?" she called, though she was also angry and unsettled.

"Don't you see, Judith," he growled. "I was manipulated. Someone took my weaknesses and exploited them. They played me like a harp!"

Judith expelled a breath. Anything less like a harp, she could not imagine. Dacian stormed ahead, his brow thunderous, his fists clenching with impotent rage.

Except it wasn't impotent: she could feel the power fluctuating in the air.

"Calm *down*," she said. "Restrain yourself, for goodness' sake,

Dacian. If you weren't so quick to anger, then none of this would have happened!"

He spun on his heel, but his hands flexed out and the roses all breathed a sigh of relief. There was a long silence. Slowly, the buzzing of insects resumed.

"I am calm," he said quietly. "I promised you that I would never lose my temper like that again, and it is true. I studied under a master Impacter in Spain; a bull runner turned monk. He taught me how to control my power."

"I could feel the pressure of it a few moments ago," she observed warily.

"Just letting off steam," he replied. "Like a kettle, so I don't explode."

"Please don't explode."

"I won't." He gave her a wry grin, then his lips compressed again. "But can you not see that this is an insult to my honour? And to yours?"

Judith put her hands on her hips. "I am well aware of the insult. You, at least, were not depicted in lustful embrace with Lord Garvey!"

Dacian's fists curled again. "The whole thing is abominable. We must find the culprit and string him up to dry. I'm going to Garvey House today and I'll shake the rat loose, whoever it was."

Above him, heavy cream blossoms nodded approval in a faint breeze.

Judith, however, shook her head. "You can't just storm off to Garvey House and make wild accusations."

"Why not?" He glowered.

"The Edicts, for one." She dropped her hands from her hips and walked a few steps closer, lowering her voice even though they were alone in the arbour. "How will you avoid talking of the magicks if you are claiming a complex Illusion was used against you? Not to mention that you will drag the whole awful matter of the duel back into light, when you have only just returned to England. There is probably still a warrant for your arrest gathering dust somewhere, and the family might demand that it be honoured, especially if you turn up full of recriminations."

Dacian's frown deepened. "Damn it."

"I am usually right, you know."

His mouth quirked reluctantly. "What do you suggest, then? I cannot let it rest, Judith. Nor should I. Someone deliberately intended Garvey's death, and used me as the instrument."

She chewed on her lip. "Who could possibly have done it? Who stood to gain from his demise?"

Dacian's eyes narrowed. "Well, we know who inherited the estate. His brother, Kenneth Garvey. They weren't on the best of terms, either, as far as I recall."

"No." Judith cast her mind back, remembering scenes from long ago. "They argued about Lord Garvey's engagement. Do you remember it? Charles announced his betrothal to Miss Selina Pelling, from the neighbouring property. Kenneth did not hide his dislike of it."

"Yes," said Dacian slowly. "He probably didn't want an heir to displace him in the line of succession."

Judith nodded. Lord Garvey had only been blessed with one daughter before his first wife had died in childbirth. "The estate would have been entailed to Kenneth, with no male children to inherit."

Dacian scowled. "Kenneth is our culprit then. I'll damn well wring his goddamn neck."

"Wait!" Judith held up her hands again. "We don't know that for certain. Is he an Illusor? You can't just throttle him!"

"Can't I?" Dacian spun on his heel and stalked away again. "I'll bloody well force the truth out of him, see if I don't."

She hurried after him. "You just promised that you can restrain yourself."

"I can; that doesn't mean I will."

"They won't let you into the house! You killed Lord Garvey, for goodness' sake. The door will be barred to you."

His fists clenched. "I'll force my way in."

"Very gentlemanly," she said dryly. "And then what? Kenneth will deny it, and you'll be worse off than when you started, having revealed your hand. We need some pretence. Something that will allow us to visit Garvey House and make discreet enquiries."

"Us? Judith - "

She cut him off. "It is my reputation that was besmirched, your grace. And I have a useful talent, do not forget. I will be able to tell if Kenneth lies."

Dacian stopped and swung round.

"No," he said. "We cannot both go. If Kenneth Garvey sees us together, he will soon realise that his little scheme has been revealed. It would only be a matter of time before you and I would talk on the matter and realise we had both been made fools of."

"Not necessarily." She gestured for him to walk beside her, hoping it would calm him. He reluctantly fell in step, and put out his arm. She took it, feeling a bolt of awareness as she touched him. Only a short while ago, she had placed her hand on his beautiful face. She had been about to kiss him, to surrender her body and heart to him. Then he had ruined it all with his mortifying revelations. She flushed again, angry that he had believed such awful things about her.

She cleared her throat. "We are English, after all. You *have* only just broached the matter to me today, after nine years' silence." That fact still hurt; that he had not bothered to write or see her since Lord Garvey's death. Though now she understood a little better why.

He shot her a look from under his brows. "Regardless, it will put Kenneth on his guard to see us together."

"If Kenneth is indeed the guilty party."

"*Whoever* the culprit may be, they will be alerted if they see us."

Judith had to admit that Dacian had a point, and she let out her breath in a long whoosh.

The solution was clear, but his grace wasn't going to like it.

"Well, then," she said firmly, "the alternative is that *I* go alone to Garvey House. Stokesford is west of here - on the way to Cornwall, after all."

They had reached the end of the arbour and he drew them to a halt by the apple trees, frowning. The leaves danced in the sunlight as a soft breeze ruffled his black hair. "I do not want you tangled up in it, Judith."

"I am *already* tangled up in it. Furthermore, my Gift can help uncover the truth better than your violence."

He heaved a sigh but did not deny it. "And what excuse will you give for calling on Garvey House, marchioness?"

"I don't know yet," she admitted. "I need time to think."

"No harebrained schemes," he admonished. "I need time, also, to tie up the loose ends here."

The last few days had been eventful, culminating with a villain locked into Dacian's cellar, and a mother and child injured. The household was in an uproar, and the duke was needed to put it in order. Judith nodded stiffly in agreement, though she rather thought she'd be better off going to Garvey House alone. She didn't want Dacian to be arrested for murder, as much as he might infuriate her sometimes.

"Though," he added, "I must report back to London soon, and see if my Gift can be of use, with the threat of invasion hanging over us. Not that I believe for a minute that Bonaparte will manage to fight past Nelson."

"Indeed not," she said staunchly, though her heart cowed a

little to think of Dacian joining the fight. Was that the real reason he had returned to England now? His refuge in Spain must have become precarious last year, with the rupturing of the Treaty of Amiens. Though she didn't believe for a moment that he had been sitting by idly while the French piled their troops into Spain.

She opened her mouth to ask, but forestalling her, Dacian hastily changed the subject. "How is little Otho doing? Has his arm improved?"

"It still pains him, I believe." Judith allowed the diversion. "He smells strongly of lavender, willow bark, and some other dreadful herb slathered all over him. I would rather advise some of that Spanish drinking chocolate as a suitable remedy."

"Is that so?" His lips twisted in amusement. "Don't forget I only let you try that recipe when you promised to stay longer at Sargenet: I rely upon your honour in this."

"Indeed," she said coolly.

"No galloping off to Garvey House." He gave her a penetrating glare.

She put her nose up. "I do not *gallop*."

"Of course not," he agreed, chastised. "We shall determine a plan together, Judith."

She nodded, but she avoided his gaze. They turned back to face the house, the massive bulk of it rising above the rose garden. Dacian pulled her a little closer. "This is not how I intended this morning to unfold," he said ruefully.

Judith drew a breath. "No doubt you were hoping I'd pull down my bodice for you."

"No!"

She raised an eyebrow, hiding her hurt under a show of asperity.

He grinned. "Well, yes - but not yet. I just wanted to...talk. Properly, for the first time in years."

"Hm." She knew the truth. Dacian had been hoping for a wanton display like the one he had witnessed nine years ago. "Talking is what you had in mind, was it?"

His cheeks flushed a dull red. Judith began walking back to the house, pulling him with her, both of them now in embarrassed silence. The intimacy that had flourished between them a short while ago was squashed and burnt in the flame of her embarrassment.

At the cold entrance hall of Sargenet, they parted ways. Judith trod with dignity up to the Gold Room and pushed the door open with relief. Sunshine poured through the curtains, lighting up the golds and maroons with warmth and splendour.

Alone at last, surrounded by opulence, Judith threw herself on the bed and cried.

She did not even have her companion Miss Marigold Cultor to confide in, for the vampiri was asleep behind the cupboard. Judith was glad, in a way, as all her frustration and mortification could pour out uninterrupted.

How *dare* Dacian think for *one minute* that she had ... *cavorted* with Lord Garvey? That she had undone her gown? And displayed her...upper body... for that cretin? What had passed through Dacian's head? Clearly not much. If he *had* been in possession of his senses he would have known she would *never* do such a thing. He must have been drunk, lustful, and stupid, as was his stupid wont.

Did Dacian not *know* her? Is that how he truly saw her: as a loose woman, freely sharing her favours at a house party? Judith gritted her teeth. She now knew *exactly* why Dacian had made his advances among the roses today. He had led her to the decadence of the secret hot spring, hoping she would undo her bodice for *him*.

The thought was mortifying. Worse, she was aware of a sense

of desolation. She had believed, for a short moment, that he loved her.

Certainly, he had claimed to be *wild with jealousy*. Judith sniffed into her pillow, squashing the tender shoot of hope that sprung up within her breast. Dacian's jealousy probably did not signify much. It was likely a matter of masculine dominance. The duke was all too accustomed to being the object of female desire: to see Judith accepting the embrace of Lord Garvey would certainly have spiked his *jealousy*.

She shuddered. The whole thing was so dreadfully sordid. Who had dared sully her own image with such a vulgar pantomime? And how dared Dacian believe it?

Tears slipped down her cheeks. Again and again, she opened her heart to him, and then he did something to show how little he valued it.

Well, enough was enough. He would soon learn that she was not to be trifled with, and she was not going to undo her bodice for him, let alone the guards around her heart.

Emotions spent at last, Judith tried to console herself with a nap. Ordinarily, she regarded naps as a cure for all ills. Yet she had slept in too late that morning, and sleep would not come.

Instead, after lunch, she sat down at the rosewood writing desk, gathered her composure, and cast about for an excuse to visit Garvey House.

She tried to remember what she knew of Kenneth, the new Lord Garvey. She had seen him often in London over the last few years, his short, plump figure a common sight in the ballrooms and drawing rooms. He was unmarried, and didn't seem intent on shackling himself down, for she couldn't recall him courting any one of London's eligible maidens. After the scandal of his brother's death, society had turned a rather cold shoulder towards the Garveys, which, now that she thought of it, seemed unfair.

Garvey had died violently and scandalously, but it had been the duke who had delivered the fatal shot.

Of course, if it were a matter of taking sides between a duke and a mere lord, society would rally round the duke. Most likely, everyone blamed Charles Garvey for his own death, and tarred his brother with the same brush, even if it had been the duke who had been in the wrong. Kenneth had not allowed it to daunt him, however, and through persistence had held onto his place in the ton - helped, no doubt, by the fact that he now possessed the title.

For Charles - the late Lord Garvey - had been a widower when Dacian killed him. His wife had died years earlier in childbirth, leaving behind a stillborn and a young daughter. Judith recalled a piquant little face peering down from the upper floors, next to her own daughter, Elinor, as both of them avidly watched the house party before they were shooed back to the nursery. What was her name? Georgina Garvey? Poor little thing, to lose her mother so young, and then her father. She was a sickly creature, too, prone to coughs and lung complaints, possibly as a result of the grief she had suffered.

Judith sat up straighter at her writing desk. The girl must be nearly of an age to enter society now. Perhaps Judith could extend a hand of friendship. As an old family acquaintance, it would not be too remarkable if she invited Georgina Garvey to visit Elinor in Devon, or even London for Elinor's wedding. Kenneth should leap on the chance to give the girl a little experience in polite company before attempting the perils of a season. And if Kenneth was reluctant, Judith could appeal to Georgina's grandmothers: the old Lady Cordelia Garvey (a bit of a battle-axe, as she recalled), and Mrs Harriet Bollopher (who was a sensible woman). Both of them lived at Garvey House, so it was the perfect excuse to call upon them there.

She smiled to herself. Dacian could not fault her plan, even if it had no room for him in it. As a dignified widow, she could simply call on the dowagers, and under the guise of extending kindness to Georgina, make some discreet enquiries. Harriet, at least, would probably welcome the visit, matron to matron.

Judith would need her most respectable mobcap.

In which a moustache makes an appearance

Charm, of a personal kind, can be most deceiving in and of itself.
- from Lady Avely's Guide to Lies and Charms

FOR THE REST of that day and the next, Judith and Dacian avoided each other. Judith occupied herself with sewing a tiny primrose gown for Marigold, and the duke had plenty to keep himself busy with his family and managing the estate, as well as employing two new footmen and instructing his steward, Mr Lewis.

Judith envied Dacian's indomitable energy, for she found she was quite exhausted after the recent events and revelations. She needed several naps and cups of chocolate to restore her mettle.

She was aware, too, that she was running out of time. She was supposed to be visiting Castle Lanyon in Cornwall, to conduct a cursory inspection before her children removed there with a roost of bats. Then she needed to travel back to London for Elinor's wedding. There was no time to dilly dally.

So at dinner, Judith made her announcement, while Dacian was safely lodged behind the dining table.

"I will be leaving tomorrow," she said calmly. "I intend to call upon Garvey House, so I must be on my way."

Dacian frowned from his seat. "Is that so, marchioness?"

Lady Agatha, Dacian's sister, was the only one present at dinner. The rest of the family had asked for trays to be sent to their rooms after the recent tribulations. Lady Agatha was there simply out of pig-headedness, determined to show that she could rise above it all with true English fortitude.

Now, however, Agatha's face became disapproving.

"Garvey House?" Her dark brows lowered, and she paused in the act of sipping from her spoon. She shared the same striking, dark colouring as Dacian. "What on earth can you want with Garvey House?"

It was a chance to see if Judith's story would pass muster. "I thought I could invite Miss Georgina Garvey to visit Elinor," she replied. "I imagine she is due to come out next year, if not already."

"Why do you care about the Garveys?" asked Lady Agatha suspiciously. "They are low ton, soaked in scandal, with which they managed to muddy Dacian too. You cannot have forgotten that ghastly duel? You should keep away, especially now that you have moved up in the world, Lady Avely."

"All the more reason to help them," said Judith coolly. "You surely do not believe that the sins of her father should be visited upon poor Miss Garvey? She will need some support if she is to appear in London."

Dacian looked unhappy but he nodded reluctantly. "It is a good notion, Judith. I would like to make amends to the family, myself. Perhaps I should come with you."

Judith frowned at him, but she was not called upon to refute this preposterous idea.

"Make amends?" Agatha set down her spoon in affront. "Dacian, whatever Lord Garvey did to provoke a duel, I am certain that he deserved it. You, as a duke, should not admit to any fault."

Dacian's face went stony. "Agatha, it *was* my fault that he died. Regardless of the circumstances, I should not have killed him."

"That dreadful man must have done *something*," she retorted. "We all know that duels are a matter of honour. I am sure society condones your actions even if the law does not. After all, you *are* a duke."

Judith took a sip of her cream of onion soup, though it tasted rather sour. "Not *all* of society condones duelling. There is a reason it is illegal: in our enlightened day and age we should not need to resort to violence."

Agatha sniffed. "Everyone knows Lord Garvey liked to seek out trouble." She shot a sideways glance at Judith and took up her spoon again. "Far be it for me to repeat what *I* heard about that night."

Judith raised her brows. Ordinarily she did not like to play the gossip, but this was a matter of murder. She could be forgiven for her interest in exactly what Agatha had heard. "I confess I am curious, Lady Agatha."

Agatha gave her a penetrating stare, then she turned her head and dismissed the butler, Broughton, from the room. Once the man had discreetly closed the door, Agatha spoke.

"If you must know," she murmured, "people said that Dacian found Lord Garvey forcing his attentions on Lady Vosse." She shuddered. "Poor Isobel."

Judith's spoon wavered in her hand, spilling a drop of soup on the white tablecloth. "Oh. I see."

Lady Isobel Vosse. Her involvement made all too much sense. There had been gossip about the duke and the attractive red-haired woman years ago, scandalous gossip that Judith had tried to ignore. It was more evidence that Dacian was nothing but a rake, but Judith hadn't wanted to know the intimate details.

Indeed, irritation at Lady Vosse was one of Judith's more vivid memories from the cursed Garvey house party. Watching her twine those auburn locks around her fingers as she widened her green eyes at Dacian had been *exceedingly* annoying.

She risked a glance at Dacian now. He was staring at his bread, a faint redness in his cheeks. Exactly how much truth had there been in those stories? Perhaps there was reason enough for everyone to have assumed it was Lady Vosse who had sparked Dacian's masculine instincts.

Agatha smiled in triumph. "So you see, everyone is in perfect sympathy with you, Dacian. For once your stupid temper was useful. I imagine that Lady Vosse was very grateful to your intervention, given that her husband is so useless."

It was true that Lord Vosse appeared to have *other* sort of interests, which did not include his wife. So much so that Isobel Vosse had been free to do as she pleased, even if it involved a handsome, libertine duke.

Dacian remained silent.

"What a sordid story." Mechanically, Judith began eating her soup. "Let us not mention it again."

"Precisely," agreed Agatha. "Dacian, you will do well to keep away from the Garveys."

"We will see," he replied shortly. "You cannot dictate my movements, Aggie, as much as you may have become accustomed to running this house."

When the strained meal finally ended, Judith made her excuses rather than suffer the perils of the drawing room. She retreated to the Gold Room once more and found Marigold awake, sprawled on her bed.

The vampiri's brown curls were in disarray, and a bare shoulder peeped from under the orange-gold silk that Judith had given her.

"You look a bit peaked," Marigold observed as Judith shut the door. "Especially for someone who ought to have been napping all day."

Judith pursed her lips and sat down on the settee by the window. "There have been unfortunate developments, I'm afraid."

"Oh?" Marigold sat up with interest, and her silk fell further down. Grimly, Judith wondered how much further it would have to fall before it mimicked her gold and black dress nine years ago.

With some embarrassment, she explained how Dacian had been provoked into killing Lord Garvey. She left nothing out. If Marigold (as she hoped) were to come to Garvey House, she would need to know the details. She could be useful in uncovering an Illusor, for vampiri could sense when magic was being cast.

Marigold's eyes widened. "Sunbeams! How dare someone take your image in vain!"

"Precisely my feelings."

"And a duel of pistols at midnight! That's a bit disgraceful, isn't it?"

Judith gave her a wry look. "No more than my exposed flesh, I wager."

"Oh, that doesn't concern me much." Marigold wriggled her naked shoulder suggestively. "Who cares if flesh is exposed? Duels, on the other hand, are usually fought at dawn, aren't they? The duke must have been very angry to ignore the usual protocols."

"True." Judith frowned. "He hasn't told me exactly what happened. I heard the gunshots, however. It must have been an impromptu fight, spurred by drink." Duelling was a terrible practice, a violent and stupid way to settle quarrels. And Dacian's indulgence in them was yet another reason to spurn his advances.

Glumly, Judith fed Marigold from her wrist, cementing their bond even though they both agreed it was a temporary measure. They had only joined forces recently, and Marigold was a flighty sort of bat, reluctant to commit to any one Musor for long. Still, while they were bonded, Judith was duty bound to feed and care for the little creature.

Sighing, she leaned back against the pillows and picked up her sewing, wondering if Dacian would try to stop her from leaving tomorrow. She would have to be prepared for his intervention.

It came sooner than she thought. Just as she was finishing a sleeve, there was a rap on the door.

Half expecting the duke, Judith swallowed her disappointment when she saw that it was Robert, her husband's illegitimate son. The sight of his rich brown hair and blue eyes still gave her a shock of recognition; even if she had been inclined to deny the relationship, it was there before her eyes, in Robert's resemblance to his father, Nicholas.

Robert gave her a tentative smile and Judith returned it. She had been carefully trying to befriend him. He was only a few years older than her own son, Peregrine, and she had decided it would be better if Robert joined their family, as was only right. When she had first learned of his existence it had been a painful thing to accept, but over the last few days of spectre hunting and foiling a murderer, she had grown rather fond of him.

Now, however, he spoke formally. "Lady Avely, his grace invites you to partake of chocolate in the study."

Robert was still dressed in the Sargenet footman's livery of green and gold. Earlier that day, Judith had tried to convince him to cast it aside, but Robert had said he was happy to be a footman while the household was short and in chaos besides. He owed the duke that much, he claimed. Judith thought that was a rather generous view of the situation, for it was by Dacian's (and her) neglect that Robert had ended up employed by Lady Agatha in menial service.

"Oh, his grace does, does he?" said Judith grumpily. "What if I were sleeping?"

Robert allowed himself a small smile. "He bade me promise you that it will be the best Spanish recipe."

"Hmm." That meant it would contain cayenne and doradozón, a rather delicious addition to the usual spices. Judith was tempted. Damn the duke. At least, she noted, Dacian was not breaching the privacy of her own room this time with his chocolate rendezvous. Good. A business-like meeting in the study was far more appropriate. Especially now Dacian knew she was unlikely to *expose her breasts*.

She bit down a flush of mortification, and stood up. "Marigold, would you like to join us?"

Marigold sprung up. "Yes, please!" She flung her gold cloth aside and Robert hastily averted his eyes from her naked form. "Just let me attire myself more appropriately."

Judith told herself that they could be a little bit lax with the Edicts in the duke's household, and the vampiri could act as a sort of chaperone.

Not that she would need it now.

ROBERT LED them through a darkened house, for everyone else had withdrawn to sleep. The study, when Judith entered, was lit by several candles. Dacian was sprawled in an armchair with a glass of whisky in his hand. He lurched to his feet when Judith came in. Marigold was tucked in her pocket, out of sight, and now (fortunately) dressed in a blue gown.

"Ah, marchioness," drawled Dacian. "Robert will fetch the chocolate. I think we should add some spirits to it tonight." He lifted up his glass of liquor suggestively.

Judith gave the duke a disapproving frown as Robert clicked his heels together and vanished.

"Don't frown at me, Judith. It's been a hell of a few days. I deserve a drink."

She sighed in acquiescence. "Very well, but we have much to discuss."

"We do indeed." Dacian sank back into his armchair. "What did I say about harebrained schemes? I don't like this plan of yours to go to Garvey House."

"It is not harebrained. It is perfectly respectable for me to call upon Lady Garvey or Mrs Bollopher." She moved forward into the room and took up a defensive position behind a table, sitting in a high-backed chair that suited an air of authority.

"You can't go alone," he insisted.

"I most certainly can. I am not a maiden anymore. I am a widow of advanced years."

"Pfft," he scoffed. "You may be a widow, but you're still young, Judith, with plenty of life in your limbs." He let his eyes trail down her body suggestively, and waved his whisky glass. The amber colour glowed in the candlelight.

"As much as you like to cast me as a *merry* widow," she snapped, "I must inform you that you are bound to be disappointed."

"Will I?" He smiled lazily. "After all these years? I really hope not, Judith."

Marigold chose this moment to pop her head out of Judith's pocket, with an interested look. "Your grace, are you propositioning a lady while drunk?"

Dacian's eyes widened. "Me? No." He cleared his throat and took another gulp. "I was trying to make a point. What was it? Oh yes. Lady Avely can't go alone to Garvey House. It might be dangerous."

"I can promise you," Judith said coldly, "that I will not be tempted to enter into any duels."

Dacian looked pained. "Miss Cultor, please tell her that I must accompany her."

Marigold looked undecided as she glanced from one to the other.

Judith shook her head crossly. "You said yourself we cannot be seen together."

"Ah," said Dacian, putting his glass down with a decisive clink. "But I have my own harebrained scheme."

"Oh, really?" Judith leaned into her high-backed chair and braced herself. This sounded ominous.

"I will go in disguise." Dacian held up his other hand to forestall her objections. "Hear me out. I will travel separately as a Mr Fortnew, a simple man of business. We can both stay at the Golden Bat, the inn closest to Garvey House. That way I am on hand to assist you."

"Are you mad?" Judith shook her head. "It is an entirely foolish notion; I cannot imagine you as a Mr Fortnew."

"Nonsense, I am accustomed to travelling under a false name. Do you imagine I travelled around Spain as the Duke of Sargen?" Dacian's lips quirked. "Be grateful that I am not suggesting I appear as the Count of Querrento."

Judith rolled her eyes. "A small mercy, indeed, but this is England, Dacian, not Spain. The odds are that you will be recognised, even after ten years' absence. People don't forget a duke. I am much more likely to go unnoticed *without* you."

"Ah, but this will be no ordinary disguise. I will take Robert with me."

Marigold clapped her little hands together. "Ooh, so he can assist you with an Illusion? This could be fun."

"Might as well fight fire with fire." Dacian grinned at Marigold, and knocked back the last of the whisky in his glass. "I was contemplating a moustache. And brown hair. What do you think?"

Judith ran her eyes over his thick, black locks. "It will scarcely be sufficient." His black hair *was* a distinctive Sargen trait, but simply changing his hair colour wasn't going to disguise his cursed cheekbones. "It is a ridiculous idea. Robert cannot constantly Illuse you. He will become Bewildered."

"Not constantly." Dacian leaned back and crossed his legs. "I'll stay in my room all the time, and you can hire a private parlour for our discussions. I'll only need a moustache when the servants come in."

Judith frowned. She didn't like the idea of being alone in a private parlour with the duke. It sounded...intimate. Like this current situation, which was far too convivial in tone.

"No," she said. "I don't have the funds for a private room. Not to mention that my reputation will suffer if I entertain a strange man there."

Dacian tipped his head thoughtfully. "You're right, perhaps you should already be acquainted with Mr Fortnew. I can be *your* man of business - assisting you with your new property!" He grinned like a child who has just performed a trick.

Judith drew a breath to refute the notion, but at that moment, a soft tap came at the door. Marigold vanished under the table, but it was only Robert, who entered the room carrying a large wooden tray, topped with molinet and two tall cups. Dacian waved him in.

"Robert, my dear boy, how are you at moustaches?"

"Excuse me, your grace?" Robert set the tray on the table. He was very formal today, Judith observed. He was probably trying to make up for his recent lapses into Bemusement.

"Can you paint one on my face? A suave brown moustache, if you would be so kind. Give it a try."

"Now, your grace?"

"Yes, now, for God's sakes." Dacian sat up. "I am trying to prove something to Lady Avely."

Robert shot a glance at Judith. She rolled her eyes and set about pouring a cup of thick, steaming chocolate. She was going to need it, she could tell.

Robert cleared his throat. "Certainly, your grace." He stared at Dacian's face earnestly and a moustache drifted into view. It was thick and brown, like a caterpillar. Judith shuddered.

Marigold popped her head out from under the table and observed it critically. "I'm not one for moustaches, myself."

Robert startled, and the moustache fell away. He nodded politely at Marigold.

"I need a mirror," announced the duke, who was peering down the end of his nose. "Robert, can you fetch one, please? There is no point in conducting your artistry if I can't see it. And next time, make my hair brown too. I need a thorough disguise."

"Certainly, your grace."

Robert retreated once more and Judith took a sip of fortifying cocoa, breathing in the soothing aroma of spices. "You shouldn't treat him like a servant, you know."

"I know. I'm treating him as a co-conspirator. Whisky in that?" Dacian picked up the decanter.

"Tsk, tsk," said Marigold, hauling herself up the leg of the table like a small monkey. Ordinarily, she would stay hidden from servants, but with Robert it didn't matter. Technically, they were all currently in breach of the new Edicts, for vampiri were meant to keep themselves separate under King George's oppressive new protocols. The Edicts, passed in the heat of the French Revolution, forbade vampiri to appear in public, or consort openly with their blood companions. Musors and vampiri had always kept apart from the uninitiated, but now they weren't given much chance to talk even to each other. Unless one simply ignored the rules, as Marigold was prone to do.

Judith sighed and proffered her cup for the whisky. "Why

not?" She was going to need more than cocoa, she suspected. Dacian poured in a liberal dose. The resulting brew was fiery and potent, and she sipped it as Dacian dosed his own cup. Marigold shook her head disapprovingly, now sitting cross-legged on the table once more.

"Where is Wooten?" Judith asked. Wooten Willoughby was Dacian's own vampiri companion, a personage of melancholy moods and immaculate attire.

"Oh, he wanted some quiet time," replied Dacian airily. "All the irregularities lately have worn down his fortitude."

"You mean, you knew he wouldn't like this moustache nonsense." The whisky glowed warm in Judith's belly.

"Ha, yes," said Marigold. "A moustache is far too interesting for Wooten."

"The moustache is a good idea." Dacian rested his cup of chocolate negligently on his thigh, though he did not deny Judith's accusation. "You might as well accustom yourself to it, my dear, because I won't let you go alone."

Judith took another sip of whisky-laced chocolate, pointedly ignoring him and his endearment.

"She won't be alone." Marigold bristled. "She'll have me."

Dacian raised a brow. "You're a bit small. And you sleep in the daytime. No offence, Miss Cultor."

Marigold huffed. Judith sighed, nursing her cup, as Robert returned carrying a large brass hand mirror. The duke took it and bade the moustache to re-appear.

Robert stood with his hands clasped behind his back, and stared fixedly. A large brown caterpillar appeared on the ducal face.

"No, that's too fat." Dacian tilted his chin up. "Make it slightly thinner. No longer than my lips."

Robert complied, until there was a rather elegant moustache

sitting atop Dacian's lip. If anything, thought Judith morosely, it simply highlighted his sensuous mouth, and counterpointed his high cheekbones.

"No," she said. "It's no good."

"I rather like it." Dacian preened into the hand mirror.

"You still look like *you*."

"Robert, what about brown hair?" Dacian's black hair became a mousy brown, matching his moustache. Suddenly he looked a bit unfamiliar, for Robert had also taken the liberty of concealing the familiar white scar on his forehead. Judith stared.

"Don't forget his eyebrows," put in Marigold thoughtfully. "They stand out a bit."

Dacian's striking eyebrows softened into a more muted colour, becoming rather less thick and untamed. Everyone examined him. He was, regrettably, still handsome.

"If I may suggest," said Robert diffidently, "a bit more of a curl?"

At his words, the moustache lengthened slightly, thinning and curling at the ends. In counterpoint, the wave in Dacian's hair deflated, becoming very straight and neat.

"Perhaps," said Judith, entering into the spirit of things, "a mole is required."

"An excellent notion," agreed Robert, grinning. In a blink, a large brown mole appeared on Dacian's left cheek.

The duke peered into the hand mirror. "Not too sure about the mole."

Neither was Judith, but it was time to assert some authority. "Your grace, if you want to come to Garvey House, you must have the mole. It is the only thing that will possibly make this work."

She took another gulp of hot, spiced cocoa. Perhaps the mole would act as its own sort of chaperone. She couldn't possibly kiss a man with a curly moustache and a mole, even if his cheekbones and dark eyes remained irrepressible.

Dacian frowned. "I don't like the mole."

"You will put your vanity aside," said Judith austerely. "Robert, it appears you will be coming on a little expedition with us. May I introduce you to Mr Fortnew, my man of business?"

In which a butler is obstructive

Servants lie all the time, usually at the bequest of their masters.
   - from *Lady Avely's Guide to Lies and Charms*

ROBERT TENTATIVELY REQUESTED AN EXPLANATION, and the duke simply replied that they were investigating the circumstances of his long-ago duel with Lord Garvey. "I may have been misled by an Illusion," said Dacian, and he spared Judith's blushes by not elucidating the exact details. "Judith thinks she can reach the bottom of it, but I insist on accompanying her, and now you must too."

Robert nodded slowly. "Very well."

Dacian's reticence reminded Judith of a pertinent fact: that she had not yet told Robert the nature of her own Gift. He knew, undoubtedly, that she was a Discernor, but he did not know the specifics.

Accordingly, when Robert led her back to her room that night, Judith stopped him outside the door. Marigold had flown off on some adventure, so unfortunately she wasn't there to smooth out the following confession.

"Robert," Judith began. "I must tell you something."

He held the lantern aloft, turning to face her. "Yes, my lady?"

"Call me Judith, for goodness' sake," she said uncomfortably. "Do not forget we are family now."

Robert said nothing to this, and she wondered if she had overstepped. He had not yet claimed the relation, even if *she* had decided it was the right thing to do. Well, perhaps taking him into her confidence would further that aim. After all, Elinor and Peregrine knew of her Gift, and they had been quite cross that she had kept it from her own children for so long.

"I must inform you that I am a Truth Discernor," she said baldly. "I can tell when someone lies, by the tenor of their voice."

Robert's eyes widened a little. "Oh."

"It is not an exact art, for although I know when someone is lying, it doesn't always tell me the truth."

"That explains quite a bit." Robert frowned. "It's why his grace had you question all the servants... and why he is letting you go to Stokesford."

"I don't know about 'letting'," said Judith. "But yes, it makes me useful in ferreting out secrets."

"I see."

"I thought you would like to know, especially if you are going to help us discover such secrets."

"Indeed." Robert cleared his throat. "I appreciate the intelligence." If anything, he looked rather discomfited by it.

"And," she added, for it seemed opportune, "are you certain you want to come to Garvey House with us? You are under no obligation to do so, you know."

He hesitated. "It is difficult to say no to his grace. And he has offered to help me choose my profession afterwards."

Judith repressed a huff of disapproval. "You do not need to

rely upon his generosity going forward. You have a place waiting for you in Cornwall as part of the Avely family."

He stiffened slightly. "Just because I am coming to Garvey House does not mean that I have decided to continue on to Castle Lanyon."

Judith coughed to cover her awkwardness, for she had indeed thought that to be the case. "I can hear *that* to be the truth, at least."

Her little attempt at humour fell flat, however, for Robert merely bowed his goodnight, and retreated down the hallway.

As she turned her doorknob, she thought dismally that he had withdrawn even more from her.

Curse it. She ought to have remembered that people didn't like Truth Discernors. No one liked having their little white lies and exaggerations exposed. Sighing, she let herself into her room, hoping that she hadn't just miscalculated.

THE FOLLOWING MORNING, Judith was set to depart in the duke's unmarked carriage. She had decried this as unnecessary but Dacian had overruled her objections, saying that it was his honour at stake and she would take the damned carriage, and he would pay for her private parlour at the Golden Bat. He had told his coachman, Patrick, to regard Lady Avely as his new mistress for the next while, and not to confess his true master.

In the cold light of day (and without the softening edges of whisky), the whole plan seemed foolish in the extreme. Judith only allowed it to persist because Dacian's little disguise meant that Robert would accompany them. It would give her further opportunity to talk with the boy, and convince him to come to her new castle in Cornwall. Surely they would both grow closer together as they endured 'Mr Fortnew's' company together.

Robert was saying goodbye to Lewis, his good friend who was also the steward at Sargenet. Lewis was scowling, as usual, his black hair scraped back to expose the enviable Sargen bone structure. He clapped Robert on the back and wished him luck, even as he looked as if he rather wished he could join the fun. But the duke needed someone to stay home and help Agatha run the estate.

A chill autumn breeze plucked at Judith's skirts as she stepped into the carriage, handed up by Dacian. Marigold was tucked into her valise, already aboard, and Robert leapt up to cling to the rear step of the vehicle. He was insisting on maintaining the role of a footman, though Judith had invited him again to dispense with formalities. At least now he had abandoned the green and gold Sargenet livery, for it was imperative that no one in Stokesford connected her with the Duke of Sargen. Instead, Robert now wore plain black and accompanied Judith as a manservant. She was determined that this little charade would only last as long as they were in sight of Sargenet.

Dacian bowed over Judith's hand as he helped her into the carriage. "God speed, marchioness." He held her fingers longer than was necessary, and lowered his voice. "I'll follow this afternoon, after I have seen to a few pesky matters. Wait for me at the Golden Bat."

Judith nodded. Of course, she had no intention of waiting tamely for him at the inn. She could visit Garvey House that very day and make her first enquiries. No time to lose, after all. It would be quite convenient if she could wrap the matter up before his grace even arrived in Stokesford.

The coachman set the horses into motion, and she leaned back, relieved to put the ducal estate behind her. She had what she came for: Robert now travelled with her.

They drove through the dark Sargenet woods and Judith heaved a sigh as she peered out at the thick trees. She had walked through these woods so many times and each time it had taken on the character of her own mood. It had been the gentle bosom of her first courtship with her husband Nicholas, and the cold witness to her stumbling grief as she left with the knowledge of his love for Anna Thane. It had been an enchanting, private world in which the duke strolled with her, soon after, and its leaves had whispered in ecstasy on the day she had walked to Sargenet in hope of a ducal declaration among the roses all those years ago. It had been dark and indifferent as she was delivered home with her heart punctured. Then black and mocking, full of shadows, when she fled again, after Dacian lied to her on that fateful night.

Returning twenty-three years later, it had witnessed her pilgrimage to confront her husband's illegitimate child, and seen her face the duke again after his long absence abroad. She had been glad to see him in the woods, with a secret hope lurking in her breast, her pulse quickening as he smiled at her.

Now the forest was cold and impassive, the trees rearing up on either side with bleak implacability. The woods were witness to her own foolishness, calmly judgmental. It was clear now that Dacian had only wanted a dalliance, a chance to ravish her in the rose garden. Like he had with Lady Isobel Vosse, and countless others before and after.

Outside, clouds gathered above, making the woods gloomier. She pulled her shawl close around her. It was time to put aside such fruitless rumination and unpick the mysterious circumstances of Lord Garvey's death. Her hand drifted to the lapis lazuli pendant resting on her bodice, hoping it would grant her clarity, serving in its function as a Talisman Stone.

Reluctantly, she conjured the memory of Lord Garvey in her mind. He had been in his third decade when he died, with swarthy good looks topped by thick blond hair. He did not, of course, compare to the Duke of Sargen for masculine beauty, but there were plenty of women who were happy to receive Lord Garvey's attentions. Lord Garvey had even flirted with Judith at the house party, she recalled, with some joking remarks and caressing looks. She had allowed it only because she'd known Dacian was watching, and she'd been so angry at him. She had reasoned to herself that Dacian wouldn't mind, because he had Lady Vosse hanging off his arm.

She frowned. Someone had been watching their tangled web of desire. And someone had taken advantage of it. The thought was infuriating.

Dacian was quick to blame Kenneth Garvey for his brother's death, and it was true that Kenneth had an obvious motive to eliminate the threat to his inheritance. Yet there may have been others at the house party eager to trouble Lord Charles Garvey. Perhaps they had not even intended his death, in antagonising the duke, but simply a cruel prank. However, they must have known of Dacian's reputation for duelling...

Tapping on the front aperture, Judith communicated her change of plans to Patrick. Then she stuck her head out the window and ordered Robert to come inside. He simply shook his head. Testily, she sat back down. Young men could be so stubborn.

Within an hour, the carriage rattled up the long drive to Garvey House. Judith looked down at her navy-blue skirts, and adjusted her matching cap with its white lace ribbons, and tucked her lapis pendant away. It was time to play the concerned matron. It was a role she was well suited to, no matter what Dacian might imply. And most people only saw the outer accoutrements of character and looked no further.

She peered out the window to see the familiar shape of the Renaissance structure. Garvey House was smaller and more elegant than Sargenet, built of white limestone and curved gracefully where the bay windows and oriels jutted out. Window panes reflected the opaque grey of the clouds, and a lawn swept down in great swathes between gravel paths.

Yet despite its tasteful lines, the house had a shuttered look. The grass was long, and the gravel unraked. Huge ash trees lined the far drive, their branches a riot of yellow and orange. The leaves had been allowed to fall unchecked, and some scuttled along the road before them. The windows were closed, curtains pulled shut against the gloomy morning.

The carriage drew up, and the rumbling wheels fell silent. No servant came out to greet her, and Judith repressed her doubt and gripped her reticule tightly. She would be roundly defeated if the Garveys were not even home.

Robert opened her carriage door, and she stepped down, boots crunching on the brown leaf litter. She tutted. A cool wind crept under her shawl, tossing her lace ribbons and rustling the leaves. Resolute, she marched up to the front door and knocked, glad that Robert was standing behind her.

She had to knock loudly twice more before the door finally swung open.

A burly man stood there, with a thick thatch of brown hair, bloodshot eyes, and a pugnacious chin. He was about the same age as Judith. He frowned suspiciously, quite unlike the manner of an implacable butler. Yet he was clothed in the neat garb of an upper servant, with a dark coat and short white gloves. Judith couldn't help but wonder if they had been hurriedly thrust on.

"Yes, my lady?" His tone, at least, was subservient enough, though Judith could hear the falseness of it.

"I have come to visit Lady Garvey," she announced. "Or, failing that, Mrs Harriet Bollopher." Either matron would do, though Lady Garvey was higher in rank, with Mrs Bollopher (Lord Garvey's mother-in-law) a poorly tolerated poor relation.

"Lady Garvey is not at home." On this man's lips, the polite refrain seemed even more like a lie. What is more, Judith's ears could detect a flat echo. She gave a sigh of relief. It was indeed a lie. At least one quarry was in the den.

She allowed him the platitude, however. "What of Mrs Bollopher?" she asked. "My errand concerns her too."

A fleeting look of discomfort crossed the butler's face, flattening his lips. "I am sorry to inform you that Mrs Bollopher passed away two years ago, my lady."

Judith stared, for no lie coated his voice this time. "Harriet? Dead?" A sharp pang of regret spun through her, that Harriet's dignity and patience had been snuffed out. The woman had been little more than an unpaid servant in the Garvey household, yet she had borne her lot with quiet fortitude, looking after her daughter's child, Georgina, and helping manage the house with an eagle eye. "When did she pass?"

"A few years ago. Good day, my lady."

The butler went to close the door in her face. Judith, recovering from her shock - at both the news and his conduct - wedged her foot in the way. "Wait a moment," she said firmly. "What about Lord Kenneth Garvey? May I speak with him?"

"Lord Kenneth Garvey does not live here," was the cold response. "He resides in London."

Again, the butler spoke the truth. Judith frowned. It was strange that the new lord and master of Garvey House had not taken up residence. "Well, I must insist on speaking with *someone*. My visit concerns a matter of some importance. Lady Garvey might not be home for others, but she *will* be home for me. Tell her-" she hesitated, "-that Mrs Avely is here." Her new title might confuse the issue, whereas Lady Garvey must surely remember Mrs Judith Avely.

The burly man returned her gaze balefully. "You misunderstand me, my lady. No one is home. Lady Garvey has gone to visit family in the north. She will not return for some time."

Judith's frown deepened. Now his words had rung with the

tinny echo of a definite lie. She doubted Lady Garvey had *any* family in the north, and she certainly wasn't visiting them. "Let me see her granddaughter then, Miss Garvey."

"Miss Garvey accompanied Lady Garvey."

Another lie. Judith pursed her lips, affronted, then fumbled in her bag for her card. "Very well, if you *must* be difficult, here is my card. I will call again tomorrow, on the chance that they have returned," she said ironically, raising her brows. She could only hope that he would carry the message to Lady Garvey, who might change her mind.

The man took the card, his eye falling upon the name written there. "Indeed, my lady, though I don't believe they will return for some time."

Judith pursed her lips in disapproval. Why didn't the man simply stick to 'not at home'? Lady Garvey must have given very strict instructions to receive no visitors, if her servant felt compelled to weave such an insistent falsehood.

"Wait," she said. Reluctantly, the man paused, though she could tell he was itching to be rid of her. She adjusted her cap. "Such a shame that the family is away. I was a good friend of Lord Charles Garvey." This was not true, but the butler had no way of knowing it. "I might pay respects to his memory, by walking his maze. I know he was so proud of it."

The butler's expression froze, but before he could object, Judith turned on her heel and descended the steps.

"A moment, my lady," he called after her.

"Just a little stroll," she called sweetly over her shoulder. "In honour of the late Lord Garvey. I'm sure you understand."

He glowered. Then, as she drew away, he shut the door with a snap.

She told Patrick to walk the horses, and nodded at Robert to accompany her. No need to take unnecessary risks. And rather than stroll, her step was quite brisk as they followed the drive around the house.

"What did you think of that man?" she asked in a low voice.

"He seemed like a groomsman elevated above his station," Robert replied thoughtfully, remaining two steps behind her, which was most irksome. "Is Garvey House in dire financial straits, that it needs to employ such bad staff?"

Judith nibbled her lip. Perhaps Charles Garvey had died in debt. If so, it was even more important that she see how Miss Georgina Garvey fared.

"He was lying," she remarked. "Lady Garvey *is* at home."

"Useful to know," said Robert, but reserve coloured his tone. She had the feeling that he didn't really like her Truth Discernment. Of course, that was why she usually never told anyone! She had thought Robert might take it in his stride, with their recent adventures, but it seemed she was wrong.

The yellow ash leaves crunched under their feet, a breeze rustling the branches overhead. Judith rounded the corner, and then pulled to a halt, surprised.

The back grounds were in stark contrast to the front. The maze, off to the left, was neatly pruned and glossy. The gravel terraces were raked. Tidy lawns framed both, interspersed with well-kept beds of roses. This side of the house showed love and care, and clear signs of occupancy.

Proceeding more slowly, Judith walked forward, looking for further signs of life. The lower back windows glinted, cleaner than the front ones, and with the curtains open to allow in the afternoon air. Yet she could not see anyone.

Sticking to her story, they approached the maze, which was set at right angles and at some distance to the house. She knew from experience that the maze was shaped like a clover leaf, with the 'centre' in the top leaf but only reached after a torturous circumnavigation of the whole. Drawing in a determined breath, she stepped in, Robert at her heels.

The green walls loomed above them, the leaves thick and impenetrable, the way only wide enough to take one person abreast. It was as she remembered: the narrow walkways providing a shelter from the wind, and a sense of being enclosed in some private world. Red berries of autumn showed on the yew branches, like bright drops of blood. At intervals, they passed white stone statues set into the yew, the first one of Pan, and another of a woman pouring water.

Judith stepped quietly, dreading and hoping that she might somehow find her way to the Apollo alcove. The grass pathways were smooth beneath her feet, and she wondered how Lady Garvey managed to maintain the grounds so well. And why not the front of the house?

Yet, as their path wound them round the back laneways of the maze, the neat clipped hedges gave way to an overgrown wilderness. The yew grew unchecked, bushy and crowding close together, making the walkway unnavigable unless Judith pushed against the foliage. Weeds marred the path below. The back - and centre - of the maze was neglected and overgrown. Eventually, unable to push further, Judith pulled to a halt and faced Robert.

"Strange," she remarked. "Why is only half of the maze clipped?"

Robert glanced round nervously. "I don't know, but I don't like it. The duke wouldn't want you wandering around in here, Lady Avely."

"Nonsense. And please call me Judith. We are friends, at least, are we not?"

"Er, yes." Still he left off her name.

Irritably, Judith became aware of a thick, cloying fragrance that hung on the air. Looking round, she could not see any flowers, despite the wilderness. It was an oddly familiar scent. Had it been in the maze nine years ago?

In the sudden silence, she also heard something, rustling low on the other side of the hedge. Some wild creature? Or human footsteps?

The sound died away. Judith put her hands on her hips and turned to face Robert. "And I give you warning that I will not allow you to be my footman when we reach the Golden Bat. You must be there as my son, even if it is only as a ruse for a while."

His eyes widened. "Er..."

Judith felt suddenly abashed. "I mean, if you would be amenable to that arrangement."

There was a short silence as she walked past him and busied herself with leading them away from the untamed hedges. It was with relief that she saw the path clear a little and the hedges recede to a more civilised distance.

Eventually Robert spoke behind her. "I don't think I should pose as your son. It wouldn't be...appropriate."

"Appropriate?" There was some note of discord in the word. Was Robert fudging some other hesitation? Still, she was glad he had finally stopped My Ladying her. "You are my husband's child," she pointed out, taking a brisk turn. "I cannot in good conscience have you in the role of my servant."

She glanced back, to see Robert awkwardly shake his head. Then he said, "It is easier to play the servant. At least then I know exactly what is expected of me."

Again she had the sense that he was not being entirely honest with her, even though his words did not sound with the concavity of a lie. "Surely Taunton inducted you into the ways of the gentry?" Robert had attended Taunton Boys' School for several years, sent there by the duke when Anna Thane died, along with another boy, Lewis.

"A little." There was a short silence. The quiet of the green maze seemed to invite confidences, so she did not press him. "Yet I was raised as the son of a blacksmith."

Judith paused before another turn, examining the different avenues while being careful not to look at him. "That need not determine your destiny."

He sighed. "Yes, but I confess that I do not want to abandon my mother's name - and my father's - so easily."

She took a sharp breath in, hearing the truth in his voice. So this is what bothered him.

Anna Thane had rejected Nicholas Avely, and raised her son as Robert Steer, son of a blacksmith. Only when Anna's husband died, and she became ill, did she write to Nicholas, begging him to take care of Robert. It was understandable that Robert held a strong loyalty to his mother, and his surname, and did not wish to claim a new mother. Especially when he had been consigned to the position of a footman due to Judith's neglect.

Perhaps he resented Nicholas too. She could not blame him.

Judith stiffened her spine. "I quite understand, and I will not press you into any relation with me." There was an uncomfortable silence, where she felt quite mortified. "Now, have I misjudged a turn somewhere? Surely we should have reached the outer ring by now."

"If we are lost," said Robert, with a cheerful tone that rung rather hollowly, "the maze is only doing its job."

"Indeed."

After a few more turns, she had to confess that she was completely disoriented. Each avenue looked much like the last, and even when she recognised a statue, she could not remember how to proceed from there. The thick walls seemed to press closer, and she began to feel concerned that they would be turning about for hours. The way was made even more difficult by coming across untamed corners which balked their passage.

Then she rounded a corner, and pulled up short again. "I recognise this."

It was the Apollo alcove.

The statue of the god was set back in a curved recess in a hedge. He held his arm aloft, holding a bow, with robes draped seductively across a muscular body. A broken quiver of arrows angled awkwardly at his side, and Judith was glad to see that the suggestive silhouette had been reduced. As was tradition, his face was beautiful and aloof. Examining it, she couldn't help but compare the god's serene visage to Dacian's beauty, and find it lacking. Dacian, after all, had more vitality and intelligence, as well as such firmly sensuous lips.

She shook her head slightly. This was no time to be mooning over a statue. Here was the scene of the crime, where the Illusion had been cast. She turned, observing that the alcove was pruned, and not let to grow wild like the further reaches.

Looking round, she saw only the opaque walls of yew hedges. Where had the Illusor hidden to cast their pantomime? The banks were sufficient to hide behind, but an Illusor would need to have line of sight to cast the Illusion.

Perhaps nine years ago, the maze had not fully grown, and there had been gaps between the leaves. Now, however, Judith could not see how someone could throw the Illusion without being seen themselves.

Unless they were also in the clearing, in plain sight.

She narrowed her eyes, examining the statue. Could someone have hidden behind it? That would take a certain boldness. Another possibility occurred to her. Who had been with Lord Garvey that night? There must have been *someone* under the Illusion of Judith.

Could it have been Lady Vosse, after all? Might she have thrown an Illusion up over her own indiscretions, to keep her reputation intact? Had she the gall to cast Judith's visage over her face, to hide her own tryst with Lord Garvey?

With an angry swish of her navy blue skirts, Judith swept past Apollo. "I think I know the way from here."

WITH SOME DIFFICULTY, Judith managed to at last lead Robert out of the maze, finding an overgrown exit on the other side. The narrow walkway opened onto a wide avenue of poplars, and the sudden sense of space provided a welcome relief. The slender trees shivered and glittered in the breeze, their leaves turning gold. It was a lovely promenade, but the path, Judith saw, was overgrown again, and the stone border in disarray. From this side of the property, it once more looked neglected and abandoned.

She and Robert slunk around the outer rim of the maze, making their way back to the house. As they rounded the last curve, they saw the gleaming edifice of a glasshouse, set on the southern angle of the house. It was a pretty structure with arching roofs, but Judith kept close to the hedge and examined the house as it came into view. As she hoped, she finally caught sight of movement in one of the windows. She froze, putting out a hand to stay Robert.

A face peered from the second story oriel. It was pale under long dark hair, and it turned as if searching the grounds. Feminine features pressed close to the glass, with a red ribbon tied above the ear. Judith shrank further into the shadow of the maze.

Just then, however, the watcher saw her. In a flash, the girl withdrew, vanishing behind a curtain.

Even at this distance, Judith could recognise the startle of fear.

That most certainly had been Georgina Garvey, in her grandmother's drawing room. Judith well knew that the second story oriels were situated in the drawing room, with a fine view of the grounds and glasshouse.

The butler was confirmed as a liar. Yet why was Georgina hiding? And why was she afraid?

Judith stepped out into the open, marching back round the house and to the carriage with her head held high. Robert, curse the boy, helped her up into the carriage and then insisted on hanging off the back step again. It seemed as if he was determined to keep his distance. She felt a pang of hurt, even as she knew it was unwarranted. Of course the boy would not rush to claim a new family when it had treated him so badly. She would simply have to endeavour to make it up to him somehow.

The carriage rolled back through the grand driveway of ash trees, and onto the country laneways. Peering out, Judith was struck by a sudden memory: walking those same laneways long ago, escorted by Lord Garvey himself...

Interlude I

Nine years earlier

It was the first afternoon of the party, after most of the guests had arrived and consumed an extravagant luncheon around Lord Garvey's dining table. Mrs Harriet Bollopher, Lord Garvey's mother-in-law, kindly suggested they all go for a walk to stretch their legs.

"Indeed," put in Lady Cordelia Garvey imperiously. "There is a lovely stream along the border of our estate; you must walk it." She raised her quizzing glass and peered through it, pointing through the terrace windows. "Start at that willow tree." She patted her iron grey hair and her walking stick, simultaneously excusing herself from the expedition while making it sound like an order for the rest of them.

Everyone obeyed with varying levels of enthusiasm. Judith politely acquiesced, though in truth she craved a long walk alone, away from everyone, and especially away from the duke.

She had not expected to see his grace here at Garvey House.

The sight of him, long limbed, dark haired, and handsome as ever, had been an unwelcome shock. She had hoped the house party would be a respite from her troubles. Since Nicholas's death a year ago, she had been in mourning and raising her children alone, in a long, grey place of grief. It had seemed advisable to finally foray into society again - especially as it would provide some excitement and companionship for Elinor and Peregrine, with the other children of the party - so she had accepted Lord Garvey's invitation.

That was before she had found the letter in her husband's effects. It was from the Duke of Sargen himself, spelling out Nicholas's failures and the fact of his illegitimate child.

Rage and humiliation swept through her anew at the thought of it, yet she had to smile politely and agree that a walk in company was a pleasant prospect.

The gathered guests followed Harriet as she led them down a picturesque path by the glasshouse and through a wooden gate onto a country lane. Careful to avoid the duke, Judith positioned herself next to Lord Garvey himself, who eagerly offered his arm as they approached the graceful willow tree.

"Mrs Avely, I am pleased you have finally emerged from your year of mourning." He smiled down at her, his swarthy countenance genial. "I see you have not abandoned your dark colours. They suit you admirably, of course, with your lovely blonde hair. Such a fair complexion you have!"

"Thank you." She smiled, a little uncomfortable with his compliments. She could see Dacian in front of her, escorting Lady Vosse, his head slightly turned. No doubt he was murmuring something equally inane into Isobel's ear. Judith had heard, in letters from London, that Lady Vosse's name was scandalously linked with the duke's. The news had caused Judith's lips to twist, but she was not surprised. There was always some scandal - and woman - linked to the duke. She was simply thankful, she told herself, that her own brief, youthful flirtation with him was not common knowledge. It would be too mortifying if everyone knew how he had thrown her over for the Widow Bleau; no doubt a widow was an easier liaison than a young girl, and more able to satisfy his excessive appetites.

Judith stifled the thought that now, so many years later, she was a widow too.

They turned onto a pretty laneway, bordered on one side by a burbling stream, and a hedgerow on the other. Lord Garvey chattered on about his plans for the party, and Judith nodded and smiled, scarcely listening. She wanted to waylay the duke alone, but certainly not for purposes of seduction. She had several scathing pronouncements on his character which burned to be uttered.

"You must investigate my maze," said Lord Garvey, patting Judith's arm. "I have a most intriguing statue of Apollo installed there now. Perhaps I should show you it myself." He gave her a sly smirk which Judith was at a loss to understand.

Suddenly Dacian pulled to a halt and faced them. His face was a neutral mask, and his dark eyes passed over Judith without expression. Her smile became even more fixed.

"Are you referring to the statue with the quiver of arrows, Garvey?" asked Dacian.

"Why, yes." Lord Garvey's smirk broadened. "Have you inspected it, Sargen? It is *particularly* good at certain hours of the day. May I suggest ten o'clock at night, at this time of year, for the best viewing?"

"Oh," trilled Lady Vosse. "It sounds most intriguing, gentlemen." Her green eyes sparkled, and Judith ignored the glory of her thick red curls cascading over her shoulder. Further down the path behind them, Lord Vosse walked with Kenneth Garvey, and hadn't noticed his wife's coquettish glances. It was well known that the pair were not close.

"Why don't you describe the details of the statue to Lady Vosse," suggested Dacian coolly. "I must speak with Mrs Avely about a certain item belonging to her husband."

Judith bristled. Could he have the gall to be referring to Nicholas's *bastard*, who was effectively in the duke's care? Dacian had taken on the responsibility of Robert's schooling arrangements and accommodation - or so she gathered from his cursed letter to Nicholas. Anger clenched her jaw. Here was certainly not the place to discuss the matter.

Yet the duke's peremptory tone did not brook refusal, and somehow he managed to swap places with Lord Garvey, sending him on with Lady Vosse. Isobel cast a slightly piqued look over her shoulder but then turned willingly enough to interrogate Charles about his Apollo. Her throaty laughter rang out as Dacian drew Judith further behind. Beside them, a stream burbled over smooth rocks, and widened into a river hung over with willows and spotted with ducks.

"Judith," he murmured. "I was not expecting to see you here. I am glad you are looking so well."

Somehow, though he only faintly echoed Garvey's compliments, coming from Dacian - with his charismatic charm - it sent a tremor of pleasure through her. Her hand tightened on his coat sleeve, and she could feel the hardness of muscle. No doubt, while she was child wrangling, he had been horse racing and boxing. And womanising.

"Likewise, your grace," she said coldly.

He cocked his head. "Do I detect a note of reserve, Judith? I was hoping we could manage to be friends now, after all this time."

She shot him a look. Was he referring to their dalliance, aeons ago? And the fact that Nicholas was now out of the picture? He could damn well go jump in the stream. Hopefully a duck would eat him.

"A friend does not keep secrets," she retorted bitterly, unable to help herself.

"Secrets?" He repeated, and glanced down at her in confusion. Then his eyes widened in sudden understanding. "My secrets, or someone else's?"

"I do not wish to discuss the matter here."

Dacian was silent a moment, then he spoke quietly. "If it is what I imagine you are referring to, I could not betray a confidence, Judith. Surely you understand that? And especially not to you."

She stopped and withdrew her arm abruptly. "I *said* I do not wish to discuss it. I see Miss Pelling is walking alone. I will join her."

"Judith, please." A black lock fell into his eyes, his gaze intent on her face. "Can we talk about it later? In a more private place? I can understand that you must be angry. I promise to take your censure meekly."

"Do not patronise me," she returned icily. "Now, if you will excuse me."

She turned away from his crestfallen expression. Quickly, she dropped backwards to reach the side of Miss Selina Pelling.

The young woman looked rather uncomfortable, though glad to see Judith. She possessed the dewy prettiness of youth, with clear skin, blonde hair, doe brown eyes, and a well-presented bosom. A flush stained her cheeks and Judith became aware that Kenneth and Lord Vosse, bringing up the rear, were having a heated discussion that was quite audible despite their attempts at discretion.

Kenneth Garvey spoke in a low tone that nonetheless carried on the still air. "She is too young, I tell you. It is disgusting that Charles should take a child-wife."

"She is of age, surely," replied Lord Vosse calmly. "I am not one to criticise a marriage of convenience, my friend."

"He must be twenty years older than her! It is repugnant." Kenneth's voice was thick with loathing. "Can you imagine what he will do to her?"

Judith cleared her throat loudly and threw a censorious gaze backward. The two men blinked, and Kenneth flushed with embarrassment, realising that his invective had been heard by Miss Pelling. Selina, for her part, looked at the ground, her complexion now white.

"Come, my dear," said Judith. "Let us take a shortcut through the poplars, back to the house - I can see it in the distance there. I find I am quite wearied already, and require solitude." On the stream, a duck quacked, a reassuring sound.

"Indeed," said Miss Pelling gratefully. "I am tired also."

Judith spoke lightly of trivial matters on the way back, until they reached the terrace. "Where is your family, if I may enquire? Are you here on your own, Miss Pelling?"

"It is unusual," agreed Miss Pelling. "However, my family live on the adjoining property, so they are content to send me to this house party alone. We are old family friends of the Garveys, and Mother will join us for dinner."

"Ah." So that was why an engagement between Lord Garvey and Miss Pelling was being hatched: to combine the two properties. "I look forward to meeting Mrs Pelling."

Was the mother the architect of her daughter's sacrifice? For it did not seem to Judith that Selina was very enthusiastic about the proposed match, for which she could scarcely blame her. Lord Garvey was a lecher, and twice Selina's age.

Judith wished she could intervene, but to do so would press far beyond the limits of her acquaintance with Lord Garvey. Exhausted, she retreated to her guest room, preoccupied with wondering how she was to survive the next four days in the duke's company - without tearing his head off with her bare hands.

In which a duke is reputed as wicked

Gossip contains a surprising amount of truth, despite its lashings of lies.
  - from *Lady Avely's Guide to Lies and Charms*

ALONE IN THE CARRIAGE, Judith sighed a little, remembering the party all those years ago. It seemed as if she had spent much of her life angry with Dacian. With the maturity of hindsight, she was starting to see that it was easier to be angry than to admit the strength of her attraction to him. It was far more dignified to be coldly furious than to be one of his adoring women.

She had adored him, a long time ago. She was beginning to realise that she had never stopped doing so. It was a rather unsettling realisation.

Looking back, she knew that she most likely would have soon forgiven him for keeping Nicholas's secrets, had Dacian not vanished from England. Even at the time, after their first riposte in the laneway, she was aware that he had only done what he thought right, in keeping her husband's confidences. She would have forgiven Dacian, and then he might have pursued her.

And then what? He would have stripped off her bodice and ravished her in the maze before the house party was over, if he had had his way.

She shifted on her seat. She could not deny the image held some appeal - the thought of his strong, caressing hands, and his mouth hot on her skin. But it was poisoned by the fact that he had thought she had done the same with Charles Garvey.

How could he have misjudged her affections and her character so? Wryly, she remembered how angry she had been nine years ago. Perhaps it was not so strange that he thought her capable of cruelty. And as much as she might wish Dacian was not so quick to temper, she could scarcely exempt herself from that fault.

Ten minutes later, the carriage rolled through Stokesford and up to the Golden Bat.

It was a low stone building, also made of limestone, but much more modest in its aspirations than Garvey House. A faint tang of smoke hung in the air as Judith stepped down, promising the warmth of a fire. Robert leapt down and although she gave him a speaking look, he busied himself with unloading her valise. Well, she would let him play the footman, for now, and keep his distance. She knew from experience in managing her own children that sometimes it was better to take two steps back in order to invite a step forward.

She repressed an anxious thought for Elinor and Peregrine, who were somewhere in the seas around Sark, or possibly on the island by now. Why had she allowed them to go? At the time, a remote island had seemed safer than London, but now a prick of premonition troubled her mind. She could, if she allowed herself the indulgence, worry about her children endlessly. It was pointless to do so, however, when she was helpless to assist them.

Perhaps that was why she was concerning herself with Robert's welfare instead; it was something she could deal with directly, if only he would allow her.

The innkeeper informed Judith loftily that the best room and parlour were already taken, but allowed her to bespeak two bedrooms and the second-best parlour. She retreated to tidy her hair, glad to see that the rooms were small but clean. Her bedroom even had an oak dresser with a lockable door, suitable for Marigold. Quickly, Judith transferred the little sleeping creature into the low cupboard, shielding her from the light as she did so. Then she locked the door with a wince. Marigold would not like to be imprisoned, but it was better than having her discovered by a curious servant.

Just then a maid knocked and offered to unpack Judith's valise. She nodded, though she was more than capable of the task herself. While she pinned her hair back before a mirror, she asked the maid her name - Phyllis - and whether the famous Garvey Maze was open to visitors, as a way to broach the subject.

Phyllis knelt by the valise and clicked it open. "Oh no, my lady. The manor house is all shut up. Lady Garvey is away with family, and visitors are not encouraged." It seemed that the lie was commonly accepted, for Phyllis's voice rang true. She began pulling out Judith's gowns and shaking them out. "Not that you should go anywhere near it, if you don't mind me saying. The old maze is haunted."

Judith widened her eyes. This was news. "Truly? By whom?"

"Lord Garvey himself. He was shot dead, years back." Phyllis smoothed out a crease. "His ghost has been seen at night, staggering through the hedges with a gaping hole in his chest." She gave a theatrical shudder.

"Goodness me. How ghastly." Judith narrowed her eyes. This sounded like the work of an Illusor. "Who has seen such a horrifying vision, if I may enquire?"

"The new butler, for one." Phyllis carefully hung a lilac gown in the cupboard, and spoke over her shoulder. "He said it gave him a terrible fright to see the old lord lurching around, bleeding from a bullet wound just like what killed him."

"Hm," murmured Judith, continuing to pin her hair. Maybe this was simply another story, concocted like the butler's other lies, and intended to discourage visitors.

Phyllis seemed to sense her skepticism. "Ay, and even our Constable Carter has seen it, and he is a sensible sort, my lady. He said he was patrolling for poachers in the Pelling woods - which adjoin Garvey's land - and he saw a well-dressed gentleman standing still by the maze, obscured by the mist. Then suddenly, the gentleman vanished."

"How intriguing. Did your constable see the bullet wound?"

"I don't know if he were close enough, my lady." Phyllis gave another shiver as she unfolded a cloak. "If it were me, I would have run in the opposite direction. Poor Lord Garvey, without any rest. That wicked duke should hang."

"Wicked duke?" Judith accidentally pricked her scalp with a pin, and winced.

"The Duke of Sargen, of course. He who killed his lordship. They were fighting over a woman, it's said. Lord Garvey tried to rescue a poor maid from his grace's evil clutches."

"Are you sure it wasn't the other way around?"

"Well, I suppose it may have been," admitted Phyllis. "Lord Garvey was a bit of an adventurer in his day, as far as I've heard."

"Indeed. I knew Lord Garvey while he was alive, and I can assure you that he was more likely to imperil a young woman than save her."

"Is that so?" The maid gave her a measuring glance. "You'd know best, my lady. I was a little lass when it all happened."

Judith gave her a resigned look, feeling rather old. Phyllis must be around eighteen, so she would have indeed been nine years old at the time, when Judith had just embarked on her thirtieth decade.

"Before your time," she acknowledged. "Do you know any of the servants at Garvey House?"

Phyllis turned back to her work, her hands respectful as she hung the gowns. "Not many stay long at Garvey House. Especially after Mrs Bollopher died. She kept the house ship-shape, I heard, but now it's falling to wrack and ruin."

Judith knew this was true of the front exterior, and she could imagine the inner rooms suffered too. She knew that Harriet had looked after the household accounts and overseen the house-keeper, for Lady Cordelia Garvey was an indolent woman, the sort who was happy to play the matriarch without doing any of the work. Like how Lady Garvey had taken Harriet's kind sugges-tion for a walk and turned it into her own order.

"How did Mrs Harriet Bollopher die?" Judith ventured to ask.

Phyllis tucked the last gown into the cupboard. "She was found dead in her bed, I believe. It must have been her heart that gave out. Mayhap Lord Garvey's ghost came upon her and fright-ened her to death," she added, with a sideways look.

"Mayhap," said Judith dryly.

"Is there anything else you need, my lady?"

"No, thank you, Phyllis." Judith passed her a coin. "Only, is there a second key to this dresser? I have some valuables which I am rather particular about, and I wish to possess both keys."

"Of course, my lady." With one last curious look, the maid dropped a curtsy and left.

Once she had both keys tucked into her reticule, Judith made her way to the parlour, trying to gather her composure before the duke arrived. At least now she was vindicated in her opinion that Dacian needed to tread carefully in Stokesford. She would be sure to tell him so.

The second-best parlour was not much bigger than the bedrooms, with a writing desk by the window, and a small dining table crammed into a corner. Three chairs upholstered in green fabric were arranged around a small fire place. A tidy blaze warmed the room, and Judith ordered some tea and sat down at the escritoire to compose a letter to her good friend Caroline Axelton, who was still in London and might have heard whether or not the law intended to pursue the duke. Judith was a little embarrassed to explain how she had become tangled up with Dacian again, as Caroline was one of the few who knew of their complicated past.

Once that missive was completed, she began one to her children, who might return to Devon soon, before they repaired to Cornwall with the vampiri roost. If, indeed, they managed to find the French roost with its sleeping queen, and then persuade it that Castle Lanyon would make a suitable residence.

She had only just begun when a sharp rap at the parlour door heralded the appearance of a handsome middle-aged man. He had brown, straight hair, a rather ostentatious moustache, a mole on his left cheek, and a twinkle in his dark eyes.

Putting down a large trunk, he bowed deeply. "Lady Avely. It's been far too long since I saw you last."

Judith rose from her writing table, her heart beating a little faster. "Mr Fortnew. Please do come in." She was glad he had assumed his disguise, after hearing Phyllis's willingness to have the 'wicked duke' hanged. His striking features were still recognisable after a few moments, but only, she hoped, because she knew to look for them. And perhaps, she admitted to herself, because they held a special fascination for her. And for many other women, of course. She was not alone in that regard.

Dacian stepped inside, Robert behind him. The door shut, the Illusion dropped, and Robert went so far as to wink. Mr Fortnew's gentlemanly pallor faded, showing Dacian's face that had seen the sun in Spain, along with the new lines that fanned out from his eyes and the scar on his forehead.

"See?" Dacian strolled over to take her hand and kiss it. "Easy as a drinking whisky."

"Ha."

"I bought some more liquor in my luggage. I couldn't guarantee that the Golden Bat would be suitably equipped."

"I think we have already imbibed too freely," she said primly. "I need to have a clear head for tomorrow, when I call on Garvey House again."

"Again?"

"We stopped by on the way here."

"Judith!"

"There was no harm. Nothing much came of it, for the man at the door turned me away."

"You mean the butler?"

"Officially, I suppose he was butlering. Yet he didn't seem like a butler, did he, Robert?"

Robert shook his head. "He was a bit rough around the edges."

"Moreover," Judith sat down again at the writing desk, "the 'butler' lied to me. He claimed the Garveys are visiting family in the north, but it was poppycock."

Robert picked up the duke's luggage. "I'll unpack Wooten, shall I, your grace?"

"If you would be so kind. Pop him on top of a cupboard. People don't tend to look up."

Judith frowned in disapproval, both to this cavalier attitude towards the dignified Wooten, and to Dacian treating Robert like a servant again. Before she could say anything, however, Robert left, tenderly bearing Dacian's suitcase aloft.

Dacian sauntered to the window to look outside. "Tea, Judith?" he noted. "I'm disappointed; I expected chocolate."

She poured him a cup. "I am partial to tea as well, you know."

He leaned against the window frame and took a sip. "Interesting that this butler seems determined to keep visitors away."

"Yes," she agreed. "When I pressed him, he only embroidered further. And apparently he has also been spreading a rumour that Lord Garvey's ghost haunts the maze."

"Ah! An Illusion, perhaps? We are in the right quarter then."

Judith topped up her own cup and held the warm vessel in her hands. "Unless the butler was simply lying again. However, the Stokesford constable has also seen the vision, according to my maid. But we must be careful not to mention the magicks or the possibility of Illusion. The locals put it down to ghosts and faeries, and we cannot breach the old rules of secrecy."

"It will make things difficult." He smiled. "However, I am confident in your ability to sniff out our villain."

She was pleased by his remark and took a sip to hide it. "I do have a question for you."

"What is that?"

"How was it that you happened to be in the Apollo alcove just in time to witness the Illusion? Why were you there in the first place? Surely it wasn't a coincidence."

Dacian frowned. "It wasn't. I was given a note, directing me to that spot for ten o'clock. It was unsigned." He paused, embarrassed. "I had hoped that it was you, actually, who wrote the note."

"*Me?*"

He nodded.

"You thought I would invite you down to the maze after dark?" Judith gave him an offended look. "You really do have an odd notion about my character."

He grinned. "Well, I *am* irresistible. I thought even your uprightness might give way before my charms."

"How insufferable...!"

"No, not really," he said, "It was more that I thought you

might want to apologise - after behaving like such a shrew the previous day. That you might beg my forgiveness for assaulting my chest."

Judith choked on her tea. "I did not assault your chest! I merely...pushed it."

"If you say so." Dacian watched her over his cup. "Just because I am an Impactor does not mean I am immune to violence, my dear."

"It wasn't violence! And besides, you assaulted me first!"

Dacian raised his brows in affront. "I was comforting you. Clearly, I must work on my technique."

Judith blushed furiously. "This is all beside the point. I did *not* write that note, which leaves us with the question - who did?"

Dacian looked down.

"What?" asked Judith suspiciously. "Do you have some idea?"

"I admit, it has crossed my mind that it might have been Lady Vosse."

A silence fell.

"Ah," said Judith at last. "Of course. *She* would invite you down into the maze. And you would go." She hated herself for the jealousy that speared her.

"Not for the reasons you imply, you wretch," said Dacian calmly. "She had been making overtures, it is true, and I planned to tell her that I was still not interested."

"Oh, *really?*"

"Yes. Quite apart from the fact that my interest was otherwise engaged-" he shot her a glance "- her husband had warned me off, the year previously. Lord Vosse felt we were making a fool out of him, and told me to back off. Which I had, and I don't know why Isobel thought it wise to pursue me again." He sighed. "Like I said, I am irresistible."

Judith rolled her eyes. Before she could (mendaciously) refute this claim, there was a knock and Robert came in. He took up position by the door, his hands clasped behind his back.

"Robert, please," begged Judith, pouring him a cup of tea. "Do sit down. You need not claim relation with me; simply be our acquaintance, Mr Robert Steer."

Robert shook his head. "Best I stay here, my lady. In case anyone comes and we need the moustache."

"True, but you may do that from the chair," she insisted, holding the cup aloft. "For goodness' sakes - Dacian, tell Robert he cannot be our footman anymore."

"Robert, you cannot be our footman anymore," said Dacian obligingly, and took a sip of his own tea.

"Yes, your grace." Robert stayed where he was, avoiding Judith's gaze.

"Dacian, you're as bad as he!" Judith accused, putting down her cup with a clatter. "Dismiss him from your service this instant!"

"Well, it might be convenient for Robert to play a servant." Dacian defended himself. "He can gossip belowstairs, and go where we cannot."

"Dacian!"

"It's true," agreed Robert, but Judith could sense some other reason for his diffidence.

"Hmph," she said, then added reluctantly, "I suppose you can provide a buffer between the staff and Marigold and Wooten. They mustn't be seen."

Dacian sat down on one of the green chairs, pushing it back so he could stretch his long legs out. "Indeed. When I passed through London, I heard rumours that King George has set up a new branch of vampiri to investigate any breaches of the Edicts. Apparently he is inspired by the success of John Fielding's establishment."

Robert tilted his head, intrigued. "You mean the Bow Street Runners?"

"Yes, except these ex-vilitia are called the Beauchamp Fliers, for they operate out of the Beauchamp Tower in the Tower of London. We must assume that His Majesty has instructed them to spy on their own kind, just like the Runners."

Judith allowed the change of subject, and picked up her tea again, taking a sip. "Using the vampiri to police their own? Dear me, I abhor these new strictures."

Robert looked thoughtful. "Do these new Beauchamp Fliers assist the Musor Custos?"

A faint look of discomfort flitted across Dacian's face. "No. I believe not. The Musor Custos are far older, and law unto themselves."

"The Keepers of Obruo?" asked Judith nervously. Those guardians were rarely mentioned in polite company, the same way that one did not speak of the hanging docks. Judith had been loath even to tell her own children of them. "What do you know about them, Robert?"

"I warned him of them," said Dacian, crossing his ankles casually. "When he told me about his Gift. Just as I warned Lewis. It is better to know the consequences of misusing your power."

Judith caught her lip between her teeth. The Obruo could wipe the magic from one's veins without a trace. It was a severe measure, usually only administered in extreme circumstances, for the Musing was rare. It was rumoured that the Musor Custos served it with a dose of Lethe as well, leaving the person as a husk, emptied and forgetful. She took a fortifying sip of tea. "The Musor Custos only intervene in desperate cases," she remarked. "They would not concern themselves with such trifling matters as the Edicts, even if King George thinks they are so important."

Robert, intrigued by the conversation, was staring at Dacian with interest. "What about the crime of duelling?"

"No." Judith answered for him. "That is a common law matter, and the Musor Custos will stay out of it. They only deal in the magicks."

"Ah," said Dacian. "Regarding that matter, I am afraid that I must tell you something."

Judith set her cup in her saucer carefully, for Dacian had put back his shoulders. "What is it?"

"I didn't kill Garvey in a duel."

Robert's brows shot up, but Judith's heart sank. She had, truthfully, suspected this was the case. It wasn't the first time that duelling had been used to hide Dacian's reckless force. She made herself speak calmly. "But I heard the gunshots myself. We all did."

"I fired them as a ruse. I thought it was better to be guilty of a duel than of killing a man by magic." Dacian's jaw clenched. "He was dead in an instant, long before I shot him. I flung him aside with my Gift, and his head hit stone."

Judith bit her lip, appalled. Dacian's eyes lowered to the table.

"Lord help us," said Robert, in awe. "So the Musor Custos *and* the Runners could be after you!" He seemed almost impressed, curse the boy.

"I doubt it," said Dacian brusquely. "Nine years have passed. Neither of them will bother with the matter now."

Judith spoke up reluctantly. "Unless the Garveys demand justice. Or the Musor Custos discover your transgression."

"Which is why we must find the truth." Dacian met her eyes once more. "If I was being manipulated by an Illusor, the Musor Custos will be far more concerned with *that* misconduct than mine."

Judith took a breath. She could hear his unspoken plea - that she also forgive him, for his fatal, heedless power. His nature was the opposite of her own; it was another reason to keep him at a distance.

Robert coughed. "There is one thing I don't understand: how did you fire two guns simultaneously by yourself?"

Dacian looked over. "Lord Triskett helped me. I found him on the terrace and asked for his help, and he fetched Garvey's own pistols from the gunroom."

Judith, about to refill her cup, stilled her movement. "Lord Triskett was on the terrace? Did he see anyone leave the maze?"

"I don't know. I've written to ask him, actually," said Dacian. "As soon as I realised that I had been tricked, I sent a note to him. He might have seen Kenneth skulk out, which would confirm our theory."

"Kenneth?" asked Robert. "Who's he, now?"

"Kenneth Garvey, Charles' brother and the new Lord Garvey," explained Dacian. "He didn't want Charles to remarry and start begetting heirs to oust him from the line of succession."

"I remember him being rather angry about it," admitted Judith, recalling the scene in the laneway as she resumed pouring. "He thought the girl was too young. He was right, too. Poor Miss Selina Pelling. I wonder what happened to her."

At that moment, a knock sounded at the parlour door. Judith nodded at Robert, and Dacian's clean-shaven countenance became marred by Mr Fortnew's smug moustache and prominent mole.

"Come in," Judith called. She glanced askance at Dacian, for he was sitting in a very casually arrogant way, leaning back with his ankles crossed. He looked much like a duke at his ease, and unlike a lowly steward, for all his neat garb and mousy brown hair.

Seeing her pointed look, he sat up straighter and pursed his lips. The maid, Phyllis, entered and dipped a curtsy.

"Would you like to have dinner served in the parlour, my lady? Sir?"

Dacian nodded. "A capital notion. And drinking chocolate afterwards, if you would be so kind."

Phyllis nodded and departed, and the moustache and mole dropped away. Robert grinned.

"See?" said Dacian, leaning back again, putting his hands behind his head. "A simple matter. Good work, Robert."

A faint red rose in Robert's cheeks.

Judith stood, annoyed that he was so easily charmed by the duke, while she had to fight for every concession. Outside, she could see that the sky had turned a pale lilac; dusk had fallen. "Marigold will be rattling at her cage. I must fetch her. And while we are eating, the vampiri can investigate Garvey House. I know it is rude to spy, but if the Garvey's won't let us in, we need to discover the reason."

In which a gentleman is prepared

Marigold

Marigold awoke to the smell of old oak, and the sense that the sun had just set. She was in some sort of wooden cupboard, with dim light seeping through the edges. Pushing against the door, she found it was locked, and waited impatiently for Judith to release her. Cursed Edicts. Why should she have to hide away all the time? The only consolation was that she knew Judith didn't like it either. And Wooten would also be out of sight, for all that he thought he was a vision.

She busied herself by dressing in her new primrose gown that Judith had sewn for her. Lady Avely was a funny old thing. Prim and proper - until the duke turned up. Then suddenly she wanted to investigate murders and ghosts and gallivant around after dark. Maybe Marigold would stay as her companion a bit longer, though ordinarily she did not like to pin herself down.

Soon an iron key thrust into the lock and released the door.

"Marigold," whispered Judith. "Are you ready to do some flying? We need you to investigate Garvey House."

Marigold huffed with annoyance. "I knew I shouldn't have dressed."

"You'll need clothes - you must wait for Wooten."

"He takes so long to garb himself." Marigold complained. "And he won't even want to go."

She was right: when they reached the parlour, Wooten did not want to abandon his immaculate cravat and coat to become a bat. He informed them that he would much rather stay by the fire and partake of whisky with the duke, despite his grace's atrocious new facial hair.

Dacian lifted his nose. "I thought I was carrying it off with suitable gravitas."

Wooten winced. "A gentleman's face should remain unadorned. And I'm not flying off into Garvey House uninvited."

Marigold stood on the parlour table and folded her arms over her new yellow bodice. "I don't need your escort," she said. "You can stay here and stroke your cravat if you like."

However, to her annoyance, Dacian insisted. "Wooten, I regret to inform you that an English bat must be chivalrous. What if there is a cat, or an owl? Or someone sees Miss Cultor in the house?"

"Precisely my point," said Wooten gloomily. "Very well, then. Robert, please would you fetch my flying cloak?"

Robert raised a brow but gave a mock click of his heels and retreated once more.

"Robert is not our servant!" expostulated Judith.

"Flying cloak?" demanded Marigold. "Are you serious, Wooters?"

"A gentleman should always be prepared," sniffed Wooten, "and *never* be exposed."

Marigold sighed. It was no wonder that she preferred lady bats.

Once Robert had returned with a scrap of black velvet - a silk ribbon hanging from it - Wooten disappeared behind the writing desk. While they waited for him to disrobe, Judith relayed to Marigold what she had discovered so far, including the brazen butler's lies, and the oddly neglected grounds of Garvey House. When Wooten eventually flew out in his bat form, the shimmering velvet hung down in front of him: a back-to-front cape.

Marigold shook her head. "Don't blame me if that catches on a tree, you dandy."

Wooten merely put his snout in the air.

She stripped off her gown while Robert and Dacian looked at the ceiling, clearing their throats. Then she and Wooten swept out the window like two swallows of the night, wheeling into the darkness.

It was glorious to be winged again, carefree and wild. Marigold shot ahead, following the road that Judith had described, allowing herself to loop crazily and zigzag between the trees. Wooten flapped more slowly behind, no doubt encumbered by his ridiculous cape. Above them, clouds streamed across a waxing moon, making the light dip and flow around her.

After a stretch of flying, some of her energy had dissipated, and she was glad to see the line of ash trees looming ahead. These must be the ones that marked the drive to Garvey House. Just as Judith said, as Marigold drew closer she saw that the manor seemed closed and abandoned. Cautiously, she led the way round to the back of the house, noting the dark mass of the maze to the left and the glint of the glasshouse to the right. And just as Judith had surmised, candlelight showed from the right-hand windows of the mansion.

A graceful oriel window jutted from the second floor. That

was where Judith had seen the frightened girl, so Marigold made a bat-curve for it. She landed to cling upside-down to the upper window frame, her wings tucked neatly around her. Wooten attempted the same, but she was amused to see that the velvet fell in his face. He wriggled until he could twist his neck around the fabric, while Marigold rolled her eyes.

She turned her attention to the room inside. The curtains provided a gap of less than an inch, but she could make out a drawing room with old, shabby furniture and a worn carpet. Within her line of sight, an elderly woman sat in front of the fire, her evening attire covered by a rich silk dressing gown patterned in peach and blue. Over her grey hair, she wore a peach, silken mobcap that reminded Marigold of one of Judith's, and she possessed a beakish nose and sharp eyes. A walking stick rested against her knee. The strength in her expression belied the frailty of her gnarled hands, which lay limp on the armrests. This must the Lady Garvey that Judith mentioned, living in her son's house. An old-fashioned quizzing glass hung around her neck, framed in ornate pinchbeck gold.

Listening, Marigold could hear a young female voice engaged in the monotonous lilt of reading, though she could not see the reader. There was an empty plate on a side-table next to the old lady, and an embroidery frame resting on the mantelpiece, next to an ugly old candelabra. It was a scene of feminine retreat and genteel poverty. A longcase clock ticked in the corner, its face round and mournful.

Other than that, there were no masculine voices or knick-knacks. It seemed that Lord Kenneth Garvey was absent from the familial hearth, just as the butler had claimed.

After a while, another figure crossed Marigold's sight. A black-clad servant, quick and skinny, with gaunt features. She took up the empty plate and interrupted the reading, asking the old lady if she would like tea. The old woman - who must be Lady Garvey - nodded.

Marigold caught the flounce of a pink skirt and the sound of a heavy sigh. Poor young Georgina, to be stuck in this house with two old crows. She, at least, would be willing to accept Judith's invitation, if only Judith would be allowed to make it.

After the tea was fetched, old Lady Garvey took over the reading. Her diction was decisive yet emotionless, and Marigold heard another soft sigh emanate from Georgina.

It was irksome not to be able to see more. There remained the possibility, too, that Lord Kenneth Garvey was somewhere else in the house. Marigold dropped away from the pane and investigated the other windows, searching for a way inside. Unfortunately, they were all tightly latched against the cool autumn air. Crossly, she swooped up to the roof.

Wooten followed, and when she landed in her human form, he reluctantly followed suit, careful to swing his cape to preserve his modesty.

Marigold ignored his theatrics, and stood stark naked on the rooftop, hands on hips. "I want to go inside."

Wooten heaved a long-suffering sigh. "How do you propose to do that?"

She pointed to the stone column of a chimney, silhouetted against the dim sky. "I'll climb down that." She clambered over to it and put her hand against the brick. "It's not warm, so there's no fire at the bottom."

Wooten looked aghast. "You'll get dirty."

"I'm not wearing any clothes," she pointed out.

"I noticed *that*." He whisked his cape a little closer, as if it might somehow become contaminated by her nakedness.

"*You* don't have to come with me. You can keep watch up here."

Wooten grimaced. "His grace will expect me to accompany you."

"I won't tell him, if you don't." Marigold pulled herself up the bricks, still in her human form. Wooten turned his gaze away from her bare bottom. She ought to spare him, but it would be easier to fit down the narrow chute without the length of bat wings to hinder her.

However, just as she was about to swing her legs into the spout, a new voice, female in timbre, came from behind the chimney.

"I wouldn't do that, if I were you."

Marigold startled backwards and slid down behind the chimney in fright. She landed with a plop on the roof tiles, grazing her rear. Cheeks burning, she darted behind the chimney again. Clutching the brick, she peeped round it, her curls bouncing against her cheek.

"Who spoke?" she demanded.

"I." The voice came again, low and sultry. "You may call me Yvette."

A vampiri was hidden in the shadow of the chimney. Her skin was pale and she was very beautiful, with full, sensuous lips, sculpted cheeks, and liquid dark eyes that looked almost violet as she stepped into the moonlight. She was clad in a soft fall of black silk, in a cape much like Wooten's. Somehow, she made it look far more attractive.

She was staring at Marigold's face with curiosity. Marigold stared back.

The strange vampiri trod forward softly, rounding the side of the chimney. Marigold, suddenly embarrassed at her state of undress, scuttled back to stand next to Wooten. She grabbed a corner of his velvet cape and held it in front of her. Wooten grabbed it back. After a short tussle, they managed to arrange the cloth so that it covered both of them, though Wooten huffed in indignation.

The woman raised her brows in amusement. "And who may you two be?"

Marigold cleared her throat. "I am Miss Marigold Cultor, and this is Mr Wooten Willoughby."

"Excuse me," said Wooten, affronted, "I'll have you know that I am blood companion to-"

He stopped on a grunt, for Marigold had employed a sharply placed elbow. She didn't think it was wise to announce that he was companion to the Duke of Sargen, especially to this stranger.

"Yes, yes," she said. "I know you like to think that Mr Fortnew will inherit the baronetcy one day."

Wooten coughed. "Hmm. I am certain of it."

The new vampiri - Yvette - raised her brows. "A pleasure to meet you both."

Marigold smiled brightly. "And who do you belong to, er, Miss Yvette?"

"I might not *belong* to anyone." The full lips curved in a smile. "And who do you belong to, Miss Cutlor?"

Marigold lifted her chin. "Perhaps I prefer not to say."

"Ah, a lady of mystery," Yvette said with interest. "How delightful."

Marigold was inclined to agree. Then she remembered that this beautiful woman had tried to curtail her adventure. "Why shouldn't I go down the chimney?" she asked suspiciously.

Yvette's violet gaze weighed her. "It breaches the Edicts, for a start."

Marigold scoffed. "I don't care about them."

"Perhaps you should. If you go down there you will land in a sooty mess and call human attention to yourself."

"Exactly what I said," put in Wooten.

Yvette ignored him. "Humans don't like bats. And if you are in your vampiri state, that might be worse. Do you know what they do to bats who breach the Edicts, Miss Marigold Cultor?"

Marigold wrinkled her nose. "They strip them of companion status. It does not overly concern me. I am never a companion for long anyway." For most vampiri, being a Musor companion was the only way to seek civilised shelter and food. Yet Marigold had never been particularly civilised, and was not so afraid of being cast out of human society.

"Oh?"

"I prefer flexible arrangements." Marigold dared a wink.

Yvette examined her, appearing unmoved. "Why do you want to go indoors, if I may enquire? I take it you do not belong to the house, temporarily or otherwise?"

Wooten interposed. "We heard talk of a ghost on the premises. Miss Cultor has a morbid fascination with such things."

Marigold nodded, glad he had come up with a plausible story. "Yes, I adore ghosts. So delightfully gothic. Have you seen any in these parts?"

Yvette pursed her luscious lips thoughtfully. "Ah, you must be speaking of the unfortunate Lord Garvey's spectre. I, too, have heard rumours of his ghost, but I am yet to witness it. Apparently, he haunts the maze."

"Oh." Marigold blinked innocently. "Where is that?"

"We could have a look together," suggested Yvette with a smile. "You are already unclothed and ready to fly." Her eyes flickered down, to where Marigold's ankles were bare in the moonlight.

Marigold found herself blushing. "I suppose we could do that."

"Must we?" said Wooten grumpily.

"You needn't accompany us," replied Marigold, her eyes fixed on Yvette.

"I will accompany you," snapped Wooten. "Now, remove your person from my cloak."

Yvette laughed and turned away. Her black silk swirled and then lifted, as she transformed into a bat. Hastily, Marigold followed suit. Wooten was the last to join them in the air, struggling to swing his velvet frontwards.

Together, they flew off over the gardens, heading for the maze.

In which a noble lowers his station

Repetition will assist one in most pursuits; even more so in the casting of a charm.

   - from *Lady Avely's Guide to Lies and Charms*

DINNER TOOK a toll on Judith's nerves. Every time Phyllis entered with a new serving platter, or to remove plates, or to pour drinks, Robert had to conjure up Dacian's disguise. It was just as well, Judith acknowledged, that Robert was playing the part of a footman, for it allowed him to keep watch at the door and listen for footsteps. However, after the first couple of interruptions, he thought it wiser to simply leave the Illusion in place.

Judith nervously watched as Dacian ate his food, wondering if the moustache looked convincing enough. He shovelled food into his mouth and winked from under his thatch of brown hair, seeming to enjoy her scrutiny. Judith rolled her eyes and tucked into the beef and vegetables. She was famished, and she could trust Robert to watch out for them.

Dessert arrived - stewed apple and custard - and then, to her horror, she saw that Robert had added a touch of verisimilitude by placing a spot of custard upon the ducal moustache.

She turned her head and gave him a disapproving glare. Robert's lips quirked, his cheeks slightly flushed. Judith's brow furrowed with concern. He was clearly becoming Bemused.

When Phyllis returned, she told her they would *not* require chocolate, after all, and that they wished to be left in peace now.

As the door shut behind her, Dacian's real face became apparent, wearing an expression of surprise and concern.

"Not require chocolate? Marchioness, are you feeling alright?"

She nodded at Robert. "Your moustache is taking a toll."

Dacian examined Robert, who stood a little straighter. "Are you Bemused, my boy?"

"No," said Robert sturdily. "Not much. Not yet."

"What about the custard?" demanded Judith.

Robert grinned. "Just a momentary diversion."

"What custard?" asked Dacian suspiciously.

"On your moustache," said Judith. "A little dribble."

Dacian looked horrified. "Good God, Robert! Have pity!"

"It is only to be expected, if we overtax him with such an onerous task." Judith paused. "Perhaps we should look into constructing a charm, to contain the Illusion. That way it can continue on without his presence."

Robert stepped forward, interested. "I've tried to do that before. Do you know the trick of it?"

"It is not a trick." She pushed a bowl of custard and apple towards him. "Sit down and eat this, and I will tell you."

The fact that Robert did as she instructed was another indication that he was not quite himself. Judith waited until he was comfortably eating custard, then continued. "A charm requires an extended casting, repeated many times to imprint the magic to an anchor. We will require an object and the flame of a candle." The element of fire assisted Illusions, just as water made Discerning easier.

Dacian nodded. "I can help you, Robert - I've made many Defence charms before, to work in my absence. It will exact a toll too, of course, but you can sleep it off."

Robert nodded eagerly, then appeared to recall his position. "Yes, your grace."

Judith cleared a space on the small dining table, hoping that the magical exercise would ease any formality between them all. "What object should he use? It has to be something you can wear on your person."

Dacian's hand went to his neatly pinned cravat and he withdrew a small silver pin, topped by a pearl. "This should do." The folds of his cravat loosened, revealing the hollow of his throat.

"Very well," replied Judith, ignoring how the lamplight played over his cheekbones. Perhaps she *should* have ordered chocolate, after all. She launched into an explanation of how charms worked, as far as she understood the theory.

Robert listened intently. When he had finished eating from his bowl, she let Dacian take over the instruction. She watched as Robert held the end of the pin (between gloved fingers) over a candle flame. He waited until the metal heated and became more susceptible to the spell, then set about imprinting the Illusion of Mr Fortnew's mop, moustache, and mole. Dacian hovered his face at the correct distance above it, so that the proportions would align.

Robert already knew the word for Illusion, so soon he was continually muttering *alucin* as he attempted to build the link between his efforts and the cravat pin, while Dacian patiently gave instructions or advice.

It took many repetitions to cast a charm, so Judith retired to the writing desk, leaving them to it. Her letter to her children lay ignored, however, for her mind kept returning to what Dacian had said: that he went out into the maze hoping to see *her*, even though she had already - the day before - given him a piece of her mind in the greenhouse. What exactly had he been hoping for that night? To seduce her, no doubt, and instead he had found her already seduced.

Who had sent him to witness such a sordid scene?

In a pause between castings, Robert rested, and Judith took the opportunity to ask a question.

"Who gave you the note, Dacian? The one that told you to go to the maze."

Dacian rolled his shoulders back and stretched his neck. His cravat now lay discarded on the table, and he looked disconcertingly casual, his throat bare. "The butler. A different fellow to the one there now, I imagine."

"Hm." Judith focused on the matter at hand. "Even if we could track him down, it is unlikely he would remember who gave it to *him*."

Robert picked up the cravat pin again, this time using tongs from the fireplace, for it was becoming hot enough to burn through his gloves. "There is one thing I'm curious on," he said, blinking slowly. "I gather that your grace saw an Illusion of Lady Avely with Lord Garvey?"

Clearly, he was *quite* Bemused, to directly address the subject. Judith bit her lip. "How did you guess?"

Robert waved the tongs in a lackadaisical manner, almost setting a painting on fire. "Easy enough. It had to be something that would provoke his grace. *I* guessed that such a portrait would provoke him. But the question is - who *else* knew of the affection between you?"

Judith looked down, her cheeks heating. "Um."

Dacian cleared his throat. "It is a sensible question, Robert, but I am afraid that most of the house guests knew that we passionately...provoked one other. We had, er, an encounter in the glasshouse, which was witnessed by most of the guests."

Judith's blush deepened. The weave of the carpet was suddenly extremely fascinating.

"Why, what happened?" Robert twirled the tongs innocently and raised his brows.

"You focus on casting the charm," said Dacian repressively, and glanced at Judith. "You need at least ten more imprints for it to settle."

Robert looked a little mulish, but fortunately, at that moment, there was movement at the window. Marigold and Wooten slipped through the gap, two winged shapes darting down behind the escritoire. Judith stood and busied herself with assisting Marigold into her gown, while Wooten vanished into the curtains. When at last he came out (immaculately dressed), he interrupted Marigold's account of their adventures to describe her utter foolishness in engaging with a mysterious lady bat named Miss Yvette.

"That hussy even invited Marigold to spin around the poplars," he finished, "and then to go back to her belfry apartment!"

Marigold huffed. "I didn't go, did I? Not to her belfry, anyway."

"Her belfry?" questioned Judith. "You mean at the Stokesford church? Is this Miss Yvette there alone, unattached to a Musor?"

"She didn't say," said Wooten. "She was very evasive. She didn't even give us her full name!"

"A lady need not reveal everything at once," said Marigold.

Wooten glared. "Oh? You should keep that in mind."

"One moment." Dacian held up a hand. "I hope you didn't reveal our reason for being here."

"Of course not," scoffed Marigold. "Though Wooten almost announced his noble companionship with you, if I hadn't jabbed him in the stomach."

"I did not."

"Did too."

Judith intervened. "Regardless, Miss Yvette is probably not remotely interested in the duke."

"Did you see any ghosts?" asked Robert, from where he leaned upon the mantelpiece; still at his ease, Judith was glad to see.

"No," said Marigold sulkily. "Not one."

"Well, Kenneth is away," said Dacian, leaning back in his chair. "If he is the culprit, maybe we should track him down in London."

"At least let me speak to Lady Garvey first," said Judith. "She might have something to say about it all. And Miss Garvey sounds as if she is quite stifled. I do want to extend the hand of friendship to her, as a matter of Christian duty."

She glanced at Robert as she said it, hoping that he would also eventually accept her friendship. But he seemed to withdraw in on himself again, abruptly shifting the tongs and avoiding her gaze.

THE NEXT DAY DAWNED OVERCAST, with a threat of rain hanging in the air. Judith, eating her breakfast in the parlour, peered out the window anxiously. Her plan today required that she walk to Garvey House, and she did not want to get drenched.

She took a bite of her hot buttered roll, her eyes drifting to where Dacian had sat the night before. He and Robert had stayed up late, long after she went to bed, taking time to construct the Illusion charm. She hoped they would both stay abed today, out of trouble. Robert would need to sleep off his Bemusement, certainly.

Yet, just as she was finishing her cup of coffee, the door opened and Dacian slipped in. He was dressed in Robert's dark blue coat and breeches, with a neat, unobtrusive cravat tied at his throat. His face was disguised, and a glint of silver and pearl showed the presence of the enchanted cravat pin. Under his mop of brown hair, Judith perceived a gleam in his eye.

"Why are you wearing Robert's uniform?" She had a sinking feeling, and she eyed his white stockings with disapprobation. Unfortunately, they displayed his muscular calves rather nicely.

"I am going to play the footman today. Robert is completely drained, the poor boy. It is my turn to escort you."

"Must you? I am perfectly capable of walking to Garvey House myself."

"Absolutely not."

"At least your new charm is working nicely." Her eyes narrowed. "Though one end of that moustache appears pointier than the other."

Self-consciously, Dacian's fingers went to the point in question, but of course his hand passed through the Illusion and it momentarily vanished. "Robert was becoming tired, and I didn't want to strain him. He can refine the details tonight. I pass muster though, do I not?"

The moustache sprang back into existence, and Judith regarded it with disfavour. "Indeed, no one would guess that beneath *that* moustache lies the Duke of Sargen."

The slight asymmetry gave his face a roughish look, not tempered by the grin he gave her now. "Then let us depart." He held out his arm, then dropped it. "Damn. I'll have to walk behind you."

Thus arranged, they set off on the walk to Garvey House. Although the clouds remained threatening, the air was pleasantly warm and still. Judith found herself wishing to talk to Dacian. However, even on the lonely country lanes she did not want to risk giving rise to comment by chatting to her footman, or ogling his calves. They fell into a companionable silence, Dacian a few feet behind her, and sound of birds twittering around them in the hedgerows.

The lane took them past the flowing stream, the same one they had walked besides nine years earlier, with some ducks of a similar descent paddling in the waters. Then Judith turned up the long drive to Garvey House, and marched through the browning, rotting ash leaves.

At her resounding knock, the front door eventually opened. The burly butler stood there, his hand still on the doorknob, and his chin at an arrogant angle as he sneered down at her.

"Yes, my lady?" He might as well have said *You again?*

"I am here to see Lady Garvey," Judith said firmly. "I know she is at home and will receive me."

"No one is at home, my lady." The lie clanged, and the man's gaze shifted to Dacian, who stood behind her. The butler's bloodshot eyes narrowed. Judith hoped he didn't notice that her footman appeared different today, and moreover possessed an asymmetrical moustache.

"It concerns Miss Georgina Garvey," pressed Judith, "and a personal invitation to a wedding."

The butler's eyes came back to her face. "Do you have the invitation?"

"I wished to *personally* invite her."

"Invitations can be delivered by the postboy," he said, and then, shockingly, shut the door in her face.

Judith spun around. "Did you see that?" she hissed in outrage.

Dacian nodded. "A butler, my foot. The Garveys must be desperate."

"I won't have it." She pushed past him, and marched along the avenue in front of the house. "We will try the back door."

However, when they rounded the back corner of the house, Dacian coughed. She glanced over her shoulder and he jerked his head towards the maze.

"Can we have a quick look in there? Before you storm the castle? Wooten remarked upon something last night."

"Oh?" Judith hesitated. "I warn you, Robert and I became quite lost yesterday."

"I have a map," he replied. "After you went to bed, Wooten drew one for me. Apparently, he flew over the maze several times, while he was waiting for Marigold to finish frolicking in the poplars. He said there is a path through the wilderness that leads directly to the centre."

"How odd. When we walked it yesterday, we could not find it." She turned and led them into the maze, away from the watchful window panes. It was a relief, in a way, to retreat within the privacy of the yew walls. They walked along the green avenue in a sudden, quiet silence.

Judith heard a rustle and looked over her shoulder to see Dacian had pulled a scrap of paper out of his livery. He showed it to her: a tiny map drawn in Wooten's fastidious hand. After examining it a moment, Dacian looked up.

"May I take the lead?"

"Of course."

To do so, however, he had to edge past her in the narrow confines of the maze. Judith pressed herself back into the leaves, but her bodice almost touched his chest as he passed.

He paused, so close, looking down at her. "We barely have a moment alone, with Robert always hovering."

"That is as it should be," she replied weakly. She could feel the warmth of him, and her hands ached to grasp his coat and pull him closer. With a force of will she kept them by her sides, clenching her skirts tightly.

"You were right, you know." His expression was serious.

"About what exactly?"

"About my misjudgment," he clarified. "I should have known it wasn't you in the maze that night. I can only say that I was drunk and didn't stop to think."

"Hm." The hedges pressed around them like a green cocoon, and she felt a little dazed. "And what about the intervening nine years? Surely you weren't drunk for the entirety of *that*."

"Wretch. That is why I asked you about it, to see if there was some explanation." He paused. "I did write to you from Spain once, you know."

"I never received it." She almost didn't believe him, except her Gift could hear his truth.

Dacian brought a hand up to brush her arm. She wondered if he had infused his touch with Impact, that it swept through her body with such power. "Even when I sent it, I doubted it would reach you, with the war on the continent." His gaze was rueful. "It must have been intercepted."

The knowledge that he had written, even once, suddenly lightened her heart. Her fingers unclenched. Then she recalled the possible contents of that letter. "Did you accuse me of seducing Lord Garvey?"

"Er, no." He hesitated. "Not exactly."

"You still believed the Illusion, in fact." Her jaw tightened and she jerked her head. "Let us not dally too long."

For a moment longer, he stared down at her. She gazed back defiantly. Then his lips twisted and he moved in front again, turning his back to her.

Judith let out her breath and proceeded after him. Was it indeed true that he was irresistible? She had almost thrown herself into his arms, just at the scent of him: cocoa, spices, and whisky.

Perhaps she just needed a good drink of chocolate. And soon.

Dacian's broad shoulders progressed deeper into the maze, until they reached a corridor that disappeared into an overgrown press of hedge. Yew banked close together in a wild, unchecked generosity. Nearing the impassable wilderness, he glanced down at Wooten's map and then turned to his right.

"Strange," he murmured. "Wooten must have marked it wrong. He drew a path here." Dacian pointed to where tendrils stretched out in a haphazard growth.

Judith came to stand beside him. "It certainly needs a trim." She reached out restlessly to tweak an errant twig.

Yet her fingers brushed through thin air.

With her groping grasp, a section of the overgrown tangle suddenly vanished. Where before there had been an impenetrable mass, a gap opened before them, showing a neatly clipped path.

"An Illusion," she breathed.

"I doubt it is being cast as we speak." Dacian glanced around sharply. "It must be held in place by a charm. Where is the enchanted object?"

After a short inspection, they soon found it: a large, brass key hanging in the yew branches, obscured by leaves and berries. Judith held it up. "A common household object, and easy enough to heat above a candle." She paused. "An Illusor must live at Garvey House, or close by."

"Kenneth," said Dacian, tucking the key away so it was once more hidden. "He must have left this enchantment in place while he resides in London."

"Perhaps," said Judith thoughtfully.

"I'll go first, marchioness." Dacian shouldered in, still bearing his map. Judith followed, wondering if it were wise to tread into a secret tract. Her eyes trailed down to Dacian's tapering waist. Was his striking figure instantly recognisable? The silly moustache would not do much at all to disguise him if they came face to face with their quarry; indeed, it would better if the duke could melt into the maze as a piece of shrubbery. She would have to suggest it to Robert for next time.

Dacian held his map aloft, but there was no need for it now.

The hidden path cut a direct, though tight, swathe through the morass which pressed upon them. After the suffocating tightness of the corridor, it was jarring when it suddenly opened onto a large, perfectly round clearing.

Judith recognised it as the centre of the maze, for standing in the middle were two thin swords set upright in a cross, as if marking the spot. Their wicked points were rusty now, and the pommels, resting in stone cradles, were dull with age. Oddly, despite the respectfully pruned clearing that encircled the swords, the stone plinth was covered in a wild flowering vine that had been allowed to grow unrestrained. The vine snaked over the stone, as if swallowing it whole, and flowers crept up the sword handles, unconfined and lush.

The blooms were large and white, with purple splotches in their centre. Yellow filaments made them look much like a cross between a briar rose and a pansy. Opposite the swords, a worn, wooden bench looked well used, its arms curling down on either side of the seat.

Sniffing the air, Judith recognised the same cloying scent that she had smelled yesterday. She and Robert must have been closer to the centre than they had realised.

"Is it someone's secret garden boudoir?" wondered Dacian. "Carefully hidden. Suspicious, don't you think?"

Judith stepped forward and sniffed one of the flowers. The sweet smell became overpowering. "This scent is familiar, yet I do not recognise this plant."

"I don't fancy it much. Better not touch the blooms, in case they are poisonous." Dacian strolled the circumference. "It seems there is not much else here."

"Check for Illusions," she advised. She demonstrated by trailing her hands along the surrounding circle of hedge. It stayed as a bower of topiary, though Judith could see small round gaps spaced throughout the wall of foliage. Dacian poked through the flowers, to test the barely visible plinth and rusty swords, but they found nothing further out of the ordinary.

"Why the concealment?" Dacian questioned. "We must be growing close, marchioness!"

"Indeed." Judith contemplated the clearing. "Unless the charm was simply purchased and installed for amusement's sake? Perhaps Georgina hides here when she grows bored of her grandmother."

"Hm," said Dacian skeptically. "Well, the house awaits us. Maybe it will have more answers."

He took the lead again, and they traversed the hidden path in silence. Once free, they turned to see the Illusion spring up again.

Consulting his tiny map, Dacian led them back through pruned avenues. Judith expected him to find the exit soon, but he stopped. Over his shoulder, with a sinking feeling, she saw the Apollo statue, with its lewdly angled quiver of arrows.

"Here it is," he said grimly.

"Yes." Judith cleared her throat, desperate not to conjure the image of herself with her hair and gown unbound. "I wonder where the Illusor hid that night."

Dacian strode into the clearing. "I heard footsteps. Whoever it was must have been obscured by the hedges." He glared at Apollo. "It still boils my blood, just thinking about it." Judith felt a tingle of pressure on her skin, and a rustle passed through the leaves.

"Think about this, then," she suggested. "There must have been a person under the Illusion: a real woman. It is entirely possible that *she* constructed the Illusion herself, rather than a hidden watcher."

Dacian stalked round the statue. "It is possible. But who would do such a thing?" He paused uncomfortably. "I suppose Garvey might even have been complicit in it, as some sort of erotic play."

Judith frowned. "What do you mean?"

"He may have asked for the woman to take on another guise, to titillate him."

Judith swallowed, repulsed. "How revolting."

Dacian's fist clenched. "He deserved to die, if that was the case." The pressure returned, with a promise of thunder. Then it dissipated, and Dacian's fingers loosened. "However, Garvey didn't show guilt when he turned to face me, so I rather think not. The Illusion must have been cast for my eyes only."

"Someone who knew of your temper and your Gift."

"Not necessarily my Gift," said Dacian. "They would have known of my reputation for duelling, at least. Perhaps Kenneth pinned his hopes simply on that."

"Maybe." Judith turned her back on the aloof visage of Apollo. "If it was indeed Kenneth."

It was easier today to find the way out, with Wooten's map once more taking them to the spacious poplar avenue. Out of the maze, Judith took the lead, and skirted round the back of the hedges, with Dacian resuming his role as a footman.

When they came in sight of the house, Judith took a breath. "We need the element of surprise. And a convincing reason why they can't refuse us entry."

"Yes, marchioness?" said Dacian. "I suspect you that have a plan."

"Can you carry me?"

He raised a brow. "With ease."

"Well, I have twisted my ankle," said Judith resolutely, as she tightened the ribbons of her mobcap. "You will need to carry me to the front door and demand assistance."

"Quite." Dacian grinned. "Come on, then."

He stepped forward. Judith frowned at his chest. "I abhor the necessity, but I cannot think of another way inside."

"Oh, absolutely, a terrible necessity." He put an arm around her shoulder, drawing her close. Judith's legs threatened to give way in reality. "If I can bear it, then you can, marchioness."

She examined his face, ostensibly to check that he was still disguised. Robert's charm was holding up remarkably well: Dacian's moustache was bushy and concealing, his scar hidden, and his eyebrows muted. A pity his eyes were so amused and direct.

"Are you ready?" He bent slightly, slipping his other arm around her thighs. Judith's blood rushed to her cheeks, but before she could change her mind, she was suddenly airborne.

It ought to have been lurchingly unstable, but instead she felt contained and steady, held by his strength. Her ribs and breast pressed against his chest, and she smelled oak, smoke, and whisky, with the tantalising fragrance of spices.

"It's not so bad, is it?" he murmured in her ear.

Mutely, she shook her head, then managed to slip her arms around his neck. "Onwards." Her voice was a little husky.

Dacian shifted slightly and began walking. He peered down at her. "You look rather flushed. Try to look pale and distressed."

"Oh, be quiet," she snapped. "Stay in character. Remember, you are my servant now."

"Always," he said. "Now clutch a little more, marchioness, ready for the pantomime, but don't dislodge my moustache. I'm about to kick up a fuss."

Judith let her head droop onto his shoulder, and contorted her face into an expression of pain. After all, it *was* torturous, she realised, to be this close to Dacian and be unable to nuzzle into his neck and run her fingers through his thick hair. She distracted herself by watching the house through half-closed lids, and was rewarded by the sight of the curtain twitching on the second floor at the oriel window.

When they arrived at the back door, Dacian began shouting.

"Hallooo? My mistress is hurt! Let me in!" He kicked the door for good measure, and Judith jiggled against his chest. She gulped.

He bellowed again, right next to her ear. She flinched, clutching at his hard shoulders, fearing that he would send her deaf. Before he could do so, however, the back door suddenly swung open.

In which they storm the drawing room

The magic in a charm is ordinarily stirred to life by a single word.
  - from *Lady Avely's Guide to Lies and Charms*

THIS TIME, the butler was not in evidence. Instead, a short, elderly servant stared up at them. Her wrinkled features emphasised a pair of watery blue eyes, sunken in her face and shadowed by a white mobcap. She wore an old-fashioned dark gown, respectable enough, with a crisp white apron tied over the top. A chatelaine of keys dangling from her waist indicated her profession.

This must be the skinny servant that Marigold had seen serving Lady Garvey last night.

"Yes?" demanded the housekeeper. "What is wrong?"

Dacian did not wait for permission and pushed past her. "My mistress, Marchioness of Lanyon, has twisted her ankle."

"Broken," moaned Judith. "I'm sure it is broken."

"Grievously broken," agreed Dacian. "She needs a couch and some medical aid."

Over his broad shoulder, Judith saw the housekeeper frown. "Very well. There is a bench in the kitchen on which she may rest, while we wait for the apothecary."

"Kitchen?" Dacian adopted the arrogant accents of an outraged footman. "Apothecary? My lady will require the Drawing Room, if you please, and a doctor."

Following his instincts, as well as his knowledge of the house from nine years ago, Dacian marched up the hall and found the central staircase. Without any apparent effort, he carried Judith upwards. She clutched at him, knowing that this moment was soon to pass. As he strode up the stairs, she caught a glimpse of the butler, his swarthy face startled, then angry. He followed, right behind the housekeeper, who hurried behind them, protesting.

Oblivious, Dacian kicked open the door to the drawing room. They burst in. Judith lifted her head from Dacian's shoulder to take stock of the scene.

In the chair by the fireplace, Lady Cordelia Garvey sat in regal splendour. She was not dressed for company, but clad in a peach brocade dressing robe, with a blanket spread across her knees. At least, Judith was pleased to see, her ladyship was wearing a satin mobcap much in the same style as Judith's. A beaky nose jutted out from beneath it, and Lady Garvey's eyes blinked in astonishment at the sight of Judith aloft.

"Lady Garvey." Judith nodded from her elevated height. "So sorry to intrude, but I am afraid I have injured myself."

"Judith Avely? Can it be you?" Her voice quavered, then grew in strength. "What on earth are you doing, crashing in here like this? Most improper."

"I'm afraid I have twisted my ankle and need to rest a moment."

The housekeeper hovered like a black shadow at the door, and spoke up skeptically. "I thought you said it was grievously broken?" Behind her, the butler scowled.

"Oh, it is feeling much better already," said Judith firmly.

Dacian carried her over to the window seat, which was framed by curtains with maroon stripes. Tenderly, he laid Judith down in the oriel settee, arranging cushions behind her. His breath was warm on her ear, his hands gentle. Then he stood to the side, clasping his hands behind him and pursing his lips under his moustache.

He looked like a handsome, tall footman, yet she worried that it was blindingly obvious that he was something more. Someone dangerous, arrogant, and powerful, merely pretending to be a footman.

"Harold," she said after a moment, "Please return to the inn and fetch my carriage. I cannot walk home in this condition."

Dacian's jaw tightened, but he dared not object. He gave short bow and retreated in good order, pushing past the butler, who went with him. Judith had the feeling she was going to hear about his summary dismissal later. And perhaps his moniker.

"Dear Judith," said Lady Garvey, raising her quizzing glass so that it magnified her sunken eye. "Can it really be you? The last time I saw you..." Her expression faltered and became overlaid with grief, crumpling her features. She dropped the quizzing glass onto the blanket, then spoke briskly. "What brings you here?"

"I will tell you." Judith's eyes slid to the housekeeper, who had not departed. The woman's pale blue eyes watched carefully, her hands folded over the white apron. "However, I am utterly parched. I don't suppose I could have some tea first?"

"Yes, yes," nodded Lady Garvey. "Mrs Froode, fetch the tea things. The nice ones."

She jerked her head, and reluctantly Mrs Froode withdrew, but not before Judith had seen her thin hands clutch each other, the veins showing.

"Thank you." Judith settled back into her cushions, glancing round at the faded furnishings and the threadbare carpet. "You have retreated from society, I see - I have not seen you in London for an age."

Lady Garvey cleared her throat, fingers playing with her quizzing glass as she eyed Judith. "Yes, you must tell me the latest scandals. I am certain you know *all* about them."

There was a dig to her words, and Judith wondered what Lady Garvey had already heard. Judith's daughter, Elinor, had managed to call some attention to herself during the season. Eager to deflect any attention from Elinor's antics, Judith imparted some intriguing tidbits about the Duke and Duchess of Planx instead, and the news of her own rise to the title of marchioness.

While they were talking, Mrs Froode returned, bearing a tray of tea and biscuits. Lady Garvey nodded as the tray was set on the table before her. "Thank you, Mrs Froode. Please tell Faske to fetch a doctor for Lady Avely, if you would be so kind."

"Oh, that won't be necessary." Judith swung her foot down and made a show of testing it. "I simply need a rest. I shall be fine in my carriage, once my footman fetches it."

The housekeeper bobbed a curtsy, and once more withdrew with a lingering, suspicious glance from under her pristine white mobcap.

Judith stood and carefully limped over to the tea table. She sat down next to Lady Garvey and offered to pour the tea.

"I suppose you may." Her ladyship's black, hooded eyes examined Judith closely over the tea pot, her slashing brows lowered. "As long as you tell me the true purpose of your visit. It seems strange to see you now, after such a long time."

"Yes, almost ten years!" Judith poured the tea, the liquid steaming and fragrant. "Lord Garvey is missed in London," she lied. "I am so very sorry for what happened that night nine years ago."

Lady Garvey gnarled hand snatched at the cup, and the liquid sloshed. "Don't spout platitudes, Judith Avely. I always knew you didn't like Charles. You thought yourself above him, if I'm not mistaken, though the Lord knows why. No doubt you think yourself proven right now, with your fancy new title."

Judith blinked at this plain talking. "Not at all. It was a great tragedy to lose Lord Garvey at the prime of his life." She paused, picking up her own cup more gingerly, the hot porcelain warming her fingers. "Did you ever discover what the duel was about, that became such a matter of life and death?"

Lady Garvey dug her chin into her peach shawl. "I heard different things," she said irritably. "None of them true, I'd say. Charles was a perfect gentleman."

Judith could hear the lie in her ladyship's voice. Even his own mother did not believe that Charles had been an honourable sort.

In contrast to their sordid subject of conversation, the tea, at least, was hot and refreshing. Judith took a grateful sip. "Was the duel over a woman, perhaps? They often are."

"How am I to know?" snapped Lady Garvey. "Sons do not usually divulge their affairs to their mothers, Lady Avely - unless young Peregrine tells you of his amours?"

Judith swallowed the scalding liquid and kept her face neutral, determined not to acknowledge the hit. She suspected there was quite a bit that Peregrine was hiding from her on that front, not the least his rather close friendship with a certain person of royal bloodline. Mustering a smile, she said, "No, indeed, and would we want to know? I am merely curious if you heard something afterwards which might explain why the duke's ire was so fatally raised."

"Oh, you assume it was the duke who issued the challenge, do you?" Lady Garvey sniffed. "Perhaps it was Charles who discovered the duke in some misdeed. Indeed, it is quite possible that his grace was attempting to seduce Charles' betrothed, Miss Selina Pelling. Perhaps *that* was the reason for the quarrel."

Again, Judith could hear the doubt in her ladyship's voice, and simply raised her brows.

Lady Garvey's nostrils flared. "Don't give me that superior look. Miss Selina Pelling was a hussy. She was very quick to marry someone else before Charles was barely cold in the ground."

Judith could hear that this last accusation *was* true. "Oh? Who did she marry?"

"Mr Southcott, local gentry," said Lady Garvey shortly. "He owns a small property nearby. Nothing compared to this, of course." She gestured to the decrepit drawing room, pride and proprietorship warming her gaze. "Not that Selina Pelling deserved any of it."

"You think that Miss Selina was dallying with the duke?" Judith frowned. Did Lady Garvey know something that she didn't? The thought that Dacian might have flirted with that young girl was like the scrape of a rusty sword over her skin. But of course, he usually went for widows. "I doubt his grace would have paid Miss Pelling much heed."

Her ladyship gave a pitying smile. "Why do you sound skeptical, my dear? The Duke of Sargen was a rake. We all know that."

This was true, and Judith's reply stuck in her throat. She took another sip of tea to try to dislodge the lump.

Her ladyship snorted in triumph. "Enough of Charles' unjust death. Tell me the purpose of your visit, Lady Avely."

She attempted a placatory smile. "I merely wish to enquire after Miss Georgina Garvey. It occurred to me that she must be quite grown up now. Is she well?"

"Still prone to illness, I'm afraid." Lady Garvey's lips turned down and her gaze drifted to the window. "She has weak lungs."

"Nothing serious, I hope?"

"It is manageable enough."

"Will she be having her first London season next year?"

That provoked a glower. "Oh no. I'm too ill to do a season in

London. And Georgina's delicate constitution would suffer. Out of the question."

"I thought Georgina might like to attend Elinor's wedding," Judith pressed. "A way to dip her toe into society, as it were. If you are too ill to escort her, you could send her with the new Lord Garvey. Kenneth resides in London, doesn't he?"

Something darkened her hostess's face. "Kenneth is not fit to chaperone a young girl."

Judith tilted her head with curiosity. "What can you mean?"

"Nothing." Lady Garvey's expression became dour. "It is a private family matter. Suffice to say, I won't trust my grand-daughter with him."

Judith frowned. It was true that an unattached bachelor wasn't an ideal chaperone for a young girl, but she could hear some other meaning in Lady Garvey's tone. Politeness dictated, however, that she could not pursue the question. "Surely Miss Georgina must have some female relatives in town? What about her mother's side? I am so sorry to hear about Harriet's death."

Lady Garvey nodded tightly, her lips pressing together.

Judith waded on. "Did Harriet have any other daughters, or sisters, or cousins, that could stand in her stead to watch over Georgina?"

"The Bollophers don't have any respectable family." Lady Garvey's mouth twisted in distaste. "Oh, there might be a second cousin somewhere, I grant you, but I'm not going to trust my Georgina to some stranger. Regardless, Georgina's health is too fragile to warrant a trip into the metropolis. It is full of pollution and disease, and I don't want to hear another word about it."

"Of course," murmured Judith. "Such a shame."

"Now," Lady Garvey put down her cup with a click in its saucer. "If you have quite finished prying, you may take your leave, Judith."

That might have been that, except then Miss Georgina Garvey herself burst into the room.

She was a slender young woman, with dark hair, a pale complexion, and pretty, even features. The same red bow that Judith had glimpsed through the oriel window still sat above her ear, and she wore a frilly gown in pink and white that was a little old-fashioned. She looked rather hale and hearty to Judith's eyes, with the vigour of youth blooming in her cheeks.

Georgina threw herself down beside Lady Garvey's chair and clasped her empty, wrinkled hand.

"Please, Grandmama, *please* let me go to London!"

Lady Garvey spoke with gentle reproof. "Now, Georgie, we've discussed it before, and we won't discuss it again in company. Have you been listening at the door, you naughty puss?"

"How could I help it? We never receive visitors." Georgina turned to Judith. "I am so delighted you have called on us, Lady Avely, and it is so very kind of you to think of me," she said prettily. "I remember Elinor so well from years ago. Is it true that she is to marry an earl?"

Judith nodded, smiling. "The wedding is soon; consider this your invitation to attend."

Lady Garvey snorted. "Don't raise your hopes, Georgie. And Judith, allow me to manage my own household how I see fit."

"Come now, it will be good for Georgina to have company her own age. You cannot keep her locked away forever."

Georgina tucked her legs under her skirts, still holding her grandmother's hand. "*Please* let me visit Elinor, Grandmama."

Lady Garvey shook her head and gently withdrew her hand from Georgina's claps. Shakily, the old lady pushed herself to her feet and made her way to the oriel window with the assistance of her walking cane, her movements jerky and slow. She peered out into the grounds. "No, Georgina. You are too sensitive for London."

"But, Grandmama–"

Lady Garvey held up a veined hand. "Your carriage is pulling up, Judith. Ah look, your footman is hopping down. A handsome fellow, isn't he?" She peered down. "Though a bit old. Footmen should be young, in my opinion."

Judith smoothed her skirts, and returned the thrust. "I have not seen any of your footmen, Lady Garvey, and I confess I have taken your butler in dislike. Where did you find him?"

"Oh, Faske." Lady Garvey turned away from the window. "He is a bit rough around the edges, I grant you. However, I need a strong man on the premises to protect us. We are two women living alone, as you may have noticed."

Soon Judith heard hasty footsteps on the stairs, and Dacian came through the door with Faske at his heels.

"My lady," Dacian bowed low. "Your carriage awaits."

The Illusion still concealed his features, but to Judith's senses it was utterly obvious who he truly was. Worse, the moustache was looking more uneven, and the mole appeared to have moved slightly. Could the charm be fading? Judith cast a nervous glance at Lady Garvey, who was now examining Dacian through her quizzing glass, her brow furrowed.

"Thank you, Harold, you may pick me up," Judith announced, hoping to distract that beady gaze. "I declare, I cannot walk."

"Certainly, my lady." Dacian slid his strong arms around her and launched her into the air. He smelled divine, and Judith had a sudden craving for chocolate, or perhaps something more... sustaining.

"Goodbye, Lady Garvey." Judith twisted her head. "Please think upon my invitation. I will call again tomorrow to further discuss the matter."

"Do not bother," snapped Lady Garvey, dropping her quizzing glass. "I have made my decision. Goodbye, Lady Avely. Good luck with your daughter's wedding. I hope no scandal attaches to it."

Dacian swept her out the room. Judith could hear Georgina admonishing her grandmother as the door shut behind them.

Mrs Froode followed them out and called after them, her voice frail but somehow containing a steely note. "If you do call tomorrow, my lady, you will be turned away."

"That is a decision for Lady Garvey," said Judith with dignity, even though she was being held aloft like a child and peering over Dacian's shoulder. He came to a halt and listened, his arms reassuringly solid.

Mrs Froode shook her head, her blue eyes narrowing. "You will be barred from here. Even if you cry wolf." She gave a slightly derisive look at Judith's exposed ankle, then turned away. "Faske, escort Lady Avely out, and do not let her return."

There was something familiar about the housekeeper in that moment. Judith stared at the black-clad figure. "You've been with the household a long time, I take it? Were you here when Lord Garvey died?"

"I was," agreed Mrs Froode. "And I advise you not to turn up old stones. You might find something ugly underneath."

The housekeeper held Judith's gaze for a warning moment, then turned away. "Faske, escort Lady Avely out, and do not let her return."

In which a footman is improper

A charm must be reinvigorated or it will fade into disrepair.
  - from *Lady Avely's Guide to Lies and Charms*

ONCE OUTSIDE, Dacian bundled her into the carriage, and then took his place as footman, hanging off the rear. The coachman, Patrick, set the horses in motion, and the carriage rumbled down the ash-lined drive. Judith sank back against the squab, relieved to be alone for a minute. It had been trying to joust with Lady Garvey, while listening for lies. Dacian's arms had been a bolstering relief, but that too was an assault on her senses. She needed a moment to put herself in order. Patting her mobcap back into place, she retied the ribbons and smoothed her skirts.

The carriage turned onto the laneway, out of sight of the house. Judith heard rattling at the side door and suddenly saw Dacian's head peering through the window. He had climbed around the body of the carriage while it was in motion.

"Let me in." He rapped again on the glass. "We need to talk."

Hastily, she unlatched the door. He swung himself inside, clicking it shut, and sat down opposite her.

Despite herself, she smiled. "You are not very good at playing a footman, are you? This is most improper." Fortunately, Patrick was solidly the duke's man, and would not turn a hair at his untoward behaviour.

"Not as improper as allowing a footman to embrace you."

Judith blushed. "I don't think we should attempt that ruse again. Lady Garvey paid far too much attention to you. What if she were to recognise you? She might call the parish constable out to arrest you for killing her son."

"No risk of that," said Dacian, with a mock twirl of his moustache, which of course did not respond but momentarily vanished instead.

When he lowered his hand, she saw that the accoutrement, though it sprang back, had started to wilt a little. The whole disguise had slipped down somehow; perhaps with his athletic swing around the carriage. The moustache now sat on Dacian's lower lip, and his mole in the hollow of his cheek.

Judith reached forward and pulled the pearl pin out of his cravat. "Take it off, for goodness' sake. It is making me twitch."

As she pulled the pin out, the brown colour washed out of his hair, leaving it black and wavy again. Now she could see the beautifully carved planes of his face, and his dark, striking eyes. The white cravat loosened around his throat without the pin to hold it in place.

"That's better," she said faintly.

He raised a brow. "If you are to take my cravat off, may I take off your mobcap? Fair's fair, marchioness."

"Certainly not." Judith resisted the urge to pat her headgear. She held Dacian's cravat pin, warm in her fingers. "Thank you for fetching the carriage."

"A dastardly ploy on your part," he said, "yet some good has come of it." He leaned back, folding his arms over his broad chest. "You recall that the best parlour is already taken at the Golden Bat? When I ran back, I saw the occupant emerge. It is Lord Kenneth Garvey himself."

Judith sat up straight, intrigued. "How very strange. Why would he stay at the inn when he could stay as master at Garvey House?"

"Guilt," suggested Dacian with satisfaction. "He killed Charles for his title and inheritance, but now he can't bear the thought of it. Or perhaps he is afraid of running into his brother's ghost."

"Or," said Judith thoughtfully, "he is afraid of a more human accusation. Lady Garvey was very scathing about her second son. Perhaps she suspects his guilt."

Dacian raised his brows. "What did she say?"

Judith thought back. "I suggested that Kenneth could be Georgina's guardian in town, and she rejected the notion with hostility. When I pressed her, she said it was a 'private family matter', but that she wouldn't trust Kenneth with Georgina."

Dacian grimaced. "I suspect I know what *that* might be about."

"Oh?"

"Kenneth likes men." His lips quirked. "Lady Garvey, because she is a fool, probably sees that as a greater moral failing than murder."

Judith's eyes widened. "He is like... Lord Vosse?"

"Indeed. In fact, I suspect Kenneth and Lord Vosse were, er, intimately involved with each other, at the house party."

She cast her mind back, remembering how the two men had been walking together behind Miss Pelling, talking with the intimacy of close friends. Perhaps it had been more than friendship. She had not paid any attention to the possibility at the time, even though she was aware that such arrangements existed. "Who knew about it?"

Dacian shrugged. "Not many. They were discreet."

"I wonder if Charles knew, and threatened to intervene to protect the family reputation," Judith pondered. "Perhaps Kenneth killed him not for the title and money, but for passion."

"Well, we can find out," said Dacian. "We must invite ourselves into the best parlour and question the man himself."

"*I* must invite myself. You must not show yourself at all. Kenneth might recognise you, and that would give the game away."

They were drawing closer to Stokesford, and reluctantly she handed the cravat pin over again. She watched as Dacian expertly redid his cravat and thrust the pin through. His disguise resumed, but the moustache was still marginally adrift.

Dacian leaned forward. "Don't think I have forgotten that you called me Harold," he warned. "I am still concocting a suitable punishment."

A smile crept onto her face. "What would you have preferred? Bartholomew?"

He winced. "Good God, no."

She pretended to consider. "Yes, I think that moustache belongs to a Bartholomew."

"Stop maligning the moustache!"

"Anyone would think it was your real one," she mocked. "We must ask Robert to refresh it. You will draw attention if you are wearing it on your chin."

Dacian ignored that and directed a speculative look at her ankle. "I must carry you out of the carriage, to continue the charade of your injury."

"That won't be necessary."

"I assure you, it is no hardship."

Judith thought of her soft body pressed against his hard one, and looked away. "We do not want to tax your Gift with such trivial matters."

"What else is my Gift worth, if not to protect a beautiful woman?" His eyes glinted.

She shook her head. "If you expect such ridiculous nonsense to convince me to undo my bodice, you are sadly mistaken."

"No, you'll take your bodice off because I'm irresistible," he retorted. Judith huffed in exasperation, and then he added, "I won't rush you, marchioness, but I live in hope." Without waiting for an answer, he swung himself out of the carriage again, to resume his position clinging to the back rail.

Left alone again, Judith's heart beat fast. He had said those very same words to her, nine years ago.

Interlude II

Nine Years Earlier

Judith avoided the duke as much as she could at the Garvey house party, but it was difficult in such close quarters. At least their difference in station meant that she was never required to sit beside him at dinner. Afterwards, in the drawing room, he was always thronged with admirers, including the annoyingly beautiful Lady Vosse. Even Mrs Pelling, a buxom widow with doe-brown eyes like her daughter, seemed determined to flatter his grace's sense of importance. Perhaps she thought better of selling off her daughter to Lord Garvey, if there was a duke to be bagged.

On the second evening, however, Dacian managed to excuse himself from their clutches, and wander over to Judith. His eyes were bright with drink, his coat well-fitting, and he swirled a glass of whisky.

He put out a peremptory hand. "Come, Mrs Avely. Step outside with me for some fresh air."

"No, I thank you." Judith stayed seated, her hands folded on her lavender silk gown. Although she wanted to give him a piece of her mind, she couldn't possibly disappear outside with him. He must be quite drunk to even suggest it. People would leap to *quite* the wrong conclusion, especially now that she was a widow - even though it had only been a year since Nicholas died.

Ignoring her cold look, Dacian sat down, dismissing her companion with a flick of his eyes. Miss Pelling hastily stood and removed her person.

"We must talk," he announced. "I cannot bear this coolness from you, Judith. Say your piece, for God's sake, and put me out of my misery."

"Not here," she retorted. "I might raise my voice."

He leaned in. "Where, then? Perhaps we could meet in the greenhouse tomorrow at midday. There we will have the privacy you desire." The gleam in his eye gave his words a double meaning.

She gritted her teeth, and straightened a pearl button on her glove. "Very well. Tomorrow at midday. Then you will receive what you deserve."

"And a duke deserves only the best," he replied teasingly, and her pulse jumped - in anger, of course.

WHEN SHE SLIPPED into the glass building at noon, however, she saw that it was already occupied.

Mrs Harriet Bollopher was there, her slight figure and greying hair recognisable among the glossy leaves of the peach trees in the far corner. She wore a brown gardening smock over her russet gown, and she was wrestling with the heavy pots, attempting to turn them round so the fruit trees could gain an even exposure to the autumn sunlight.

With her was Miss Selina Pelling, providing some assistance.

Between the two of them, they managed to swivel a massive porcelain pot around so that the hidden branches now faced the southern warmth. Opposite them, a neat stand of orange trees bore the first small green orbs that would ripen in winter.

"There." Harriet straightened. "That should do it. Thank you so much, Miss Pelling."

Judith approached, wondering how she could be rid of them quickly, or if Dacian would hear their voices and retreat. "Do you require some assistance?"

Harriet looked up and smiled. "Oh, no. It is bad enough that I have roped Miss Pelling into this menial task. Lord Garvey has put all the gardening staff to work on the maze, so the greenhouse has been quite neglected. I am lucky that Miss Pelling is a woman of unsuspected talents."

Harriet winked at Selina, who looked down at the ground with a fixed expression of embarrassment. Judith wondered at the girl's lack of poise, and then realised that the poor child was hiding in the glasshouse, trying to escape the machinations of her mother and Lord Garvey.

"Indeed." Judith glanced around. "Such a beautiful greenhouse must require a lot of work." The tall glass walls were lush with climbing roses, and a crescent of camellia plants gave off a delicate scent. Beds of vegetables grew next to the peach and cherry trees, and oleander plants flanked a row of vividly blue delphiniums. "A pleasant past-time, however," she added. Perhaps once married to Lord Garvey, Selina would find some solace here.

Harriet seemed to follow her thoughts. "Yes, Miss Pelling enjoys it, do you not?" She smiled kindly at Selina. "And she is quite capable of managing it, I'm sure. Anyone who sees you as a weak or empty-headed female will be surprised."

Judith pressed her lips together. She abhorred the practice of marrying young girls off to old men. Was there something she could do to intervene in this instance? Any interference would not be taken kindly by Mrs Pelling, or indeed, Lord Garvey.

Harriet brushed her hands off. "It must be time for morning tea. Do you know the time, Mrs Avely?"

"Almost midday," said Judith, and cast a nervous look at the glass door. She had arrived early, thank goodness, but at any moment the duke might stride in. It would be immediately apparent to anyone that they had made an assignation.

Harriet's shrewd gaze weighed her. "I must see to our guests. Miss Pelling, if you come with me, I will acquire some lemon cake for you."

Selina looked gratified. "That would be lovely, Mrs Bollopher."

"Would you like some too, Mrs Avely?"

"Er, no," said Judith. "I will stay here and enjoy the lovely garden."

Harriet nodded and led Miss Pelling out of the greenhouse. Judith chewed on her lip, expecting them to bump into Dacian on the way out. Yet he did not appear, and she gave thanks for his arrogant tardiness.

She looked around for a private nook that would not be visible through the large windows overlooking the lawns and house. Fortunately, vines and foliage, luxuriating in the sunshine, grew to obscure the glass walls. A charcoal brazier glowed in the southern corner, adding to the warmth that heated the window panes and caused condensation to blur the view. Judith found a stone bench in the middle of the camellias, and waited several minutes, her heart beating rapidly, before she saw Dacian's figure at the door.

He pushed the glass open and stepped in. His dove-grey morning coat and high boots were immaculate - probably because he had only woken up an hour ago, thought Judith irritably. He crossed the paved floor quickly and came to stand before her, looking down with a glimmer of a smile.

"Alone at last." Mock tenderness coloured his voice.

She looked up crossly. "You needn't be glad of it."

"Ah, but I am. Come, Judith, tell me what is in your heart."

She pursed her lips, annoyed at his continued double entendre. As if she had brought him here to seduce instead of berate him! "You know very well why I am angry."

"I have my suspicions," he agreed.

Feeling at a disadvantage, she stood. Yet Dacian did not take a step back, and she found herself staring at his chest while he smiled down at her. Infuriated, she prodded it, pushing him away.

"I found a letter hidden in a book," she said grimly. "Addressed to Nicholas, from *you*."

A look of discomfort flickered across Dacian's face. "Perhaps you should not have read Nicholas's private correspondence."

"He is dead," snapped Judith. "What else was I to do? It might have been something important. It *was* something important. It regarded nothing less than his bastard child, whom you *both* kept secret from me."

Dacian opened his mouth to speak, then shut it again.

"How dare you not tell me about it?" she continued, her voice shaking with anger. All her feelings of mortification and betrayal surged up. "You have known about this boy for at least two years, and you didn't think I would want to know?"

"It wasn't my secret." Dacian groped for words. "I thought that Nicholas would tell you."

The fragrant scent of the camellias was suddenly acrid. "Well, he didn't. Nicholas *died* before he could tell me. And still you didn't visit and inform me of this pertinent fact about his legacy."

"You were grieving him," said Dacian. "I didn't want to sully Nicholas's memory... I wanted you to have the chance to mourn him properly."

"Mourn him properly?" Judith's voice quavered. "Why should I mourn Nicholas, when I didn't even *know* him? When he loved the woman who bore his first child?" The terrible knowledge of it knotted her shoulders and made her nauseous. Her marriage had been a lie, her husband a false idol. She had known about Anna Thane before she married Nicholas, it was true. But she had not known there was a child. Would Nicholas have chosen Anna over Judith, if he had known?

Dacian shook his head, as if sensing her question. "Of course he loved you best." He shifted closer, putting a tentative hand on her arm. "How could he not? You eclipsed Anna in his heart, I can assure you of that."

Judith could hear the truth in his voice. It undid her defences, and tears sprung to her eyes.

Dacian held out an arm, his expression sympathetic. With a sob, Judith stumbled forward. All the rage and sorrow of the last year rose to the surface and spilled out. She had not spoken to anyone of Nicholas's dreadful secret, and it was a relief now to put it into words, and to air the private humiliation that had stiffened her whole being for months.

"How could he not have told me?" she wept, barely aware that Dacian had dropped his other arm to curve around her waist. "If he loved me, he should have trusted me with the knowledge."

"No doubt," soothed Dacian.

"He didn't trust me. Or he didn't love me."

Dacian drew a breath. "No, he feared your judgment. And your pain."

Judith snuffled into his coat, and voiced her deepest fear. "Did he know about the boy all along? Did he abandon him?"

"I don't think so. Truly, I don't, Judith."

Again, Dacian spoke the truth, but Judith didn't trust it this time. Her faith in Nicholas had been trampled upon. "How can I be sure of that? How do I know he didn't just turn a blind eye, to both Anna and Robert?"

Dacian pulled her a little closer. "Nicholas was a good man," he sighed. "You can believe in that. I wouldn't have let him marry you, otherwise."

Judith stiffened, suddenly aware that she was held close in the circle of his embrace. He smelled of smoke and leather, and his chest was firm beneath her cheek. She could feel his chin resting on her head, and his fingers smoothing the fabric of her gown down her back.

What was he doing? What was *she* doing? Abruptly, she lifted her head and stared at him, her eyes still blurry with tears. "What did you just say? You *let* me marry him?"

Dacian's expression froze. "I mean..."

She placed her hand on his grey coat and pushed angrily. "How dare you imply that you had anything to do with it?"

"Well, Judith... I just mean that..."

She took a furious step backwards, knowing exactly what he alluded to: their ill-advised dalliance long ago. Before she had married Nicholas, she had been waylaid by the duke's manifold charms. She'd even been willing to call off her engagement to Nicholas, and throw herself at Dacian's feet. Until he showed her his true libertine nature, and she had saved herself from a terrible mistake.

Except now it seemed she had made a mistake in marrying Nicholas too.

Dimly, she noticed that Dacian's grey coat was now marked by the moisture of her tears. "It was my choice to marry him."

"Yes." There was a bleakness in his voice. He raised a hand across the distance between them, and placed a finger under her chin. "But Nicholas is gone now."

She stared into his dark eyes. It was reprehensible, but the truth was that Dacian only gave voice to the secret hope hidden in her heart. Now that her husband was long buried, could she and Dacian once more indulge in each other and love one another? Her eyes drifted to the sensual curve of his lips then back to his intent gaze.

Only, she reminded herself harshly, it had never been *love* for Dacian. To him, she had been a flirtation, a distraction; a momentary infatuation at most. She had been quickly replaced.

With a wrench, Judith stepped sideways, out of his reach. "How dare you?" she uttered. "How dare you think I will fall into your arms now?"

His arm fell, his expression pained. "I spoke too soon."

"No, you are simply falling into old habits," she snapped. "You really think that I will rush into your embrace, after everything you have done?"

"I only ever did what I thought was right, Judith."

She spluttered, astonished that he should try to justify his detestable tendencies like this. Then she took a deep breath, remembering suddenly that Nicholas had died in debt to Dacian. "Indeed, as much as I abhor it, I owe you a debt of gratitude, I suppose. I must thank you for looking after my husband's child." She raised her chin stiffly, trying to recall her dignity. "How is the boy? Is he happy at Taunton?"

"I believe reasonably so."

"Has he shown any sign of Musing?"

"Not as far as I know. Stop trying to change the subject." Dacian gave her a long look. "I won't rush you, Judith. But I live in hope."

Judith blinked, her mouth going dry.

Before she could answer, however, a tapping noise caused both of them to turn quickly. Through the foliage of camellias, she could see the slender form of Lord Triskett outside, his knuckles raised to tap on the glass.

Seeing that he had gained their attention, he tentatively pushed the door open and came into the greenhouse.

Dacian took a discreet step away from Judith. "Yes, Anthony?"

His lordship advanced, pulling at his cravat. "Ah, Sargen, Mrs Avely. Most sorry to interrupt."

"What is it?" Dacian said brusquely.

Lord Triskett cleared his throat. "I just thought that you might like to know - you have an audience."

"An audience?" repeated Judith.

"Ahem." Lord Triskett jerked his head upwards, rolling his eyes backwards.

Judith stared at this contortion, but Dacian's gaze lifted.

"Damn," he said. "He's right. We are being observed, Judith."

She followed his gaze, up through the roof panels made of glass. To her horror, she realised she had a direct line of sight to the oriel windows that protruded from the house. The windows to the drawing room, where the guests were all gathered for morning tea.

If she had a direct line of sight, so did they.

Lord Triskett coughed. "Just wanted to warn you, that's all."

Judith swallowed. She could make out two figures in the oriel bay window. One, the green clad lithesomeness of Lady Isobel Vosse, who seemed to be looking down with venom. And two, her husband, Lord Vosse, his head inclined with interest.

What had they seen? Judith cast her mind back, flushing with embarrassment as she recalled her moments of intimacy with the duke.

"Damn it," said Dacian. "Shall we brazen it out? Biscuit, a turn about the greenhouse. Walk with me. Both of you."

Rigidly, Judith followed his lead. An awkward circuit of the peach trees followed, with Lord Triskett muttering something about the weather, and Dacian in stony silence. When at last they finished their perambulation, Judith nodded to them both. "Thank you."

Then she fled the greenhouse, her face aflame, not daring to look up.

In which a mobcap is removed

Those who speak or Discern the truth are often shunned.
  - from *Lady Avely's Guide to Lies and Charms*

BACK AT THE INN, Robert was waiting anxiously outside the parlour for their return from Garvey House. He confessed he had slept very late, repairing his Bemusement, but he wished that he could have gone to see the fun.

"We stormed the drawing room with Judith aloft," said Dacian. "It was masterfully done."

Judith tutted and told Dacian to change out of livery before someone noticed that her footman had doubled. Robert turned to follow, but she called after him.

"Please, Robert, take a seat." She gestured towards one of the upholstered chairs by the fire. "Enough of this nonsense."

Robert remained uncomfortably standing. "I don't think..."

"As Mr Avely's son, you should most certainly not be gadding about as a footman," she said firmly. "I cannot countenance it any longer. Please, put us out of this misery."

Robert raised his brows and folded his arms. "I will not renounce my position just to assuage your guilt, my lady."

Judith eyed him speculatively. That was just the sort of impertinent remark her own son, Peregrine, might make. Disrespect, she decided, was a good sign. It was far better than distant formality.

Fortunately, she was well equipped for such battles. "Such a shame," she said sweetly, "that you refuse to lessen the burden that weighs on my heart."

He regarded her uneasily. "Er..."

"At least sit down so I may tell you about our morning," she continued gently. "If you loom over me, you will give me a crick in my neck, something I can ill afford at my age."

"Er..." he said again, but he glanced at the chair. "What *did* happen this morning?"

"I will tell you." She looked up expectantly, rubbing her neck as if it pained her.

Either her conniving or his curiosity won the day, and Robert crossed to the chair and reluctantly sat down. "Very well, you win this round," he said. "What happened?"

Pleased, Judith told him about the false screen of yew, hiding a passage to the centre of the maze. He leaned forward, intrigued, and pointed out that it might be the unlikely butler who had put it in place, or indeed anyone from Garvey House, even Kenneth. The question of why, however, was baffling. Was the centre of the maze used for secret meetings, perhaps? The fact that Kenneth Garvey was staying at the Golden Bat indicated he had some covert business in Stokesford. But then why not stay at Garvey House?

When Judith recounted the 'storming of the drawing room', Robert chuckled at the introduction of 'Harold'. Yet when she concluded her tale, he sprung up again.

"Thank you for telling me, but now I must see if his grace needs help changing out of the livery."

"Nonsense. Dacian is perfectly able to change his clothes. Tell me, have you been drawing at all since we left Sargenet?"

"I've scarcely had time..." Robert trailed off.

"Precisely." Judith stood and crossed to her writing desk. "Here, take some foolscap and my charcoal nibs, while we are stuck at this inn."

Robert accepted the proffered items, but his expression became shuttered.

She ignored it. "Have you already tried your hand at landscapes?"

"Ah, a few, here and there."

"And are they any good?"

"Not really."

She raised an eyebrow at the white lie, and smiled. "Well, I can't wait to see them, if that is the case."

His jaw tightened even more. Dratted boy. He might think she was trying to force her way into his affections, but she had an obligation to ensure his welfare. Children! As they grew up, it seemed they became less receptive to parental love. Yet in Robert's case, she could hardly blame him for being wary.

Briefly, she wondered what Elinor and Peregrine would say to their new half-brother, then she put the thought aside. There was plenty of time to sidle up to *that* particular confrontation. At this rate, it seemed like Robert did not want to meet his half-siblings.

"Well," she said, "you would have plenty of time to paint landscapes in Cornwall, if you decided to go with me."

Robert looked uncomfortable. After an awkward pause, he put his chin up. "I am afraid that I must tell you that I won't be joining you in Cornwall."

"What?" Judith stared. "I thought you were growing accustomed to... the idea."

He shifted on his feet as he held the paper and nibs. "After some consideration, I have decided that it is inadvisable."

"Why?" It seemed to her, rather, that he had only just decided on the matter.

"His grace told me that Lewis is going to manage another one of the duke's estates, in Hertfordshire. I think I should go with him."

"Oh," said Judith blankly. She knew that Lewis and Robert were very good friends, both being born on the other side of the blanket and going to Taunton together. She had extended her invitation to Cornwall to Lewis too, but now it seemed that Dacian had mucked things up, by offering to transfer Lewis to Hertfordshire. Devil take his thoughtfulness!

Yet it seemed to her, also, that Robert had not been entirely honest in his excuse.

"Well," she said, after a moment. "I am sorry to hear it. Of course you must do as your loyalty demands, and I well know that you don't owe me anything. However, are you sure that is the only reason you won't accompany me?"

Robert nodded quickly. "Of course."

The words fell with a hollow clunk.

She did not want to flaunt her Gift by pointing out the lie, especially when she would rather invite his confidences. Yet Robert seemed to realise her speculation, for he looked up guiltily. "Thank you for these papers." He gave a small bow and rushed out of the room.

Confounded, Judith stared after him. Clearly, he felt uncomfortable around her Gift, just as she had suspected. She sighed, reflecting that Truth Discernment was its own sort of curse. People didn't like being an open book. If only Robert knew that she was completely baffled by him.

What was bothering the boy? It must be his loyalty to his

dead mother, something that she could not fault. His duty, too, to Lewis, was something she could admire.

Frowning, Judith retired to her bedroom for lunch, needing to gather her composure after the morning's adventures. After a large plate of shepherd's pie and roast parsnip, she felt much restored, if somewhat heavy with food. Marigold still slept in her cabinet, and Judith likewise indulged in a nap. She might be required to conduct some nocturnal investigations, after all. There was still the matter of the alleged ghost of Lord Garvey tramping about the maze, and possible secret meetings taking place in the hidden grove.

When she awoke, she turned her mind to the problem of how to beard the *new* Lord Garvey in his den, in the Golden Bat's superior parlour. Could she simply waltz in and force an acknowledgment? It was a little rude to do so. She didn't like to play the role of a pushy matron (too often), but perhaps certain circumstances required it. If Kenneth was the killer, it would be better to establish that fact without delay.

The best parlour was on the ground floor, directly beneath their own. Robert had said that it opened onto a small garden courtyard. An idea occurred to Judith.

She made her way into her own little green parlour, and found Dacian reading a newspaper. He was back in his guise as Mr Fortnew, with the moustache once more returned to its former glory, or lack thereof.

He stood and bowed. "Lady Avely. How is your ankle? Shall I call for some chocolate?"

She gave him a reproving look. "Perhaps later." She crossed to the window. "I must find a way to interrogate Kenneth now. I thought I could drop something into his garden, as an excuse to venture into his parlour."

Dacian folded the paper up. "I will come with you, of course."

"No, you won't." Judith pushed the window open. The hinge

grated a little. "If Kenneth recognises you, he will be put on his guard - or worse, have you arrested. Now, what should I drop outside?"

She turned, looking for some small object that she might conceivably have left on the windowsill and knocked over. Briefly, she considered a teacup, but she didn't want to risk it breaking. A book, too, might be damaged.

Dacian was watching her with a gleam in his eye. "I have a suggestion."

"Yes?"

"Your mobcap. If you hung it on the window handle, a breeze might have caught it."

She pursed her lips. It was a good notion. Reluctantly, her hands went to her ribbons.

In three strides, Dacian was in front of her. "Here, let me. You do owe me after all, for the cravat."

She was about to refuse him, when she remembered his words from earlier. *He lived in hope.* A breath of hope ran through her also, like a bellows whooshing onto coals. She let her hands drop. Perhaps it would do no harm to allow him some familiarity, if he had been hoping for it for nigh on ten years.

She cast her lashes down.

There was a charged silence, then he accepted her tacit permission and stepped forward. The brush of his fingers moved against her throat, then came the tug of lace, gently pulling. The ties loosened and his hands lifted the silk away, whispering past her ears.

As he pulled the cap off, her scalp tingled. Heat rose in her cheeks as he threaded his fingers through her hair, tugging it loose from her pins and softening the tightness of her coiffure. In fact, her whole body tingled, as if he were removing her very gown.

She felt as if she were unravelling.

After a few minutes, pins lay scattered on the floor, and he lowered his hands. In a daze, she saw that he was presenting the cap to her.

"Marchioness." His voice was hoarse. "Your cap."

He took a step back. She felt bereft, as if some great gift had been suddenly snatched out of her grasp. She blinked, staring at the crumpled silk in his hand.

"Throw it out the window," she managed, "if you would be so kind."

Some of his old sardonic manner returned. "With pleasure." He crossed to the window and tossed the blue silk out, then peered down. "Ah, it has landed on a blackberry bush. I fear, much to my dismay, that it might be rent and unwearable."

"Hmph."

Dacian turned, concern now etched on his face. "Please take Robert with you."

"On the subject of Robert," she said, remembering her grievance, "how could you arrange for Lewis to transfer to Hertfordshire without consulting me?"

"I was not aware you were intimately involved in the matter." Dacian raised a brow.

Judith flushed, realising she was being rather presumptuous. She put her hands on her hips. "Well, Robert wants to go where Lewis goes, so now he won't come to Cornwall with me!"

"Hm," said Dacian skeptically.

For a moment, she considered asking Dacian what other reason Robert might have, then she decided against it. After all, she wanted Robert to trust her, so she should not pry behind his back.

And it would be extremely irksome if Dacian knew more about it than her.

Turning, she left the room in a huff.

After fetching a subdued Robert, Judith knocked loudly on the best parlour door. Her blonde hair now bare, she braced herself for a tricky interrogation.

If Dacian's guess was true, Kenneth must be wily and conniving. Surely, as soon as he recognised her - the feminine object of his fatal Illusion - he would be on his guard. She would have to be careful, and equally as cunning.

The door swung open and she was given her first surprise. Not Kenneth, but some other man greeted her.

He was lean and tall, smooth shaven with a bald head, and in the elegant garb of a valet. His features were gaunt, punctuated by a rather long nose.

"Yes, my lady?" He gave her a quick perusal down that long proboscis. "How may I help you?"

She clasped her hands in feminine dismay. "I am so very sorry, but I think I dropped something into the garden." She jerked her head at Robert, who stood just behind her. "I would have trusted my footman to fetch it, but it is my favourite cap, you see, and I wanted to extricate it myself from the blackberry bush, in case it should tear."

"Your cap?" said the valet, with pardonable aloofness and a hint of disbelief.

"Indeed." Taking a leaf out of Dacian's book earlier in the day, she wasted no compunction in pushing past the servant. The valet stepped out of her way, taken aback, as she swept in, looking around. Robert edged into the room behind her, and took a place opposite the valet, by the door.

The Golden Bat's superior parlour was certainly much larger than the tiny parlour she had been allocated, and more plushly furnished. A thick red patterned carpet led up to a broad fireplace, where two armchairs rested in splendour. A small piano sat against the rear wall, its keys covered, with a vase of flowers upon the doilys. The glass door onto the garden was closed against the day, where it had finally begun to rain. Judith was glad to see it, as it lent her story more urgency.

Opposite the fire was a rosewood writing desk, similar to the one in Judith's parlour. Papers were strewn across it, with an inkwell open and a quill lying upon the sheets.

Kenneth Garvey's plump figure sat at the writing desk. He swung round to stare at Judith, his bushy eyebrows going up. He sported a luxurious moustache which quite put Dacian's to shame. It was grey, to match Kenneth's thick hair and brows, with a dashing curl. His tailoring, likewise, showed the smartness of town, with a well-cut coat in walnut brown and cream pantaloons.

Judith made a show of pulling up in surprise. "Why - is that Kenneth Garvey? Your lordship, fie, I did not expect to see you here!"

"Mrs Avely?" said Kenneth slowly. He stood and bowed in reluctant recognition.

"Oh, it is Lady Avely now," she said airily. "My husband was granted a title for his military services. I am on my way now, actually, to visit my new property in Cornwall. What are you doing here, if I may be so bold to ask?"

"I live nearby," said Kenneth shortly, while his valet looked on woodenly.

"Oh, indeed!" she exclaimed. "Garvey House is in Stokesford! But why on earth are you staying at the Golden Bat, my lord?"

Kenneth's hand drifted across the paper on his desk, palm down. "I find this inn far more agreeable," he said, after a moment, and seemed disinclined to expound on the matter.

Judith dared to sit herself down on one of the armchairs, and Kenneth sat, too, though hesitantly. However, good manners forbade that he promptly turn her out of the room.

"Why is that?" she pressed. "Don't tell me you subscribe to these ridiculous notions that a ghost haunts your property? Oh! Is it possible that you have seen it yourself?"

Kenneth shot her a look and shifted the chair so he could face her - thereby also blocking her view of his correspondence. "No, no ghost," he said uneasily, and Judith could hear the lie in his voice. So he *had* seen the ghost. Or had he cast it? He continued, waving a deprecating hand. "Garvey House is merely draughty, which is not good for my health." He coughed unconvincingly, to match the lie in his voice. "I must stay warm, and I find that the Golden Bat is better at keeping the chill out."

Judith's eyes narrowed. There was some other reason at play, given his mendacity. Was it indeed guilt, as Dacian suggested?

"It must be a great burden," she suggested, "to take Charles' place."

Red crept into Kenneth's cheeks. "No one can take my brother's place." He spoke with a note of bitterness, and Judith felt a surprising flash of sympathy. Charles had always been Lady Garvey's favourite son, despite his vile character. "Yet I do the best I can. I live in London, and simply visit Stokesford regularly, to fulfil my responsibilities. Believe me, it is easier to manage them from here, in the village, than in that ramshackle place. For one, the servants here are more efficient."

His valet's eyebrow twitched in supercilious acknowledgement, while Robert took a step sideways - closer to the escritoire, Judith was pleased to see. Perhaps he could manage to see what Kenneth wished to hide.

She attempted to distract her host. "Indeed, good servants are hard to find," she said. "I confess I visited Garvey House this morning, and found your current butler to be an odd sort."

Kenneth sighed, his guarded manner seeming to relax. "I agree, Faske is atrocious. He is my mother's man; she insists on employing him. You can see why I would prefer to stay here."

Judith wondered what talents Faske hid, that made him a desirable employee. She saw that Robert had edged closer to the desk, his gaze lingering on the strewn papers, out of Kenneth's line of sight.

She hurried on. "Well, in fact, I am very glad to have found you here," she said, with an air of confession. "This morning I invited Miss Georgina to my own daughter's wedding, but Lady Garvey was reluctant to give her permission. Perhaps you could grant it in her stead? I venture to say that you are better fit to make such decisions." She repressed an internal wince as she appealed to his sense of patriarchal right, which lurked in all men. "Indeed, I would go so far as to suggest that Lady Garvey is not a fit guardian for a young girl."

Kenneth's lips thinned. "No doubt she would say the same about me."

This was so close to the truth that Judith did not know where to look. Kenneth gave a short, mirthless laugh, and pulled on his moustache. "I will, however, speak to my mother. I thank you for the invitation, Lady Avely, and I will do my best to persuade her to allow Georgina to gain a little town polish - but the fact of the matter is that I do not think she will listen to me any more than you."

"Perhaps if we join our entreaties?" suggested Judith. "Lady Garvey said she won't see me again, but if I arrive with you, she cannot turn me away. Perhaps we can go this evening."

"Not tonight." Kenneth's eyes darted away. "Perhaps tomorrow you may accompany me? I quite agree that poor Georgina is wasting away in that mausoleum."

Judith could hear a note of sincerity and smiled in sympathy. But then he leaned forward, his moustache bristling.

"But that cannot be the reason you knocked, Lady Avely?"

"Ah, I quite forgot!" Judith blushed. "I am staying in the parlour above, you see, and my cap blew out the window. I believe it is hanging off your blackberry bush and likely to catch the rain."

She stood. The valet, lean and noiseless, crossed the room and opened the terrace door. Judith trod past him. "Yes, there it is!" she said brightly. "How silly of me."

Advancing into the soft rain, she carefully unpicked the blue silk from the thorns. A particularly sharp one tore at her thumb, and a pin drop of blood stained her mobcap. Ignoring it, she retreated all the way to the parlour door. "Thank you and good day, Lord Garvey."

"A moment, Lady Avely."

She turned at the door. "Yes?"

Kenneth had stood, folding his arms across his soft belly. "When I was in London, I heard a rumour that the Duke of Sargen has returned to England. You knew him well, I believe? Can you confirm whether or not the gossip is true?"

Judith blinked, uncomfortable that the tables had turned. "I don't know, your lordship," she lied, as smoothly as she was able. "I have not seen him."

"Hmm." Kenneth fingered his moustache. "I hope he doesn't have the gall to show up around Stokesford."

"No." She hesitated. "Do you intend to press charges against him?"

Kenneth gave her a shrewd look. "I ought to. He did kill my brother, after all." The statement rung with truth - but it did not absolve his lordship of any hand in the matter. "Yet even if I were to bring the full force of the law against his grace, I expect Sargen will find a way to squirm out of it. He is a devilish slippery sort of fellow, the duke. And the scandal of a court case would adversely affect my own family - and Georgina's chance of a good marriage."

Judith nodded. "Though one would want to see justice served, of course." She paused. "Yet sometimes justice is a complex matter."

"Indeed." Kenneth's brown eyes examined her closely. "Good day, Lady Avely. A pleasure to see you again."

His last phrase sounded with a note of discord. Was it simply social hedging, Judith wondered, or something more?

HURRYING BACK to her little green parlour, Judith found Dacian pacing restlessly, his brow thunderous. Dusk showed at the window, which was still open, rain pattering on the darkening sill.

At the sight of her, Dacian pulled up short. "Thank God. What happened? You were gone an age." Pressure rose in the air, against her skin, and then faded, as if it had ascertained she was whole before withdrawing.

Judith came in and sank down on an upholstered chair. It was not as comfortable as Kenneth's armchair. She wrung her stained mobcap in her hands, casting her mind back over the conversation. Robert came in and carefully closed the door behind him.

"Did Kenneth guess her purpose?" Dacian demanded of Robert.

Robert shrugged. "He was a bit suspicious, but Lady Avely played her part well." Judith was glad that accord seemed to be established between them once more, despite the awkwardness of their earlier conversation. Then Robert added thoughtfully, "Lord Garvey does have a magnificent moustache. I felt quite inspired."

"Never mind that," snapped Dacian. "What did he say? Is he our man?"

"Hush," said Judith. "We must talk quietly, for Kenneth is right below us. He lied to me, certainly. He would not tell me the real reason he stays here rather than Garvey House. And he attempted to hide his correspondence, didn't he, Robert?"

Robert nodded. "I managed to have a peep. It looked like accounts to me. And an invoice of a large sum, directed to a Mr Poleney."

"Poleney?" Judith frowned. "That name is familiar."

"Yes," agreed Dacian, then he shrugged. "Probably a local tradesman in Exeter."

"I didn't recognise the name," said Robert. "And I know most of those who do business with the Sargenet estate. Besides, it was an invoice, not a bill. Lord Garvey was selling something to Mr Poleney, not the other way round."

Judith set her mobcap aside in a crumpled heap. "Something he didn't want us to know about."

"Intriguing," said Dacian, "but I cannot see what this has to do with Kenneth arranging his brother's death nine years ago."

Rain pattered against the window. Judith frowned. "I am not so certain that Kenneth is the guilty party. He seemed quite bitter about taking his brother's place, if anything, and expressed a distaste for Garvey House. Furthermore, he showed kindness when I taxed him about Georgina. I confess I find it hard to imagine him as our villain."

Dacian snorted. "One kindness does not exclude a person from villainy."

"No, but I cannot see his motive so clearly anymore." Judith folded her hands in her lap, her mind wandering back to the drawing room at Garvey House. "I find myself curious about Miss Selina Pelling, who is now Mrs Southcott."

"Charles' young fiancé? What of her?" Dacian frowned.

"She had a stronger motive: to escape a predatory marriage with Lord Garvey, and to marry the man she loved. Also," Judith added, "today I recalled Harriet Bollopher mentioning that Selina was a girl of 'unusual talents'. Perhaps she was referring to Selina's ability to cast Illusions."

She felt another pang of grief for Harriet's passing. It would have been useful to discuss the entire matter with Harriet; she had been observant and might have noticed something on the night of Lord Garvey's death. Judith sighed. "As we cannot speak to Harriet, we must at least question Mrs Selina Southcott.

Robert, could you please take my card to the Southcott residence now, so I can call upon her tomorrow?"

"Certainly." Robert gave a small bow, smirking. "It seems it is convenient for me to play the footman, after all, Judith."

Judith fixed him with a reproving stare, but inwardly she felt some relief at the return of his impertinence. Surely it was only a short step from there to accepting her as a parental figure. Indeed, the two were practically synonymous.

Although perhaps neither would result in Robert telling her his private concerns. She pursed her lips. Maybe someone younger or more carefree would have more success. Perhaps she should ask Marigold to make some overtures to Robert, in a discreet sort of way, and determine what bothered him.

"Forget Selina," snapped the duke. "The idea is ludicrous. It is dark now; let us wake the vampiri. Perhaps they can spy on Kenneth and prove me right."

JUDITH RETURNED to the parlour half an hour later, wearing her red paisley shawl over her shoulders to hide Marigold, who hung as a bat within its folds. The vampiri had refused to don her gown, rightfully pointing out that she would just have to remove it again.

Judith saw that Dacian had delivered Wooten to the dining table, sporting his black velvet cloak, ready for a quick transformation. When Wooten saw Marigold flutter out of Judith's shawl, however, he was clearly unimpressed. He folded his arms where he stood on the table.

"Absolutely not," he said. "I refuse to go gallivanting about with Miss Cultor like that."

Marigold gave a high-pitched noise of disdain and spun in a lazy circle around the parlour.

"It is bad enough," retorted Wooten, "that I must play third wheel if that conniving Miss Yvette shows up again. I will certainly not do so if you are *naked*, Miss Cultor."

Marigold flapped her wings impatiently, while Robert stifled a laugh.

Wooten shook his fist. "You will snatch at my own cloak again, to cover your modesty!" He turned with entreaty to Judith. "That is what she did last time, almost revealing my own nakedness! I utterly refuse to be so mortified again. If we are to go out together, I *insist* that Miss Cultor also take a cape."

Marigold whistled scornfully and seemed inclined to fly off without him, but Judith intervened. "He has a point, Marigold," she said gently. "Yvette was wearing a cape, wasn't she? You would not want her to feel overdressed."

With a flounce, Marigold became human and vaulted onto the writing desk. Wooten let out an inarticulate noise of protest and covered his eyes. Indeed, the little vampiri's naked limbs were a shocking sight in the prim and proper setting of the parlour. Robert and Dacian hastily turned their backs, while Judith sighed.

"If I must," Marigold huffed. "Make it something pretty, if you please."

"This is *not* a party," huffed Wooten.

"Yes, do be careful," said Judith, reaching into her reticule for a piece of cloth she kept there. "Do not reveal the duke's presence - and try to determine Kenneth's movements. And also, if you can, Miss Yvette's business in Stokesford."

"With pleasure," replied Marigold, taking the orange-gold cloth and tying it around her neck.

In which a name is obtained

Marigold

Their first port of call was to spy on Kenneth.

Marigold had heard about Judith's foray into the best parlour. It sounded as if Kenneth had behaved suspiciously, even with a lady sitting in his armchair. An unseen watcher might gather further evidence of misconduct.

Accordingly, Marigold (now with a pesky orange-gold cape tied around her front) dropped down from Judith's windowsill to the French doors below, protected from the soft rain by a small eve, and clung upside-down on a vine. The damn cape, now damp, hung in her face. After a short struggle, she wriggled it aside and looked in.

A portly man with a magnificent grey moustache sat by the fire. He moodily picked at a plate of food, while his bald-pated manservant stood by with a pitcher of beer.

After twenty minutes of watching Lord Kenneth Garvey desultorily eat his steak and potatoes, Marigold was convinced that he was a person completely without interest, and far too boring to be a master villain. Fortunately, the rain had now subsided. She let go of the vine, and flew off in the direction of the church, hoping that Wooten would not notice her departure.

She hadn't liked to mention it, but on the previous evening, Yvette suggested they meet again at the belfry tonight. Marigold wasn't certain of the tenor of the invitation, and a flutter of anticipation quivered through her wings. Yvette had certainly seemed intrigued by her company. It was *possible* that Wooten would be *de trop*.

Unfortunately, when Marigold cast a look back, she saw the flicker of his black wings following. With an irritated sigh, she swooped up the church tower and through the arch of the belfry.

The large iron bells hung still in the night. Marigold slowly flapped round the pale stone cavern that housed them. Thick ropes were affixed to the wheel, hanging in the darkness. The belfry overlooked the village of Stokesford, quiet and blockish below, and the aloof spire above was an ideal place for a bat to take refuge (except, of course, for the noise). Yet Marigold, looking around eagerly, could not see any other creature, supernatural or otherwise, hanging from the arches.

A ledge jutted out two-thirds of the way up. With an uncomfortable tumble, Marigold landed in her human form. As nonchalantly as possible, in case Yvette should be watching, she shifted her golden cape so it fell round her shoulders and covered her limbs.

"Hello?" she called tentatively. There was no need to shout, for vampiri had very good hearing.

Silence met her. Then came the hushed flap of wings. Yet it was only Wooten who flew into the belfry, his furry bat nose wrinkled in distaste. He, too, landed on the stone ledge and fumbled with his cape.

"What are we doing here?" he demanded, once he could speak.

"Just looking," Marigold lied. "I thought we could see if there is sign of Miss Yvette's occupancy."

Wooten cast a disparaging glance around. "It appears not. Who would want to reside in such a dusty, dark tower?"

"It seems swept and clean."

"That is not enough to indicate a permanent residence."

"No," agreed Marigold. "She might be a bit of a vagabond, like me."

"She is nothing like you," enunciated Wooten. "Miss Yvette, at least, had the decency to wear a cape while abroad. Her manners, too, seem to indicate a level of sophistication that you lack."

"Don't be snide," huffed Marigold. "I'm dressed now, aren't I?"

Yvette's voice rose from the darkness. "Of a fashion."

Marigold spun round and saw the vampiri emerge from beneath the lower ledge of the belfry. Her dark hair was swept up into a knot, with ringlets falling over her ears in the current fashion, and she wore a soft lavender cloak. It brought out the violet colour of her eyes, which gleamed in the faint light of the tower. Her hair and cloak seemed to be damp; she had been out already that evening, in the rain.

Yvette hauled herself onto the stone ledge and fixed those startling eyes on Marigold. "You came."

Marigold nodded, suddenly bashful, and looked round the belfry. "A delightful residence you have here."

Wooten looked sharply between them. "You invited us, Miss Yvette?"

"I invited *her*." Yvette's lips curved with amusement. "I have a little apartment hidden below. I won't take you there now; it is a bit too cosy for all *three* of us."

"Another time, perhaps," said Marigold diffidently and glared daggers at Wooten, who was glaring knives at her.

"We could do some sightseeing instead," suggested Yvette, "and fly to the next church tower. The night air is moderate with the clouds amassed, yet we might catch a glimpse of the full moon later."

Marigold swished her cloak. "It would be my pleasure."

"A moment," interposed Wooten. "I would like to know more about you, Miss Yvette, before we fly off into the full moon with you. You will oblige me by telling me your full name and title, and your blood companion."

Yvette turned with faintly arched brows. "My name is Yvette Belfleur, and I have told you that I belong to no-one."

"No one?" Wooten folded his arms over his cloak. "How do you sustain yourself, then?"

"That is my business, not yours." Yvette's tone became super-cilious.

Marigold spoke up hastily. "I apologise for Mr Willougby. He does not mean to pry, but we are seeking an Illusor in these parts, and we wondered if you were bonded to one."

Yvette stared between them, violet eyes opaque. "I am not."

Marigold found herself wishing that she possessed Judith's ability to discern lies. Then she shook away her slither of doubt. Yvette was from France; it was unsurprising if she were to shun a formal Musor companionship, after what had happened in that wretched country. Even without having experienced the horrors of the revolution, Marigold found it better to change her human companions often. Besides anything, it was boring to stay in one place for long. Perhaps Yvette was a kindred spirit like her, eager to explore the world.

Marigold smiled. "Maybe you can help us then."

Wooten bristled. "I don't think-"

Yvette tilted her head. "I gather you are trying to gain entrance into Garvey House."

"Yes," admitted Marigold.

"I do," said Yvette slowly, "as it happens, know a way inside."

"Oh?" said Wooten. "And how do you know *that*?"

"I have been exploring a little myself," replied Yvette. "Call me curious, but I wished to know what you were looking for."

"And you found a way in?" said Marigold eagerly. "Can you show us?"

"First tell me: why do you seek entrance?"

This was too much for Wooten. "We won't tell you why," he snapped. "Allow us to have some secrets too."

"Secrets?" Yvette smiled. "Intriguing indeed. But I will show you, for it amuses me to watch you play your games. Come with me."

Before Marigold could say a word, Yvette took a flying swallow dive into the belfry. Marigold watched with admiration as the graceful human form became a bat and looped away. She stepped forward to follow.

"Be careful," said Wooten grumpily, behind her. "I don't trust her."

Marigold scoffed and dived into the night.

YVETTE'S PASSAGE into Garvey House turned out to be a loose window pane on the second floor. She became human, clinging to the frame in order to gently lift it out, and Marigold was treated to a glimpse of Yvette's delightfully shaped backside and elegant shoulders as she led the way in, her lavender cloak proving insufficient to maintain her modesty. Marigold didn't bother to see if Wooten managed it better, for she was too busy struggling with her own cape. Cursed conventions.

The uppermost floor was in darkness. The room they found themselves in was unused, the furniture covered in white drapes. A scent of dust and mould hung in the air. As Judith and Dacian had observed, the house must be on a skeleton staff, leaving most of the rooms empty and neglected.

Becoming a bat again, Yvette flitted through the partly open door and led the way towards the occupied quarter of the house, past the drawing room that Marigold and Wooten had spied on from outside. Peering in, Marigold saw that it was now empty, though still lit by the ugly candelabra on the mantelpiece. The flickering light made the large room seem eerie and somehow sad.

Yvette had continued on down the corridor, but she pulled up to hover in a dark corner. She lifted her wings expressively. *There you go*, she seemed to say. *Now what?*

Marigold also hovered cautiously and pricked her ears. Down the turn, light crept from under a closed door, along with the sound of a monotonous girlish voice. Georgina, reading aloud again to Lady Garvey.

Creeping up to the door, Marigold clung to a ceiling cornice and listened.

Georgina was reading *Belinda*, but just as she reached a particularly interesting bit, she broke off and heaved a deep sigh.

"Why are you stopping?" Lady Garvey's voice was impatient.

Georgina sighed again. "Oh Grandmama, *please* won't you let me visit Elinor Avely? I am half inclined to stop reading until you allow it."

Marigold's sharp ears heard a blanket rustling. "Don't be ridiculous, Georgina. It is beneath you to attempt to manipulate me on this matter." Lady Garvey sniffed. "Quite besides the considerations of your health - and mine - I have heard unsavoury things about Miss Elinor Avely."

"Unsavoury? What can you mean?"

There was a pause. "Accusations of theft, for one."

Listening, Marigold found herself surprised. Judith hadn't mentioned any scandal attached to her daughter's name. Indeed, Judith had hardly mentioned her children at all. She was probably relieved to have a moment's respite from them, though Marigold couldn't imagine that any child raised by Judith would commit theft. Peregrine and Elinor Avely were probably very well-behaved young persons.

Georgina gasped. "Goodness me. That cannot be true!" There was a pause while she rallied. "Furthermore, as a Christian woman you should not make such judgements based upon heresay, Grandmama. At least allow Lady Avely to call upon us again, and ask her about these rumours before you banish her."

"Certainly not," grumbled Lady Garvey.

"You can't just turn her away!"

"I can do what I like," came the irritable reply. "I am mistress of this establishment and don't you forget it. Now, keep reading, pert miss."

"Yes, Grandmama." Georgina's voice became subdued and she resumed her tale.

Marigold, listening intently, felt a soft touch upon her wing. It was Yvette, reaching out beside her, and jerking her head in warning. Marigold became aware heavy footsteps climbing the stairs.

The three bats retreated from their position above the bedroom door. From the shadows at the end of the corridor, they saw Mrs Froode tread onto the landing. She carried a tea tray laden with a steaming pot of tea. As she drew closer, the scent of the brew wafted towards them. It did not exude the crisp smell of black tea, but some kind of herbal concoction. Marigold wrinkled her nose, for it was an oddly sweet smell.

Mrs Froode manoeuvred the tray inside, leaving the door slightly ajar. Cautiously, Marigold drifted a closer again, hoping to hear the conversation.

With the advent of Mrs Froode, Georgina's voice fell silent once more.

"Your medicine, my lady," said Mrs Froode's raspy voice.

"Is it that time already?" complained Lady Garvey. "I hope you have brought me some biscuits too."

"Of course," said the housekeeper. There came the sound of liquid pouring, and the clink of a cup and spoon. "Here you go. It will help you sleep."

The sweet smell became stronger. Lady Garvey murmured something indistinguishable, but she took a slurping sip. "Ergh, it never tastes any better, does it? Georgina, rub your salve on now, if you please."

"Must I?" Georgina sighed.

Marigold's sharp ears caught the sound of a bottle opening. A silence followed, broken only by Lady Garvey's sips.

"There," said Georgina, putting something down with a clink. "I still think it is nasty, even if my mother made it. Mrs Froode, won't you tell Grandmama that we should see Lady Avely tomorrow?"

"No, Miss Georgina," replied the housekeeper. "It would be dangerous to let Lady Avely in again, as you well know. She might see something she oughtn't."

There was a silence that seemed suddenly weighted. Fascinated, Marigold flew closer, hoping that Mrs Froode would reveal more. What might Judith see, that they were so afraid to reveal?

"Quiet now," Lady Garvey's tone was harsh. "We have nothing to fear, Mrs Froode, unless it is catching a disease from London. I won't hear anything more about Judith Avely, do you heed me?" She coughed, a rattling, dreadful cough that went on for a long time. Then she cleared her throat with one last hacking sound. "Oh, this dreadful condition. I wish everyone would just leave us alone and stop making demands of me."

Teacups clattered. "Very well, my lady. I will keep all visitors away, as you have ordered, and ensure that Faske does the same." Mrs Froode's tone was now mild and obedient.

Realising that the servant was withdrawing, Marigold hastily backed away from the bedroom door. Just in time too, for it swung open and Mrs Froode carried the tea tray through, and the saccharine smell drifted up. The housekeeper made her way to the drawing room, where Marigold could hear her tidying up, then finally retreated down the stairs again.

Georgina's voice had resumed her reading once more. Marigold perched again above the door, hoping for more revelations now that the housekeeper had gone. Wooten hung back, but Yvette joined her, clinging to the cornice right next to Marigold.

Yet after ten minutes of the monotonous recitation, Marigold was utterly bored. Lady Garvey must have been too, because a faint snoring sound now emanated from the room.

With another weary sigh, Georgina stopped her reading. There was the sound of a book being laid down, and a chair scraping. Marigold and Yvette scattered backwards, and Georgina slipped out of the room holding a candle. But she only made her way to another bedroom, and, by the sounds of it, into bed. Soon the candle darkened, though Georgina tossed and turned in her soft captivity.

Marigold abandoned that avenue of investigation, and set off to explore the rest of the house. Despite their decorous conduct, the Garveys were hiding something. What did they fear Judith would see? Perhaps she, Marigold, could uncover the mystery.

Carefully, with Yvette and Wooten following, she navigated down to the ground floor, looking for anything out of place or suspicious. Unfortunately, most of the doors were shut, and even without being locked, this was sufficient to keep the vampiri out. Neither bat claws nor tiny human hands could manage to turn the knobs. Sniffing around the edges, however, Marigold could smell that most of the rooms were dusty and unused.

Only one smelled different; a room fragrant with ink, paper, and books. A study, or a library. Marigold wondered if Lady Garvey ever managed to descend the stairs to use the room, or if

it was Georgina's refuge. Or perhaps Mrs Froode had comman-
deered it.

The kitchens and scullery were clean, rich with the smells of
fat, coals, bread, and herbs. Peering in, Marigold saw Mrs Froode
tending to the stove fire, while someone else clanged dishes in the
scullery. Faske, perhaps, or a scullery maid. Wary of being seen,
Marigold retreated with Yvette and Wooten down a narrow
passageway to the servant quarters. Only three beds showed signs
of occupancy.

The poor creatures, to have to run even a small household on
so little - even if help came in the daylight hours. Judith had
seemed to think it was simply poverty that dictated Lady Garvey's
reduced household, but Marigold knew it was also caution, born
of a desire to hide something. The question was what?

She became aware that Wooten was beckoning with a wing,
hovering above a high shelf set in one of the servant's rooms. He
vaulted down into his human form, hastily arranging his cloak to
cover his unmentionables.

"Miss Cultor!" he hissed. "A word!"

Rolling her eyes, Marigold landed beside him, and as an
afterthought, adjusted her cloak. Yvette flapped above them in
slow circles.

"That smell," continued Wooten. "From the teapot - I recognised it."

"You did?" Marigold wrinkled her nose, remembering the
sickly scent.

"It was the same as in the maze. Very distinct."

Marigold frowned, trying to recall. "Perhaps you are right."

"We should check. It might be significant."

She was loath to abandon access to the house, but the smell
was unusual. "I suppose. The scullery door is open; let's leave that
way."

Marigold leapt off the high shelf and became a bat again. She did not look to see if Wooten followed, for she could sense him close behind as she darted above the scullery maid hunched over a sink, and winged her way outside.

The full moon made the gardens seem even clearer than the candlelit shadows of the kitchen. Marigold revelled in the cool night air and the sense of wide, open space. Stretching her wings, she flew rapidly towards the maze, ignoring her billowing cape. When she reached the centre, she pulled upwards and did a showy loop and nose-dive, hoping that Yvette observed her.

With another loop, Marigold landed on the rusty pommel of a sword, taking her human form. Her cloak fluttered around her and she impatiently shifted it out of the way.

With a deep breath, she realised immediately that Wooten was right. The thick, cloying smell of the flowering plant was the same scent that had wafted from Mrs Froode's teapot.

"You're right," Marigold turned in a circle, swishing her cape. "The housekeeper must use these flowers in the tea that she served to Lady Garvey."

White petals shone in the moonlight, marred only by their dark purple splotches. It was unusual to see flowers open at night; these had not closed with the setting of the sun, and the smell hung heavy on the air.

Wooten landed on the other pommel of the crossed swords, fumbling among the vine that grew over it. "I don't know this plant. Do you?"

"No," admitted Marigold, "but I'm not one for gardenology."

"Botany."

She ignored him, for she had suddenly realised that Yvette was not with them. "Where is Yvette?"

In which a ghost walks

Marigold

Marigold turned, staring into the vibrant night. Soon they saw a small black figure winging their way towards them. Yvette became human as she landed on a stone bench nearby, tossing her cloak round her shoulders and pulling it close, but not before Marigold had seen the pale shape of perfect curves.

Marigold raised her brows, while Wooten folded his arms.

Yvette, seeming to understand some explanation was required, said, "I wanted to have a closer look at the housekeeper's belongings."

"Oh?" said Wooten.

Yvette shrugged. "Just a curiosity I have."

"You are rather full of curiosities," observed Wooten.

"Indeed," replied Yvette smoothly. "I have another one: why are we here in the maze?"

Marigold hesitated. They were both permitted to keep cards close to their bosoms. Especially if one had such lovely bosoms as

Yvette. Yet perhaps if Marigold confided in her, Yvette would return the compliment.

"Do you know this plant?" Marigold gestured at the white flowers. "It was in the tea Mrs Froode served, implying it has some medicinal attributes. Yet I have never come across it before."

Yvette glanced round. "It must be a healing herb. There is nothing unusual in that, is there? Humans are always consuming all manner of things to aid their constitutions."

Marigold frowned. "As long as we are certain the plant is not poisonous. I find it curious that Lady Garvey's cough seemed to worsen after she drank that concoction."

Yvette quirked a brow. "Sometimes that is the way with medicines."

Wooten spoke up. "Maybe we should continue our investigation of the house. We have yet to spy the butler, and I would like to see for myself his alleged incompetence."

"Who says he is incompetent?" asked Yvette.

"My companion, Lady Judith Avely, told me he was rude and hostile," explained Marigold. "You make a good point, Wooten: we haven't seen the butler yet, but he wasn't in his bed."

She swung herself off the pommel, twisting into her bat form. Once she was certain that the other two both followed her this time, Marigold flapped slowly over the meandering walls of the maze, back towards the house.

Candlelight showed from the kitchen door, a faint luminescence around the servant's entrance. Marigold was distracted by the glow, until Wooten gave a high-pitched whistle of warning behind her.

She spun in the air, searching.

A tall figure lumbered on the outside of the maze. The shape was masculine, and for a moment she wondered if it were Faske. However, this man was clad in gentleman's clothes: a black tail-coat, dark breeches, elegant stockings, and shining boots. Furthermore, as he ambled along the hedge, Marigold saw that his evening dress was spoiled by a gaping, bleeding wound in his pale yellow waistcoat.

The black hole bled sluggishly, the liquid somehow managing to achieve a rusty red colour even in the washed-out moonlight.

Ah, here walked the ghost of Lord Garvey! Heartened by this development, Marigold flew towards the spectre with alacrity. Was it an Illusion, or was it Faske playing at charades? Or, indeed, both?

The ghost's face was unfamiliar, swarthy and handsome, despite the slight puffiness and the vacant look upon it. Hatless, Lord Garvey's blond hair gleamed in the moonlight, and he walked in an odd, lurching way. Reaching the corner of the maze, he heaved round and retraced his steps, almost as if he were a sentry keeping watch. Perhaps, in a way, he was.

As Marigold drew closer, she felt the distinctive vibration of magic. It was sharp against her bat senses: the echo of Musing.

The ghost was an Illusion then, cast by a Musor. It was just as they had all suspected. Yet was there a real person beneath the gruesome depiction of Lord Garvey?

Speeding closer, Marigold did not hesitate. As she drew in line with the apparition, she dived down. At the last moment, she tilted upwards, extending her tiny claws.

Aiming at the lank, blond locks, she was unsurprised when her grasp went through thin air. The phantom head vanished without a sound, and Marigold spun round in a victory twirl to have vanquished the ghost.

Yet even as she whirled round, she saw out of the corner of her eye that a figure still remained below her. As the Illusion of Lord Garvey disappeared, it revealed another shape beneath it, shorter and wider in proportion. Marigold recognised this man's plump face and bushy, silver moustache.

It was Kenneth Garvey.

His lordship turned, scowling. He tucked his chin into his waistcoat, which was now unsullied, and marched rapidly towards the house.

Two Lord Garveys in one night, Marigold reflected. What was Kenneth up to? Then, belatedly, she realised she could still sense the vibration of Musing, emanating from the lord of the manor as he fled.

Was Kenneth an Illusion too? Or was he employing some other type of magic?

Marigold grinned with her tiny fangs, filled with the joy of the chase. Speeding after him, she lifted high again, ready to strike.

Vaguely, she was aware that Wooten gave another small shriek of warning, but she didn't care. Whoever this Illusor was, they had caused Judith a great deal of anguish. Marigold need not remain polite. Claws could be employed without compunction.

She dived. Flashing through the night air with exhilaration, she extended her talons. As she reached her victim, she swiped them across Kenneth's cheek.

This time, her claws met resistance. Lord Garvey shrieked, high pitched, and threw up his hands. His face, however, did not change, not even to show the mark of Marigold's claws. The sense of Musing was now very strong. It seemed that he was maintaining the magic even in the face of attack.

Marigold swooped again. Her claws once more dug into soft flesh and she felt a satisfying sense of triumph. It blinded her from the quick, angry hand that flashed upwards and snatched her out of the sky.

Hard fingers grabbed her, gripping her wings to her body. Shattering pain shrieked through her left wing as bones snapped. Struggling, she tried to break free, but the hand that held her was ruthless, squeezing violently.

Her head swooned. The pressure round her chest and wing

tightened. She could barely breathe, her wing in agony, as her vision began to darken.

Dimly, she was aware of two black shapes darting down. One flew viciously into her attacker's face, clawing at his eyes, and the other stabbed at the hand that held her. It was Wooten and Yvette, flying to the rescue.

The inexorable hand loosened. With a startled grunt, her captor released Marigold. She dropped like a stone to the ground, unable to fly. Her body was wracked with pain. Through half-closed lids, she saw Kenneth turn and run towards the house. One bat gave chase, while the other landed beside Marigold.

It was Yvette, vaulting into her human form. She flung her cloak aside and knelt beside Marigold. "Oh, divine Nyx. Are you alright?"

Marigold was too wretched to become human. She gave a low grunt of pain. Through her lashes, she had the satisfaction of seeing Yvette's face whiten further in the moonlight.

"What can I do?" Yvette asked, desperation tingeing her voice. "You will heal, you just have to endure it. You poor darling."

Marigold was distantly pleased at being called a darling, even as the hurt intensified.

Yvette's hands fluttered. "Shall I put your head on my lap?"

When Marigold managed a nod, the vampiri stretched her bare legs out. Folding her cloak across them, she lifted Marigold's head to rest on the silky fabric, then brushed a hand down Marigold's narrow bat cheek.

Marigold, still agonised, wished that she was in a fit state to appreciate her position, for Yvette's beautiful face looked down with concern. Her violet eyes were wide and liquid.

Of course, Yvette was right. Marigold would heal, with the supernatural ability of vampiri to do so. It would just take time and fortitude. Wincing, she did her best to unfold her damaged wing. It would mend better if it wasn't all scrunched up.

Pain swept over her like a wave, drowning her senses into blackness.

When she rose back into consciousness, she was still lying in Yvette's lap. She felt immeasurably better. The agony had receded to a dull ache, and she found could breathe freely again. She took a deep, shuddering breath, and stared up at Yvette's lovely countenance. How much, she wondered, did the vampiri know about healing times?

Yvette stared down, her brow peaked with worry, her full lip caught between white teeth. "Marigold? Are you waking?"

"Ohhh," Marigold groaned. She was still a bat, and could not reply in words. Yvette's thigh was a soft pillow beneath her head, and Marigold turned her cheek to rest upon it. "Mmmrghh," she moaned. Yvette smelled of pine, moonlight, and lavender, and Marigold was determined to stay there as long as possible.

"You poor thing," murmured Yvette. "Are you starting to feel better?"

"Mmmm." Marigold moaned again, noting that 'darling' had been replaced by 'thing'. Yet a gentle hand tucked her golden cloak closer. Her skin felt cold and shivery, and she turned her head restlessly. "Mmrgh?"

Wooten's voice came from somewhere to her left, thick with disapproval. "Lord Kenneth Garvey - or the person appearing as such - ran off. I gave chase, but Faske let him into the house, and slammed the door before I could follow."

"Hmm," said Marigold, a bit woozily. Her wing still distracted her with occasional vicious stabs. She glanced over to see Wooten give a dire frown.

She gritted her teeth, then transformed into her human form with a lurch. Gingerly, she tested her arm, and it felt the better for it; as she had suspected, the transformation had helped to speed up the process of healing.

"Then what happened?" Her voice was croaky, and she settled

her head back onto Yvette's lap before she could move away. "Did you go through the window on the second floor and follow them?"

"Yes," snapped Wooten, "but by the time I reached the ante-room, the humans were enclosed in the study."

Yvette looked down with worry. "Never mind all that. Are you alright, Miss Cultor?"

Curse it. 'Thing' was now 'Miss Cultor'.

"A bit tender." Marigold tried for a cheeky smile. "Maybe we should search the house again, once I have recovered."

"Nonsense," said Yvette. "We must take you to safety, not pursue further risk, little one. You almost died. What possessed you to attack that man?"

"It was necessary," said Marigold, admiring the curve of Yvette's cheekbone. "We have to find out who dwelt beneath the Illusion."

Wooten tutted. "It was rash, and furthermore you will give vampiri a bad name with such disgraceful behaviour. No wonder King George has introduced the Edicts, if this is how English vampiri behave."

"It was special circumstances," Marigold protested. "I wouldn't ordinarily attack a human in broad moonlight."

Yvette's voice was velvety. "Mr Willoughby is right. You must be careful to respect the Edicts, Miss Cultor. The law will not heed your excuses."

Marigold grinned, glad that Miss Mysterious seemed to care. "There is no one to witness my transgressions, except both of you. And I doubt you will report me to these new Beauchamp Fliers."

"Hm." Yvette's expression became inscrutable, even as her fingers tightened on Marigold's shoulder. "You don't know who else is watching, little one. I would be more careful, if I were you."

In which a hat is purchased

A gesture can tell a lie of a thousand words.
   - from *Lady Avely's Guide to Lies and Charms*

JUDITH, Robert, and Dacian stayed up late, waiting in the parlour for the vampiri to return. It gave Robert some time to reaffix the moustache charm, and then they played cards, though Dacian insisted they use sign language to communicate the play. Bereft of her Discernment, Judith was unable to see through the duke's bluffs, and he gloatingly amassed a pile of winnings.

Dacian's cravat pin lay on a side table. He wore his own visage now that Phyllis had delivered a last tray of chocolate and withdrawn. His black locks were disheveled as he took a long gulp and teased Judith for relying too much on her Gift instead of skill. She didn't mind, for she was rather pleased that Robert was slouched in one of the chairs, grinning at her losses.

"I swear you two are siding together," she grumbled. Her cards were woeful, and it certainly couldn't be *her* fault.

"Not at all," said Dacian. "You are merely discovering what it is to be a mere mortal, deprived of your omniscient powers."

"Hmph. Hardly omniscient."

"And look at me." Dacian gestured to his broad chest, his eyes gleaming. "A mere Mr Fortnew, no longer a duke. We are brought down together, my dear. I even played a footman today."

Judith rolled her eyes. "You're still a duke on the inside; accustomed to having your way in everything."

"That's not true!" Dacian said in mock affront. "I have endured deprivation before. In Spain, I had no whisky for months."

She turned to Robert. "He is still being ducal, isn't he? Would a lowly Mr Fortnew insist on depriving a lady of her natural advantages?"

Robert's lip quirked. "Perhaps not. Though as a footman, I am glad he did so."

"You *are* siding against me!" Judith huffed.

Robert lay down a ten of spades. "No, but you should keep in mind that Illusion could equally well be used to win at cards."

Before their eyes, the ten of spades became an ace of diamonds.

Judith's mouth fell open. "How dare you...! Dacian! Did you see that?"

Robert laughed. "I'm only teasing. I haven't been cheating."

"That is true," she replied with a smile, hearing it in his voice, and Robert rolled his eyes at her. She felt quite satisfied indeed.

"This is why the Musor Custos exists," put in Dacian dryly. "To keep two such reprobates as yourselves in check."

"Nonsense," said Judith. "It is to police the shameless misuse of moustaches."

"Wooten does that."

"As if you would listen to him."

"Do you see me ordinarily wear a moustache?" objected Dacian. "This subterfuge is my only opportunity."

"I wonder where Wooten could be?" Remarked Robert. "They've been gone a while."

They continued to bicker over their play, and the candles were near to guttering when movement finally came at the window. Judith set down her cards, then stood hastily, for Marigold was flying slowly, favouring one wing. She collapsed dramatically on the rug by the fire, sprawled in a heap.

"What happened?" Judith rushed forward. "Are you hurt?"

Wooten circled the parlour once, then vanished behind a curtain. His voice emerged, though he kept discreetly hidden as he dressed.

"Miss Cultor attacked a ghost, and the ghost attacked her back," he called out. "She was grabbed and crushed. I fear that her wings and ribs were broken in the experience, but she is better now. She certainly spent enough time laying in Miss Belfleur's lap to aid her recovery."

Marigold gave a theatrical whine to indicate otherwise, and Judith knelt down beside her.

"Quick, have a drink." Judith offered her wrist, and Marigold propped herself up in order to sink her tiny fangs into the vein.

Once she had fed, Marigold transformed into her human form (under a handkerchief) and told them of the night's events. Wooten interpolated from behind the curtain, and they described the Illusion they had seen.

Judith was horrified and angry, but Dacian was almost satisfied, though sorry that Marigold had to suffer for it.

"Well," he said, gathering up his cards, "at least this proves that I was right all along. Clearly Kenneth is up to no good."

"And," said Robert, "we know that Faske and Kenneth are co-conspirators."

Wooten stuck his head out of the curtain, frowning. "I'm not so certain of that. Faske seemed very surprised to see Kenneth."

"Odd," said Judith, "and why would Kenneth need to sneak into his own house late at night?"

"Unless it wasn't Kenneth after all," pointed out Marigold, supine beneath her handkerchief, her hands behind her head. "It could have been another layer of Illusion. I could still sense Musing emanating from him."

"Yet," said Wooten, "when we flew back much later, I saw Kenneth returning to the inn by foot, from the direction of Garvey House. So we cannot rule out the possibility that it *was* him."

"Either way," said Dacian, "it is a good sign. The ghost is walking again because it means to scare us off. Now we know for certain that the Illusor is here, and furthermore, that he is uneasy."

Judith leaned back in her chair thoughtfully. "And I'm intrigued about the plant from the maze, Wooten." She paused, smoothing her sleeve back down. "I find myself a little concerned for Lady Garvey's wellbeing."

Dacian set the cards down in a neat stack. "You mean the tea? I did warn you that the plant could be poisonous. Do you think the housekeeper is slowly doing away with Lady Garvey?" He frowned. "I always thought that I hadn't used enough Impact to kill Lord Garvey. Perhaps if he was weakened beforehand by poison, it might explain why he keeled over so quickly."

Judith tutted disapprovingly. "Don't underestimate your own strength, Dacian. Besides, if our killer had resource to poison, why bother to involve you at all?"

"They needed a scapegoat," said Dacian. "And perhaps they became impatient."

"Yes," agreed Robert. "A duel is a much quicker method, and placed the blame squarely on the duke."

"And put him in the sight of the law, as well the Musor Custos." Judith narrowed her eyes. "But why bother with the ghost now? Is it simply to frighten us off, or is there some other plot afoot?"

THE FOLLOWING MORNING, they were all rather tired, despite rising late and being fortified by drinking chocolate. A small fire blazed in the green parlour, and outside the rain had cleared, showing an unfeeling blue sky.

Judith held a fresh cup of chocolate in her hands, taking comfort from its warmth. She considered her plan for the day. "I feel we ought to warn Lady Garvey about that herbal tea, and see if we can gather any evidence about Mrs Froode. Only I am check-mated, because neither Faske nor Froode will let me into the house. And I doubt Kenneth will escort me either, now."

"He is sleeping late," put in Robert. "I checked downstairs."

Dacian chuckled from under his false moustache. "I shall be interested to see if Miss Cultor managed to leave a mark on him."

"He might sleep 'til noon." Judith sighed and put down her cup. "Is it too early to call on Mrs Selina Southcott? It is unbearable to sit around doing nothing. Quite apart from anything else, I am running out of time. I was supposed to visit Cornwall before I return to London. All this gallivanting has disrupted my plans."

"Don't fuss yourself about that," advised Dacian. He reached into his waistcoat pocket and stretched out a hand. An object glowed in his palm, circular and ornate: a topaz ring. "You can use this Travel charm to speed your journey. It will take you straight to Falmouth in the blink of an eye. From there it will be only a few hours' ride to reach Lanyon Castle."

Judith stared down at the gold ring with its blue topaz stone. "That is a valuable trinket."

"A gift from the Trisketts, a long time ago," replied Dacian. "Lord Triskett comes from a family of Travellors. His younger brother taught me how to imbue charms, actually, just like I'm teaching you now, Robert."

Robert nodded in acknowledgment from his station by the door. Despite the camaraderie of the previous evening, he had retreated into formality once more.

Dacian extended his palm in offering, but Judith looked away. "I cannot use something so precious for my trivial journey. You might need it - especially if the law comes after you."

He closed his fingers over the ring and tucked it back into his waistcoat. "If you are determined. Just remember that it is here if you need it." He glanced out the window. "It is a pleasant day. Perhaps we should make the most of it, and wander around the village. We might learn something, if we keep our ears pricked."

So it was that they spent the next hour strolling around the tiny village of Stokesford, with Robert acting as footman and Dacian in his disguise as Mr Fortnew, man of business. They sampled buns at the bakery, and circumnavigated the church, peering curiously up at the belfry. Around them rolled a bucolic view of hills and valleys, interspersed by the vivid colours of autumnal leaves.

Dacian squinted at the darkly shadowed dome of the bell tower. "Do you think that is where Miss Yvette Belfleur lives permanently? Or is she simply passing through Stokesford?"

"It does concern me," confessed Judith. "Especially now you have mentioned these Beauchamp Fliers. What if she should report Marigold's unorthodox behaviour?"

"Let's not worry about it now." Dacian took her arm. "I propose we visit that little dressmaker we passed, and buy you a hat."

She gave him a wry look, but he insisted escorting her to the little modiste that doubled as a milliner. Its walls were crammed with silks, caps, and bonnets, but Dacian determinedly led her away from the subdued, matronly selections to the window display.

"After all, you will need it, for your daughter's wedding, will you not?" He plucked up an extravagant confection made of cream lace and pale blue satin, and presented it to her. "*This* is much better than your mobcap."

"It is far too … showy." Nonetheless, Judith found herself reaching to caress the smooth curve of satin.

"Try it on," he insisted, and she was both disappointed and relieved that he did not offer to divest her of her current head-wear. He did, however, step forward to receive the object in question, rather than have the shopkeeper take it. She wondered if he was planning another mobcap-themed seduction later, and then firmly repressed the thought.

Judith admired her reflection in the mirror, flushing slightly at the ridiculousness of it. Yet the cream and blue suited her complexion, and the elegant shape of the bonnet framed her face nicely.

"She will have it," declared Dacian, "and the blue shawl to match."

"To whom shall I make out the bill, sir?" The shopkeeper named an outrageous price.

Judith widened her eyes and shook her head, but Dacian was already reaching for his purse. "Ah, I've been abroad, and I am accustomed to paying for things in the moment. We can settle it now."

The shopkeeper bowed, and Judith found herself leaving the shop with a hatbox and a new shawl draped over her arm. Reluctantly, she allowed Robert to take them from her, to give credence to his presence as a footman.

"Thank you," she murmured, then she turned to stare at Dacian. "You, however, are presumptuous."

"It was to please myself," he said, "and give me respite from your damn caps."

"At least you do not have to gaze upon that moustache," she retorted.

Dacian looked down his nose. "It is a fine moustache. Robert, do not be offended."

Robert winked from above the hatbox. "I am not offended, your grace. It is an honour to have you wear my creation."

"Indeed, you quite improve his countenance," said Judith with asperity.

"Impossible!" retorted Dacian, and Judith, a Truth Discernor, could not bring herself to refute him, though she could hear he did not believe his own words. She gave him a small smile instead.

Dacian looked smug and held out his arm. They began strolling back down the main street, enjoying the sight of late blooming foxgloves set beyond the cobblestones, and the smell of freshly baked bread in the air.

A neatly clad gentleman with red side-whiskers nodded as he passed, a truncheon swinging from his waist. Judith stiffened, suspecting that this was the Constable Carter that Phyllis had mentioned. Fortunately, he did not seem to pay them any undue attention, and moved further up the street. Of course, any thought of the exiled duke would be far from his mind. It had all happened so long ago, but the constable might have an opinion about the ghost he had reportedly seen. Judith wondered if she dared question him about it later.

Her eye travelled towards the Golden Bat. An expensive carriage had just drawn up, its wheels clean as if it had not travelled far.

A gentleman emerged, slender and well-dressed. He turned to help a lady disembark. Her moss-green skirts swished as she stepped down, and her russet-red hair gleamed in the sun.

Judith tensed, clutching at Dacian's arm. "Is that... Lady Vosse?"

His step faltered briefly. "Good God, you're right. With Lord Triskett."

"What are *they* doing here?"

Dacian frowned. "I wrote to Biscuit, remember. I didn't want to put anything too incriminating in a letter so I asked him to come to Sargenet. I didn't tell him to meet me at Stokesford." He glanced down at Judith. "And I certainly didn't request Lady Vosse's presence."

Without realising it, they had drawn to a halt. Wary of drawing attention, Judith turned to examine a shop window, pulling Dacian with her. Dazedly, she stared into an apothecary, its display full of colourful glass jars and bottles. The sight of Lady Vosse was causing old feelings and suspicions to come roaring back. Yet Dacian's voice had rung true: he had not expected her company.

Robert stopped close by. "Might they recognise you, your grace, and give you away?"

Dacian raised his brows. "So little faith in our disguise, Robert? I am sure it will pass muster. Though Lord Triskett has known me for a long time, it's true." He didn't add that he had known Lady Vosse in a far more intimate way.

Judith stared at Dacian's reflection in the window. "They will probably take one look at you and announce your name to all and sundry. And I just saw the local constable pass us."

"Nonsense." Dacian pursed his lips at himself, turning his jaw this way and that. "This is a chance to test the moustache out. I bet you another bonnet that they won't even blink twice."

Robert winced, not so confident. "Perhaps I could pass you this hatbox to conceal you better?"

"I will not hide behind a hatbox," said Dacian with disdain.

Judith released his arm. She had just noticed something else. "Poleney," she breathed.

"Excuse me?"

"The name of the apothecary." She pointed to the white lettering that arched across the window. "Poleney and Assoc. To whom Kenneth Garvey made out his invoice."

"Good God," said Dacian blankly. "You're right."

Robert leaned in. "What on earth would Kenneth sell to an apothecary?"

They all looked at one another, then said together: "The flowers."

"Maybe they are medicinal, after all," said Dacian, but he turned away to look down the street at Lady Vosse and Lord Triskett. "We can examine the question later, however. Judith, we'd better head Biscuit off before he starts asking the inn-keeper if he has seen me. Quick now."

With trepidation, Judith turned down the main street again, with Dacian and Robert falling behind her in formation.

The two newcomers were scanning their surroundings. Judith was glad to see that the red-whiskered parish constable was at the other end of the street. She glided towards the Golden Bat, wishing that she was dressed in a slightly more dashing gown than her navy cambric. Next to Lady Vosse's stylish green muslin, she felt positively dowdy. Lady Vosse was of a similar age to herself, yet the woman dressed like she was in the market for a lover.

Which, Judith supposed, she was. Lord Vosse still allowed his beautiful wife every freedom, it was clear, if Isobel was allowed to jaunt off in a carriage with Lord Triskett. Yet not when it came to the Duke of Sargen, Judith recalled. His grace had been too notorious, or their affair too obvious, for Lord Vosse to stomach.

Jealousy, annoyingly, churned in her own gut.

Lady Vosse, with some instinct, spotted them first. Her green eyes narrowed on Judith and she tapped Lord Triskett on the arm. His lordship turned, blinked, then bowed.

Judith advanced, smiling, conscious of Dacian behind her right elbow. A constable might not recognise the duke, but these two certainly might. "Ah, Lord Triskett, Lady Vosse, a pleasure! How strange to see you both in this corner of the world!"

Lady Vosse inclined her head. Her eyes were set rather far apart, giving her a gamine charm which gentlemen seemed to find extremely attractive. Judith thought it made her look cross-eyed. A young, handsome footman with blond hair stood behind her, holding the carriage door.

"I am equally surprised, Mrs Avely, to find you here." Lady Vosse fluttered her lashes. "Perhaps we seek the same quarry?"

Judith gestured to Robert. "I am not sure: are you seeking to buy a hat? There is a lovely milliner here. You simply must visit it."

Her ladyship's gaze took in Robert, with his chestnut hair, blue eyes, and firm chin, and lingered there with some appreciation. Oh dear, thought Judith. The damn woman was paying far too much attention to her male escorts.

"Ah, hats!" put in Lord Triskett jovially. "Nothing like a hat to distract a lady! Isobel, I can take you shopping, if you like."

Lady Vosse ignored him and turned to the duke, who stood diffidently behind Judith. She examined his even taller, broader form, and frowned a little. Judith saw out of the corner of her eye that Dacian had adopted a slight hunch and jutted his chin in as if nervous, his eyes cast down. It did almost more than the Illusion to disguise him, for she had never seen the duke take such a cowering stance.

"And who is this, Mrs Avely?" asked Lady Vosse. "Pray, won't you introduce us?"

"Oh, ahem." Judith coughed. "This is Mr Fortnew, my man of business. He is accompanying me to my new property. In fact, I have a new title as well: Marchioness of Lanyon. You may address me as Lady Avely now."

She was glad to see that this news momentarily distracted her ladyship. Her eyes widened, making her seem even more impish as she stared at Judith. "Goodness me, Lanyon? You cannot mean the Lanyon Castle?"

"I do, indeed."

"How intriguing. My cousins live in Cornwall," confided Lady Vosse, in her guileless manner. "They have reported some rather strange stories about your castle. Its cellars are rumoured to be desperately haunted."

"Oh?" A quiver of apprehension slid through Judith. The royal steward had warned her that there was some trouble afoot in her new residence: it was worse to know that the cellars were implicated, as they were needed urgently to house a roost of vampiri. At least, however, it seemed that Lady Vosse had not yet recognised the duke. "Perhaps you can tell me all about it, if you would be so kind? Would you like to step inside? I have taken a parlour at this inn, to break my journey, and can offer you some tea."

"Charming," replied Lady Vosse, then waved her hand at her footman. "Edward, I shall stay here tonight. Unpack my things." The young man hastened to untie his mistress's valises, while Judith blinked in consternation. She had meant to offer momentary respite only, not for Lady Vosse to take a room.

Lord Triskett gave another bow. "We would be delighted, Lady Avely. We have just come from Gurney, nearby, and I'm afraid their breakfast and accommodation were rather inadequate."

Judith sighed in defeat, while also noting that the two had been staying in the county the previous evening, not far from Stokesford. She led the way in, requesting tea from the innkeeper as she did so.

She nodded at Robert, allowing him to retreat with the hatbox, but Dacian stayed at her side, his face expressionless below the flat brown hair. Arrogant man. It was only a matter of time before Lord Triskett realised he was in the presence of his childhood friend, despite Dacian's ridiculous hunch. Or perhaps Lady Vosse would recognise her old lover first.

Judith's hands clenched in her skirts, as she examined the gleaming russet curls that cascaded down Lady Vosse's back. The woman should really be wearing a mobcap, at her age.

Soon they were all crowded into the tiny parlour. Judith took a seat, and Lady Vosse joined her at the dining table, throwing her cream muff aside and looking around with an air of disdain. Dacian remained standing by the fire, his arms clasped behind his back, still adopting a downcast pose. Judith sighed. He was determined to test how long his moustache would prevail.

Lord Triskett strode over to the window then turned to face them, speaking in a low voice. "Lady Avely, I confess we are in Stokesford not for hats. We are looking for his grace, the Duke of Sargen. I don't suppose you have seen him anywhere near here?"

Judith carefully avoided looking at Dacian. "Er, I am afraid not, my lord, but I suggest that you don't mention the possibility to the local constable."

Lord Triskett's eyes widened, but Lady Vosse leaned forward. "Yet you've just come from Sargenet, haven't you? You saw the duke there?"

Judith hesitated. "I did."

"That was quick, wasn't it?" The green eyes were speculative.

Judith stared haughtily. "I do not know what you mean to imply, Lady Vosse."

"You must have been the *very* first to visit, when he returned."

Briefly, Judith considered telling this sly woman that she had been at Sargenet on other business entirely. But she could not reveal Robert's connection to her without his permission. Instead, she nodded reluctantly. "I saw his grace in London, and he invited me to break my journey at Sargenet."

Lord Triskett frowned. "I thought you said you are breaking your journey here."

"Hats, my lord," said Judith. "I am afraid hats waylaid me. Yet why do you look for his grace in Stokesford?"

His lordship laughed uneasily, and avoided a direct answer. "I don't think Sargen has come to buy hats."

Judith purposefully did not look at Dacian, but raised her brows in question.

Lady Vosse folded her hands in her lap. "We heard from his sister, Lady Agatha, that Dacian had some odd notion to visit Lady Garvey and apologise. We thought we should stop him, before he provokes another quarrel."

Of course, Lady Vosse *would* feel comfortable using Dacian's name. Fortunately, Judith was distracted from her own irritation by the arrival of Phyllis with the tea tray. She thanked the maid then set about pouring the tea, wondering as she did so how Lady Vosse had managed to attach herself to Lord Triskett's journey. Were they intimately involved now? Would Dacian be jealous? And how much did Lady Vosse know about what happened on that night nine years ago?

Manners dictated that she offer a cup of tea to Mr Fortnew as well, and Dacian stepped forward to take it. Then he retreated back to the fireplace, hunched over his teacup, his moustache maintaining its curl and the mole firmly in place.

Lady Vosse watched him curiously.

"So!" said Judith, once Phyllis had gone. "I must warn you that it is best not to mention his grace, if you can. The Stokesford imagination paints him as the 'wicked duke' who callously killed Lord Garvey."

Lady Vosse raised a brow. "That is the truth, isn't it?" she said archly. "His grace *is* very wicked."

Dacian choked a little on his tea and Judith ground her teeth. "Maybe so, but nonetheless, we do not want him to hang," she said firmly. "Memories are long here, longer than nine years, I'm afraid, and they might not be willing to let the whole matter slide."

"Dear me," said Lady Vosse. "Poor Dacian. I hear he has become quite *browned* in Spain. Is it true, Lady Avely?"

"Er," Judith glanced down at her tea rather than look at Dacian. "Yes, I suppose he is not quite so pale as when he left."

"A price to pay for his misdemeanours," sighed Lady Vosse. "While poor Lord Garvey was cut down in his prime. Do *you* know how it all happened, Lady Avely?"

"I am quite in the dark," replied Judith blandly. "Do *you* know how it happened, Lady Vosse?"

The delicate shoulders shrugged. "Something about a woman, no doubt."

By the fireplace, Dacian took a deliberate sip of tea, gaze averted.

Judith sat up straighter, deciding to grab the cat by the tail. "I *did* hear that Lord Garvey went to meet a woman in the maze that night. It wasn't you, was it, Lady Vosse?"

Her ladyship blinked. "Me?" She gave a rather brittle laugh. "No, it was not. What a suggestion!"

Judith held her gaze over the teacup. Lady Vosse's words did not echo with the hollowness of a lie. Yet even if Lord Garvey had not met with her, she might still have orchestrated the whole thing from a distance. Or from within a disguise.

Avoiding Judith's speculative look, Lady Vosse's eyes slipped sideways and landed on Dacian. She frowned thoughtfully at his hands, holding the teacup. Then her gaze slowly lifted to his face, where she became riveted. Her mouth fell open.

"Devil's horns," she uttered. "Dacian? Is that you?"

In which hands are revealing

JUDITH SIGHED. Lord Triskett spun to stare at Mr Fortnew, eyes widening in shock.

The duke lowered his teacup and straightened his shoulders. "Isobel, you wretch. What gave me away?"

Her ladyship grinned, arch sharpness giving way to something like joy. It lit her face into beauty, and even Judith found it mesmerising. "Your hands, Dacian. I would know them anywhere."

Suddenly, she was less mesmerising and more annoying. Everyone looked at Dacian's hands: his long fingers curled around the teacup. Isobel clearly admired the strength and shape of them. Then a frown settled on her face, and she stood abruptly, slamming down her own cup.

"How dare you?" she uttered. "How dare you leave England and never send word!"

She marched over to him and leaned forward threateningly. Dacian backed up against the mantlepiece, his expression alarmed. Judith was torn between satisfaction that he was receiving his due, and irritation that she wasn't the only one who had waited in vain for a letter from him.

"You cruel man!" continued Isobel. "I thought you were dead! Why didn't you write?"

"Ah…" said Dacian. "Correspondence was difficult… likely to be intercepted…"

"So you *did* send word?" Isobel thrust her chin forward.

"Er…"

"No, you did not." She jabbed a finger into his chest. "While I was wasting away with worry, I suppose you were frolicking across the continent, wreaking a trail of seduction!"

"Er…" said Dacian again, but he did not deny it. Instead, his cheeks flushed a dull red. Judith shook her head and took a sip of tea.

"Yes," said Isobel bitterly. "Exactly." She spun around with a swish of green muslin and retreated in disgust. "You are monstrous." She sat down with a huff.

"By God, it *is* you, Sargen!" Lord Triskett spoke at last. "I can't believe it!"

Dacian turned with gratitude. "Biscuit! What do you think of my disguise? You didn't know me, at least!"

Lord Triskett walked over and clapped Dacian on the back, smiling. "Good God, no. What is that ridiculous thing on your face?"

"The mole?" Dacian's finger came up to hover over it. "An inspired touch, I thought."

"No, the moustache." Lord Triskett grimaced. "You look like you've come from a circus. Where did you find that thing?"

Dacian put his cup on the mantlepiece, avoiding an immediate answer. Lord Triskett might know about the Musing, realised

Judith, but she was not certain of Lady Vosse. They ought not speak of Illusion until they were certain.

"A little shop in London," said Dacian finally. "I thought it best to be careful while travelling in these parts. A local might turn me in, if they recognise the *wicked duke*." He cast a sideways look at Isobel.

Isobel blushed prettily and seemed to recover from her sulks. "Oh, don't tease me - you know very well you are wicked. But why are you in these parts?" she demanded. "Why did you send for Biscuit? It is all very mysterious."

Dacian raised his brows. "I might ask why you accompany him, my dear."

Lord Triskett coughed nervously. "Er, Isobel was with me - when I opened your letter. I was thunderstruck, as you can imagine, and she insisted on reading it. I hope you don't mind, Sargen."

Judith flicked her eyes between them, seeing Isobel's creamy cheeks crimson further. It seemed they were indeed intimate, as Isobel had been at Lord Triskett's home in the morning when he read his post.

Dacian also eyed them. "Is that so? It is a private matter, but I suppose you might be able to help me also, Isobel." He paused, weighing his words. "I find myself curious about the night I shot Lord Garvey and I wanted to ask you about it, Biscuit. Did you see anyone else come up from the gardens that night, before me?"

Lord Triskett frowned. "I don't think so. No."

He wasn't lying, Judith observed, and took another sip of her tea.

Isobel stared from one to the other. "But why do you ask that, Dacian?"

"It is a private matter," said Dacian. "Suffice to say, I don't think everything was exactly as it seemed that night."

"Goodness me, how intriguing!" Isobel clapped her hands

together. Then she turned to look at Judith with sudden suspicion. "It this something to do with her? Why are you here together?"

Judith spoke coolly. "I came to visit Harriet Bollopher, on an unrelated matter."

"Mrs Bollopher?" Isobel seemed disbelieving. "Garvey's mother-in-law? She's dead; has been for years."

"I didn't know that," replied Judith. "I am sorry for her loss. I wish I had known her better."

Isobel looked down. "Yes, quite."

Dacian held up a hand. "Lady Avely wished to invite Miss Georgina to London. Hearing of her proposed visit, I thought I would accompany her, to make my own enquiries."

Isobel's eyes flickered between them with obvious suspicion. Suddenly Judith was reminded how her ladyship had watched them from above the greenhouse, nine years ago while Dacian had tried to comfort her.

She decided to turn the tables. "Lady Vosse, you say you did not meet Lord Garvey that night, but perchance you sent a note to his grace, instead?"

Her ladyship sat up straight with hostility. "Excuse me? What is it to you if I sent Dacian a note? Are you his postboy now?" She gave a throaty laugh. "It would be a demanding position, I'm sure. Not that he bothers to send any correspondence worth mentioning." She gave him a bitter look, remembering her grievances.

"I don't know why you expected any word from me, Isobel," said Dacian, with a hint of asperity. "I was on the run; I couldn't write letters, and then I took refuge in a monastery."

Isobel laughed in genuine amusement. "You? A monastery? Come now, I know very well you were causing havoc in Spain for the Crown. Either way, you must be very glad to be returning to the comforts of home."

Judith narrowed her eyes; Isobel's presumption was no less

than what she had wondered. Dacian would not have sat idle in Spain while it was allied with France against England. His talk of the monastery might be true, but it wouldn't account for his whole nine years' abroad.

"Ahem," said Dacian, and frowned Isobel down. "I enjoyed the monastery, I'll have you know. A welcome respite from females."

Isobel chortled in obvious disbelief. "You can't go a week without female company."

Dacian's jaw tightened, but he did not deign to reply.

"Well, Sargen," said Lord Triskett hastily, "I did not suspect you of asceticism! I have that money I owe you from all those years ago, if you need it now. A thousand pounds, wasn't it?"

Dacian looked surprised, then nodded slowly. "I'd forgotten about that." He shrugged uncomfortably. "You know I don't need it, Biscuit."

"He's a duke," scoffed Isobel, and fluttered her lashes at Dacian. "Of course he doesn't need it. Are you well? You look hale and hearty as always."

Judith was aware of a desire to put her hands around that graceful neck and squeeze tightly.

"Well enough," Dacian replied. "My return to England has not been a gentle enfolding, I confess. There have been all manner of thrilling events at Sargenet." He then proceeded to distract them all from his current quest by giving an expurgated account of the misdeeds troubling his own estate. These were melodramatic enough to cause much interest, and Judith, seeing that Lady Vosse and Lord Triskett were utterly enthralled, decided that she would retreat to her room. The three were old friends and could do without her company. And she could do with some time alone.

Dacian did little to stop her, and Isobel was politely dismissive, waving a hand and turning again to stare with admiration at her old lover.

JUDITH HAD a lunch tray sent up to her room. The cauliflower soup and bread were rather tasteless and sat in her stomach heavily. When she laid upon her bed, she found that the call of an afternoon sleep was overpowering. Dacian might think he was irresistible, she told herself, but nothing was more seductive than a nap. She allowed herself to succumb to its soothing embrace.

When she arose half an hour later, she had a new sense of fortitude and determination. If Dacian was busy entertaining his old friend and past paramour, it was now time for her to call on Mrs Selina Southcott.

Opening her door, she saw that Robert stood outside the parlour, staunchly keeping to his role as footman. Well, she could play that game too. Casually, she asked if he had managed to deliver her calling card to Mrs Southcott; when he affirmed it, she requested his company for the follow-up visit. He nodded and they crept past the parlour together. Judith could still hear the rise and fall of conversation between the three friends, punctuated by Isobel's throaty laugh. It seemed Dacian would be well occupied. Perhaps he was, in his own way, trying to find out more about what had happened at the house party.

Robert was quick to call the duke's carriage out and assist Judith in, then swing himself up to the rear. Judith sighed. It was all very tiresome, and she had a strong suspicion that both Robert and Dacian simply liked hanging onto a moving vehicle just for the sport of it. It was the kind of thing that Peregrine would do if he could find any excuse.

They arrived at Southcott Hall shortly; it lay only ten minutes south of Garvey House. As she dismounted, Judith examined the small two-story cottage. The redbrick building lay behind a gate that was covered in a flowering briar rose. 'Hall' was a rather grand name for the residence, and any air of dignity was further punctured by the chickens pecking in the yard. Judith could also hear the braying of a donkey close by. This was a farmer's home, no doubt, and did not measure up to the elegance and wealth of the Garvey property. Miss Selina Pelling had chosen her suitor according to the dictates of love, not money.

Lifting her skirts, Judith nodded to Robert as he opened the gate for her. "Keep close, won't you?"

"Of course." Robert lowered his voice. "And you be careful."

Judith glanced around, and her gaze lighted on a glimpse of a girlish figure disappearing behind the stable. She narrowed her eyes. That had looked very much like Georgina Garvey's slim form. What was she doing here, at Southcott Hall? And why did her movements seem furtive?

Robert stepped forward to knock, and Judith turned back to face the house. A cheerful, round housekeeper opened the door, wearing a sensible navy gown and white apron. Any similarity with Mrs Froode was vanquished by the curtsy and welcoming smile she gave Robert. He announced Judith's title and stepped aside.

"My lady," said the housekeeper. "We are honoured. Mrs Southcott is expecting you. This way, if you please."

Reluctantly leaving Robert outside, Judith followed the housekeeper, stepping out of the autumn sunlight and into the dark hallway. As her eyes adjusted to the light, she saw a small, untidy boy disappear round a corner. The servant led her to a comfortable drawing room and went to fetch her mistress. Judith took a moment to admire the warm tones of the rugs and cushions, and the sleeping dog in front of the hearth.

Then Mrs Selina Southcott stood in the doorway, holding a young girl by the hand. They both stared at Judith curiously.

Selina was still pretty, Judith saw, though her face had lost the smooth plumpness of youth. Her fine bosom was no longer on display in the ruched, ornate gowns of nine years ago, but now contained in a much more practical garment, with simple lines in blue cotton. Her light blonde hair was done up, under a matching blue mobcap. The little girl had blonde ringlets, tied up in a ribbon, and blinked at Judith warily.

Mrs Southcott dropped a delayed curtsy. "Lady Avely." She turned to the housekeeper who hovered close behind. "Please, some tea and bread, Mrs Kendall, and take Sophia with you." Ushering the girl away, Selina gestured Judith towards a cosy armchair. "To what do I owe this honour, my lady?"

Judith did not answer straightaway. "I thought I saw Miss Georgina Garvey outside just now. Has she come to call upon you today as well?"

Mrs Southcott looked surprised as she took her place across from Judith. "Not today." She paused. "She does visit me sometimes; we are old friends and neighbours."

Judith folded her hands in her lap and leaned forward. She had put some thought into her excuse and stated it now with confidence. "Miss Georgina is the reason for my visit, actually. I called on Lady Garvey for the first time in years, and I find myself a little concerned about Miss Georgina's welfare. I hoped to speak to you about it, as her nearest neighbour."

Mrs Southcott bent to pat the golden-haired dog by the fire, shooting Judith a shrewd look. "Ah, yes. Are you concerned for Georgina's health, as is Lady Garvey?"

"Quite the opposite. Miss Georgina seemed strong and full of vitality to me. My fear is that Lady Garvey's anxieties are keeping her granddaughter unduly stifled..." Judith trailed off, leaving a suggestive silence.

Mrs Southcott sighed. "I fear you are right. It isn't right for a young girl to play nursemaid and gardener all the time, shut up in that mausoleum."

"Gardener?" said Judith sharply.

"Oh yes. At least Georgina has some sunshine and activity in that way. She has a green thumb like her mother reputedly did. She spends long hours in the garden and greenhouse. Yet," added Selina, "she is of an age where she should be spending more time with her contemporaries, and looking for a husband. I invite Georgina here, but I am afraid I don't provide much society for her. There are not many young men in the village, and even if there were, Lady Garvey keeps her cloistered."

"She needs a season in London," said Judith. "I invited her to my daughter's wedding as a sort of introduction, but Lady Garvey will have none of it. Would she listen to you, if you spoke on my behalf?"

Mrs Southcott pursed her lips. "I doubt it. Lady Garvey is selfish and fixed in her ways, and does not want to exert herself. She keeps the house shut up and pretends she is out to any visitors - I only know the truth because I walk over there myself to meet Georgy when I can, though I am so busy now, and Georgy sneaks over here."

"It is curious that Lady Garvey keeps it so shuttered," agreed Judith. "Do you know why she does so?"

Selina gave a little shrug and patted her dog again. "Perhaps she is simply lazy. It was much better when Harriet was alive - you know, Georgina's other grandmother. She kept the place in order, but now that Harriet is gone, it is falling to wrack and ruin."

"Hm," said Judith. "How *did* Harriet die?"

"They say it was heart trouble," said Selina cautiously.

Judith leaned forward. "Often the heart gives way at times of sorrow or anger. Was Harriet burdened with anything like that, when she passed?"

Selina stiffened, drawing a breath. Unfortunately, before she could respond, Mrs Kendall returned with the tea tray and disrupted the moment. Only once she had poured the tea - slowly and distractedly - did Selina respond to Judith's question.

"You are perspicacious, my lady. In the week before she died, Harriet visited me. She appeared to be under some sort of strain."

"What sort of strain?" Judith pressed, as she took her tea.

"I'm not sure. She was nervous and preoccupied. She said she had argued fiercely with someone, but she did not say whom." Selina sighed. "Whoever it was, they must feel dreadfully guilty."

Hot tea scaled Judith's tongue. She narrowed her eyes. "Guilty? Why?"

"To have contributed to Harriet's death," said Selina, with raised brows. "If, as you say, anger can make the heart seize up."

Judith took another cautious sip to gain a moment. What had Harriet discovered? Had she, by some awful chance, realised that there was more to Lord Garvey's death than met the eye? Or was the quarrel over some other matter?

She grasped the opportunity to make enquires. "Do you have any idea with whom she might have argued? Was Lord Kenneth in town? Or any other visitor?"

Selina frowned. "Lord Kenneth was staying at the Golden Bat at the time. Though if he was to argue with anyone it would be his own mother. They detest each other, I'm afraid to say."

"It *is* odd, I must say, that Kenneth doesn't reside at his own home."

Selina winced. "He can't bear to be around his mother. She always favoured Charles and she was heartbroken when he died. Kenneth knows Lady Garvey would rather have lost him. It is a burden for him to bear, and I cannot blame him for keeping his distance."

Judith was glad that Selina had brought the conversation around to Charles' death of her own accord. "Ah, that was a dreadful night, wasn't it? You must have been devastated to lose your fiancé."

Selina gave her a direct look. "It was not so great a loss to me as one might suppose. Indeed, as I think you saw for yourself at the time, I entered the engagement with a sense of oppression. I was grateful to the Duke of Sargen for dispatching Lord Garvey, for he saved me from an odious marriage."

Judith held her gaze. "You did not seem to be an eager bride." She paused, weighing her next words. "Would you have taken measures to escape the marriage, perhaps?"

Selina blinked. "I had little choice but to proceed," she said carefully. "I was so young, and my parents had arranged the match." She gave a deep sigh. "I owe his grace an undying debt of gratitude."

She shivered slightly, and the tea quivered in her cup. Beside her, the golden dog stirred in his sleep.

Judith's eyes narrowed. She had a sudden suspicion, and she was determined to ask the next question, even if it was intrusive. "Were you with Charles on the night that he died? In the maze?"

In which a tryst is witnessed

A charmed object - just like charismatic charm - flaunts itself to all and sundry.

    - from *Lady Avely's Guide to Lies and Charms*

SELINA'S LASHES FLUTTERED DOWN, and she was silent a moment. "Yes," she admitted. "He took me down to see that awful Apollo statue and press his attentions upon me. I did not know what to do, for my own father had ordered me to accompany my fiancé, to compromise my virtue and commit me to the marriage."

"So you went into the maze, reluctantly. Did you resist Charles' advances?"

Still Selina did not look at her. "In truth, I did not want them." There was a brief silence. "And then the duke rescued me."

Her last sentence rang with admiration. Selina might love her Mr Southcott but she reserved a special worship for Dacian, it seemed. Or perhaps Mr Southcott was the only man who would take Selina, after the scandal of the house party.

"What were you wearing that night?" asked Judith abruptly.

Selina looked up, startled. "Er - I cannot recall - my white muslin, perhaps? Yes, it was that. I remember I felt like a virgin sacrifice." She laughed uncomfortably.

Judith recalled the gown. Selina had been wearing it that night, at the announcement of her engagement. A similar metaphor had crossed Judith's own mind, seeing Selina's pale bosom and slender form clad in flowing white, while Charles had leered over her.

One question was answered: Selina had been the real woman under the Illusion of Judith. Had she been the one to cast the Illusion, to save herself? Or had it been a hidden watcher, Lady Vosse perhaps, sneaking into the maze? Or indeed, anyone who heard Lord Garvey invite Selina down into the gardens for a stroll that evening. It would be easy to guess that he would choose the hour of ten o'clock, when Apollo's shadow was at its most suggestive. Then it would have been a simple matter to send the note to Dacian and arrange for the fatal confluence.

Judith put her teacup down and rubbed her forehead. Even as one strand came loose, she could see other knots. Had Selina known of Dacian and Judith's own entanglement? She might have seen their confrontation in the glasshouse, but withdrawn from the window before Judith looked up.

Selina spoke. "I will try to visit Georgina soon, if that puts your mind at ease." She seemed eager now to change the subject. "I will encourage Lady Garvey to untie the leading strings. Perhaps if enough of us plead with her, she will take heed."

"Yes," said Judith distractedly. "That would be useful."

Standing, Mrs Southcott smiled, bringing the interview to a close. "It is strange to see you now, after all these years, Lady Avely. I hope you can see that I have grown past my uncertain girlhood."

"Indeed." Judith stood too. "It seems that some good came of that night, after all."

Selina nodded. "If you ever see the Duke of Sargen, be sure to tell him so."

Judith stiffened slightly, but she hoped it was not apparent. "I will, if the occasion should ever arise." Indeed, she was aware of a burning desire to tell Dacian that his violence had not been completely unwarranted. Perhaps it would lift some of the burden on his conscience to know that he had rescued Selina from odious encroachment.

As she followed Selina out the room, Judith's eye caught on a dollhouse, partly hidden in the corner behind one of the armchairs. It was a sturdy, two-storey wooden box, complete with tiny furniture and brightly coloured cloths. The little chairs looked rather familiar. They were in the Vember style Judith had seen before in London: crafted by and for vampiri.

She came to a halt. "Mrs Southcott, what a charming dollhouse! Wherever did you find such delicate furniture for it?"

Selina turned with a jerk. "Oh - those! Can you believe it: I found them in a forgotten corner of an attic. Charming, are they not? My daughter loves playing dolls with them."

She spoke the truth, but Judith wondered if it was the whole truth. Did the dollhouse also serve another purpose, to house a vampiri companion? Or were there more of the Vember pieces hidden away in the attic, for the use of a certain Miss Yvette Belfleur?

Once again, Judith cursed the Edicts that forbade any mention of the vampiri or the Musor arts. She would give much to ask Selina directly if she knew of any magicks. Perhaps, she considered, it was worth the risk, to put aside the etiquettes of the Edicts while on the search for a murderer.

"Mrs Southcott," she said bluntly, "does a bat ever frequent your household?"

Selina's eyes widened. "Goodness me, you do ask strange questions. Bats! Whatever next!" She tilted her head consideringly. "I am sure we do have bats in our stable, Lady Avely, and perhaps one or two make their way into the house. But please do not hold it against us. It is as much we can do to keep the mice at bay."

She turned and swept out of the house. Judith was left somewhat irate, for Selina's answer had neatly told the truth while avoiding any revelation.

ROBERT WAS WAITING OUTSIDE, while the coachman walked the horses. Judith bid Selina farewell, and then turned to Robert.

"Would you like to walk back with me?" she asked. "We can send Patrick ahead with the carriage."

Robert hesitated, glancing up at the sky, where grey clouds gathered in the distance. "The sun might not hold."

"The walk is not long."

He shook his head stiffly. "I'd best hurry back. His grace might need me."

Judith did not want to beg for his company. "Very well." She paused. "I will walk, however. And if you find the duke still occupied, please use the time for yourself."

"The duke might not like you to walk-"

"The duke is overly anxious, and treats me as if I am still a maiden," said Judith, somewhat snappishly. "The whole advantage of being a widow is that I may have a little freedom."

"Yes, my lady."

She sighed. "Please, call me Judith. It is vastly improper that you should still be carrying on as my footman, when we are related by the bonds of family and duty."

Robert nodded soberly, but did not unclasp his hands from behind his back. "Very well, Judith. And I will take the opportunity to ask around about this Poleney fellow, while you are walking."

"An excellent notion."

The carriage rolled away with Robert's tall form hanging off the back. Judith followed it, glaring after him. Irksome child! It was almost as if he *was* her son, with such inconsiderate behaviour. If she had been any other lady, he would have politely accompanied her on the walk, or at least accepted her suggestion that he take some time for himself! She supposed she should be grateful he was so prickly, for it was better than indifference.

The sound of wheels faded into the distance, to be replaced by the cooing of wood pigeons and the chirping of finches. Judith had much to ponder, as she walked along the country laneway. Several things had emerged from her conversation with Mrs Selina Southcott.

It was curious indeed that Selina had possession of Vember furniture. Then there was the worrying intelligence that Harriet Bollopher had been troubled by something before she died. Had Harriet discovered a dark plot and been silenced?

Surely the incriminating evidence could not have concerned Selina herself, for Selina had been the one to impart the news to Judith. Yet perhaps Selina had been dancing a delicate minuet, revealing truth while keeping her own secrets. The fact remained that Selina had possessed a strong motive for arranging Lord Garvey's death, using the duke as her tool to do so. She knew all too well when Charles would be in the Apollo alcove in a compromising position, and she may well have known of Dacian's pursuit of Judith. The duke had not, after all, been particularly subtle about it, even if one put aside his advances in the greenhouse.

Yet why would Selina bother to use Judith's image, when Dacian might have called Lord Garvey out anyway, upon witnessing his unwanted attentions upon the innocent young woman? Judith grimaced to herself. It was true that Lord Garvey had been engaged to Selina at the time, so his behaviour could be construed as within his rights. Dacian might have abhorred it, and intervened, but not with the instinct of rage that led to immediate violence. Selina - or whoever cast the Illusion - must have known that.

Judith tried to assemble any other relevant facts in her mind. One, Lord Kenneth avoided his own house, only visiting the inn. Did that point to his guilt, or some other knowledge? Two, Selina had said this was because there was ill blood between him and Lady Garvey, citing Lady Garvey's fondness for Charles - but there might be more behind her hostility than that. Three, Garvey House was neglected and shuttered, yet parts of the garden were well tended, including a secret path through the maze, hidden by an Illusion. Four, at the centre of the maze was an unfamiliar plant with a familiar smell, which Mrs Froode brewed in a tea and Kenneth perhaps sold to the local apothecary. And five, both Charles Garvey's ghost and a live Kenneth had appeared to lurk around Garvey House late last night. Oh, and six, there was an unattached vampiri flying about: Miss Yvette Belfleur.

A pang of worry creased Judith's brow. Marigold had spoken of Miss Belfleur in fond accents and defended her character vehemently last night. Wooten had not been so complimentary or trusting, and Judith was inclined to agree, even though Yvette had seemed to care for Marigold in her time of injury. The elusive vampiri could be with the enemy. Or she could be with the law. Either way, they ought not to trust her, as much as Marigold seemed eager to pursue her acquaintance. Judith would have to mention the Vember furniture, and the possibilities that it entailed. For if Miss Belfleur was a companion to Selina, why were they keeping the relation a secret?

The dirt path was muddy under her feet and Judith lifted her skirts slightly as she walked. Hedgerows on either side made the avenue feel protected and private, much like a larger version of the maze, though the branches also enclosed overhead. She rather felt as if her mind was caught in a labyrinth, trying to find the way to the truth at the centre of the puzzle. A greenfinch darted past, in a flash of lime and yellow, and her gaze followed its graceful, twittering path through the branches.

There was also Lord Triskett and Lady Vosse's arrival to consider, and the fact that they had been staying in the neighbouring village last night - the very time when the Illusion of Lord Garvey was abroad.

At first sight, neither his lordship or her ladyship appeared to have any reason to rid the world of Lord Garvey nine years ago. But perhaps Judith had been overly focussed on Charles' death. Perhaps his lordship had simply been a casualty.

Perhaps the real motive had been to rid England of the Duke of Sargen.

Judith chewed on her lip. If that was the case, whoever had orchestrated Dacian's exile would not be pleased to see him returned.

The laneway curved. A gap in the hedgerows showed an open field and a copse of conifers. Judith glanced through, admiring the sturdy greenery that rose up like pointed domes. Then she froze, her breath catching in her throat.

Two figures stood by the tallest conifer, hand in hand, facing one another. One was tall and broad shouldered with black hair, and the other wore a pretty muslin gown of green, with long curls of red hair trailing down her bodice.

Judith took a step back into the shelter of the hedgerow. Her heart beat fast, as if it were losing blood. It was Dacian out there, holding Lady Vosse's hand.

Gathering her courage, Judith parted a branch in the hedge and watched them.

She could see Dacian's eyes crease with a smile as he looked down at his companion. Isobel stepped closer, coquettish, and raised a hand to his face. She stroked gently, and Dacian turned his head, placing a tender kiss on her palm. Then he moved his mouth to trail two more kisses down her wrist, while Isobel smiled in triumph.

Judith's heart thudded loud in her ears. She stepped back, unable to watch. Pain shot through her like an arrow, winding her. The hedgerow prickled into the back of her gown, and her skirts dropped into the mud, unheeded.

Blessedly, the hurt was soon followed by anger - at herself most of all. Why should she be hurt? Why should she feel anything at all? She, of all people, knew that Dacian was fickle. She knew that he was lustful, and pursued his pleasures with alacrity. Isobel was simply giving him what Judith had withheld.

Her teeth clamped down on her bottom lip, threatening to draw blood. Better than tears, she told herself. *Do not cry* over that libertine. Not again.

She drew back the way she had come. Blindly, she found a fallen log she had passed earlier and sat upon it, careless of damp moss and crawling creatures. Another greenfinch flittered past her, but this time she did not notice its flash of colour. She stared angrily at her muddied hem, her hands clenched in her lap, tears welling in her eyes.

Only when a long time had passed did she rise once more, and set out again for the Golden Bat.

ROBERT MET HER BY FOOT, half a mile from Stokesford, where the lane broadened. His expression was rather worried, and only deepened into guilt when he spotted her. There was no sight of Dacian or Isobel, thank God. Judith kept walking, mechanically. The outskirts of the village were a picturesque arrangement of pastures, cottages, and barns, with a chattering stream running along the road once more.

"There you are!" said Robert as he approached. "Did something delay you?"

"I was waylaid by bird-watching."

At her flat tone, he gave Judith a more careful look. "Truly? You will land me in trouble with the duke. I am sorry that I left you to walk alone. I dared not tell him I had misplaced you, so I set out to look for you."

"He was busy enough, I'm sure." She felt a flash of irritation that Robert cared so much for the duke's opinion. If only he knew that Dacian was nothing but a charming liar with the morals of a rabbit.

Robert fell in beside her, frowning. "What has happened? You seem...upset. Did you discover something from Mrs Southcott?"

Judith gladly followed the diversion, and reported the conversation to him, stressing her suspicions about Harriet's death, hoping it would explain her low mood. In truth, she was unsettled by the thought that Harriet had laboured under some trouble and died unhappily.

"So," she concluded, "we must consider the possibility that Harriet's death wasn't as innocent as it appeared."

Robert frowned. "Are you suggesting...?"

"Perhaps Harriet discovered something incriminating."

Robert kept his long stride to match Judith's shorter steps, as they walked between the churned tracks of carriage wheels. "If that is the case, it narrows down our suspects. Who had the opportunity to harm Harriet? It must be someone from Garvey House."

"I did wonder that, but we don't really know the circumstances of her death. The story of her heart failure could simply be that - a story, put about. The truth of the matter might be quite different." She paused as the lane curved past a herd of incurious cows, searching for further distraction from her grief. "Did you discover anything about the apothecary this afternoon?"

"I did," Robert replied. "Mr Poleney has a popular new medicine, a bottled remedy which he calls the Poleney Elixir. He claims it contains a secret ingredient which will cure all ills, yet from what I can gather in the village, it has been a mixed success. Some people swear by it, and others dismiss it as quackery."

"Intriguing. Do you think Kenneth is providing the special ingredient, from the maze? Perhaps it was itemised in the invoice you saw."

"Yes," said Robert. "And it might explain why he visited in secret last night, and it would give him a motive for killing his brother, if he knew that the flower was very valuable."

"I wonder how the plant became infused with Healing properties," said Judith thoughtfully. "I shall have to engage Kenneth in conversation about it. If I catch him in a lie, it might give us a clue."

The road was muddy where carriage wheels had dug a rut, and Judith stepped around a particularly large puddle. She glanced over at Robert. "And did you find any time to draw?"

"A little," he said evasively.

She dared another question. "Which do you prefer: sketching, tinted drawings, or oil painting?"

After a moment, he replied. "Oil painting, I think. It takes far longer, but it is more versatile."

"Perhaps frustrating, when your Illusions arise so quickly to hand?"

His lips quirked in acknowledgement. "Real art does require patience, I find."

Judith nodded. "I hope that the end result is more satisfying to you. I was taught how to do tinted drawings, myself, as part of my education, and I passed on what I knew to my own daughter." There was an awkward silence, and she hurried on. "I'd be happy to share any technical knowledge with you. Your Illusions are exquisite, of course, but perhaps it is difficult to translate your artistic skill into another medium."

"That is very true!" said Robert. "The one doesn't guarantee the other, but I enjoy the challenge."

"Just don't tell the duke that I think his moustache is exquisite. He is already too fond of it."

Robert cracked a smile, which Judith shared. "By the way," she added, "you should also find yourself a vampiri companion, if you intend to keep practicing Illusion. And Castle Lanyon might soon host a whole roost from which you could choose."

Robert raised his brows, but she did not explain further, just left it as an enticement. She did not want to mention the King's mandate for the Avelys to set up a Musor school in Cornwall, for the whole conception was in its very early stages, and might frighten him off.

At her silence, Robert abruptly changed the subject. "We will be in sight of the village soon. It is best if I retreat."

Judith sighed with annoyance as he fell back apace, adopting his position as footman. It was always one step forward, two steps back with the boy (literally, in this case). Dared she believe she was making some sort of progress with him?

As they breasted Stokesford's main street, she welcomed the chance to compose herself before she entered the inn. She did not want Dacian, too, to notice that she was upset. Her pride would not allow it. She drew her shoulders back and set her lips into a small smile, as if she had traversed a most pleasant walk in the countryside.

Fortunately, she did not encounter his grace in the corridors, and she hustled past the parlour, determined to retreat to her room. At the door, she turned and nodded at Robert, dismissing him like a servant. She could keep to their assigned stations if he was going to be so damn stubborn about it. He gave her a curious look, but said nothing, taking up a position outside her door.

Alone in her room, Judith tore off her gloves and lay on her bed, wretched, as the memory of Dacian's perfidy returned. Oh, for the oblivion of a nap! But sleep would not come; she was too overwrought, her mind lurching from one unpleasant speculation to the next.

Eventually, she sat up and pulled out her knitting, to make some progress on the bridal stockings for her daughter. The repetitive motions, along with thoughts of the wedding, calmed her a little, and she sighed. Perhaps some chocolate would further soothe her nerves.

She called for Robert, and when he cracked the door open, she asked him to order a molinet for her. He smiled and withdrew quickly.

However, ten minutes later, it was not Robert nor Phyllis who delivered the tray. The door swung open and Dacian stepped through, holding the chocolate aloft.

In which chocolate is ignored

A liar can use both charm and charms to evade detection.
  - from *Lady Avely's Guide to Lies and Charms*

HE NOW WORE his disguise as Mr Fortnew. Startled, Judith dropped her knitting. Fearing that she had paled at the sight of him, she bent to gather it up again as calmly as possible.

"Dear God," she said, "your moustache gave me a fright."

Dacian grinned as he bore his burden inside. "Good afternoon, marchioness. Robert said you required drinking chocolate, and possibly some company to cheer your spirits."

Inwardly, she cursed Robert's officiousness, even if it had been born of kindness. "I am fine, thank you," she replied coolly. "I merely require solitude."

The rich smell of spices and cocoa wafted into the room. Dacian raised his brows as he set the tray down on the oak dresser. "You dismiss me, in fact." He turned to stare at her over his moustache, as if she had announced an intention to clang the silver molinet against his head. She was aware of a desire to do so - except that she would not endanger chocolate in that way. He was not worth the passion he invoked, she told herself firmly.

She clacked her needles together with a grim focus. "You need not sound so surprised that I do not wish for your company."

"Is it the moustache?" His hand went up and pulled the cravat pin out, placing it on the tray. The facade of Mr Fortnew vanished, revealing Dacian's dark good looks, fine jaw, and lined cheeks. Judith tried not to glare, remembering that same cheek turned towards Lady Vosse.

"I thought I was irresistible." He tried for his charming smile. When he saw how flat it landed, he wiped it off his face, much like the disguise. "Are you quite alright, Judith?"

"Really, Dacian," she snapped. "Just because I am not desperately glad to see you does not mean I am labouring under an illness."

"No," he agreed slowly, "but what has happened to put you out of colour? Robert said you had an illuminating chat with Mrs Southcott."

"I do not wish to discuss it right now."

Dacian was silent a moment. "Very well. If it is peace you want, I will give it to you." He paused. "May I at least pour your chocolate?"

"If you must," she said peevishly, and turned her attention to her knitting. She could hear the slosh of creamy milk and the clink of the cup, and smell the fragrance of cardamon and nutmeg. Somehow the sweet scent did not have its usual allure, for she felt sick to her stomach. Dacian's footsteps crossed the room, and she saw his hand reach out and place the cup on her bedside table. The same strong, long fingers that had clasped Lady Vosse's in the meadow.

"There you go." His tone was subdued. "I wish you would confide in me, Judith."

Rage curled through her. How dare Dacian try his duplicitous charm on her now, a mere few hours later?

"You cannot have everything you wish," she said flatly, "as shocking as that may seem."

"I thought we were in this plot together?" His eyes narrowed. "Is your foul mood something to do with the arrival of Lord Triskett and Lady Vosse? Do you feel that they intrude?"

Judith shook her head. "There is nothing to intrude upon."

He folded his arms across his chest. "Why, Judith, I believe you are jealous!" Satisfaction coloured his tone. "You *do* care, after all! My dear girl, there is nothing to be jealous of in Isobel, believe me."

His words rang true, but fury rose in her, along with an unwanted vein of sympathy for Isobel. Dacian might dismiss such dalliances as nothing, but she was certain Isobel hoped for more of his affections, as did Judith, if she was truthful with herself. Not this casual intimacy, with whomever happened to be on hand.

She stood and threw her knitting aside. "Oh, I suppose you are encouraging her advances for the sake of our investigation?" she said dangerously.

Dacian took a step back and held up his hands, his face incredulous. "Encouraging her advances? I was being friendly, I grant you, to put Isobel at her ease, but I wouldn't go so far as to say..."

"I saw you," said Judith, her colour high. "Do not fudge the matter, Dacian, with your prevarications. I *saw* you."

"Saw me *what*?"

At his confused expression, the first inkling of the truth began to bloom in her mind. "I saw you with Isobel - next to the conifers in the meadow."

"What conifers?" He was now patently bewildered. "I have been inside all afternoon, I swear. Isobel went for a walk and I chatted with Biscuit, and then I wrote some letters, including one to Lewis. I haven't been in any meadow. You must believe me, Judith!"

She stared at him, hearing the truth in his voice. Rage ebbed out of her, leaving her limbs shaky and her heart tumultuous. He had not been with Lady Vosse. She had seen someone else. Or something else.

He came forward and grasped her elbow, as if to steady her. "What did you see, Judith? What meadow?"

"I saw you and Isobel, clear as day, standing by some conifers." She swallowed. "You were...intimately engaged."

His grip tightened. "An Illusion? Good God." Then he dropped her elbow, his eyes hardening. "And of course you believed it at once."

Judith gaped at the sudden harshness in his voice. "It was right in front of me!"

His jaw clenched. "You are all too quick to believe the worst," he retorted. "Just as you were on the matter of Mrs Bleau, when I told you she was in my bed chamber that night. You would not have believed the worst if you had not already possessed a low opinion of my character."

"You deliberately misled me then! As I was misled today!"

Dacian's face was cut in rigid lines, his black eyes snapping. "Yet both times it aligned with your true appraisal of my worth. It is quite obvious what you think of me, Judith."

"What - that you are a rake?" Judith gathered her wits, trying to defend herself. "Everyone thinks *that*, Dacian. All of society knows that you cannot resist any...*moderately* pretty woman. I've seen you chase any number of skirts over the years. You cannot blame me now for painting your character accordingly!"

"What was I supposed to do?" he growled. "You were married, for God's sake!"

Their gazes locked. There was a fraught, heavy silence. Judith's heart beat in her throat. His mouth pressed in a hard line, his eyes sparking with anger, and something else. Pressure, subtle yet powerful, gathered in the air. It hung around them for a long moment, then faded.

Dacian heaved a sigh, though his fists still clenched by his side. "I cannot believe you thought I would march out there and ravish Isobel at the first opportunity!"

She swallowed. "I am sorry. You are right, I should have known better." She wrung her fingers together. "It seemed so real! Yet forgive me. It seems I allowed my emotions to cloud my judgement."

Abruptly, he rubbed his hand across his brow. "No matter. I should not be angry at you. No doubt anyone would have been fooled, and thought the same." He took another step backward, putting some space between them, while avoiding her gaze.

"It did look *exactly* like you."

He sighed again. "Describe the scene to me, please."

"Um," said Judith reluctantly, "you were holding hands with Lady Vosse, and...smiling at one another."

Dacian raised a brow. "We cannot simply have been exchanging affectionate grins, to have put you in such a rage."

"I was not in a rage," said Judith faintly. Indeed, now she felt an overwhelming relief and confusion, to discover that she had been tricked.

A smile broke across his face, like sunlight after a storm. Judith felt her knees weaken with relief, and something else.

"Interesting," he observed, "that our Illusor shows *you* merely the chaste clasp of hands, while for *me* he reserves the sight of bare bosoms."

"It was not just hand-holding! You kissed her hand."

"What, like a gentleman?"

She shook her head. "No, Isobel touched your face and then..."

Dacian's eyes gleamed. "Show me."

Her breath caught. "Don't be salacious."

"Not at all," he protested. "I need to know what you saw, to examine what we are dealing with here. How exactly was I painted? How was the scene cast? It might give us some clue as to the culprit." He stepped close to her and took her right hand in his. "We were holding hands like this?"

His fingers were warm, closing firmly round her own, which were ungloved. Speechless, Judith nodded. This close, she could see the faint line of the scar on his forehead.

"And then?" He pulled her closer, lifting her hand to his mouth. "Like this?"

"Dacian," Judith managed. "It was the other..." She brought her left hand up to his face and cupped his cheek, avoiding his gaze, studiously examining her own fingers. "Then you turned your head and kissed the palm."

She could feel his eyes intent on her. Then he did as she instructed, slowly turning to press his lips against her palm. The warmth sent a bolt of awareness spinning through her, as if the world had shivered under her feet.

"Like this?" His voice deepened.

Her own vocal cords, she found, were somewhat tardy. "Yes," she gulped. "Then her wrist."

He lowered his lips, brushing the inside of her wrist. She was tethered by the sensation. The rest of her felt as if it might burst into flames.

"And this?" He kissed just below her wrist. When she said nothing, he placed her other hand on his chest. Involuntarily, her fingers splayed, feeling the hard breadth of him. Her breath came out in a rush.

"And this?" He kissed the inside of her arm again and, shockingly, licked her bare skin. She quivered, affronted yet aching for more. His breath warmed the spot, then he put his open mouth on her again. She felt as if she were going to expire from need, the pull of it low and sweet in her body.

Of its own accord, her hand moved up from his chest, and she grasped his shoulder, bracing herself before she could fall over. His teeth pulled gently at her skin, his tongue flicking, and a moan fell from her.

He turned his head. Black hair brushed her arm, and she saw that his pupils were wide. "Then what?" His voice was husky.

"I didn't see," she confessed, her voice a breathy whisper. "I hid in the hedgerow."

"Judith! For shame." He paused. "I will have to use my imagination"

She gulped.

He traced his fingers along the underside of her bare arm. The sensation was exquisite, torturous, and dimly Judith wondered if she might faint from desire. Then he lifted his head and found her mouth with his.

He kissed her slowly and gently, as if he were afraid he might frighten her. Judith opened her mouth to him and thrust her body closer, desperately eager for more, too overcome to be afraid anymore. Dacian murmured with approval, and deepened his kiss hungrily.

She spun backwards in time. The magnetic force between them was the same as it had been all those years ago, by the river when he first kissed her, when they were young. Except it was stronger now; so powerful that Judith did not think it possible to ever move from his embrace again.

All she wanted was him; to devour the nectar of his touch. He returned the sentiment with a ravenous heat, his hands warm, curving round her lower back to pull her close.

Then a soft tapping came at the door.

The sound broke through their hazy awareness. Dacian stilled in her arms.

"The door," he murmured huskily.

Judith clung to him, but the knock came again. He released her, pushing her away. Awkwardly, she ran her hands down her skirt and up to her hair. With a start, she realised that she still wore her mobcap, though it felt as if she had been completely disrobed.

Dacian was now five feet away, adjusting his breeches and smoothing his coat. His own hair remained in some disorder, black locks in disarray. His cheeks were flushed and he grinned at her, like a boy on Christmas morning. "Tell them to go away."

"No, I can't! It might be Robert," she hissed. "Put on your disguise!" She cast a guilty glance at where her cup of chocolate lay untouched next to the bed.

"Must I?" He reached for the tray, where the cravat pin lay, and stuck it into the cloth at his neck. Mr Fortnew reappeared, thankfully overlaying Dacian's roguish twinkle.

Judith cleared her throat, aware of her own high colour. "Come in," she called.

The door opened and Robert peered inside. He looked from one to the other, and the full cup of chocolate. His brows raised in interrogation, then he recalled himself and shifted his gaze to the window like a good servant. "Excuse my intrusion, but Phyllis wants to know if you would like your supper now in the parlour."

"Ahem," said Dacian. "Now? Can it wait? Maybe for an hour or so?"

Judith frowned. She was beginning, with the advent of Mr Fortnew's moustache, to recover her senses. She glanced out the window, to see that dusk was falling, the trees becoming silhouettes. Marigold would soon stir in her dresser, if she had not already been woken by their...argument.

"Nonsense, Dacian. It is time for supper. Thank you for notifying us, Robert. We will join you in the parlour shortly."

Robert bowed. "Shall I fetch Wooten, your grace?"

Dacian was frowning at Judith, but he turned his head at this. "Perhaps after we eat. He needs a long sleep after his recent tribulations."

"And I must change," said Judith firmly. "As must you, Dacian. Enough of this nonsense."

He straightened his shoulders. She could not quite be sure under the disguise, but she thought his face went blank. "Indeed, marchioness." He paused. "I will see you in the parlour."

When the door shut behind them, Judith sank onto her bed. She was shaky and charged with a confusing cacophony of sensations. Her body still ached with want, yet her surging desire was tempered by fear and doubt. What had just happened? How had he managed to seduce her, even as she had sworn she would not be seduced?

Curse the man. He would be insufferable now, convinced that he was indeed impossible to resist.

He had not dallied with Isobel. The relief of that still swirled in her mind. Yet why should that paltry fact make Judith throw herself into his arms? Was she so flattered that he would choose her to satisfy his masculine urges? Drawing a deep breath, Judith admitted to herself that it was true. Jealousy did indeed change one's perception. Whereas before she would have kept Dacian at arm's length, the thought that he might seek solace in Lady Vosse was untenable. Seeing it painted in front of her had driven that truth home with shocking vividness. Judith could not bear the sight or the thought of them together. She would much prefer that *she* be the Merry Widow of Dacian's pursuit, rather than the Discreet Wife that Isobel offered.

It was a lowering reflection. Her desire and infatuation for Dacian had trampled upon her dignity and good sense.

She put her hands to her cheeks. They were still hot, her breath still ragged. What did she want of him? Having tasted his lips and felt his body against hers, she knew exactly what she wanted. She wanted all of him, every inch, around her, inside her, driving and wild. His hands and mouth, demanding and masterful, and her own hands tracing every hard, muscled plane and firm part of him, and drawing him close, as close as possible.

Lust. She drew a shaky breath. She was experiencing lust. It was a familiar acquaintance who had been away for some years. Its return was rather overwhelming. That was all. She was simply in lust, and so was he. What of it? They were two grown adults. They might indulge in it. They might give themselves the pleasure, even outside of marriage. She was past the youthful innocence that such strictures were meant to protect.

She rather thought she might die if they didn't...

And Dacian - could it be that he wanted this as much as she did? He had looked so pleased. She shook her head. He was simply triumphant that he might pull down her bodice at last, a hunter closing in on a particularly elusive prey.

She straightened. Even now, her insistent need was fading, the fire receding to the burning of coals. She could refuse to stoke them. Throw water over them, even. She was here to solve a mystery, after all, and uncover the villain who had sentenced Dacian to exile, and perhaps even killed Harriet. There was no time for such trivial matters as *lust*.

Needlessly, she retied her mobcap ribbons twice, and took a few gulps of the now-cooled chocolate. It was time to reaffix her dignity, and prepare for supper. She would simply act as if that unfortunate interlude had never taken place.

Never mind that it was seared on her being, indelible and irrevocable as the Musing itself. And it seemed just as liable to give rise to Bemusement, for she felt shaky, befuddled, and quite confused.

She would not give him the satisfaction of seeing it, for it would stoke his already excessive self-regard.

In which the companions argue

Always remember: a lie is a clue.
   - from *Lady Avely's Guide to Lies and Charms*

SUPPER WAS A RATHER AWKWARD AFFAIR.

Sensing Judith's withdrawal, Dacian also became cool. Furthermore, he took it upon himself to become autocratic.

"You must leave, Judith," he said, after Phyllis had delivered the first course to their little table: a rich vegetable soup that Judith set into with alacrity. Her appetite, she found, was suddenly ravenous.

She looked up. "Leave? What do you mean?"

"You saw an Illusion today, aimed at you. Someone is trying to chase you off."

Robert pricked his ears from the door. "An Illusion? Where?"

Dacian's lips pressed together. "On her walk back, Judith saw an Illusion of me in a meadow, with Lady Vosse."

Robert stared, then red crept into his cheeks. "Oh! I see!"

"I doubt you do," said Judith crossly. "His grace wasn't cavorting naked in the field, if that is what you are imagining."

Robert coughed, looking rather startled. "Er, no, indeed." He paused. "What *was* he doing?"

Judith was trying not to imagine the duke cavorting naked. "He was kissing Lady Vosse's arm." The memory of Dacian's lips on her own skin further deepened her confusion. "Like lovers."

"And," said Dacian unfeelingly, "it was clearly meant to upset you, drive a wedge between us, and make you storm off. I am of the opinion that this is exactly what you should do. Pretend that you are convinced, and retreat in a huff. That way you will not be in any danger."

"I am not upset!" she lied, then added with more conviction, "And I am not going to retreat in a huff!" Though it occurred to her that the amorous Illusion might have indeed succeeded drumming up hostility between them, had she not been a Truth Discernor and able to hear the truth of his denials.

"Retreat with dignity then." Dacian tapped his spoon impatiently against the table. "Or you can simply vanish, using my Travelling charm, and pop straight into Falmouth and trot along to your castle. Just use the word for Travel."

"What's that?" asked Robert with interest.

"*Veho.*"

Judith set down her spoon with a snap. "Just as things are becoming interesting? I'm not going to vanish! Don't you see: by casting that Illusion today, our quarry must have given us several clues."

Robert nodded thoughtfully. "That's true. Whoever it was, they know that you are here, your grace, and moreover travelling with Judith."

"Yes." Judith tore a piece of bread with a sharp movement. "*You* are the one that should retreat. Furthermore, the Illusor *also* knows that Lady Vosse is here." She glanced around. "I am afraid that we must conclude that someone has been spying on us."

Dacian frowned. "The maid, perhaps? Phyllis?"

Judith gave a cross sigh. "It is much more likely that Lady Vosse herself is our villain." At Dacian's skeptical look, she hurried on to explain her thoughts from earlier in the day, before she was interrupted by scenes of romance. "All this time, we have assumed that the purpose of the charade was to kill Lord Garvey. What if, in fact, it was all to punish you, Dacian? You had rejected Lady Vosse's advances, and she saw us together in the glasshouse. Perhaps she was a woman scorned, and wished to provoke you with a sordid Illusion."

Dacian shook his head dismissively. "I highly doubt it. Isobel does not care *that* much for me, Judith, that she would orchestrate such a scene."

"Yet the fact remains," gritted out Judith, "that whoever cast today's Illusion knew of Lady Vosse's arrival this morning. So that means it was cast by one of her party - including herself - or perhaps it was Lord Kenneth after all, watching from his window." She paused. "The one person it rules out is Mrs Southcott, for she cannot have known about Lady Vosse's appearance. The same applies to Froode and Faske."

"Except that," put in Robert, "Lady Vosse and Lord Triskett were staying nearby last night, in Gurney, the next village over. Perhaps more knew of their presence in the vicinity than we realise."

"Don't be absurd," said Dacian. "It must be Lord Kenneth. Anything else is ludicrous to imagine."

The mention of Mrs Southcott had reminded Judith of something she had not yet disclosed, in all the upheavals of the afternoon. "I must tell you, Dacian, that I have discovered that it was Selina Pelling with Lord Garvey that night, in the maze."

Dacian's brows shot up. "Under the Illusion?"

She nodded. "Selina told me that Lord Garvey was pressing unwanted attentions upon her, and she was grateful for your intervention. So it turns out that your violence was not completely unwarranted."

"Oh," said Dacian blankly, then his eyes met Judith's. A spark of understanding passed between them: that he might forgive himself a little. The truth was, she had already forgiven him. Dacian might have killed Garvey, but he had been directed by an unseen hand. And now she had some inkling of the violence that jealousy might wreak.

Judith cleared her throat. "However, if Selina was there that night, that places her firmly under suspicion. She might indeed be grateful to you - for falling in with her plans to kill off her suitor."

Dacian shook his head in repudiation, still thoughtful, but Robert agreed with Judith. "It is a possibility. I confess I also want to unravel it to the end, Judith."

She picked up her spoon again, grateful for Robert's support. "And if you think I'm going to leave before discovering the truth, you are sadly mistaken. What do you propose to do without me? Barge in there tomorrow, and throw your ducal weight around?" Judith took a large mouthful of soup, savouring it (and Dacian's look of chagrin) slowly. Once she had swallowed, she spoke again. "Tomorrow I will gain admittance to Garvey House under the aegis of Lord Kenneth, and I will ask a few more *direct* questions."

Dacian toyed with his own spoon crossly. "Very well, but I am coming with you - and no arguments about it!" he said, as Judith opened her mouth to protest. "I will wear my disguise, and be your footman again, but there is clearly less need for prevarication, if our quarry knows I am here. We might as well take advantage of the fact."

"There is also the matter of what Lady Garvey might do if she realises your presence," she pointed out. "It is more dangerous for you to lurk around Garvey House, than I."

"I'm not letting you go without me, and that is that."

"So ducal," Judith murmured, and had the satisfaction of seeing him glare.

AFTER SUPPER, Judith retreated to feed Marigold and inform her of the recent events. Marigold was not as agog as Judith expected at the news of the Illusory tryst, and she admitted that she had overheard the argument between Dacian and Judith.

"Oh." Judith flushed.

"Sounds to me like you rather jumped to conclusions," said Marigold, with characteristic frankness.

"I was completely justified in doing so!"

"Poor duke, to be so maligned."

"He wouldn't be so maligned if he showed a skerrick of restraint in his life," said Judith, then realised she was being unfair. After all, Dacian could have seduced her twenty-three years ago, but he had refrained. Yet somehow that was the worst part of it all.

She told Marigold of their speculations over supper. Marigold was inclined to think, like Judith, that Lady Vosse herself was the guilty party. Dacian himself had said Isobel had gone out for a walk, so she could have been in the meadow herself, casting the Illusion so she might stroke Dacian's cheek.

"Perhaps," suggested Marigold, "she was simply amusing herself, if she fancies the duke so much, as you say."

Judith pursed her lips. "No, I fear I was meant to see it. If only I had the wit to look around for who else might have cast it." She paused. "I saw something else today that you might find curious."

"What was that?"

"Vember furniture. In a dollhouse in Mrs Southcott's drawing room."

Marigold's eyes widened, then with quick comprehension, she said, "You think they belong to Miss Belfleur."

"It is possible."

"Well, then," said Marigold cheerfully. "That just shows us that Yvette is perfectly innocent, if she is a companion to Mrs Southcott. Have you not just said that Selina cannot have cast the Seduction Illusion?"

"I suppose," agreed Judith, though doubt still lingered in her own mind. Perhaps Selina had followed her along the road. "Yet why keep their relation a secret? Selina was rather evasive when I questioned her about the doll furniture and the possibility of bats. Why would she hide the truth from me?"

"These stupid Edicts. She is only being cautious, like you."

Judith sighed. "Yes, and I hope you are being cautious too. Will you venture out again tonight?"

Marigold sat up on the bed, nodding. "I find myself vastly curious about this dollhouse. Maybe I should pay it a visit."

"Only if Wooten accompanies you," warned Judith, "and you stay away from grasping hands. Promise me!"

Marigold grumbled at length, but eventually agreed to refrain from attacking any suspect, and also to don her new cloak. Then they had a long chat about Robert, with Judith complaining to Marigold about his contrariness, and asking the vampiri to casually raise the subject of Cornwall with him.

"He seems set against it," said Judith, "and I wish I knew why. Please won't you talk to him?"

Marigold wrinkled her nose and promised to try.

When they reconvened in the parlour, Wooten wore a long face and his own cloak, ready for the night's adventures. They flapped off into the night together after both swearing to behave with circumspection.

However, when they returned to the parlour later, they did not have much to report. Southcott Hall was closed and dark, the dollhouse visible from the drawing room windows but seemingly unoccupied. Miss Yvette, too, had not made an appearance. Judith could tell that Marigold was disheartened and confused by this, giving short answers to their questions.

"Did you investigate the belfry?" Robert asked. He was sitting round the table with Dacian, playing cards again. Judith was relieved he had allowed his formality to drop once more with the imbibing of decent whisky. His cheeks were flushed and he was smug about his pile of winnings, even as he cocked a questioning eyebrow at Marigold.

Marigold remained silent, worrying at her golden cape with restless fingers.

"We did," said Wooten, "and there was only a scrap of sheepskin and a length of silk there. They smelled of Miss Belfleur's presence, but I do not think she has stayed there long."

"Yes, a faint scent of lavender and pine." Marigold dropped her cloak and shrugged. "She must have passed through. There is no need to make a mystery of it."

Wooten sniffed. "She has simply moved on to her next destination."

"Albeit without saying goodbye," said Judith sympathetically.

Marigold folded her cape around herself. "Yvette did not owe me any civilities." She paused. "I only hope that she is not in some kind of trouble."

THE FOLLOWING morning breakfast was rushed, for Robert reported that Lord Kenneth Garvey was up and about. After her pound cake and chocolate, hastily drunk, Judith trod downstairs. She was clothed in one of her more fashionable gowns in a delicate lavender hue, and a matching mobcap that looked well on her honey-gold hair. She told herself it was because she wanted to impress Kenneth and Lady Garvey with her society credentials. Lady Vosse's wardrobe had nothing to do with it at all.

Dacian, at her heels, was dressed in Robert's livery, and wore his enchanted cravat pin. His moustache looked perkier today, after Robert had recast it overnight.

They set off to catch Kenneth in his den, but in the narrow confines of the upper corridor, they came face to face with Isobel and Lord Triskett.

Isobel widened her green eyes, taking in the sight of Dacian dressed in livery. "Oh hoh! Dacian! You are lowered, indeed! What is afoot? Can we join the fun?" Pointedly, she ignored Judith.

Annoyed, Judith said, "Nothing that concerns you," and pushed past.

"I'm in disguise," explained Dacian. "So nobody knows I'm a duke, of course. Don't give me away, for God's sake."

"Oh! I am a vault of secrecy," burbled Isobel merrily.

Judith looked over her shoulder to see the smile vanish from Isobel's eyes as Dacian reached Judith's side.

"My lady," he said. "What do you command?"

Flushing slightly, Judith turned and led the way down the stairs, aware of Isobel's narrowed gaze on her back.

Putting aside all thoughts of jealous women, Judith tapped on Kenneth's parlour door, for there were more important matters to attend to than Isobel's wounded pride.

As before, his lordship's lean manservant opened it, and as before, he seemed disinclined to grant her entry. But she could see Kenneth over his shoulder and gave him a winning smile, trying for something a bit like Isobel's bewitching charm. "Ah, Lord Kenneth! So lovely to see you again!"

A brief look of chagrin crossed Kenneth's face, but he bowed. "Lady Avely."

She examined him carefully. He had already donned his hat, which shadowed his face. She could not make out any scratches upon his cheek, left by Marigold's grasping claws, for his curling moustache obscured her view. Surely the wounds would not have healed already, in the space of a day and night? Were the scratches hidden by a subtle Illusion? Was Kenneth, after all, the man they sought?

Judith hurried on. "Are you leaving for Garvey House soon? I hope you have not forgotten your promise to support my petition to Lady Garvey."

Kenneth's lips thinned. "Indeed not. Your arrival is fortuitous, I suppose. I was just about to depart." He smoothed his luxuriant moustache.

Judith glanced back to see that Dacian was frowning at Kenneth's facial hair. Perhaps he was comparing it to his own flat, brown moustache, and feeling some sense of inferiority. She would be glad of it, though Dacian could hardly feel inferior to any man.

"How fortunate," she said, and stood aside for Kenneth to join her. Politely, he offered his arm, and they made their way out of the inn.

Fortunately Isobel and Biscuit were nowhere in sight. Mindful of her task, Judith began chatting glibly about a fictional liver complaint. "I don't suppose you know of any medicines that might help?" she asked. "I am willing to try anything that might ease my nightly pains."

"Ah yes," said Kenneth carelessly. "You should try the Poleney Elixir. It is a local product; quite new but very efficacious, I believe."

To Judith's ears, his words rang with truth. She opened her

mouth to ask more, but at that moment Kenneth turned to frown at Dacian. "Is your footman coming with us too?"

"As a matter of propriety," Judith replied, with a touch of hauteur. "I may be in my dotage, but I must still have regard to the dictates of decorum."

Kenneth coughed. "Indeed."

So it was that Dacian sat awkwardly in the carriage with them, ensuring that Kenneth could not ravish Judith in the short time it took to drive to Garvey House. She was surrounded on all sides by moustaches, and she could not say that she enjoyed the experience. Determinedly, she brought the conversation back to the Poleney Elixir.

"Does this recommended remedy have some special ingredient, perhaps? I hope it is not mercury and camphor, like in some medicines."

Kenneth shot her a look. "None of that!" He paused. "I believe that the Poleney Elixir contains a newly discovered botanical species called the Galenia flower. The bloom is so named because of its healing properties. It is quite potent; you should try it."

He spoke the truth. Judith kept her face carefully blank, and did not look sideways to Dacian. Kenneth must be referring to the strange flower in the centre of the maze, and he wholeheartedly believed in its curative power. The fact that he had mentioned it - despite Poleney's secretiveness - was probably because he wanted to increase his profits from the apothecary.

More intriguingly, his words hinted at Healing magic. Could the flower be infused with Healing? And if so, who could have cast the catholicon? With a start, Judith remembered Selina's throwaway reference to Georgina being put to work in the gardens. Could the girl be another victim to the plot, forced to cultivate the Galenia flower? The possibility made Judith's errand today even more pressing.

All too soon, the carriage drew up the long drive of Garvey House. A brisk wind was blowing, spinning the ash leaves from the branches, like embers of coal. Dacian leapt out first and helped Judith down. He gave her hand a brief squeeze then stood aside as Kenneth clambered out.

In which a dowager is defeated

Gossip mixes kernels of truth with exaggeration, speculation, and malice - so it is difficult for a Truth Discernor to navigate.
  - from *Lady Avely's Guide to Lies and Charms*

KENNETH RAPPED ON THE DOOR. Faske must have seen from the window that it was Lord Kenneth Garvey himself arriving, for this time he responded promptly.

The burly butler gave an almost creditable bow to his master, but he slid a nasty look to Judith. She smiled back benignly. He could scarcely refuse her entry now, on the arm of the lord of the manor.

"My lord," said Faske. "What a surprise to see you." This was the truth, according to Judith's perception, but she saw the butler give Kenneth a measuring glance, unlike that of a servant's respectful gaze into the middle distance.

"Is it?" said Kenneth dryly. "It is my house after all. Tell Mother that I am here to see her, along with Lady Judith Avely. We have something important to discuss."

Faske backed away, and Kenneth gestured for Judith to enter before him. She did so, feeling as if the dark hall pressed upon her. Casting a glance back, she saw Dacian sidle in after Kenneth. To justify her footman's presence, she made a show of taking off her cloak and handing it to him. Carefully, Dacian folded it over his forearm, keeping his eyes lowered above his moustache.

Faske returned. "Lady Garvey is in the greenhouse," he said sullenly. "She will see you there."

They followed Faske to exit on the southern side of the house, and down a paved path to the glass monument.

The large doors swung open without a creak, into a cave of greenery. The climbing roses that had crept up the walls nine years ago now grew in profusion in every corner, wrapping the whole room up as if it were a leafy nest. The peach trees were larger in their hefty pots, though their branches were now bare and spindly with the season. Showy dahlias bloomed beneath, warm with colour. The scent of damp soil and bark permeated the air, along with the faintly rotting smell of spent roses. And the sickly-sweet smell of the maze flower; the Galenia flower.

Judith looked around sharply, seeking the source, and saw that the group of orange trees no longer stood in their neat formation. One of the citruses was completely covered in the strange flowering vine, suffocating the branches and obscuring its fruit. Moreover, at least a dozen more small pots nursed cuttings of the vine, staked and straining towards the light.

Looking away, Judith tried to disguise her interest, and followed Kenneth obediently through the curving crescent of camellias where Dacian had comforted her nine years ago. Their delicate flowers were in bloom again, though some petals decayed on the floor.

Georgina was standing on a wooden step, pruning one of the chaotic climbing roses. Perhaps her alleged green thumb was entirely innocent, after all. Hearing their approach, she glanced over, and her face lit up with a startle of surprise. Then it shut-tered, and she looked nervously at her grandmother.

Lady Garvey was in a cane chair by the brazier fire, her walking stick leaning against the wall. The glowing coals that heated the glasshouse also warmed her ladyship's frail form, hunched in a thick woollen cloak and furs. The old woman looked more grey and ill than she had two days earlier, and Judith shot a troubled look at the tea that stood on a spindly iron table, wondering how Mrs Froode had prepared the brew.

However, as they progressed into the room, Lady Garvey sat up straighter, sharpening her eyes on Kenneth with a deepening frown. Faske withdrew to the glass door, but did not leave the room entirely, taking up a stance that was vaguely threatening. Judith was glad that Dacian took up a position on the opposing side, still holding her cloak.

Kenneth strode over to Lady Garvey, and gave a perfunctory kiss on her hand.

"Mother, why aren't you wearing the lorgnette I purchased you?" he said. "I promise you that they are all the fashion in London now."

His tone was placatory, yet Lady Garvey withdrew her hand and clutched at her quizzing glass. "I don't need confounded London fashions, boy. Don't try to worm your way into my good graces with your frippery gifts."

Kenneth flushed slightly. "I am only trying to be useful, Mother. Considering that you cannot visit London anymore..."

Lady Garvey sniffed and turned her ire upon Judith. "What are *you* doing here?" she said rudely. "I told you to leave us alone."

Judith curtsied. "My lady, Lord Kenneth invited me..."

"Ha!"

"I did," interposed Kenneth. He took a step back and clasped his hands behind him, gathering his courage, as Judith could see, even as he almost backed into a peach tree. "Lady Avely told me of her kind invitation to Georgina, and I think you must accept, Mother. It is past time that Georgina sees more of the world."

Georgina gasped and stepped down from her wooden perch, aglow. "Oh, Uncle Kenneth! There is nothing I would like more!"

He smiled. "I'm certain you will find a husband quickly, Georgy, if we let you loose upon the town."

"Nonsense," snapped Lady Garvey. "Georgina, you don't want to be married off in some distasteful marriage. Much better to stay a spinster."

Kenneth frowned. "I thought you wanted Georgina to make a good match. You should not be so selfish as to keep her here, tending to your every need."

Georgina flushed and put her pruning shears down, looking guiltily at her grandmother.

"How dare you!" The old woman's gnarled hands clenched on the cane arm rests, and she scowled at her son. "I may do as I see fit, for I am the one caring for Georgina! Much more than *you* ever have!"

Kenneth cleared his throat and stood his ground. "Well, as her legal guardian and as patriarch of this household, I must insist that Georgina goes to London. It might do something to salvage the family's reputation if she is seen to attend such a fashionable wedding as the Earl of Beresford's."

"Patriarch!" expostulated Lady Garvey. "An undeserving and inadequate one at that. I don't know why you think you can suddenly order me about, boy. You have no moral right to do so, whatever claims you might air."

Judith decided it was time to intervene, for she could hear that Lady Garvey was not as certain in her defiance as she pretended to be. "My lady, I know it is only concern for Miss Georgina that stirs you, but I swear to you that she will come to no harm in London. She may stay at Lord Beresford's town house, and I will personally escort her to the church."

"Hmph." Lady Garvey glanced at Georgina's anxious face, and her gaze softened. "Well, it seems I am overcome at every quarter." She heaved a sigh, and twitched her furs. "Drat you all. I suppose you may go, Georgy, if you must."

"Oh, Grandmama!" Georgina stepped forward, excitement radiating from her face. "Truly?"

"Only if you return quickly," said Lady Garvey reluctantly.

Georgina spun round in a delighted circle, then flew to Kenneth's side, a thousand questions pouring out of her about how she should travel and what she should pack. Kenneth indulgently answered, while his mother looked on with disapproval.

Judith took the opportunity to inch up to Lady Garvey's side. Her ladyship's countenance was rather mournful as she watched Georgina's raptures. Judith made a show of warming herself near the brazier coals.

"It makes us feel quite redundant, does it not?" she murmured. "Saddening, when we are no longer the centre of their world - and yet only right."

"Hmph," said Lady Garvey again. Her eyes slid to Judith with a hint of defensiveness, then back to Georgina. "I suppose you are correct, Lady Avely, in this instance."

Judith turned her hands above the coals. "It must be hard, when you are ill, to part with her," she suggested. "Can Mrs Froode care for you in Georgina's absence?"

"Mrs Froode already does so," snapped Lady Garvey.

"Indeed," said Judith, though Mrs Froode had been conspicuously absent today. "Are you undergoing a treatment of the Poleney Elixir? It is rumoured to be most efficacious."

Lady Garvey turned to look at her again. "What are you blathering on about?"

"The herbal remedy that you take in your tea." Judith fanned her hands out. "Is it not the new Poleney Elixir, that the Stokesford apothecary produces?" She carefully avoided looking at the flowering vine that strangled the citrus trees, though she could still smell its fragrance.

"No," said Lady Garvey blankly, and her voice rung true. "I have not heard of this Poleney Elixir. It sounds most intriguing."

"It is available in Stokesford, and it is said to be a general cure-all - though I have my doubts."

"Nothing is a cure-all." Lady Garvey rapped out. "We are each too individual in our complaints." She paused and added thoughtfully, "Yet perhaps I should try it."

"Indeed." Judith turned her back to the briar. "If you do not use the Poleney Elixir, what is your preferred remedy?"

Lady Garvey's gaze shuttered. "It is merely a little concoction that Mrs Froode prepares for me."

Judith tilted her head with gentle interest. "Mrs Froode has been with you a long time, has she not?"

"Yes." Lady Garvey hesitated. "She was Harriet's lady's maid previously, but she proved herself most capable, and I appointed her as housekeeper. She has become indispensable." There was a note of discord in her voice, and Judith wondered if there was some conflict between the two older women, one lady and one servant.

"Are you certain that her herbal concoction is safe?"

"Safe? Of course it is safe." The response was surly, yet showed no trace of doubt. Lady Garvey did not suspect Mrs Froode of any ill intent.

"Sometimes that which heals can also be lethal in large doses," pressed Judith. "I would advise caution in your consumption of it."

Her ladyship smiled faintly. "A large dose would rarely be required. Your concern is unwarranted, Lady Avely, but I thank you for it." She examined Judith with a softer glance. "I suppose you mean well, for all your meddling. You'd best take care of Georgina in London, like you promised."

At that moment, there was a commotion by the glass door. Through the camellias, Judith saw Faske step aside for Mrs Froode, as if summoned by her speculation. The housekeeper's lined face was harried under her white mobcap, for Isobel and Lord Triskett crowded behind her, pressing into the glasshouse.

Judith raised her brows. What were *they* doing here? She almost had to admire Isobel's effrontery in barging in without an invitation. And she wasn't even using a twisted ankle to do it.

"Ah!" Isobel pushed past Mrs Froode and sailed up to the tableau by the brazier. "Lady Avely! You are here too! Hasn't it been an age since we were last in Garvey House? I had quite forgotten this lovely greenhouse."

She wore a ravishing gown of green velvet trimmed in fox fur, which quite cast Judith's pale lavender into shade.

Lady Garvey lifted her quizzing glass. "Good God, is that Isobel Vosse? Am I to have no peace?"

Isobel gave a demure curtsy.

Lady Garvey was unimpressed. "This garden is meant to be my sanctuary. Faske, remove these persons!"

Faske, by the door, almost shrugged. It was clear he had no idea how to eject the well-heeled visitors, especially one as assured as Isobel.

Lord Triskett sidled up, looking about curiously. "Good morning, Lady Garvey, Lord Garvey, Lady Avely. Please excuse this incursion. We were in the county and ... and..."

He seemed quite unable to explain himself further and lapsed into silence. Isobel took up the mantle, sweeping over to a climbing rose that still bore a few blooms. Judith cynically thought that she had probably selected it as a suitable backdrop for her own beauty, as Isobel slid an amused glance towards Dacian in his livery by the door.

"We bear some news!" Isobel announced. "Last night, I saw the ghost of Lord Garvey!"

A stunned silence met her. A coal popped in the brazier as they all stared at Isobel.

Kenneth spoke, his voice husky with outrage. "Utter poppycock! Do not talk nonsense!"

"No, I implore you to listen!" Isobel wrung her hands together fetchingly. "I heard rumours in Stokesford and I inveigled Lord Triskett to walk me to the maze last night, at dusk. I did not really expect to see anything, you understand! It was just a little adventure. And then! As we came up the poplar avenue, we saw Lord Garvey himself lurch out of the hedges."

Georgina gasped. Kenneth wore a deep scowl as he glared at Isobel, but Judith could see his jaw was clenched tight, in either fury or fear. Judith watched with interest, as she knew that Isobel had not conducted such a walk. Quite besides the lie clanging hollowly in her voice, Marigold and Wooten would have seen her in their evening reconnaissance.

"Oh?" said Judith. "How did you know it was Lord Garvey?"

Isobel was not put off her stride. "I recognised him after all these years: his fair hair glinting in the moonlight, his admirable masculine form, even the fine clothes he wore on that fatal night! And he had a bullet wound weeping from his chest, blood darkening his golden waistcoat."

Her voice broke. Judith leaned forward, fascinated by the performance. The whole story was indeed poppycock, though delivered with convincing fervour. What could be Isobel's purpose? Her gamine green eyes were darting around the room, as if nervous, but Judith could detect a watchfulness there.

Judith, likewise, turned her head slightly to pass her gaze over those present, to see how they received the tale. Georgina was pale with fright; Mrs Froode was rigid with anger, her watery blue eyes glaring. Lord Triskett seemed utterly mortified, staring fixedly at the carpet. Kenneth continued to grind his jaw. Faske, observing by the door, was the only one who seemed amused. Dacian was frowning.

Lady Garvey was white with fury. "Do not tell such stories, you harlot!"

Isobel reared back as if struck, laying a hand upon a heaving bosom. "It is not a story! And I warrant that I am not the only one who has seen him, I am sure of it! Ask everyone here!"

Judith felt a flash of surprised admiration. Isobel, in her own dramatic fashion, had turned the tables. Everyone glanced at one another then looked away, wiping their expressions blank.

Yet Isobel pointed to the door, triumphant. "See! Your butler! He knows something! He smirked!"

Everyone turned to stare at Faske. At this barrage of attention, he shifted uncomfortably, and winced.

"Well," said Judith, into the silence, for she agreed with Isobel. Faske had been smirking. "Have you seen the ghost, Faske?"

In the expectant tension, Faske cleared his throat. "Er, well. I have seen a figure lurking around the maze, it is true. Perhaps it was a ghost. It *appeared* to be a gentleman."

"What!" cried Isobel. "Did you not recognise your old master? Did you not see his blood?"

Faske coughed awkwardly. "I am late to this establishment, my lady, and would not recognise the late Lord Charles Garvey. And as far as I recall, the figure did not wear a golden waistcoat. Not the one I saw." His lips twitched again.

Lady Garvey's voice was hoarse with rage. "My dear man, this is the very reason I hired you: to keep thieves away. If you see a creeping figure, you must dispatch him, not examine his waistcoat."

"Indeed, my lady," said Faske, but his smirk threatened to re-emerge. Judith narrowed her eyes. What could be so amusing to Faske about the ghostly prowler? He clearly knew more than he was saying. Mrs Froode's black figure edged closer to the butler, as if to shoo him out of the room, her brow furrowed.

Lord Kenneth took a hesitant step forward, in an attempt to exert some authority. "Faske, next time you see anything untoward, I expect you to inform me of it. If there are poachers or intruders on the estate, we must deal with them."

"Certainly, my lord." Faske straightened his shoulders, his gaze fixing somewhere in the middle distance, finally adopting the proper attitude of a servant. "Of course, my lord. I will tell you at once."

Judith heard the lie, and wondered if she was the only one.

In which a duke displays restraint

A lie can become so embedded in one's own mind that one forgets that it is untrue.

    - from *Lady Avely's Guide to Lies and Charms*

"Enough!" said Lady Garvey. "Out of my garden, all of you. I cannot bear another minute of this outrage."

Georgina flew to her side, taking her hand. "Indeed, Grandmama, we have tired you. I am sorry."

Lady Garvey did look rather frail, sitting hunched in her cane chair, her skin in a waxy pallor despite the warmth of the brazier. An ugly cough now wracked her thin chest. "Even you, child. Begone, leave me in peace! You have what you want now."

Georgina's profile crumpled a little, but she backed away. "Yes, Grandmama." She turned to the assembled company and put on a brave, polite voice. "Everyone, please leave us now. Grandmother must rest."

Another paroxysm shook Lady Garvey as they all trooped out of the glasshouse. Judith's worry renewed, and she glanced at Mrs

Froode. The housemaid's arms were akimbo and her expression grim and unreadable as she herded everyone out.

It was a relief to pass Dacian at his post by the door. He gave Judith an expressive look as she passed, and followed at her heels as she marched up the stone path and through the house. Isobel and Biscuit came close behind him, though Judith saw that Kenneth had elected, despite orders, to stay behind in the glasshouse.

Faske informed them that the Garvey carriage would take Judith home, then return for his master in due course. The butler shut the front door behind them with a bang, not even bothering with the courtesy of waiting with them for the carriages.

It began to rain, and they cowered in the portico. Judith's head ached a little. She was Bemused from following the conversation so closely. Her blood bond with Marigold kept the effects of Musing somewhat at bay, but untangling all the lines of deceit in company was exhausting, and, furthermore, confusing. Which lies were trivial, and which covered a larger, nefarious plot? At the moment, her mind was not clear enough to hazard a guess. She felt as if she had imbibed too many glasses of champagne.

Rain continued to slant inwards, angling under the roof and dampening her hem into a deeper lavender.

Dacian stood a few feet behind them. "What the hell was that, Isobel?" he muttered.

Isobel turned her head with a coy smile. "Did you like it?"

"No, I did not," said Dacian. "Did you really see the ghost? Biscuit? Were you there?"

Biscuit gulped, looking guilty. "Er, well..."

Isobel laughed. "No, of course we didn't. I was simply trying to help."

"Help?" put in Judith coolly. This was *their* investigation. They did not need Isobel throwing rocks into it.

"Yes." Isobel ignored her and directed a fluttering look at

Dacian. "I know something must have happened that night with Lord Garvey, and it is worrying you. I thought to stir the hornet's nest, to see if it brought anything to light. And if you are to have fun playacting, I don't see why I cannot."

This was not the whole truth, Judith detected, somewhat hazily. She clasped her gloved hands together to counteract her own dizziness.

Perhaps Dacian heard the lie too. "Hm," he muttered. "You do like to perform theatrics."

"Wasn't I brilliant?" gurgled Isobel. "The moonlight glinting on his hair, forsooth!" She turned and cast an appreciative look over the duke. "I rather like you as a footman, by the way. I have a position available, if you would desire it." She pursed her lips into fullness and blinked alluringly. Beside her, Lord Triskett looked forlorn and stared at the ground.

Judith spoke before she could stop herself. "I am afraid that you will find Dacian quite inadequate as a footman. He is not very good at taking orders."

"Yes," agreed Dacian, amused. "I lack the necessary subservience."

If anything, that made Isobel bat her eyelashes more furiously over her shoulder. Judith ground her teeth together.

"Besides," added Dacian, and Judith could hear that he had taken a step closer to her. "I am content with my current position, as it happens."

Isobel slid Judith a venomous look. "Really? It seems you have chosen a hard mistress to please."

Judith stiffened, but before she could respond, Dacian spoke again. "This is not all a game, Isobel, and it may very well be dangerous. You must keep out of it." He paused. "Judith, you must leave Stokesford too. Both of you. Biscuit and I can handle it from here."

"Yes, indeed," said Biscuit uneasily. "Er, what exactly are we handling?"

Isobel sniffed in disdain. "Leave? I don't think so. Don't forget your place, footman."

For once, Judith was inclined to agree with her, even if Bemusement was clouding her thinking. There was nothing that would induce her to leave now. And something was tugging at the back of her mind about the scene she had just witnessed in the glasshouse: something important. What was it?

The carriages pulled up to the portico then, and they bundled into their respective vehicles, Dacian helping Judith into the cab. Despite everything, she was relieved that he sat next to her, rather than hanging off the back in the rain. It was now falling fast, making her mobcap droop damply. She resisted the urge to take it off, in case Dacian interpreted it as a gesture of seduction.

She cast a sideways look at him, and he grinned. With a start, she realised he still wore his enchanted cravat pin; listening to his warm voice behind her, she had forgotten that he was disguised, his moustache still valiantly in place. She shook her head, feeling a little dizzy. She was aware of a desire to climb into his lap, snuggle into his arms, and give him her wrist to kiss again.

Cursed Bemusement.

"Harold," she said firmly. "We will need chocolate upon our return."

"Harold?" Dacian raised his brows. "Did you just call me *Harold?*"

"Oh, sorry," she corrected. "Bartholomew."

Suddenly, Dacian loomed closer. She edged away, and found herself pressed into the side of the carriage. She stared into his amused, black eyes.

"I think I know why you call me Harold," he said dangerously.

"Oh?" Her voice was faint.

"It is so that you are less inclined to kiss me."

Her throat was dry, and she tried to moisten her lips. He was right, damn it. "The moustache is repellant enough, believe me."

At the same time her fingers itched to grasp his shoulders and pull him close. The moustache, after all, she considered distantly, was an Illusion. It would vanish at the touch, and she would have his firm lips on her own, his thick hair entwined in her fingers, his warmth against her breasts...

He grinned. "There is a remedy for that, Judith. Simply close your eyes."

She stared at him for one, long moment. Then she fluttered her lashes closed.

She heard his breath catch. Parting her own lips in anticipation, she tilted her head back. A warm finger brushed down her cheek, and she quivered.

"Judith," he breathed. "I am not made of stone. If you keep your eyes closed, I will kiss you, Bemusement be damned."

She smiled and kept her eyes shut, waiting.

Yet when he next spoke, she could hear his voice had moved further away, grim and hoarse. "No, Judith, I won't."

She opened her eyes, adrift and wanting. Dacian had retreated to his side of the carriage. He cleared his throat and fiddled with his cravat pin. "We are almost returned to Stokesford," he said tersely. "You need a nap."

"A *nap*?" Judith sat up. "I thought you said I am *not* a matron."

"Even a young maid sleeps off intoxication."

"I am not drunk! I am perfectly able to understand that... I want you."

"God, Judith." He groaned. "Don't say that, or you'll find yourself in a very compromising position, very shortly."

She stuck out her chin. "A widow can't be compromised. She can dally with a rake if she likes."

A cloud suddenly darkened his brow. "Oh, is that so? You've taken a fancy to be ravished by a libertine?"

She stared at him. "And why not? You have bedded many other widows." She paused, her eyes tracing the long length of his body. "Perhaps I don't mind, after all, being added to the list."

At that moment, the carriage came to a halt. Scowling, Dacian said nothing. He leapt out and held the door. He put out his hand, playing the role of a footman, stiffly helping her descend. But she could tell that, bewilderingly, he had retreated behind a stony wall.

He followed her inside. She led the way to her room, hopeful. But when she reached her door, she turned to see that he had vanished.

JUDITH STUMBLED into her room and lay down in a daze. Annoyingly, she felt herself drifting off into asleep almost immediately. It was vastly irritating when Dacian was right.

When she awoke, her mobcap was pressing into her cheek. Yawning, she sat up and undid the ribbons, casting it aside. She rubbed her temples. God, what had she done?

She had humiliated herself, and probably Dacian too.

Yet the memory of his deliberate, possessive kiss from earlier threatened to undo her again. If only he had followed her into her bedroom, and laid with her. If only he was now tangled in the blankets with her... Why had he not?

Restlessly, she went to her window, staring out at the grey landscape, now awash with rain. Had she offended him somehow? How could he possibly be outraged by the truth? He was a rake; it was undeniable. Why on earth was he being missish about it now? The man was infuriating. Did he want her to be desperately in love with him? She wasn't going to admit that!

Except to herself.

Staring at the endless grey sky, she could allow the truth in the silence of her room. If she Discerned her own heart, she knew that she loved him. She was dreadfully, irredeemably, *appallingly* in love with him.

God. She clutched at her own face. The pain that had lurked deep within her for so many years now threatened to overspill. Of course she was in love with him. She had been in love with him since she first knew him. Yet every step of the way he had hurt her, pushed her away, and consigned her love elsewhere. So she had pretended to herself that it did not exist.

She swallowed down the dizzying ache that swept through her, and gritted her teeth. Surely she was too old for this sort of tumult? Infatuation was an affliction usually reserved for the young. So why did every glance and touch from him send her into such agitation?

Enough about Dacian. Much better to think about the scene in the glasshouse, and Isobel's dramatics, and Faske's amusement, and Kenneth's repudiation. Something still bothered her about the whole performance. Some detail that rang false, and tugged at her mind, demanding to be acknowledged. What could it be?

Her eyes traced the path of raindrops down the pane. What did Faske know? His barely concealed smugness indicated that he knew quite well that the ghost was a farce. Or perhaps, even, that *he* was the prankster behind the performance; or that he knew who was. Mrs Froode had looked like she was about to have an apoplexy. Was she outraged by his antics, or was she part of them, and afraid of exposure?

Isobel had claimed that she was trying to help Dacian, but did she have some other motive for her theatrics? Perhaps to muddy the waters, and throw up the spectre of Lord Garvey again? Yet a female Illusor could easily conjure the image of a man. Just broaden the shoulders, lengthen the legs, sculpt the jaw...

Judith found herself thinking of Dacian again and shook the thought away. Her feelings for him were too tumultuous, too unbridled, to dwell upon them now. Or indeed ever. She was not accustomed to being unbridled in anything. She was a matron in her fifth decade, for God's sake; she was past the age of being in love. It was unbecoming. It was foolish. It was an invitation for a broken heart, especially when it came to Dacian.

She sighed. She needed something to distract her. Knitting stockings was not going to cut it this time. She needed something more...enthralling.

Her fingers tightened on the windowsill, with a sudden thought. A ghost hunt might do the trick.

Yes, she could accompany Marigold back to Garvey House tonight. She could prowl around the maze, just like Isobel had claimed to do. Secrecy was not even essential. Indeed, an overt, matronly nosiness might summon the Illusion just for Judith's benefit.

Then Marigold could ferret out the source of the Musing - and thereby lead them to the master villain.

It might just, Judith told herself, work sufficiently to distract her from Dacian's sudden coldness.

AT SUPPER, Dacian was distant, avoiding her gaze. Robert was present, so she dared not broach the subject of their misjudged intimacies. When she airily announced her plan to visit the maze again that night, Dacian was predictably and staunchly against it.

"You want to creep around that godforsaken maze after dark?" He put down his knife and fork, and glared. Robert watched with interest from the door.

Judith calmly continued cutting into her steak. "How else are we to find the Illusor and catch them in the act? All we have now is conjecture and flimsy theories."

"I doubt the ghost will make an appearance, not after today's discussion."

"The ghost doesn't strike me as particularly shy," she observed, "And it might be my last chance to witness his perambulations and curtail them. I should leave Stokesford tomorrow. If I draw the Illusion out tonight, it will allow Marigold to track the source."

Dacian frowned. "Then I will come with you."

"And I too," put in Robert.

Judith glanced between their determined faces, and saw that she would be unable to dissuade them. "Very well. But you must wear a different disguise, Dacian, if Robert is to accompany me as my footman. I can't possibly have two footmen."

"Is that so?" He leaned back and folded his arms. "And what would you have me be, then?"

Judith shrugged. Then an idea of manifold brilliance occurred to her as she speared another piece of steak. "I know. You may be a piece of shrubbery."

"*What?*"

She turned to Robert. "You are very good at landscapes, are you not? You could make Dacian into a yew tree."

Dacian spluttered. "You cannot relegate me to the landscape!"

Robert was hiding a grin, but Judith persevered. "It is an excellent notion. You can be part of the maze itself: if you keep perfectly still, no one will even know that you are there. Robert is particularly adept at sketching trees."

"Then *he* can be a tree!"

"Nonsense. You are the right height for a maze shrub, and you are the one that might be interrogated and arrested, if someone suspects you are the duke. Whereas no one will suspect a bush."

"Oh, so now I'm not even a tree?" Dacian let out his breath in a whoosh. "Are you trying to punish me, Judith?"

She felt heat rise to her cheeks. "There is nothing to punish." She cast her eyes down and added, "I am trying to protect you."

There was a skeptical silence. Chewing on her steak, Judith admitted to herself that in the guise of a topiary, Dacian might be less of a temptation. Though he would probably remain attractive even as a yew tree, curse the man.

Robert, laughing, professed himself eager to cast the necessary Illusion. Dacian sulkily allowed that he might try it after supper. Once the plates had been removed, Robert set about conjuring a wall of greenery, the yew leaves thick and judiciously interspersed with tiny red berries. Dacian only sighed as his face and figure became concealed.

"Will that do?" His voice came disembodied from the bush that had sprung up in the parlour.

"Very nicely," said Judith. "Well done, Robert. Most realistic."

Wooten pursed his lips from where he sat upon the mantle-piece, fully dressed in gentleman's clothes. "At least you do not have to contend with bosoms this time, your grace, as when you pretended to be Lady Mary."

A long-suffering sigh drifted from the leaves. "I am not certain which is more emasculating. Here I do not even have legs."

Robert grinned. "Yew is a symbol of transformation, I believe." He clicked his fingers for effect, and the bramble vanished.

Dacian scowled. "I thought it was a symbol of doom."

Judith ignored that. "You'd better put the Illusion into a charm, to be safe, Robert. Then we can leave the duke in a bush if we have to. We don't want to rely upon your presence all the time."

"Within your ring?" suggested Robert, glancing down at where Dacian now wore his topaz ring.

Grudgingly, Dacian held it out, like a prince proffering a languid hand to be kissed.

"Is that safe?" asked Judith. "The ring already holds a charm. We do not want to overburden it."

"The Travel charm is in the topaz," replied Dacian wearily. "Robert can ensorcel the silver. That way I can turn into a hedge whenever it pleases you."

Robert grinned and slid the ring off the noble finger. There wasn't enough time to do more than a rudimentary casting, but after seven repetitions the ring could conjure a fairly respectable bank of yew. Judith examined it critically. In a dark, moonlit night, it might pass very well to hide the duke from hostile eyes.

"You are invaluable," she said to Robert. "You could very well be saving the duke from a frightful end."

Robert was a little flushed from the effort of Musing, but he gave a bow. "Delighted to be of service, marchioness."

Dacian glared. "You and I will have words later, Robert, on the correct order of noble precedence."

Marigold, when Judith fetched her to the parlour, was far more enthusiastic than the duke about the proposed adventure, and remarked cheerfully that she and Judith were making a delightful habit of ghost hunts.

"Indeed." Judith busied herself putting on her cloak and gloves. She still wore her gown of pale lavender, but she was not particularly worried about being seen.

"At least this time I don't need to wear a cloak," Marigold sighed. "Miss Belfleur appears to have left Stokesford, so I need not worry about offending her sensibilities. That silly cape was most inconvenient."

Wooten tutted. "What about *my* sensibilities?"

Marigold shrugged and tossed off her orange cloth. They were subjected to only a short glimpse of her petite, naked form before she leapt off the table and twisted into the shape of a bat, fluttering impatiently to the window.

"No," said Wooten firmly. "I will not."

Dacian stood up. "Then you can ride on my shoulder, Wooten. Be part of the hedgery with me."

"Hedgery is not a word," said Wooten sourly.

"Bushery then."

Wooten sighed, but allowed himself to be lifted to Dacian's shoulder.

Judith undid the window latch for Marigold, and ran a finger over her soft head. "Meet us beyond the curve of the road. And be careful."

In which a cravat is creased

JUDITH WORE her warmest cloak and her boots, but the night still held an autumnal chill. She walked with 'Mr Fortnew' at her side, and Robert behind her as footman, but as soon as they were out of sight of the village, she called for Robert to draw abreast with them and walk together.

It was very quiet. Only their steps sounded, and the occasional call of a night bird. The moon was almost full, a glowing, misshapen pearl in the sky. Clouds drifted overhead, and the trees seemed larger somehow in the moonlight, their presence more noticeable and mysterious. The smell of damp earth released with the rising dew.

Judith cast a sideways look at Dacian. He was silent, walking with his hands thrust into his coat, staring at the ground. He was clad in gentleman's clothes again, elegant and fine, and Judith felt a momentary doubt.

"Perhaps you should be in livery, after all," she said hesitantly, "in case you are required to emerge from the hedge."

"Too late now," he said moodily. "Be happy with me as a topiary."

"We could return for Robert's spare clothes." She chewed on her lip, seeing Dacian's cheekbones sharper in the moonlight, his hooded eyes somehow more piercing as he glared at her. "You appear rather...ducal. Even with the moustache."

He shrugged. "The Illusor knows that I am here. And to be quite honest with you, Judith, if anything goes amiss, I will not stand quietly by as a shrub."

Judith sighed, annoyed and worried. She could just imagine that Dacian might leap into the fray with 'Lord Garvey' just as Marigold had recklessly done. Overhead, she caught sight of her companion wheeling across the sky, and wondered if they were all flying into danger.

"Lady Garvey does not suspect your presence yet. And do not forget my theory that Lord Garvey's death might have been simply to exile *you* from the country. You *must* be careful, Dacian."

"Don't be ridiculous," he replied shortly. "Why would anyone want to exile me?"

"Hm." Right now, she could think of several reasons.

Robert spoke up. "What of Lord Triskett? Didn't he owe you a large amount nine years ago?"

Dacian snorted. "Enough to want me out of the country?" Then his mouth twisted. "People have killed for less than a thousand pounds, I admit, but I refuse to believe it of Biscuit. He doesn't have it in him to concoct such a scheme. He's as harmless as a lamb, and besides, he knew I wouldn't press him for payment."

"As a matter of honour, he was bound to pay you." Judith pulled her cloak closer. "And it might not have just been money. I rather think he has deep affection for Isobel. Perhaps he was jealous of you as a rival."

"Utter nonsense," said Dacian. "Honestly, Judith, you've been reading too many gothic novels, to come up with this sort of tripe."

Wooten sniffed from Dacian's far shoulder. "Says he who is wearing a villainous moustache."

"It is not," said Dacian. "Kenneth's moustache is far more villainous than mine. If you ask me, it is further proof that he is our killer."

"Hush," said Judith. They had reached a crossroads, the wooden signs indistinguishable in the shadows, but she knew which way to go. "We should approach the maze from the poplar avenue, around the back. That way you can take up your position, Dacian, before I stroll out and invite the ghost to join me."

Dacian shrugged gloomily. Judith called up into the sky for Marigold, and explained to her circling form that she wanted Marigold to go with Robert and approach from the front, staying hidden and watchful. "Keep an eye and ear out for Musing in the house," she said softly. She did not mention that she wanted Marigold safe from grasping hands. "Wooten will stay with me and the duke."

Robert folded his arms. "So you are to parade about as ghost bait? Is that wise, Judith?"

She smiled, glad that Robert was being more direct with her, even if it was a product of his slight Bemusement from conjuring yew hedges. "The ghost won't do anything to me, except perhaps loom a little."

"It's no use, Robert, you won't dissuade her," said Dacian. "Just be glad that you're not a tree."

Robert laughed and set off with Marigold towards the main driveway of Garvey House. Judith took a more indirect route round the fields with Dacian and Wooten. They walked in silence at first, and briskly, to warm their limbs against the creeping cold. Soon they were at the bottom of the poplar avenue.

The trees stood tall and shivering in the moonlight, their spindly branches bare where their leaves had fallen. Towering shadows leaned across the avenue, slicing it into strips of darkness.

Judith slowed a little, steps crunching on the fallen litter, and glanced uneasily at Dacian. It was unusual for him to remain so quiet, but she dared not broach the subject of their indiscretions while Wooten still sat upon his shoulder. Goodness know what Wooten might have to say about it all.

At that moment, the vampiri murmured something softly into Dacian's ear. It was indistinguishable to Judith, but she heard Dacian's side of the conversation.

"Follow her... Confront her if you must..." Dacian came to a halt and tilted his head. "Come now, Wooten, I know you don't feel the cold. And we need to find out more about the lady in question."

Ah. It must be Yvette of which they spoke. With difficulty, Judith restrained herself from looking skyward. It seemed that Wooten had sensed the presence of the other vampiri. Had Yvette returned to Stokesford? Was she looking for Marigold, or up to some other mischief? Judith would be glad of an opportunity to question the vampiri herself, to gauge the truth of her statements.

Wooten grumbled. Judith, craning to see past Dacian's profile, quickly averted her gaze, for Wooten was reluctantly disrobing. He passed his delicate cravat into Dacian's large hand, followed by his coat, waistcoat, shirt, breeches, and underclothes, all neatly folded. Dacian stuffed them into his own pocket, and Wooten let out a moan of distress.

"Careful, I beg of you! Those are tailored by the Duchessel of Planx herself."

"Off you go," said Dacian implacably.

"This is *not* proper British conduct," whined Wooten, but then his black shape lurched into the air and faded into the shadows of the poplars.

Dacian began walking again. Judith followed, wondering if she had the courage to speak now, to ask him why he was so cross. It could not simply be about his impending stint as shrubbery, could it?

But even as she drew a breath to speak, he held up his hand, warning for silence.

They had drawn close to the entrance to the maze. The opening looked darker and narrower than in daylight.

"Through the maze or around?" he murmured. "I have Wooten's map with me."

She eyed the ominous passageway. "Around, I think." She did not want to be lost in there again. "There are two or three more entrances on the other side, which we can use if necessary."

Dacian turned wordlessly and led them around the outer edge. From this perspective the maze appeared as a massive bulk, solid and impenetrable. Judith was glad when they reached another entrance and paused, listening.

The only sound was the call of an owl and her own beating heart.

Dacian cocked an eyebrow.

"Not yet," she muttered. "The next one."

As they walked on, she heard the frightened rustle of a creature, disturbed by their progress. She jumped, and the animal retreated noisily into the undergrowth of the maze. She stayed frozen, listening intently.

Dacian reached back and took her hand in his warm grasp. The touch made her heart leap anew. Blood rushed to her face, yet Dacian said nothing, merely pulling her forward and walking in silence, holding her hand.

In the dark, Judith felt as if she were a girl again: treading on air and utterly enchanted by such a trivial touch.

She looked down at his fingers, so sure and strong, and barely stopped herself from raising them to her lips and kissing them.

"Dacian," she whispered.

He turned his head. Their gazes met.

"Yes?"

"I'm sorry," she whispered.

His face lightened with a faint smile. "For insisting that I be a tree, or a rake?"

She drew a breath and pulled them to a halt. "Both."

He turned to face her, his eyes intent. But at that moment, a sound came crashing from the maze. Not an animal this time, but a human blundered through the corridors, large-footed and clumsy. The noise stopped, then just as quickly began again, brushing against the yew, snapping branches and sending birds and creatures scurrying.

Judith and Dacian stayed very still. It sounded as if someone were drunk or mad, lost and panicked. Or perhaps the sounds were simply magnified in the darkness. As Judith strained to listen, the crashing halted again and there was a long silence.

Then a small, high-pitched shriek pierced the air. A girl, or a woman, in danger?

Dacian squeezed Judith's hand, and let go. Then he pelted away, and vanished through a shadowy entrance into the labyrinth.

Judith stared after him, horrified. She did not move, but listened with all her might. She could hear his progress, but it soon became muddled with the sound of the other stumbling figure. There was no other scream, but the lack of human voices somehow made the muddled cacophony all the more frightening.

Suddenly there was a loud grunt, and a deep yell of pain. It was masculine and agonised, and followed by the sound of a heavy body falling.

Then footsteps running.

Which one had been Dacian? Judith found herself moving too, blindly and wildly. She ran into the maze and, by instinct only, followed the path she had heard him take. Please God, she prayed, let him not be hurt. Please, let that tormented cry not have fallen from his lips.

She realised that she could only hear her own thudding footsteps now. Her heart beat in her throat and she strained her eyes desperately against the darkness, turning frantically deeper into the maze. Where had he gone? She dared not call his name, and announce his presence. There was still a chance that he was the one who had cast the blow, not received it.

Coming to a gasping halt, Judith realised she was lost. Silence fell eerily, blank and suffocating. The walls of the yew loomed up on either side, casting thick shadows. An opening showed to her right but she did not know whether to take it or not. She clenched her gloved hands in front of her, too overwrought even to curse.

For a long while, she listened. There was no sound at all, as if even the little creatures had all frozen in fear. Then a thought occurred to her; that maybe Dacian, too, was listening and waiting.

She swallowed. "Harold?" Maybe it would prick some response from him.

Anything was better than this dreadful absence.

"Harold?" she called again, quietly.

When the silence continued, anxiety tightened in her chest.

Not knowing what else to do, she called once more, and took the right-hand turn, progressing further into the labyrinth.

In which a maze fulfils its function

Violence never lies.
  - from *Lady Avely's Guide to Lies and Charms*

A FEW STEPS IN, she heard an awful crashing, wrenching sound. It went on for long minutes, a dreadful violence that rent the air. It was impossible to hear where it came from in the darkness. Judith stood petrified, her senses assaulted. When it finally died away, she took a shaky breath and pressed forward again. She was determined to find Dacian, even if it should take all night in this hellish landscape.

For an interminable age, she stumbled through the twisting pathways of the maze. She cursed its construction, Dacian, and herself, in an internal stream of invective to try to keep her spirits up. For all she knew, she was uselessly travelling in circles while Dacian lay unconscious a few feet away. The thought was unbearable, and her anxiety was at a peak when she finally stumbled upon the secret passage to the centre.

The brass key charm had been wrenched from the yew

branches. It lay on the ground, barely visible, the narrow entrance revealed. Judith did not stop to wonder who had torn it aside, and took the path without hesitation.

She emerged into the circular clearing. A sword gleamed in the moonlight, thrusting its point to the sky, the stone plinth covered in its blanket of flowers. The sweet, ghastly smell of the blooms assaulted her nostrils as she scanned the clearing. Then she saw that the second steel sword was missing from its pommel.

And Dacian was sprawled upon the wooden bench, bleeding.

His head lolled on his shoulder, unconscious, his black hair limp. Blood ran from his scalp, down his cheek, in a terrible river that had frozen and stilled. The other sword lay on the ground beside him, and more blood pooled beneath his body. His arm trailed, lifeless, so that his elegant fingers brushed the liquid.

Judith's own breath threatened to suffocate her. A crashing devastation rolled over her like a wave, and she ran towards him, full of terror.

Throwing herself into the pool of blood, she grasped his hand and brought it to her lips. His fingers were cold and lifeless. He did not move, his face slack and empty.

Grief choked her, with the crippling fear that her life was now utterly desolate.

"Dacian," she whispered. "Please no."

She stared at his beloved face: even in the shadows cast by the hedge, she could see the black fan of his lashes, the strong line of his jaw, his parted lips firm and full. All waxen now with death.

His moustache was gone, she noted distantly. He must have cast it aside.

The first slither of doubt crept into her tumultuous mind. Why would he cast aside his disguise? And why could she still see his cravat pin in place?

Her eyes sharpened and she looked more closely. Shuddering,

she released the hand that she held. It dropped back to the ground with a thud.

Her heart slowly lightened as she stared at the face before her. The brows were too elegant, too arching. The handsome features were not quite right: a little too perfect in its symmetry. And while there was a small white scar on his forehead, it was angled slightly wrong.

It was an Illusion.

Tears once more flooded her eyes, this time with relief. It was not Dacian. Thank God, it was not him.

Yet the blood seeping into her skirts was real. She could see the spreading stain, and feel the awful wetness as she ran her fingers over the sticky damp.

She stayed still, kneeling in the blood, her mind racing. The hand she had held was real enough; and cold enough. Judith looked over the fallen body, and realised that she had no idea if it were male or female, under the depiction of the duke's fine clothes and face. And the fact that the Illusion had not vanished upon the touch meant that the Illusor was still present, keeping the mirage in place.

To be sure, she steeled herself, and reached to grasp the limp shoulders. The flesh under her hands was solid and broad, and she shook it, as if trying to rouse her beloved, overtaken with grief.

Briefly, her violent shaking showed a dissonance. Dacian's elegant coat wavered, revealing a coarser cut: the garb of an upper servant. Another face showed a glimpse under the planes of Dacian's.

It was Faske.

A terrible gladness swept through Judith at this final confirmation, even as new fear thudded through her. Flinching, she slipped her fingers to his neck. No pulse thudded in the butler's throat. The column was cold and clammy. He was dead.

She dropped her hand and bowed her shoulders, as if in

sorrow, while her senses sharpened. Who cast the Illusion? Whoever it was, they were still present, watching.

Awareness prickled between Judith's shoulder blades. She swallowed and stared at the ground, hoping she painted a convincing picture of shock and grief. With an awful lurch, she remembered the small gaps in the circling hedge. Small enough to act as peeping holes.

For a long moment, she stayed there, bowed and listening. Silence met her, along with the growing sense that someone was there, observing her.

She stood.

The killer was here. She could feel the knowledge of it on her skin. Somewhere in the glade, or just out of it, the Illusor was watching.

Judith bent, ignoring her bloodstained skirts, and picked up the steel sword that lay beside Faske. The hilt of it was bloodied and marred. She grit her teeth and swung round.

The clearing was empty. With shaky steps, she trod round the centre plinth, searching. In the awful quiet, she thought she could hear someone breathing. The sound sent icy shivers down her back.

"Show yourself," she said hoarsely. "Stop hiding behind tricks, you fiend."

For a moment, nothing happened. Then footsteps padded. Judith gripped the sword, raising it higher. But the sound was retreating behind the hedge, as the watcher moved away.

Angrily, Judith turned and ran through the secret path, determined to see who it was. She careened left, trying to follow the steps. Yew branches clawed at her sodden gown, and the sword was heavy, weighing her arm down. Her face was stiff with dried tears, and she was wracked with guilt and fear. What had she missed, that had doomed Faske to his death? Why hadn't she discovered who was playing such cruel games?

Soon she was hopelessly lost again, in a dreadful purgatory, stumbling in the dark. Once she thought she heard footsteps, and terror spiked through her. When she stilled, she heard her name hoarsely whispered from somewhere beyond yew walls. Her heart thudded erratically, with the hope that it was Dacian, but she dared not speak, for fear of another trap. She waited a long moment and the grim cry did not repeat. She pressed on.

When she passed a statue of Pan for the third time, she halted, breath heaving, and rested the sword on the ground. Worry clawed at her. Where was Dacian? Robert? Would the killer hesitate to harm them as well?

At that moment, a black shape swooped in front of her, as if in warning. It materialised as a bat, with long black wings flapping urgently, and Judith felt relief surge through her. The bat twisted into human form and landed on the shoulder of Pan.

Judith blinked. It was not Marigold who stared back, but another feminine vampiri. Wide, dark eyes glared from a beautiful face, set above a velvet cloak.

"Lady Avely, hush." A slender finger held up in warning. "I take it that you wish to find the Duke of Sargen?"

Judith stared. This must be Yvette, and obviously she *did* know something of their purpose, if she could mention Dacian's title. But Judith was too anxious to prevaricate. "Where is he?"

"I will show you. Follow me."

Yvette stepped off the statue. The cape billowed up, showing a glimpse of curves, then she plunged into her bat form. Spiralling up, she flew just above the height of the hedges, but close enough for Judith to see.

At first, Yvette led her on a winding path, then suddenly straightened into a broader swathe. This path looked new and ragged, as if it had been impatiently cut through the serpentine twists. The sharp smell of sliced wood hung in the air. Judith's breath caught, for she perceived the work of an Impactor. This must have been how Dacian found his way out, in that violent, crashing cacophony she had heard.

Judith followed the brutal swathe until it emerged on the right-hand side of the maze, facing the house. She drew a breath and strode forward, holding her sword aloft like Athena herself, careless of who might see her.

"Where is he?" she demanded of the dark sky.

Yvette flew in the direction of the glasshouse. Judith followed, warily scanning the gardens. There was light glowing in the oriel windows again, warmly, as if someone did not lie dead nearby. She could see no sign of Robert, or Dacian, or their vampiri companions. Was Yvette leading her into a trap? Could she trust her? Could she afford *not* to trust her?

She heard her name called, low and urgent. "Judith!"

It was Dacian's voice, to her great joy. Judith halted and stared about, unable to see him anywhere.

"Put that bloody sword down." His voice was close by, tense with worry. "Is that blood on your gown? Are you alright?"

Judith lowered the point. "Where are you?" she hissed.

To her right, a bushy hedge suddenly dissolved and Dacian appeared. His lips quirked under his moustache. "Don't you recognise Robert's handiwork when you see it?"

Judith dropped the sword and flung herself at him.

"Judith?" His arms came round her. "Good God, what happened?"

"Dacian." She found herself weeping again. She did not care, just pressed as close to him as she could manage. "Thank God you are safe. I saw you dead."

Grimly, he processed her meaning. "You saw another Illusion? Of me murdered?"

"It was Faske." She swallowed back more tears. "He lies dead in the maze."

Dacian arms tightened around her, as a pressure gathered in the air. "Damn it, Judith, you were meant to stay put!"

"I thought you might be hurt." She lifted her face from his chest, to check that he was indeed unharmed. She ran her fingers down his cheek, and the moustache and mole vanished, showing his rigid jaw and concerned gaze.

His own hand came up to gently brush the tears from her cheeks, then her lips. She leaned in, and kissed him long and hungrily, then abruptly pulled away in a daze. What was she thinking? This was not the time for passion. A murderer stalked the gardens, and moreover, knew that Dacian was here.

Reluctantly, she let go of his coat, gathering the shreds of her composure and looking away. The moonlight cast dark shadows around the maze, imbuing it with threat.

"What is it?" asked Dacian. "Don't stop, Judith, my dear."

She cleared her throat. "You are in danger. Whoever cast that Illusion meant it as a warning. And where is Robert?"

Dacian shrugged, and his hand fell from her shoulder. "I do not know, curse the boy. Have you seen Marigold or Wooten?"

Judith shook her head and explained that Yvette had led her out of the maze. Yet when she called out, the vampiri did not deign to reveal herself again. "Find Marigold," Judith pleaded to the empty, dark garden. "Please. She trusts you."

Silence was the only response, but Judith hoped that her plea had not gone unheard.

Dacian drew Judith behind the shelter of a tree, and told of his own movements. After he had run into the maze, he had become lost. Then he had seen a figure pass briefly through an avenue: the disappearing back of Faske. Dacian had followed it, only to be further led astray. Fearing that while he ran in useless circles, Faske might leave the maze and find Judith, Dacian had grown impatient. When he heard Judith's faintly calling for 'Harold', he cast Wooten's map aside and cut a path through the yew. That had been the dreadful crashing sound that Judith had heard.

He had come out on the southern side of the maze and rapidly walked the circumference, searching for Judith, hoarsely whispering her name. It had taken him several minutes to complete the circuit in the dark, which must have been when Judith was trying to find her way out with the sword.

"I couldn't find you." He pulled her close again, in the shadow of the trunk. "I was sick with worry. Then as I came round the southern side again, I saw a figure emerging from the maze. I thought it was you at first, but then I saw it was another woman, unfamiliar to me. She had blonde hair and a mobcap like yours."

"It sounds like Selina Southcott." Judith frowned. "What was *she* doing here?"

Dacian shrugged. "She walked towards me. I was in shadow, and had the presence of mind to press into the side of the maze and turn on Robert's charm. She went straight past me and into the glasshouse, keeping to the shadows."

"The glasshouse?" Judith turned to stare at the glass dome. "Is she still in there?"

"I haven't seen her emerge. But then I heard someone walking about in the maze again and thought it might be you, and thank God, I was right."

Judith stared unseeing at the sword she had left lying on the ground. Part of her wished to run away now, pulling Dacian to safety, and put the whole awful business far behind them. Yet Faske, for all that he had been boorish and hostile, had not deserved to die like that. She shuddered, remembering his blank face and the pool of blood. He might even be the third victim, if Harriet's death was also due to this vile plot. Judith could not let the culprit go unpunished, especially if they still threatened Dacian.

"It is unlikely to be Selina behind it all," she said slowly.

"Why not?"

"Simply because you saw her." Judith turned to look at the opaque windows of the glasshouse. "The Illusor would not be foolish enough to appear as themselves. Ergo, it is not Selina."

Dacian grimaced. "You might be right."

"We must go into the glasshouse, and find whoever it is."

"I will go alone," said Dacian firmly. "And bring the whole edifice down around their heads, if I must."

Judith rolled her eyes. "If you think for one moment that I am going to allow us to be separated again, you are mad. I have my sword. You have your Gift. We will be fine."

Dacian's lip twisted. "I'll only allow it because I can't trust you to stay put, God damn it, Judith."

Together, they crept up to the glasshouse, Judith lugging her steel weapon. She pushed the door open while Dacian held his bare hands at the ready.

They stepped into an eerie silence. The creeping vines and potted trees cast deep shadows. Grime on the ceiling panes filtered the moonlight into haziness.

Cautiously, they proceeded through the various obstacles: pots, shovels, plants, and trees. Yet after twenty minutes of careful searching, they could not find anyone crouched behind the black shapes.

Dacian pulled Judith to a halt, and they stayed still and silent. There wasn't a sound, not even a breath.

"Curse it," muttered Judith. "Is there another door, perhaps?"

After another ten minutes searching, they found it: a low, wide entrance hidden in the southeast corner. It was obscured by a lush oleander plant.

"Damn it." Dacian pushed the door open, and it opened without a sound. "She must have left through here."

"No doubt in another guise." Judith chewed on her lip. "Cunning."

"Yes," Dacian sighed. "Let's leave this wretched place, and go home."

Judith clenched her hands in frustration. "No! We must find out where all the players have been, and who might be Bemused. We cannot let them defeat us like this!"

Dacian nodded reluctantly. "True. Whoever it is, they cannot have carried off so many Illusions without paying the price."

In which there is only one horse

Discernors often have a strong sense of duty, arising from a wish to honour the truths that they perceive.
  - from Lady Avely's Guide to Lies and Charms

FIRST, Judith marched up to the back door of Garvey House, Dacian close behind. She banged loudly on the door several times and yelled a demand for entrance - much like Dacian had as a footman - and eventually the door opened a crack.

Mrs Froode's weathered face peered out, blinking. She was not wearing her usual apron and mobcap, and her head showed thick grey curls. Her gown was unrelievedly dark, though it was difficult to see past the narrow gap in the doorway.

"What is it?" the housekeeper said irritably, yet the whites of her eyes showed as they took in the sight of Judith's stained gown and Dacian's grim face.

Judith put her foot in the crack. "Where have you been in the last hour? Answer me now, and truthfully."

The housekeeper's face shuttered. "I don't have to answer any questions. Especially at this time of night." She pushed the door against Judith's foot so that pain shot through it.

Dacian put his hand on the wood with a threatening fluctuation of power. "Answer now, or I will force this open."

Mrs Froode's eye twitched. "Very well," she sniffed dourly. "I've been doing my work, as usual. I was in the study, going over the household accounts."

"That is a lie," said Judith. At the same time, she noted that the housekeeper seemed to be in possession of her wits, and not as if she had been casting Illusions willy-nilly all over the place. Or perhaps she was keeping a careful hold of herself.

"Is it now?" Mrs Froode stared back, impassive, her pupils dark in the dim light. "And what gives you the right to say so, if you don't mind me asking, my lady?"

Judith pressed her lips together. She could not announce her Gift. Indeed, it was a hidden tool in their arsenal, and she should not reveal it. Yet it galled her that Mrs Froode could calmly lie to their faces without consequence.

"Faske is dead," said Judith abruptly. "What do you think of that?"

The housekeeper's eyes widened and her mouth fell open. It was a convincing facsimile of shock, but Judith did not trust it. Mrs Froode knew something; she could see it as the housekeeper's eyes darted to the gardens outside.

Dacian, too, shifted behind her. "We'd like to know your thoughts on the matter."

After a long moment, Mrs Froode spoke in a low whisper, with a faint note of hysteria. "If he is dead, it is because he was stupid."

"What do you mean?" demanded Judith. Was Mrs Froode Bemused, after all?

"He laughed at the ghost, didn't he?" She grew louder, her fingers white on the door frame. "It's unwise to mock that which you don't understand."

Judith stared. The housekeeper's voice was thick with some meaning which she could not decipher. Not a lie, that much was clear to her Discernment. A warning, then?

Or the truth, from the lips of a clever dissembler?

"A ghost didn't do this," said Dacian sharply.

"I never said it did," was the cryptic reply. A grim smile flitted across Mrs Froode's face. "How was it done? A gunshot, perchance? You'd better watch out, your grace. You might be blamed."

Judith pulled her foot back in surprise.

"You know who I am?" asked Dacian. He still leaned his hand against the door, unyielding.

"I recognise you right enough, with your handsome face under that foolish moustache," said Mrs Froode, giving him a contemptuous look. "And I won't be the only one. I advise you to leave this property. I will have to call the parish constable now, to deal with Faske, if what you say is true. You'd better make yourself scarce, or you might find yourself blamed."

Judith backed away from the door, uncertain. It almost seemed as if the housekeeper was trying to help them, for no lie coloured her voice. Or perhaps she was threatening them.

Then Mrs Froode shut the door in their faces.

Frustrated, Judith retreated with Dacian to the terraces.

"She lied about doing the household accounts," she said angrily. "And yet we cannot prove it."

"You think she is our quarry?"

"I don't know! She did not seem Bemused, though she *was* being rather insolent." Judith hesitated. "We must find Kenneth, Isobel, and Lord Triskett, and see how they fare."

"You cannot possibly still think that Biscuit..." Dacian trailed off. "Very well. Just to eliminate the possibilities. With any luck we will find Biscuit asleep and Kenneth quite Bewildered."

They walked quickly around the house, keeping to the shadows. The moon was high now, small and bright in the sky. Judith gnawed at her lip. "It will take too long to walk back to the inn. I think we should steal some horses."

Dacian grinned. "You surprise me again, Judith."

They made their way to the stables, the cold night air seeping through Judith's cloak. Yet when they sneaked in, there was only a single horse sleeping in the stalls; a dappled grey mare.

Quickly, Dacian bridled it and led it out. "You can go ahead without me," he suggested reluctantly.

"Absolutely not. We ride together." Yet she hesitated, looking back over to house. "Where is Robert? Do you think Yvette found him and led him away? If not, we must tell him to withdraw."

"Cover your ears," instructed Dacian, and proceeded to bellow loudly into the night. "Robert! Return to the inn! We go there now!"

Judith winced. Dacian had probably roused the whole of Stokesford with that directive. However, she was relieved when she saw a shadow detach from a tree in the distance and wave acknowledgment.

Dacian mounted the horse and put out a hand to hoist her up with his effortless strength, pulling her to sit behind him.

"Are you comfortable?" he asked.

Judith muttered an agreement, feeling a little embarrassed that she was astride behind him, his warmth between her thighs. As he guided the horse out into the night and into a trot, she grasped his waist with cold fingers, then eventually slipped her arms around to hold him more tightly. He was all muscle and strength, and she sighed as she leaned into his back.

The ash trees sped by as they passed down the drive. Dacian turned his head to murmur, "I must say that I was heartened by your earlier display of concern, my dear."

Judith breathed him in; the smell of freshly cut yew and

smoke. "I was simply happy that I didn't have your death on my conscience," she said into his shoulder.

"Yes, it was only a sense of duty that moved you." There was a laugh in his voice, and it caused a frisson to run through her. Or perhaps that was the friction of his body against hers.

"I have a strong sense of duty," she said primly.

"Very passionate," he agreed. "I would like to see it roused again."

She blushed. The horse thundered beneath as he guided it into a canter. For a long while, they were silent in the thrill of the ride, and Judith revelled in the pleasure of being so close to him, even as she mulled over what they might find at the inn.

Halfway back to Stokesford, Dacian suddenly slowed the horse, and Judith soon saw why: darting glimpses of movement suggested that a bat circled them. Dacian put out an arm, and the creature landed to swing from his elbow, then claw its way up to his shoulder.

Wooten. Judith whispered a greeting, glad to see that he, too, was safe. He remained as a bat, clearly reluctant to shape-shift without ready access to his clothes, which were tucked away in Dacian's pocket.

When they reached the inn, Dacian became grimly focused on the matter at hand. Dismounting, he shook Wooten off and helped Judith down, then barrelled inside, heading straight to Kenneth's parlour.

Yet his insistent pounding on the door obtained no response. The room lay dark, its occupants seemingly determined to ignore them.

Dacian scowled. "I'll break down the goddamn door! Kenneth! Open up!"

"I say, sir!"

Judith turned to see the disgruntled innkeeper behind her. Testily, he informed them that Kenneth had departed the inn that afternoon for London, and moreover he would thank them not to damage his property.

They retreated in disorder. Judith was displeased that their questions had been balked, and wondered if Kenneth truly had fled Stokesford and why. Could it be a cover for his murderous hunt that night? Then she bethought herself of a different quarry, and spun on her heel, making her way to Isobel's quarters.

Dacian kept close behind, muttering. At Judith's forceful knock, a maid opened the door and reluctantly went to fetch her mistress.

After several minutes, Isobel came forward, tying a green silk dressing gown around her slender waist. She appeared to be half asleep, blinking confusedly at Dacian and Judith.

"What is it? Is there a fire?" She yawned. "You both look very fierce."

"No fire," said Judith grimly. "There has been a murder, and I want to know where you've been this night."

Isobel snapped her mouth shut, her eyes widening. "What? Do you dare impugn me in the matter?"

Dacian held up a hand. "We just need to know everything we can, Isobel. Please help us."

Mollified, Isobel gave him a coy smile. "I've been alone in my bed, more's the pity."

Judith narrowed her eyes. It was a lie, and moreover, Isobel seemed to lack her usual sharpness. Was she not yet fully woken, or was she Bemused?

Isobel put out a dreamy hand to brush Dacian's arm. "Did you kill someone again, my fearsome man?"

"Isobel!" Dacian pushed her hand away. "You know I would not. It was Faske who died, the butler at Garvey House, and we don't know who killed him."

Isobel blinked innocently. "Is that blood on your gown, Lady Avely?"

Judith looked down. The deep red stain stood out starkly against her lavender skirts. It brought bile to her throat, recalling how she had knelt before Faske's mauled body, seeing his face overlaid with Dacian's, stricken with violence.

She spun on her heel. "Indeed, I must change."

Dacian followed, and she heard Isobel's door close behind them with a pointed snap. Judith stalked past her own door and headed for the stairs.

"Well," Dacian caught up with her on the landing. "At least we know that Isobel can't have done it."

"She lied," snapped Judith. "When she said she was alone in her bed, it wasn't true."

"Hm. Perhaps Lord Triskett was in there with her?"

Judith darted him a glance, relieved to see that Dacian suspected the same, and did not seem to mind the vagaries of Isobel's affections.

"Well, let us see if Lord Triskett is in *his* room."

Judith pulled her cloak round her to hide the ugly stain on her skirts and marched down the corridor. There was no time to change. They had to find Lord Triskett to see if he knew anything about the matter.

LORD TRISKETT WAS NOT in his room. His manservant said that his lordship had gone to partake of dinner at the local tavern, and had not yet returned.

Dacian frowned at the news, and Judith raised her brows. So Lord Triskett had not been safely ensconced at the inn all evening - unless the story of the tavern was simply to cover his presence in Isobel's bedroom.

Quickly, they made their way down the cold street to where the Stokesford tavern still glowed with light and chatter. With a shock, Judith realised it was not yet midnight. It felt as if an eon had passed since they had left the village at dusk.

She let Dacian take the lead, following him into the pub and pulling her cloak close. Warmth assailed her from a fire, roaring heartily at one end of the room. Several men sat around nursing their ale, turning to look at the newcomers. The smell of beer and meat hung in the air.

Dacian ignored their audience. He scanned the room, then strode towards a dark corner at the back, where a figure slumped over a table.

Judith followed. As she drew closer, she could see that it was Lord Triskett, his slender wrist flung out, holding a glass of spirits loosely. His head lolled on his upper arm, his eyes half closed, and he did not seem to notice their approach.

"Biscuit!" Dacian stepped close. "Wake up."

His lordship straightened, blinking. "Ah, Shargen. What are you doing here?" He lifted the glass in a half-hearted salute. "Shplendid whisky, this."

He was drunk. Judith examined him narrowly. Or was it a cover for Bemusement?

Dacian seemed to realise her thoughts, for he slid her a reproving look. "Have you been here long, Biscuit? We need to know."

His lordship frowned, confusion clouding his eyes. "A while. Long enough to soften the harshness of life." He tilted the glass again, and the golden contents sloshed wildly.

Judith grimaced. There was no point questioning Biscuit in this state; his lordship was either too drunk or too wily to answer them directly. She turned and marched over to the counter, to ask the tavern owner for a more reliable account.

"That man there." She jerked her chin. "How long has he been sitting at that table?"

The tavern-keeper was a large man with a huge beard to

match. He tipped his head, considering. "Aye, his lordship has been there since sunset, drowning his sorrows."

Judith did not want to believe it, but she could hear the truth in the man's voice. Her shoulders drooped, and she turned, finding that Dacian had come up behind her. He put a hand on her arm.

"He's as drunk as a wheelbarrow," he said. "I'll come back for him, once I've put you safely to bed."

Despondently, she allowed herself to be led out the tavern, into the cold night air.

In which a discrepancy hints at villainy

Truth can be layered over a lie.
  - from *Lady Avely's Guide to Lies and Charms*

"WELL, THEN," murmured Dacian in her ear, as he led her back to the inn, his arm warm and firm beneath her cold fingers. "Biscuit certainly cannot have traipsed out to Garvey House to murder Faske, if he has been here all night."

Numbly, she agreed. Her own wits were beginning to fray at the edges. The effort of expending her Gift was exhausting, and she felt battered by the night's events. "What of Isobel's lie then? She said she was alone in her room."

Dacian frowned and did not reply. Yet as they trod up the stairs to their parlour, the question was answered for them. Isobel's young, blond footman was sneaking down the corridor, his golden locks in disarray.

With an amused grunt, Dacian stood aside for the footman, grinning at Judith. It was clear he believed that the young man was the reason for Isobel's lie. Judith was not so certain. And if it were true, she felt sorry for Lord Triskett, whose reason for drowning his sorrows was now apparent.

Everyone, it seemed, could evade her questions. She was no closer to finding out who had killed Faske, Harriet, and Garvey. And the spectre of Dacian's fallen form hovered at the edges of her consciousness, frightening her.

"Bedtime, marchioness," said Dacian firmly. He took her arm. "We can do no more tonight."

"What about Robert?" The thought surfaced with a pang of worry. "Has he returned yet?"

"Let us see."

When they made their way wearily into their parlour, Robert was there, pacing anxiously. When he saw them, he let out an exclamation of relief and demanded an account of their evening.

Dully, Judith obliged. After expressing his horror, Robert told his part. He had gone, as instructed, round the front of the house with Marigold. The vampiri had insisted that she investigate inside, gaining access through the loose window pane on the second floor, to see how Lady Garvey and Georgina fared, and espy the movements of Mrs Froode. She had vanished and Robert had waited patiently for her return.

Only, she had not come back.

Time had stretched out, and Robert could not say how long he had waited. He heard distant crashing from the back gardens - Dacian's violent passage through the hedges - and he had been torn between coming to Judith's aid or staying at his post. Deciding that they would never forgive him if their quarry escaped round the front, he stayed, in an agony of suspense. Yet the noise had quietened to silence, and neither ghost nor Marigold had appeared.

Eventually, he had seen a horse led out of the stables and

heard Dacian's yell. Relieved, he watched them ride down the ash-lined driveway. He had followed on foot, hopeful that Marigold was with Judith.

"She is not!" Sharp worry twisted through Judith as she stared at Robert. "I have not seen her since she left with you!"

Dacian held up a hand. "Wooten? Are you here?"

A black creature emerged from the curtains: Wooten, still in his bat form.

"Have you seen Marigold?" demanded Dacian.

Wooten shook his head mournfully.

"Oh, God," cried Judith. "What if she is captured? Killed? I should not have let her go anywhere near that house!"

"It's my fault." Robert looked pale. "I'll go back for her."

"Let's not panic," said Dacian. "It is quite possible that Marigold has flown off with Yvette. She might yet return." He frowned at Wooten again. "Become human, for God's sake, Wooten, and tell us what you saw."

Wooten just stared back, his black eyes twin pools of despair.

Dacian heaved a sigh and fumbled in his pocket. He withdrew a pile of miniature clothes, sadly creased, and threw them down along with a large linen handkerchief. The vampiri glared at his crumpled coat, then twitched the handkerchief to hide himself. A moment later, his human head emerged.

"Well?" demanded Dacian. "Where did you go?"

"I shadowed Yvette," said Wooten bleakly, "and she led me a merry dance. We flew round the glasshouse and across many fields, until I lost her in a copse of trees." He gave a gloomy sigh. "It is my belief that she was well aware of my pursuit."

Robert frowned. "Or you simply lost her."

Wooten drew himself up. "Or she wished to be rid of me so she could pursue her own villainy."

"Or perhaps she pursued Marigold, as I asked her to do," said

Judith tentatively. "She did help nurse Marigold when she was fallen, remember."

Dacian raised his brows. "You think she might be courting Miss Cultor?" He glanced over to Judith.

She shrugged helplessly. "Yvette has shown herself to be on our side at least once. We must hope that the two of them are together now."

Dacian grinned. "No doubt they are cosily ensconced in the belfry."

Judith tried to smile, and take some solace from this possibility. A part of her wished urgently to ride back to Garvey House and search for Marigold on the instant, but her limbs and mind ached with tiredness. "Wooten," she begged, "please, can you look for her again?"

"No, I thank you," said Wooten. "*I* don't want to interrupt any tryst. Marigold will bite my head off."

Judith frowned, but she did not press the matter. After all, if there was danger, she could scarcely send Wooten off to face it alone.

"I'll go," said Robert.

"No," said Judith. "Definitely not." Robert would be a much larger target than Wooten. And there was every chance that Marigold would insouciantly flap through the window before dawn, looking very pleased with herself.

Robert looked mutinous but Dacian shook his head at him. "We can give Miss Cultor until dawn to return, and worry then." He took Judith's hand again. "Now it is time to change out of those awful clothes and go to bed."

Robert's eyes fell with interest on their clasped hands, but this time Judith was numb to the sensation of Dacian's fingers.

Vaguely, she registered that he had ordered her to bed, but if she nurtured any hope that his words hinted at seduction, she was to be disappointed. Dacian called for Phyllis and ordered a hot bath to be poured, and left Judith to the maid's ministrations. Only when she was dried, dressed, and settled in her bed with a large cup of chocolate did Dacian reappear.

He, too, had changed out of his evening wear, into loose breeches and a white shirt, and without the disguise of Mr Fortnew. He looked down at her and smiled. "You look rather spent, my dear."

Her mind was still fuddled with Bemusement, fatigued and scattered. But Phyllis had put a hot brick between the sheets, and the warmth soothed some her tension.

"I am weary," she admitted, and took a long sip of chocolate, eying Dacian. He looked very beautiful in the candlelight, like an oil painting of a king at ease. The top of his shirt was open, showing the planes of his collarbones.

"I intend to sleep in your room tonight," he announced.

Judith's eyes widened. "Oh?"

"Not like that, you hussy. I will sleep on the floor. It is simply that I refuse to leave you alone, with a killer prowling about."

She opened her mouth to object, and then remembered the ghastly vision she had seen of Dacian dead. She nodded instead.

He raised his brows. "You don't mind?"

"I can keep an eye on you too," she pointed out. "Though, really, you could share the bed. The ground is far too hard and cold."

He laughed, even as his eyes darkened. "I've had plenty of practice with hard beds in Spain. And you are still Bemused, my dear." He paused. "It is beyond irksome that every time I find you alone, I cannot take advantage of you."

She batted her eyelashes at him. "I won't mind."

"Hm. Perhaps I should send for Wooten, so he can play chaperone."

"Please don't." She snuggled deeper into her blankets, wriggling her toes against the warm brick. "I'll be good."

Dacian took a step closer, then turned away to busy himself with doubling the rugs and pulling woollen blankets out from the cupboard. Judith admired the heft of his shoulders, and took another slurp of chocolate.

"Do you want some?" she asked, holding out the cup.

He finished laying a blanket out, and looked across. "Why not? I'll need all the help I can to put me to sleep."

He came to sit on her bed, and she handed him the cup. His eyes did not leave her face as he took a long, slow sip.

She sighed dreamily. "You are very handsome, you know."

His lips quirked. "I do know."

"Have I ever told you?"

"Not in words." He handed her the cup. "Though I like the way you look at me sometimes."

She blinked. "How is that?"

"Like I am the first cup of chocolate you've seen in a year."

She chuckled and took a sip. "I'm not the only one. Even Lady Garvey said you were handsome. Though she did remark that you were too old to be a footman."

Dacian pulled his shoulders back, mock affronted. "I make a fine footman!"

"I agree." Her hand crept out across the covers, and he took it. The warmth of his grasp was far more satisfying than any cup of chocolate, and she closed her eyes with bliss.

"I'm sorry," she said quietly, "for trying to seduce you."

His laugh was wry. "That is my line, I believe."

She smiled at him, then her lids closed again, involuntarily. Dacian sighed and withdrew his hand, taking the empty cup from her lax fingers. She heard him moving away and lying down, and within minutes she was asleep.

When she awoke, daylight was filtering round the edges of the curtains. Turning her head, she could see that Dacian still lay on the piled rugs, his tall figure obscured by blankets.

Dreamily, Judith stared at him. In the dim light, and asleep, he looked younger again, like he had when she first met him. The strong jaw, the thick hair, and the sharp cheekbones softened into youthfulness; it was as if she had travelled back in time to an earlier version of his vitality.

Yet she did not want to travel back in time, she realised. They had both been so blind and arrogant then, and not yet fully themselves. It had taken years to teach them both humility and awareness. Only now did she see the world and herself more clearly. Growing older seemed to have widened and deepened her perception, and it made a stronger foundation on which to build.

And he was still extraordinarily handsome. Perhaps that was why he was still recognisable after all these years, even by Mrs Froode, a servant who had only seen him briefly at the house party.

She idly traced the planes of his face, then her eyes suddenly widened.

It was the misaligned piece of the puzzle, the nagging thing out of place. The small fact that Lady Garvey had mentioned to Judith in the greenhouse.

"Mrs Froode," she uttered. "Mrs Froode used to be Harriet's lady's maid."

"Hm?" Dacian blinked awake. "What?"

Judith struggled to sit up, her heart beating wildly. "I've just realised something. Mrs Froode used to be a lady's maid, and yet she said she recognised you!"

He rubbed his brow, still blurry with sleep, and gave a soft huff of amusement. "No need to rub it in." He paused, yawning. "Didn't she also say how handsome I was?"

Judith rolled her eyes, even though he echoed her own

thoughts from a minute ago. "She shouldn't have known you well enough to make either observation. Mrs Froode would have only tended to her mistress upstairs. When would she have laid eyes upon you?"

All traces of sleep vanished, in the harsh light of her realisation.

"Perhaps she spied on us from the landing?" said Dacian blearily.

"She would scarcely know your face well enough to see through your moustache!"

"True." Dacian rubbed his fingers over his upper lip, as if to caress his beloved moustache. "I have always cut a rather dashing figure, but it may simply be my title that made her pay attention to me."

"She might have noticed you, indeed, but enough to recognise you now?" Judith's brows shot up with a sudden, startling thought. "Perhaps she was at Garvey House nine years ago as a guest, not a maid."

Dacian sat up at last, now scraping a hand over his jaw. He frowned. "Are you suggesting that Mrs Froode...is *not* Mrs Froode?"

"Exactly." Judith blinked, overwhelmed. "Her Illusion charm is probably in one of those huge keys she wears at her chatelaine!"

"If she is an Illusion," he said slowly, "then who is hiding beneath the mask?"

Her mind tumbled through the possibilities. Suddenly, she caught her breath, the truth springing up before her. "I think I know."

Dacian raised his brows.

"Harriet Bollopher." She clenched her hands into fists.

It was the only explanation that made sense.

Harriet would be an elderly lady now, like Mrs Froode, so she did not need to disguise her hands and figure to pass as the housekeeper. Just her face, hiding her plain features under Mrs Froode's watery blue eyes and thick, curling grey hair, helped by the concealing mobcap. If Harriet was a powerful Illusor, it would be simple enough to cast the Illusion into a charm each night, into one of those heavy iron keys in her chatelaine.

"Harriet?" said Dacian, his tone incredulous. "Do you mean to say that *Mrs Froode* is the one who died a few years ago? But why would Harriet Bollopher take the place of her housekeeper? And why would she want Kenneth dead?"

Judith frowned. "Harriet was already treated as little more than a servant, yet she stood to lose her position in the house when Kenneth remarried. She was the mother of Charles' first wife, and she wouldn't be assured of a home anymore. As an upper servant she could stay on at Garvey House, close to her grand-daughter."

Dacian nodded slowly. "And close to the Galenia flower."

Judith agreed. "She must have ensured that Mrs Froode was promoted to housekeeper before she died, to entrench her position. Lady Garvey would have allowed it - she let Harriet run the house." She shook her head in amazement. "For her to take the position of housekeeper has a certain ironic justice to it."

Dacian leaned on his elbow and stared at Judith. "It is a crazy theory. How can you be sure you are right?"

She gnawed on her lip. "We will have to prove it somehow. Search the house for evidence if we must." Belatedly, her eyes swung to the dresser with a pang of fear.

The oak door still hung slightly open. Her heart sank. Marigold had not yet returned.

Dacian saw the direction of her gaze. "We will get her back," he said quietly. "For now, we must tidy ourselves up, before Phyllis arrives with breakfast."

He stood, and Judith saw he was still clad only in his white shirt and loose trousers. Quickly, she averted her gaze, remembering with embarrassment how she had burbled on last night. Dacian seemed disinclined to talk, however, and set about putting the rugs and pillows away.

Once he had pulled his coat and shoes on, he put his hand on the door knob. "I'll fetch Robert and Wooten, and we can make a plan."

In which an attic is alluring

Marigold

Marigold had been rather grumpy as she flew above Robert, making their way to the front drive of Garvey House, even as the moonlight had cooled her wings. She knew exactly why Judith had sent them to this boring post: to keep them away from all the excitement.

And also to give her some time to talk to Robert. Judith seemed to think that Marigold might gain his confidences in some subtle, cheerful, guileless sort of way, but how was she to do *that*, exactly? If she tried to be guileless, surely that was full of guile? Truth Discernors had twisty sort of minds.

Rather, Marigold decided, the situation called for a direct approach. When Robert was hidden in place, standing in the long shadow of a tree trunk, she became human and perched on an ash branch above him. As she peered down, a withering leaf fell to the earth in a slow tumble.

"Robert," she said, without preamble, "why don't you want to go to Cornwall with Judith?"

Robert glanced up, then looked away hastily. "Er."

Marigold folded her arms across her small naked breasts. "What is it? Do you mistrust her gesture? Do you fear that she will rescind it later?"

"Er, no," he hesitated. "I suppose not."

"Then what is it? Does her ability to Discern lies unsettle you?" This was Judith's secret concern, and Marigold thought it best to air it.

Robert sighed, and kicked his boot against a tree root. "Well, that *is* part of it. I can't even fudge the little things - even whether I think my paintings are any good."

"Ah." Marigold nodded wisely. "I can see why that would be annoying. Your own hubris is on display."

Robert scowled, and stared gloomily out into the night. "Ha."

"That cannot be all."

"Well." He sighed heavily. "If you must know, I don't want to betray my own mother."

"Oh." Marigold felt a sinking sensation. "How...?"

"She hated Judith. She was envious, I suppose, that Judith married Nicholas Avely. Even though Mother didn't want him anyway." Robert's lips twisted, and Marigold imagined that such knowledge must be a blow to his heart and pride. "She told me that Judith was a pious Rector's daughter, naive and righteous, who had everything laid out on a silver plate for her."

Marigold winced. "Do you think that is true?"

"A little." Robert folded his arms and cast a defiant look up, before once more looking away hastily.

"It may have been true once," admitted Marigold, "but hardly now, and she has suffered in her own way. I am certain your mother wouldn't mind if you went to Cornwall with Judith, in the circumstances."

"Mother would hate it," said Robert with certainty.

"She is no longer here," Marigold pointed out.

"Which is why I must protect her memory and her wishes!"

Marigold frowned, scuffing the bark of the branch with her toe, and wondered if Robert's secret fear was that he might actually begin to *like* Judith. "Why, then, did your mother write to Nicholas Avely? She must have accepted that you would become part of his family."

"With great reluctance only," said Robert. "She assumed I would be taken in by Nicholas, not Judith. Besides, it goes the other way as well. Judith had no love for my mother. Most probably, she didn't even like my father, in the end. If anything, she must resent me as well."

Marigold sighed. She felt sorry for the boy, that he felt like an unwanted chess piece in a game not of his choosing. "That may have been true once, but I believe Judith has grown fond of you."

Robert looked skeptical. "She doesn't show it. She acts out of duty, because she feels guilty, and ashamed of her husband's past. Offering me a place in Cornwall is a sop to her conscience."

Marigold winced again. There was some truth in that, but she pressed on valiantly in Judith's defence. "*Any* person is a muddle of motivations, the good mixed up with the bad."

Robert merely grimaced, and leaned against the trunk.

Marigold shrugged her bare shoulders. Enough of family dramas. They were exhausting. People would persist in remaining closed off from one another, for the silliest reasons. She had tried to reason with him, to no avail.

It was time to stretch her wings again.

"I'm going to investigate inside the house," she announced.

"What? No!" Robert pushed himself off the tree. "It might be dangerous."

"Fiddlesticks," Marigold scoffed. "You stay here and study the formation of ash branches. The duke might need to be deciduous next time."

Robert frowned, but there was not much he could do to stop her. Marigold dropped off the stark branch and became a bat again, whisking away to the second floor where the loose window pane waited to grant her entrance. The glass grated over the wooden sill, reflecting the rising moon.

When she slipped through the gap, however, she found that she was expected.

"Good evening." It was Yvette's smooth, melodious voice. "I thought you might try the house again tonight."

Marigold spun on the sill. Yvette was standing on a cabinet, her silhouette stark against the white dustcloth. She wore a dark blue cloak tonight, the colour of a lake at midnight. Her hands were clasped before her, her expression bland, her cheekbones sharp.

Marigold transformed, regretting her decision to forgo her cloak this evening. Once human, she grabbed a corner of a dusty curtain and pulled it across her body, stifling a sneeze.

"What are you doing here?" she demanded. "And why did you vanish last night?"

Yvette gave an elegant shrug. "I had my own errands to run. Did you miss me?"

Marigold felt herself flush. "A little, I confess. We might have run errands together, you know."

"So sweet," Yvette murmured. "I confess, I missed your company too, Miss Cultor."

"Please," she stuttered. "Call me Marigold."

The violet eyes blinked. "Did you discover anything of interest while I was gone, Marigold?"

"Not really," she grumbled, and twitched the curtain irritably. "All the interesting things happen while I am asleep." She had missed the Illusor's attempt to upset Judith, and the reported glasshouse dramatics where Lady Isobel Vosse had thrown a fox among the rabbits. "I hope to find something damning tonight, hidden in the house."

Yvette nodded slowly. "I have, actually, found something intriguing."

"Oh?"

"I decided to investigate myself, seeing as you were so inquisitive." She lifted one shoulder casually. "Come, follow me."

Yvette flung her cloak back and stepped off the cabinet with studied grace, plunging into her creature form. Marigold, admiring, followed suit without half as much style, and flapped after her.

Once out the door, Yvette ignored their previous route down the stairs and took a left-hand turn. She led Marigold to the end of the corridor, and pulled up.

Hovering, she gestured with her wing.

With a start, Marigold saw narrow wooden steps, leading up to an attic. The attic door was slightly ajar, its top half angled with the slope of the roof. The narrow strip of opening was enticingly dark.

Curious, Marigold flew through it.

Looking around, she immediately saw what Yvette meant by *intriguing*. This was undoubtedly the home of a vampiri. The corner of a larger attic had been bricked up, enclosing a small triangular space. The rest of the attic, she speculated, must be accessed through a different door on the other side, for this one was complete unto itself, and obviously equipped for a bat. Ropes hung across the gabled roof, for easy hanging, and pieces of Vember furniture stood against the wall: a small table, armchair, and settee with the distinctive curling legs. A blue patterned Turkish rug on the floor added a cosy touch, along with scarves and cushions strewn about, in both vampiri and human sizes.

Marigold took this all in within an instant. At the same time, she became aware of a smell. It was the delicate scent of pine and earth, with a subtle overlay of lavender. The smell of Yvette.

Her instincts worked faster than her conscious mind. Marigold arrived at the obvious conclusion before she was even aware of it, and spun back toward the door.

It was too late. The door thudded shut, with Yvette on the other side.

Marigold threw herself forward, even as she heard the metallic click of the lock turning. Battering her wings uselessly, she twisted into her human form and beat her fists against the wood.

"What are you doing?" she shrieked. "Let me out!"

Yvette's voice was soft through the crack. "I'm sorry, Marigold."

"Don't call me that! You liar!"

"I serve my companion," said Yvette patiently, "just as you serve yours."

Marigold's fists crumpled to her side and she leaned her forehead on the door. Betrayal hollowed her out from the inside. "You lied to us!"

Silence came from the other side, then Yvette said, "Yes."

"You've been spying on us! You serve the Illusor." As she said it, Marigold cringed, realising how stupid she had been. Even that very first night, Yvette had been on the roof, preventing Marigold from entering the house. She had only shown them the way in when it was safe to do so, and then hung back when they headed to the maze. No doubt to notify the Illusor that it was time for a nice little ghost show.

"Yes," said Yvette again. "But now I am just trying to keep you safe."

"Ha," said Marigold bitterly. "By locking me up? How convenient."

"I don't want you snatched out of the air again like last time. She might do worse than break your wing, if it happens again."

"She? Who is she?" demanded Marigold. "Who snatched me?"

Yvette gave a small laugh. "I cannot tell you that."

"Someone in the house."

"It doesn't matter," said Yvette. "What matters is that you must rest and stay out of it now."

"Why? What is planned for tonight?"

Yvette sighed and did not answer. "Believe me, it goes against my sense of honour to lock you up like this, but it is partly your own fault for being so reckless."

"Honour!" Marigold spluttered. "And you say it is *my* fault I'm locked up? What spurious logic! If you have any scrap of honour you will release me at once!"

To her deep chagrin, Yvette declined to answer and Marigold soon realised that the vampiri had withdrawn.

She was left to stew in her own reflections, which were not pleasant. She had been a naive fool, and to add sunlight to the wound, Wooten had been right.

Right from the start, Marigold realised gloomily, the villains had been watchful and prepared. Judith had effectively betrayed her hand by knocking on the manor door that first morning. Yvette must have been sent to spy on them that very night at the inn, and returned to Garvey House in time to warn the Illusor that Marigold and Wooten were on their way.

The second night, too, must have been orchestrated: their tour of the house, with every door locked. Yet - Marigold remembered Mrs Froode's slip, in the bedroom, speaking out against Judith with the suggestion that the Garveys had something to hide. Indeed, they were concealing the Illusor's identity, in a careful charade that must cost something to be maintained.

No wonder the grounds were neglected and visitors discouraged. Marigold angrily knocked the delicate Vember chair and it fell to the ground. How could she have been so stupid?

She paced the attic room, furious, and with a gnawing sense of danger. Why would the Illusor need to lock her away? What villainy was planned for this evening? Whatever it was, Judith would innocently walk right into it. Moreover, Judith only had Wooten to act as her eyes in the air, and he was probably too concerned with arranging his cape.

At least, Marigold consoled herself, Judith also had the duke accompanying her this time, with his violent power. Gripping her hands together, she hoped that it would be enough. Then she kicked over a spindly table to relieve her feelings.

Time passed excruciatingly slowly. Marigold stalked round the room, ears pricked. Annoyingly, even in her state of extremis, she could observe indications of Yvette's seductive femininity everywhere: an oval-shaped vampiri-length mirror set into the wall, a bottle of lavender scent perched on an elegant table, and a silver cloak flung on the end of the soft bed. Everything was arranged tastefully and comfortably. Marigold was aware of a passing wish that she was there in different circumstances, and then became filled with bitter anger towards herself. She was a fool and an idiot, and when she saw Yvette again she was going to use that pretty silver cape to strangle her.

At some point, she heard a terrible ruckus coming from behind the house. Marigold threw herself in desperation against the door, but it remained irrefutably closed. The crashing noise outside faded, leaving a silence thick with ominous threat.

Marigold began to worry what her own fate might be, as well as Judith's.

She searched the room thoroughly for some avenue of escape, but there were no gaps, windows, or chimneys: as a vampiri abode it was securely closed against any chance of sunlight or discovery. Then, just as she was creeping along every inch of the walls as a bat, she heard a voice raised in the distance. Her sharp hearing could make out the masculine bellow of the duke, somewhere out the front of the manor. He shouted Robert's name, along with the instruction that they were all returning to the inn.

Marigold dropped off the wall and sank onto the blue Turkish rug with relief. The duke would not leave without Judith. They must be safe, and retreating. Thank Nyx.

Only, they were leaving her behind. Marigold swallowed, and told herself it was for the best. As a bat, she was quick and small. She had more chance of escaping this house than anyone else. And if Judith returned to fetch her, it would only be foolishness.

Hours passed, the night lengthened, and no one came to rescue her. Time became its own kind of torture. Fruitlessly, Marigold sifted through Yvette's belongings, rifling through her wardrobe and drawers. Yet there were no clues or weapons to be found, only indications that Yvette was a creature of comfort and solitude. No sign, thought Marigold angrily, of her duplicitous nature.

Dawn grew near; she could tell by the fatigue growing at the edges of her mind. Despondent and becoming frightened, Marigold sat on the edge of the bed and chewed on her knuckles. What next? As the sun rose high over the horizon, she knew that sleep would be inevitable. She was exhausted and in desperate need of rest. And asleep, she would be vulnerable.

After some consideration, she curled up as a bat, right next to the triangular door. That way, she might grasp the opportunity to escape, if her captors returned and she woke in time. Glumly, she tucked one of Yvette's stupid, soft shawls over her.

In her bones, she could feel the sun rising, with a sense of impending doom. Despite herself, with a sigh, Marigold fell into a deep sleep.

SOME HOURS LATER, she was woken out of heavy slumber by the sensation of a hand pinning her wings to her side. It was a familiar experience, and a familiar hand: the same sure grip of 'Lord Kenneth Garvey' by the maze.

Marigold struggled and bit viciously. She was thrust back into Yvette's room, and only when she heard the door close again was she released. Only this time, she had company in the attic.

An old woman stood by the door. Her face was unknown to Marigold: pale and plain featured, with barely any eyebrows, and thinning grey hair to match. Yet faint red scratches marked one cheek. She was examining Marigold closely, with watchful grey eyes. She wore a gown of pale grey, edged in white lace.

"Who the devil are *you*?" asked Marigold, once she was human again.

A smile tugged at the corner of the thin lips. "You don't know? I am glad to hear it."

Marigold stared, not wanting to give any more away. Then her impetuous nature overcame her. "You are a villain, I know that much. I've tangled with you before."

"Yes, you are a vicious little thing." The old woman's eyes narrowed, then she sighed. "But I am not a villain. I have only tried to do what is best for Georgina. And me, of course."

Marigold tried to make sense of this, but she was distracted by movement at the corner of her eye. She turned swiftly to see that Yvette hung from one of the ropes across the rafters. As a bat, it was difficult to read her expression, but Marigold thought bitterly that it most likely depicted some sort of scheming guile.

"You," she snarled. "You held my head in your lap, you treach-erous rat."

The old woman chuckled. "Did she now? Well done, Yvette, for playing your role so convincingly. Or have you begun to care for this little creature, after all?" She weighed Marigold with new interest. "She is a little scrappy, which is not usually to your taste."

The bat in the rafters gave a scornful sniff and shook her head rather too vigorously.

Marigold glowered. "What are you planning to do with me, you evil old crone?"

The grey head tilted. "Nothing much yet, Miss Cultor. We will merely keep you as our guest for the day. We can't have you running off telling tales, after all. And I want to ensure that Judith comes looking for you, as she most assuredly will."

"Judith knows I can look after myself."

Too late, Marigold realised she had confirmed their companionship. She pressed her lips together angrily. Then she remembered that the old woman was well aware of her status, thanks to Yvette's treachery. Marigold shot the bat another fuming look, but Yvette remained hanging, unruffled, above.

The old woman blinked. "I suspect that Judith rather likes you. She will come charging back here with her duke in no time."

Marigold's eyes bulged.

"Yes, yes," continued her tormentor. "I know his grace is lurking around Stokesford. As if I couldn't see through his ridiculous disguises. I especially like him as a hedge, I must say. If only I could plant him in my maze and keep him fixed. But it will be easy enough to dispose of him. Sargen is his own worst enemy."

Marigold said nothing to this. The old lady might be bluffing, trying to confirm her theories. Why else was she here, chatting to Marigold?

But the pale eyes creased, amused. "You've told me enough, Miss Cultor. Judith does not yet suspect me. Of course, Yvette tells me that Lady Vosse is higher on the list than I, which I find unsurprising. Judith was always jealous of Isobel."

Marigold maintained her stony silence. The old woman seemed to abruptly grow weary of the discourse, for she lifted her head to speak to Yvette. "Grab her, would you, dear? I must leave now. I need to make things ready for our visitors." Her hand crept up to the scratches on her cheek. "No need to be gentle."

Marigold shot up, twisting into her bat form. But Yvette was equally quick. Mid-air, they grappled. Yvette dug her claws into Marigold, and muffled her face with a wing, her soft body writhing against Marigold's. With fury, Marigold felt the hated human hand grip her neck, bony fingers pressing close against her windpipe.

She squirmed and twisted to no avail. Without ceremony, and with some violence, the old woman thrust Marigold into Yvette's fashionable wardrobe, and propped something heavy against it. In her battering fury, Marigold heard the attic door close and lock again.

Her convulsive attempts to escape did not work. And if she had thought her captivity was bad before, this was infinitely worse. The closet was cramped, and suffocating, even as it smelled of that dratted lavender. Gritting her teeth, Marigold closed her eyes and folded her wings tight around herself. She must simply pretend that she was in her oak dresser at the inn, and that Judith would shortly open the door with a smile.

She must trust that Judith would prevail.

Otherwise, Marigold suspected she would not be allowed to live another night.

In which clothes maketh the man

A cunning liar will use their body and gestures instead of their words.
  - from *Lady Avely's Guide to Lies and Charms*

AFTER DACIAN LEFT, Judith dressed hastily, and paced around her room restlessly, her mind too busy to look at the breakfast tray that Phyllis soon delivered. The maid opened the curtains, but as soon as she was gone, Judith carefully shut them again, for Wooten's sake.

She was growing very anxious for Marigold. If the vampiri had not returned, it might mean that she was still with Yvette - or that she was captive. Alone, in enemy territory, while Judith had been sound asleep. They must besiege Garvey House again to find her.

She had the beginnings of a plan too, though Dacian would not like it.

He and Robert came in, and Wooten's head popped out of Dacian's pocket.

"What a brilliant insight, Lady Avely," Wooten said with admiration. "It explains why Selina thought Harriet was preoccupied before her death. She must have been concocting her evil plan to change places with her housekeeper."

Judith nodded distractedly. Selina had mentioned that Harriet had argued with someone too. Perhaps it had been her own granddaughter. Did Georgina know of the plot? It would have been hard to keep it from her. Judith remembered how Georgina had ducked out of sight in the window. She had perceived the movement as one of fear, but now she realised it may also have been guilt. Georgina might have helped her maternal grandmother to maintain the charade, especially if she believed her life depended upon it.

And they must have gained Lady Garvey's cooperation through threatening to withdraw the Galenia flower. Judith would have to make a counter-proposition to the old battle-axe, if only she could gain entry into the house.

Dacian put Wooten down on the empty dresser. "Harriet's alleged preoccupation before she died is scarcely proof enough that she is now masquerading as a housekeeper. I can't imagine how we are to make this wild accusation."

Robert shut the door. "Perhaps accusations can wait, until we find Marigold. I feel awful that I left her alone."

Judith nodded, and proceeded to explain her plan.

Dacian folded his arms and leaned against the dresser. "It will not work."

"Of course it will," said Judith. "Do you not have faith in Robert's Gift?"

"I have perfect faith in him," said Dacian calmly. "But you will not pass as a man, Judith. The idea is ludicrous."

"Kenneth is plump, like me," she argued. "And his moustache will hide most of my face. If I claim to be ill, I can cough into a handkerchief, and you can do all the talking, as his valet."

"You just want me as your servant again," Dacian grumbled.

"And your curves look nothing like Kenneth's, I can tell you that for certain."

Judith blushed and turned to Robert. "Did you have a good look at Kenneth and his manservant, when you were in his room?"

Robert nodded hesitantly. "Perhaps." He stared at a wall, and a face materialised over the wallpaper. It was Kenneth, complete with bushy grey brows and the luxuriant moustache, his hooded eyes blank.

"I will need it in a charm," said Judith. "I rather fancy myself in a cravat."

"God help us," said Dacian.

Wooten spoke up in a pained voice. "Not a cravat, if I may say so, my lady. It takes years to master the art of tying one properly. You are much better off having a shawl wrapped around your neck, particularly if you are pretending to be ill."

"A good notion," she acknowledged. "And Dacian, you will suit the role of Kenneth's superior valet; you must simply lean into your natural arrogance."

Dacian lifted his nose. "I assure you, I will be superb." He paused. "What does this valet look like? A handsome fellow, I hope?"

Robert closed his eyes, his brow furrowing. The image of Kenneth was replaced by one of his supercilious valet: gaunt cheeks, long nose, and a bald pate.

"No." Dacian's tone was shocked. "Absolutely not. He has no hair."

Judith rolled her eyes. "Your vanity knows no bounds. You will do this to save Marigold. You might even look quite dignified without hair."

"Not with a nose like that," he protested. His eyes drifted to her breakfast tray. "Eat, Judith. You'll need your strength today, I suspect. God save me, but I will try to find some breeches for you."

He took Wooten with him for sartorial advice, leaving Judith alone with Robert.

"Are you up for the task?" She smiled at him. "We are asking a lot of you, I know."

Robert straightened his shoulders, pulling his chin in like a soldier readying for duty. "It is the least I can do."

"You don't owe us anything. If anything, it is the opposite."

Robert's gaze shuttered. "Mm."

Judith frowned. "You must let me repay you by hosting you in Cornwall."

"No, I thank you, my lady." He took two steps backward. "I will construct the charms now."

He left, shutting the door quietly, and Judith's shoulders slumped. Curse the boy. And curse herself for pushing when she should have stayed silent. She had thought they were growing a little closer in the extremis of their circumstances, but it seemed that Robert persisted in that characteristic trait of young men: refusing to acknowledge the superior understanding of those twenty years older than themselves.

With her own children far away, Marigold missing, and Robert so distant, Judith felt suddenly quite alone in the world. At least, now, she told herself, they must work together to foil a killer, which should surely build the bonds of comaderie. Hopefully, they would also horrify Wooten in the process.

TWO HOURS LATER, they set off in Dacian's carriage, leaving Isobel and Lord Triskett still abed. With any luck, Isobel was prone to leisurely mornings, while his lordship would be preoccupied with a pounding skull.

Halfway to Garvey House, Dacian ordered his driver to stop the carriage, and they donned their disguises.

Robert had decided against another cravat pin, on Wooten's advice, and instead had enchanted a pocket watch that Dacian had purchased in the village. It lay on top of Judith's new coat, which Dacian had obtained from the milliner, along with a natty pair of gentleman's breeches and boots.

The men waited outside while Judith climbed into her new clothes. The coat was rather tight across her chest, despite her attempts to bind her breasts. To counter the curve of them, she stuffed her paisley shawl into her waistband, so that she appeared unrelievedly round.

Unfortunately, Wooten was now asleep in her (Dacian's) trunk, and was not there to witness her depredations upon male fashion.

Next she put a beaver hat upon her head, and tied a thick woollen scarf round her neck, and said the word for Illusion.

A faint warmth settled on her face. She peered past her own nose, glimpsing a protrusion of grey. The excessive moustache now adorned her, and, she hoped, would distract anyone from looking too closely.

She stuck her head out the carriage window and cleared her throat.

Dacian and Robert turned to look, and their eyebrows shot up.

"It might even work," said Dacian reluctantly. He had donned Robert's livery again, now equipped with a magical button, and he wore the long, gaunt face of Kenneth's valet, topped by a bald dome without any telltale scar. His expression was doleful. "You, at least, have a virility of hair. Can you cough in a manly way?"

Judith gave the deepest cough she could muster. Dacian winced. "Fortunately, Kenneth doesn't have much of a baritone."

Robert grinned through a yawn. He had been casting the new charms for the last two hours, and was thoroughly Bemused, his hair tousled and his cheeks pink. "Judith, that moustache is a masterpeesh."

"I miss mine." Dacian looked down his lengthened nose and sighed.

"Never mind," said Robert consolingly. "I can make it bigger next time."

Dacian stiffened. "I do not like your implication, my boy."

Judith interrupted hastily. "Robert, perhaps you should have a little nap in the stables when we arrive."

Robert was to accompany them as a groomsman and stay outside nearby, to be on hand in case anything should go wrong. He was garbed in a coarse brown coat and matching hefty boots, with a jaunty kerchief around his neck.

"Yesh, my lady," said Robert, bowing.

She frowned at him. "When I said to give up your role as footman, I did not intend you to go even lower," she said severely. "This is the last time I will countenance any sort of role of service from you, Robert, whether you like it or not."

"Yesh, my lady," said Robert, with a deeper bow.

Judith glared.

"You can argue about that later," said Dacian with amusement. "Let us hurry. My head might catch a chill."

As their carriage rolled up the drive to Garvey House, Judith's chest tightened with fear. A lot depended on the next few minutes: whether or not they could manage to gain access to the house, and find proof of Harriet's duplicity before they talked to Lady Garvey. Judith knew where to find it too: in the household accounts, which Harriet had always kept. If she was still alive, her hand would still show in the neat columns.

But the household accounts were kept inside. Judith had to be convincing in her role as Kenneth: plump, harassed, and ill.

The vehicle pulled to a halt. Outside, the sky was heavy with clouds and the threat of rain. Dacian leapt down and held the door open, his bald head gleaming, his lips pressed close together.

Judith took a deep breath, wrapped her thick scarf more

tightly, and descended, holding Dacian's cambric handkerchief aloft. She was rather self-conscious in her breeches, with her limbs so exposed. It was not at all what she was used to, compared to the layers of a gown. Dacian's eyes trailed down her body, then whipped up again.

He turned smartly on his heel and rapped on the front door. After an interminable five minutes, it opened. Yet, in a stroke of luck, it was not the visage of the indomitable housekeeper who greeted them, but the youthful countenance of Georgina.

She frowned at the sight of Dacian, then her gaze slipped past him to Judith.

"Uncle Kenneth! I thought you had left for London!"

Judith coughed as deeply as she could manage, and shook her head behind her voluminous handkerchief.

Dacian intervened. Peering down his long nose, he said, "His lordship has taken a cold, and wishes to sleep here tonight."

Georgina looked surprised, yet a brief expression of anxiety crossed her face. "We don't have any rooms prepared, I am afraid...I thought you preferred the Golden Bat for comfort, Uncle?"

"No," Judith croaked, and proceeded to have a fit of coughing into her handkerchief, as if unable to speak.

Dacian carried on with aplomb. "The innkeeper's maid is sick. His lordship does not wish to dally there any longer." When Georgina still seemed reluctant, Dacian's tone sharpened. "As this is his lord's ancestral home, he will sleep here tonight."

Georgina did not dare protest any further. She backed away from the door. "Yes, of course. I will take you up to the old master bedroom, Uncle, and send Mrs Froode to air it. It hasn't been used in some time."

"No need," said Dacian austerely. "I am accustomed to seeing to my lord's needs, in various *inferior* establishments."

Georgina grinned, but she did not object. Her step light, she led them up the first flight of stairs and opened the door to a large bedroom.

She was correct: the furniture was covered in white sheets, and the air smelled musty. Judith, huddling behind her handkerchief, wondered why the household was so certain Kenneth would not wish to stay there. And where was Harriet now? Why was Georgina reduced to answering the door?

Dacian seemed to have the same thought, for he turned imperiously to Georgina. "What occupies your housekeeper? We shall need a hot brick for my master."

Georgina bit her lip. "I think Mrs Froode has been called to discuss something with Lady Garvey."

Judith frowned at the uncertainty in Georgina's voice. It was far more likely that Harriet was giving Lady Garvey instructions. She raised her brows in question.

Georgina shrugged, leaning forward with an air of confession. "I believe they are plotting something to do with Lady Avely. Grandmama says we are to expect another visit from her, and I fear she will take the opportunity to rescind her promise. You mustn't let her, Uncle!" Georgina took a step closer, lowering her voice. "If you do not uphold my visit to London, I will not help you with the Galenia plant anymore."

Judith tried to remain impassive at the determined glint in Georgina's eyes. So the girl was indeed in the plot - or in two plots, it seemed. She was helping Harriet maintain her deception, while also making a ploy for freedom by assisting Kenneth in his venture.

Dacian was listening, even as he wrestled with the window locks, thrusting the panes open. Judith merely nodded at Georgina, and coughed again to disguise her voice. "You'll go to London, child."

Georgina, relieved, withdrew to the door. "I will fetch the hot brick myself. We are a little short on staff at the moment. Faske seems to have disappeared. I know you always thought he was shifty, Uncle, and it seems you were right."

Judith and Dacian exchanged a look. So Georgina did not know the whole of it.

The girl gave a small curtsy and vanished through the door. Dacian shut it carefully behind her, then whipped the dust sheets off the bed and bundled them into a corner.

Judith sank onto the bed.

"I don't think she suspects," she whispered.

Dacian shook his head. "No, I was the one who had a view of you from behind."

Judith blushed. "The breeches are rather tight."

Dacian cleared his throat. "Indeed. It seems that Georgina is muddled up in her grandmother's schemes. Do you think she will obstruct us?"

"It is hard to say. She will scarcely want to act against her own blood. Lady Garvey, on the other hand, might be more willing to throw off Harriet's iron rule over her household."

"Should we seek the domestic accounts now? As master of the house, you have a right to simply demand them."

"No," said Judith. "We do not want to alert Harriet to our interest. We must steal into the study when no one is looking. And first we must find Marigold. I fear for her safety."

"I will look for her," said Dacian. "You climb into bed. Georgina will be back soon enough, and we must stick to our parts."

Obediently, Judith crawled into the blankets, relieved to hide her legs beneath their weight. Dacian set about pulling the rest of the dust sheets off the furniture, and unpacking the trunk, careful to transfer Wooten to Kenneth's old wardrobe. It was easily done, as the vampiri was deeply asleep, curled up in a startling purple silk brocade dressing gown that suited his dark hair and swarthy colouring. Dacian then knelt by the fire, where dusty twigs lay ready for lighting, and set a small blaze to warm the room.

Judith kneaded her hands together, grateful for his efforts but anxious for him to start the search for Marigold.

She was glad he remained, however, when Mrs Froode herself appeared at the door instead of Georgina.

The housekeeper held a swaddle of cloth that presumably contained the hot brick. Her white mobcap was as pristine as ever, yet her blue eyes looked even more washed out as she narrowly examined Judith.

"My lord." She dropped a curtsy, and took a step forward, proffering her bundle. "This is to keep your feet warm."

Judith was relieved that Harriet – if it were indeed her – was keeping to her part, perhaps afraid of exposure if she questioned Kenneth too directly. Harriet's caution might keep Judith from being revealed too.

She stared at the housekeeper's weathered face, trying to see some hint of Harriet's plain, pleasant features behind the Illusion of servitude.

Mrs Froode trod towards the bed, but Dacian stepped in briskly, taking the bundle. "Thank you," he said in his most supercilious tone. "My lord will require some broth too, with fresh bread and butter."

Judith rather suspected he was asking for himself.

Mrs Froode nodded. "Certainly, my lord."

She gave another curtsy, and withdrew after another glance around the room. Once the door shut behind her, Judith let out a sigh of relief.

She waited a moment before whispering, "She didn't seem to suspect, either."

"I hope not." Dacian pushed the brick under the blankets to rest by her feet. Then he trod to the door with a warning glance. "I'll prowl around the place, pretending to look for a compress or something. You will need to eat, after all, so I'll leave the door unlocked for the soup, and take the key with me."

Judith nodded and lay back against the pillows, watching as Dacian slipped out into the hallway.

Left alone, she was prey to her own doubts. Was she wrong about Harriet? Perhaps she really *had* passed away, and Mrs Froode simply knew all visiting nobility by sight. It would be rather awkward if Judith attempted to rip off the Illusion, only to find that it really *was* Mrs Froode behind the chatelaine. It was essential to see the household accounts, and determine if they bore out her theory.

As for Marigold - Judith's jaw tightened with fear, even as she told herself that the vampiri could simply be sleeping somewhere safe, away from sunlight.

The slow hands on her new pocket watch showed the minutes ticking by. Dacian did not reappear, but Georgina did, bearing a tray of broth and bread from the kitchen. Judith, huddled in her blankets, nodded her thanks, relieved when the girl set the tray beside her bed then left again promptly. Thank God, she was not being overly solicitous.

Judith had just settled her shoulders into the pillows with a sigh, when she heard new footsteps in the hall, accompanied by the tapping of a walking stick. She tensed as a knock rapped on the door, knowing it would be Lady Garvey. Would her ladyship see through the hastily cast Illusion of her own son? Should Judith confide in her now, and tell her of Harriet's part in Charles' death?

She remained silent, frozen and undecided, and then Lady Garvey thrust the door open and advanced, tottering, into the room.

Her beaky nose jutted forth with irritation, under a thunderous frown. "Good God, what are you doing here, Kenneth?" Her pinchbeck quizzing glass glinted on her bosom, and she lifted it to peer at Judith, her eye sharp beneath the glass. She was wearing a pale grey gown edged in white lace.

Judith gulped nervously, and hoped that Kenneth would have done the same. She had just seen Mrs Froode standing behind Lady Garvey, a hovering black crow: Harriet, wearing the guise of her old servant's face.

"Mother," she croaked, and took refuge in another bout of coughing into her handkerchief. "I am ill, take pity," she said hoarsely, from under her bushy moustache.

"Lord, do you think I care?" Lady Garvey's penetrating glare turned into an impatient glance heavenwards, and she dropped the quizzing glass. "It is the worst possible time for you to thrust your presence upon us. You must not move from this room, do you hear? You might expose Georgina to your illness, and you well know that she has a delicate constitution."

Judith nodded meekly, and coughed again. She dared not petition Lady Garvey right in front of Harriet, without Dacian's support. She must wait until their plan could come to fruition, along with their incontrovertible proof.

"And," continued her ladyship crossly, "we are expecting Lady Avely to call this afternoon. You would not want to infect her too, would you, now?"

Judith peered nervously over her quilt. "Oh?" she mumbled, and tried to deepen and roughen her voice. "Visiting again?"

Lady Garvey's lips thinned. "So I gather. We have something she wants returned, I believe."

A chill crept into Judith's heart. Marigold. They had Marigold. She blinked, and tried to remain expressionless, while her pulse beat erratically in her throat.

"You look rather pale. You need laudanum," said Lady Garvey decisively. "Mrs Froode, fetch some for Kenneth, would you?"

"Yes, my lady," came Mrs Froode's rasping voice.

Judith grunted in agreement, and added another cough for

good measure. She would certainly not consume any medicine provided by Mrs Froode.

Lady Garvey gave her a last disparaging look as she stalked to the door, sweeping her housekeeper before her. "Stay abed, if you know what is good for you, Kenneth. God knows you will just lower the tone of Garvey House if you are seen in its halls."

Judith did her best to look cowed, which was not difficult.

The door shut with a snap behind them. Judith lurched up, blood humming in her ears, grateful that Robert's Illusion had held up.

Yet she was clearly expected. They were planning something, that much was certain. And they held Marigold hostage.

Judith gripped the blanket tightly, her eyes going to the window. Heavy, grey clouds still covered the sky, which was a minor comfort. Direct sunlight would be far worse. Marigold might endure filtered, gloomy daylight for a short time, if only they could find her.

Broth wafted at Judith's elbow, but she ignored it, too tense to stomach a single mouthful. Georgina arrived again, this time bearing a bottle of laudanum, which she set on the table. Judith eyed it with suspicion, and hoped that the untouched soup was a convincing sign of Kenneth's illness. She nodded weakly, and tossed fitfully as Georgina left again, shutting the door behind her.

It seemed an age before Dacian returned. When he finally slipped through the door, he had one hand thrust into his pocket. His face was grim as he undid his Illusion charm with the other, and seated himself on the bed.

He proceeded to confirm Judith's fears.

"I found an attic abode," he said quietly. "A vampiri residence, with signs of struggle. It looks like Marigold was held there for some time, as she has torn the place apart. Unfortunately, I could not see her. Perhaps she has escaped, or they moved her."

"Where? Not outside..."

"I also found *this*," said Dacian.

He pulled his hand out of his pocket. His long fingers were wrapped around the body of a black bat. Its head stuck out from his fist. Little black eyes stared up at Judith defiantly.

"Yvette?" Judith breathed. "Where?"

"Under the attic stairs, sleeping. I grabbed her without much difficulty. So it is one for one now."

The black eyes snapped with scorn, but Judith was glad the creature had been wrenched from slumber so unceremoniously. For it was undeniable now that Miss Belfleur was with the enemy.

"Well," said Judith icily, "let us hear her story. Release her, so she may talk."

Dacian looked unconvinced, but he proceeded to lock the door and windows one-handedly before he released his grip, placing Yvette on the bed.

The bat stretched out her wings with a shudder, then transformed into a beautiful, miniature woman. Thick waves of black hair fell around her shoulders. Her eyes were an odd colour of violet, and her figure boasted long legs, a slender waist, and a full bosom.

"Hm," said Judith. Without the covering of darkness and a cloak, she could now see why this exquisite creature might exert an undue fascination on Marigold. "You are Miss Yvette Belfleur?"

"I am." Yvette inclined her head and spoke in low musical tones. "That is a remarkable moustache you are sporting, Lady Avely. An improvement upon the last time I saw you."

Judith frowned at this sally. "I thank you for helping me escape the maze last night, but I must now ask: have you entrapped Miss Cultor?"

Yvette cleared her throat. "Indeed, and I am sorry for it."

"Oh?" said Dacian sceptically. "Where is she then? What have you done with her?"

"May I have something for my modesty first?" replied Yvette coolly.

Judith dug crossly for her cambric handkerchief and flung it at the vampiri. "Now tell us everything. Or you will find that the duke's grip is not so kind next time."

Yvette tucked the heavy fabric round her shoulders and drew it calmly across her breasts. "I trapped Miss Cultor in the attic, it is true. But I have freed her again." She paused. "I began to realise that my blood companion has violent tendencies, and I feared for Miss Cultor's safety."

Judith could hear the truth in her words, and her shoulders relaxed infinitesimally against the pillows. It seemed that Yvette was not going to obfuscate matters. "Your companion, Harriet Bollopher?"

"Yes," said Yvette, with a piercing, approving glance, along with a modicum of surprise. "Last night, I saw Harriet kill the butler in the maze, with nary a hesitation. It caused *me* some consternation, however. Now I wonder what other crimes she may be capable of." She paused. "I feared if I left Marigold sleeping in the attic, Harriet might return and simply snap her neck."

Judith shuddered, appalled to have her suspicions borne out. Yvette's tale rang with honesty, mixed with shame.

"Then Harriet has played a part all this time?" Judith narrowed her eyes. "Faske might not be the first murder to her name."

Yvette's eyes dropped to the coverlet. "It is possible. I always thought she simply grasped the opportunity presented to her. But now I wonder if perhaps Harriet orchestrated it."

"To what end?" demanded Dacian. "Simply so she can be sure of a roof above her head?"

"That, and retain access to the Galenia flower in the maze,"

Yvette explained. "Its healing properties keep her illness at bay. She feels she has a right to it, as her daughter made it."

There was more Judith wanted to know, but it could wait. "Never mind all that," she said. "Where have you put Marigold?"

Yvette licked her lips. "She was reluctant to trust me, but I managed to convince her to hide in the longcase clock in the drawing room - she only agreed when I mentioned the aforesaid possibility of her neck being snapped. We sneaked across to it only an hour ago, despite the daylight. I reasoned that if Harriet notices the escape, she will search all the other rooms first, before thinking to look in the drawing room."

"Clever," said Dacian, "and I suppose you locked Miss Cultor inside?"

For the first time, a trace of discomfort crossed Yvette's features. "I am afraid so. I wanted to keep her safe. She hates me anyway, of course."

Judith sighed. "You wanted to stop her from flying into Harriet's grasp again." Despite herself, she found herself glad of Yvette's action. God knows what Marigold might do, addled with rage and lack of sleep. At least this way, she was safe and contained.

"Yes," said Yvette. "I fear that my mistress is filled now with some kind of exultant fire, after last night. I must warn you - she has sent for the parish constable. She plans to have the duke arrested as soon as he appears." Her eyes slid to Dacian. "I don't think she suspects yet that you have snuck in beneath her nose."

Dacian glowered over his own long proboscis. "You mean you didn't tell her of our plans this time?"

Yvette shrugged. "I thought I'd give you a fighting chance. I even told her that I heard you make plans to visit at dusk, which is why she doesn't suspect Kenneth yet." She nodded at Judith, then paused. "I find I don't approve of murder."

"Good of you," growled Dacian. "Nonetheless, there is a trunk that you are about to become intimately acquainted with, Miss Belfleur."

"I think not," replied Yvette calmly. "I must return to under the attic stairs. You wouldn't want Harriet to look for me and notice anything amiss."

Dacian's power momentarily fluctuated in the room, then he controlled himself and turned to Judith. "What do you say? Can we trust her?"

"I am afraid we must." Judith frowned at Yvette. "She has been truthful, as far as I can tell."

Yvette gave an ironic nod, and turned to Dacian. "If you want further proof of my good faith, I will tell you that Harriet means to blame you for Faske's death. She returned to his body and plunged the duelling sword through him, to make it look like a fight between men. So be careful, or you might end up charged with two murders, not just one."

This echoed Mrs Froode's warning to them the previous evening, and Dacian's brows lowered with the reminder of his own crime long ago.

Yvette, finished with him, casually tossed the cambric cloth aside.

"Wait," said Judith, raising a hand. "What if Harriet should demand to know where Marigold has gone?

"I shall simply pretend to search for her," replied Yvette. "And fail to do so."

"You're a sneaky little bat," said Dacian.

"Why, thank you." Lifting into the air, she flew peremptorily to the door. Dacian stalked over and opened it a crack, watching as Yvette glided out the room.

"Conniving creature," he said grimly.

Judith sighed. "We must be thankful that she has belatedly found her conscience and warned us of Harriet's intentions. It gives us time to take countermeasures."

"Throw Harriet out the second-floor window, perhaps? Or force Lady Garvey to speak out against her?"

"No," said Judith reluctantly. "Not in front of the constable. His presence will certainly complicate things." She felt a little sick at the possibility that Dacian might be snatched away, this time by forces that were backed by authority and legality. "If we betray the Musing to the local constable, that will unfold all sorts of trouble for us. Especially if you are concerned about the Musor Custos."

Dacian paced around the room like a caged dragon. "She has us checkmated."

"Perhaps not," Judith said slowly. "But I require Robert to run another errand for me, curse it."

In which a scene of seduction is thwarted

We all lie to those closest to us, because it is their judgment that we fear the most.

- from *Lady Avely's Guide to Lies and Charms*

JUDITH SCRAWLED A HASTY NOTE, and sent Dacian downstairs to deliver it to Robert in the stables. This time, he locked the door behind him, not trusting to leave Judith unprotected in the room. When he returned, he was scowling under his long nose and bald head. He locked the door once more and flung himself around the room in a fury of impatience.

"I say we charge into the drawing room," he said. "Throw some things around. Yank the chatelaine off the old hag."

Judith tutted. "You know we cannot do that. We must fetch the accounts first, as our proof, and let Robert recover his wits and do his part. It is better we wait until dusk, regardless, so that Marigold is fully awake and able to move quickly."

Dacian growled and threw himself onto an armchair. "I cannot bear to sit around all that time." He thrust his jacket off, thereby casting aside the Illusion of the valet's features. Black hair and smouldering eyes sprung back into view as he threw a hungry glance at the soup. "Can I have some of that?"

When Judith nodded, he took the bowl and rapidly consumed half of its contents. Then he insisted that Judith eat the rest. She found she was more able to stomach the thought of it, now that she knew Marigold was safe. To make eating easier, she removed her pocket watch charm. It was a relief to have her own face again, even if she still wore a coat, shirt, and breeches.

She dipped the bread into the broth. It was tasty beef stew, and she breathed in its warmth gratefully. Garvey House possessed a good cook, at least. No doubt that was part of Harriet's hold over Lady Garvey: that she ran a good kitchen.

Dacian calmed down now that he had something in his stomach and had his hair back. He watched her from the armchair and Judith studiously avoided his gaze. Now that the rush of planning and action had faded, she found she could remember with prickling clarity how she had told him how handsome he was, and apologised for trying to seduce him last night.

Why the devil had she apologised for that? She was half inclined to try again, except that she was in breeches. She didn't feel quite as confident without her feminine accoutrements. After all, she didn't even have a mobcap for him to seductively remove.

Nonsense, she told herself. Don't be a ninny. You can proceed without a mobcap. Now is the time for courage. You don't know what will happen this evening...

The thought of Dacian's slain body in the maze was all that was needed to give her spirit a kick of resolution.

"Come." She put her empty bowl aside and patted the bed. "Sit with me."

Dacian jumped up with alacrity and was at her side within a moment, taking her hand and smiling.

Judith, flustered, put her other hand over his. "Dacian."

"Judith."

"I am not Bemused."

"Are you certain?" He cocked an eyebrow, even as his voice deepened, taking her meaning. "You were listening rather closely to Miss Belfleur."

"She was telling the truth, and I think that perhaps lies are more exhausting to me."

"Is that so?"

"Yes." Judith took a deep breath. "Therefore I am quite in possession of all my wits... and I want you to kiss me."

"Oh?" He leaned forward and undid the scarf from around her neck. The soft cloth trailed over her skin. The sensation was exquisite, and she tilted her head back slightly. Yet he paused, leaving her exposed. "Is this because I am a convenient rake?"

She brought her chin back down, and met his eyes. "It is because you are you."

"Judith." His voice was husky, but he simply trailed his finger under her chin, then down her neck, leaving a line of fire. "I have always wanted you, ever since I first saw you."

He leaned forward and kissed her.

He took his time: deliberate and masterful, as if to relish the moment that she was finally becoming his. Soon her whole being was aching with impatient desire, heightened by all the danger they still faced together. She grasped at his arms, pulling him closer.

Following her directive, Dacian climbed onto the bed, and all pretence at restraint vanished. He thrust her against the bedhead, pushing her blankets aside and claiming every inch of her with the length of his hard body.

Judith pressed back, to be as close as possible, glad now that only thin breeches and not thick petticoats separated them. Dacian's kiss became devouring, and she returned it with fervour. She ran her hands over his dear shoulders and through his thick, darling hair. His embrace reverberated through her entire being, tilting her life on its axis as it did so. She was more than content, now, to surrender her whole being to him.

A soft tap came at the door, and they froze.

"My lord?" The low tones were hard to identify. Mrs Froode? Harriet? "Are you awake?"

Dacian's head withdrew, his eyes widening. There was a taut silence.

Then, with admirable presence of mind, he let out a huge snore.

Judith jumped. The sound reverberated right next to her ear, and it was quite shocking to her tightened nerves. After a moment, he did it again, sounding much like a horse with a bad case of influenza.

She pressed her lips together to hold back a laugh. Dacian grimaced and backed away another arm's length, only to expel another grunting snore.

There was silence from the door, alert and listening.

Judith gestured in encouragement, and Dacian continued to snore, snorting at intervals. Judith bit the inside of her cheek. His warm hand still rested on her shoulder, fingers pressing through her coat, and his legs were tangled with hers.

She ached to run her hands all over him, but she dared not distract him from his current duty.

After an excessive number of snores, they heard the footsteps finally recede. To be safe, Dacian kept on with his performance for another minute, while Judith rubbed her own cheek with relief.

"That was close," she whispered.

"Fortunately, we were simply kissing," he murmured, and finally desisted. "Perhaps we should return to that activity?"

Her eyes traced his beautiful lips. "What if it were Harriet? And what if she should come back?"

"Damn it, she might." Dacian grimaced.

"I do not trust us to hear her, not in the heat of passion."

He scooped her close again, and claimed a searing kiss. "I like it when you talk of the heat of passion." He kissed her again, warmly on the cheek, then throat, leading lower as his hand deftly undid her waistcoat buttons.

Judith placed a finger on his lower lip to stop him. "We must be cautious. It would be a shame to toss our cards on the floor now."

Dacian groaned, but he settled back on the pillow, renouncing her waistcoat. One arm still possessively embraced her, however, keeping her close. "You will drive me mad, Judith."

She blushed, yet drew away a little. "The feeling is mutual." She hesitated, wondering if she should confess that it was not just desire that muddled her senses, but love: deep, ridiculous, heart-wrenching love. Then she closed her lips, remembering that Dacian had done this sort of thing a thousand times before. Lustful dalliances were nothing new to him, only to her.

He frowned, examining her face. Then his head shot up, listening. After a moment, he launched into another ear-splitting snore. Judith bit her lip to hold back her amusement, and extricated herself from his arms. She didn't trust herself within his embrace, and they could ill afford to drop their guard now. It seemed that Harriet was growing suspicious.

Dacian continued snoring for another few minutes, his expression pained. When he was sure that no one still lingered outside the door, he leaned across to nuzzle her neck.

"Scenes of love-making are futile in these circumstances," he murmured, pulling her close again. "How am I to convince you of my passion?"

Her hand crept down his front, to grasp the long length that, despite everything, still strained against his breeches. It was, she felt, very hard, large, and incontrovertible. "I find that I am convinced, your grace."

"Lady Avely!" His voice was mock outraged, and he moved her hand away to rest on his heart. "This is the organ you should seek to interrogate, my dear."

She snatched her hand away, distracted by the sound of floorboards creaking outside. "Hush!"

He gave a wry grimace and folded his hands over his chest.

Judith was too busy listening to notice. When she was certain that no one lurked outside, she let out a sigh of relief. "Do not attempt to convince me of anything, I beg you," she whispered. "We will become carried away."

"God, Judith. I am already carried away. Let me be carried."

"I thought you said that you learned restraint in Spain?"

"Mmrgh," said Dacian, and sat up a little.

They spent the next few hours in a tense, listening silence, three feet away from each other on the bed. Twice, Dacian had to resume his room-shattering snoring, which Judith found to be a rather good antidote to lust.

Nonetheless, it was torture to be within reaching distance of him and yet be unable to crawl into his arms. She swallowed at the sight of his broad shoulders against the pillows, his black hair in disarray, his dark lashes against his cheek. For he had closed his eyes, and after a while, Judith did so too, simply out of a sense of self-preservation, while they listened for the sound of floorboards creaking in the corridor.

A brief distraction came after one of Dacian's excessive snoring demonstrations, when Wooten popped his head out of the cupboard.

"What the devil is that noise?" he hissed. Then his eyes widened as they fell upon Judith. "Good God, what sort of waistcoat is that? You look like a rustic."

"Watch it, Wooten," snapped Dacian, lifting his head from the pillow. "A little respect, please."

Judith ran a hand down the herringbone tweed in apology, swallowing a smile. "It's the best we could do in the circumstances."

"It's tight in all the wrong places," said Wooten, wincing. "Didn't you say Kenneth was a man about town?"

"Well, only you would notice," said Dacian. "I'll have you know that we have managed to fool everyone, except that damn Miss Belfleur. The snoring is to keep up the ruse."

"Yvette knows we are here?"

"She is on our side now," explained Dacian reluctantly. "She locked Marigold in a clock."

Wooten looked faintly impressed. "A female of taste and discernment, after all." He looked round the master bedroom. "Well done, I suppose, on making it thus far. Keep the noise down, would you? I'm trying to sleep." And he disappeared back into the cupboard to return to his slumbers.

At long last, dusk fell, darkening the window. Judith peeked through her lids and drew a relieved breath, pushing herself up from the bed.

"I must change," she announced in a low voice. "I do not wish to face Lady Garvey in breeches and coat, especially if Wooten is so scathing about it." She swung her legs over the side of the bed and stood.

"I disagree," said Dacian, running an appreciative eye down Judith's lower half. "You look very fetching in those breeches."

"I will feel more myself in a gown. And they are expecting *me*, after all."

"Then I will help you dress."

Judith eyed him skeptically. He held up his hands.

"I swear, I will be as if I were your lady's maid," he said. "Or your valet. Purely in the role of assistance, not a rake."

She didn't believe it for a moment. "I'd rather not risk it."

He quirked his eyebrow and folded his arms, waiting.

Flustered, she realised she would have to undress before him, and that he was not going to be a gentleman and look away. Hastily, she turned her back on him and shed her coat, then undid her waistcoat and shirt.

In the mirror, she could see Dacian's eyes darken. He held himself very still. Typical man, to have to keep such a tight rein on his lust. Rather enjoying herself now, Judith slipped her shirt off, then unwound her bindings so her breasts sprung free. She drew a long breath with the relief of it, and saw Dacian swallow hard, his arms tensing across his chest.

She smiled and undid her breeches. Stepping out of them, she said sweetly. "My gown, please."

Dacian leapt forward to shake out her blue gown, and then hold it out for her, an appreciative gleam in his eyes. With dignity, she let him place it over her head, the silk sweeping over her skin. She waited as he did up the ties, biting her lips, clamping down on the desire that swirled through her. His fingers brushed her back, and caressed her neck.

It was only the thought that he might have to start snoring again that stopped her from pushing him onto the bed immediately.

The thought of Marigold also sobered her. Her little companion was still locked in the longcase clock, and they were relying on Yvette's cunning to keep her undiscovered. Harriet might at this moment have realised she had lost her pawn, and be searching the house high and low for Marigold.

So Judith stayed rigidly still as Dacian did up the final buttons along her neck. He, intuiting her mood, also became serious, and did up the last bow at her waist with deft fingers.

She turned to see in the mirror that her cheeks were flushed, her pupils enlarged.

"There," he said, with regret. "I hate to say it, Judith, but now all you need is a mobcap."

In which a dandy is dismayed

As a general rule, one must not give credence to the continental belief that one's handwriting can reveal character. In some circumstances, however, writing can reveal its owner.

- from *Lady Avely's Guide to Lies and Charms*

WHILE JUDITH TIED up her mobcap, Dacian woke Wooten up from his wardrobe den. The vampiri's purple silk dressing gown was miraculously uncreased as he stepped onto Dacian's hand, yawning.

Dacian explained the plan and Wooten nodded in approval, though he shook his head gloomily when Dacian resumed his disguise as the long-faced, bald-pated manservant. Then they encountered a problem, as they searched Dacian's trunk for Wooten's velvet cloak.

"I cannot see it anywhere," said Wooten, in a worried tone. "Where is it?"

"Hm." Dacian also rifled through the contents, which currently consisted of Judith's masculine attire, a charmed pocket watch, and some spare clothes of Robert's. "It looks as if we might have forgotten it in the rush."

Wooten stared. "What am I going to wear?"

Dacian straightened, eying him. "What about your dressing gown?"

"This old thing?" Wooten said in horror. "Most certainly not. Apart from anything, it is purple!"

His face was a mask of dismay.

"Perhaps," suggested Judith, "you must simply stay in your creature form. We can carry extra handkerchiefs, in case of an emergency."

Dacian produced one with a flourish. "Like this one." It was a large flannel square that he had borrowed from Robert, while Judith had been employing his own fine cambric one.

Wooten wrinkled his nose. "Are you serious? Handkerchiefs are for peasants."

Judith raised her brows. "Fortunately, Marigold isn't here for that remark."

Wooten sniffed. "I think I will make do with my dressing gown," he muttered, "though it is a little voluminous for flight."

"Buck up, Wooten," said Dacian. "At least this means you won't spoil your cravat."

Wooten simply gave a gusty sigh, tucked his purple silk closer, and crawled into Dacian's pocket with an air of dejection.

After listening closely at the door, Dacian finally eased it open and they crept out. The corridor was quiet. They trod along the length of thin carpet, ignoring the main staircase and slipping into the servants' stairs.

Judith shut the door behind her, and followed Dacian down the narrow, dark stairwell. The silence felt tense, their footsteps too loud. At the bottom, Dacian again opened the door a crack, and peered out.

"Wait here," he whispered. "I'll be as quick as I can."

She grimaced but allowed it. He was still disguised as the valet, so his presence would not occasion too much comment. He vanished through the door, shutting it behind him.

Judith stood on the second step, waiting, all thoughts suspended in the silence. It seemed an age before the door opened again and Dacian crowded into the confined space. He held a heavy tome under one arm.

He lifted the large book up as if it were a pillow. "Success."

"So easily?"

He shrugged. "I had to force the study door open, and I broke the locks on the desk. It was quite a satisfying exercise."

Judith tutted and took the accounts ledger, laying it on a step. She flicked the pages open. It was too dark in the stairwell to read easily, so she gestured for Dacian to open the door a crack.

In the slither of light, she knelt to peer at the dates. With difficulty she found the year of 1801, when she was certain Harriet had been alive. Strong, slanting script marked out the bills and receipts in black ink.

Scrolling from there, Judith tracked through the years: 1802, 1803, 1804... the same distinct hand continued to record the household accounts, remarkable in its continuity and legibility, even in the faint light.

Judith reached 1805 - the current year - and the last, active page of the accounts. It was noticeably similar to the first one she had read, though fewer in its list of expenses.

"It is as I thought." She looked up, triumph thudding under her breastbone. "The handwriting remains the same. It is our proof that the same woman still lives here. We just need a witness to say that Harriet used to tend to the accounts, and this shows that she still does."

Dacian's eyes gleamed. "Excellent."

"Is Robert waiting?"

"As instructed."

As Judith stood, her knees gave a faint crick, while Wooten vanished again. Dacian wrenched off his charmed button, and with it, his Illusory face. She was glad to see it again, and lifted a hand to brush his cheek, before she could help herself.

He caught it and kissed the back of her hand, smiling. Then he lifted the tome from the step, and reached for the door. "Are you ready?"

For the next part, they had to step out of hiding and make their presence known. Judith bit back a pang of cowardice, which sprung purely from her fear of losing him again. She nodded, smoothed her skirts down, and stepped out into the hall.

To her great relief, no one accosted them in the entranceway. Of course, Faske was no longer there to keep guard, and Harriet was no doubt embattled with housework in her role as house-keeper, or plotting something dastardly.

Dacian quickly led the way through a rear corridor to the back door. Outside, Robert was waiting impatiently, his task completed, his lower lip clenched in his teeth with apprehension. Beside him stood Mrs Selina Southcott.

Mrs Southcott wore walking boots and a fine cambric gown of apple green. A delicately patterned paisley shawl draped over her shoulders, the soft greens setting off her blonde hair, which hung in ringlets from under her mobcap. She curtsied deeply, sliding a startled glance towards Dacian (who was revealed as himself), then turned a wary gaze to Judith.

Judith nodded greetings and exchanged a few quick words with her, while Dacian passed the book to Robert for safekeeping. Then they all proceeded up the main staircase, the very same one Dacian had carried Judith up a few days ago.

Dacian removed Wooten from his pocket and set him on the floor in a bundle of purple silk. "Keep a look-out," he instructed quietly, "in case you must fetch help."

Wooten nodded. Judith had barely a moment to observe that

Selina did not seem to be overly taken aback at the sight of the vampiri, then Dacian flung open the drawing room door.

Leaving Robert, Selina, and Wooten stationed outside, Judith took a deep breath and followed him in.

Lady Garvey was no longer in her usual place, huddled in the armchair by the fire. Instead, she stood at the oriel window, watching the front drive, leaning on her walking stick. At their entrance, she turned abruptly and stared.

"You!" she exclaimed. "How did you mount my staircase without me seeing your carriage?"

Judith dropped a curtsy. "Good evening, Lady Garvey. I confess, I walked here. I apologise for the lateness of my visit."

An odd look of relief showed in Lady Garvey's eyes, but then she turned a grim gaze upon Dacian. "And you - I recognise *you*." She raised a quivering finger and pointed dramatically. "That is the Duke of Sargen, the man who killed my son."

Judith became aware of another presence in the room. From behind the door, a soberly dressed man stepped out. He was the red-haired constable from the village, with the long sideburns, flushed cheeks, and brass buttons straining over his black coat. He held heavy iron manacles in one hand, and his truncheon hung from his belt.

Yet Judith's attention was also distracted by the hollow sound of Lady Garvey's last word, ringing with the tenor of a lie. Judith turned to look frowningly at her hostess.

"I introduce you to Constable Carter," continued Lady Garvey triumphantly. "Arrest that man, Carter. Not only did he kill my son, but he has turned his violence upon my butler, who now lies dead. You saw yourself the duelling sword thrust through his body."

Her ladyship's words still rang hollowly, and Judith's eyes narrowed. Lady Garvey clearly knew that Dacian was not the culprit, and yet she was willing to have him arrested on false charges.

The policeman took another step forward, his face set with resolution. "Are you indeed his grace, the Duke of Sargen?"

"Indeed." Dacian, in the centre of the room, raised his hands placatingly. "I see my reputation precedes me. However, I swear to you, good sir, that I did not kill Lady Garvey's butler."

Constable Carter eyed him with a touch of nervousness, as well he might, facing down a man known for his violence and rank. Yet, admirably, he clenched his jaw and marched up to Dacian, rattling the irons a little for courage. "Nonetheless, you are under arrest for killing Lord Charles Garvey, by means of an illegal duel to the death nine years ago."

Dacian gave his most charming smile and held out his wrists. "By all means, take me to the magistrate and he may decide whether to press charges."

Constable Carter hesitated, thrown by this apparent placidity, while Lady Garvey frowned by the window.

Judith intervened. "There is something you must hear before you proceed, Constable. You would not want to arrest and manhandle a peer of the realm without due cause."

"There is nothing to discuss!" snapped Lady Garvey. "Sargen's flight was proof of his guilt. Arrest him, Arnold. Do not bow to his rank."

Constable Carter's lips pressed together. He extended the manacles out, readying to do his duty and clasp them over Dacian's wrists.

"Wait." Judith stepped forward. "There is a witness you must hear first."

She turned. With a gesture to rival Lady Garvey's denouncement, she grandly indicated the door.

Hearing his cue, Robert pressed it open, and led Mrs Selina Southcott into the room.

Selina ran her hands nervously down her apple-green skirts, and curtsied, her face pale and determined.

A startled silence fell. Constable Carter's hands dropped, and he gave a small bow to the newcomer in recognition. Most likely they were neighbours, and well known to one another.

Judith cleared her throat. "May I present Mrs Selina Southcott, previously Miss Selina Pelling, who was present at the scene of Lord Garvey's death."

The constable's brows drew together in a frown. "Were you, indeed, Mrs Southcott? This is the first I have heard of it."

Selina inclined her head. "I am afraid that I kept my presence a secret, Mr Carter."

Lady Garvey blustered. "It doesn't matter if she were there or not! Sargen still shot Charles!"

Selina held up a gloved hand. "Yet I think you should hear my testimony, Constable Carter, before you proceed."

He gave a short, sharp nod. Dacian, who had been obediently holding out his wrists, dropped them, and turned his attention to Selina.

She was staring at him, a faint blush in her cheeks. "Your grace." She dropped a low curtsy. "I must thank you for saving me from Lord Garvey's cruel, lascivious attentions when I was a girl."

Spluttering came from Lady Garvey, but Selina continued, turning to look at the constable.

"The duke has honourably kept quiet upon the true circumstances of the duel, but I will speak out on his behalf." She drew a breath and Constable Carter frowned, as the room hung on her words. "His grace came across myself and Lord Garvey in the maze. Lord Garvey was forcing his attentions upon me, even though I had begged him not to do so. His grace intervened, and called his lordship out." Here she lowered her eyes. "I am eternally grateful for his intervention, which was the chivalrous action of a true gentleman. I was a helpless young girl, unable to defend myself."

For the first time in this shocking recitation, Judith heard the clang of a lie. Her eyes sharpened on Selina, but no one else noticed anything amiss. Constable Carter took a faltering step backward, the irons now swinging limply in his hand.

"So you see," Selina finished, "no jury would convict the duke. You would be wise to leave him be, and not embroil our families in scandal." She gave a small nod at Lady Garvey, who looked apoplectic.

"And why," demanded her ladyship, in fulminating tones, "would you wait 'til now to share this convenient story?"

Constable Carter nodded, his attention still on Selina. "Yes, you constrained the duke to exile with your silence, Mrs Southcott."

Selina winced. "I know, and I am sorry for it. In my defence, I was very young, and frightened. If I had spoken up, I would have been cast as a harlot, though Lord Garvey's attentions were unwanted."

The constable shifted uncomfortably. Judith knew it was true: the female victim was often blamed in these circumstances. Lady Garvey scowled.

Selina's voice strengthened, hearing the acknowledgement implicit in everyone's silence. "If the true story emerged, I would have lost any chance of marrying, and moreover, I may have lost the regard of Mr Southcott. I could not bear that to happen, and so I allowed the duke to carry the burden of exile." She straightened her shoulders. "Now, however, I am a married woman, and my reputation can only suffer a fraction of what it would have. I am happy to testify in the duke's defence."

Lady Garvey ground out a rebuttal. "You were Charles' betrothed, Selina. He could scarcely molest his own fiancé!"

Selina met her gaze squarely. "Yet he did. Until the duke intervened."

"It was nothing," said Dacian modestly. "Anything to protect a lovely young woman from harm."

Selina blushed and stared at him with devotion. Judith carefully did not roll her eyes. Nine years' exile was not *nothing*. There was still the matter of Harriet's lies and Illusions to account for, but they could not address such matters in the presence of the worthy constable.

Lady Garvey snarled, "You cannot believe this poppycock, Arnold!"

"Hm." The constable coughed, and looked from Lady Garvey to Selina. "Perhaps if you come with me, Mrs Southcott, and make a written statement to that effect, describing the scene as you experienced it. Then I can pass it on to the Bow Street Runners, to see if they still wish to pursue the issue. I think you are right that your evidence changes the complexion of the matter."

Lady Garvey glared. "You are a coward, Arnold. When I think of how many excises I have paid to you!"

"I apologise, my lady," returned Constable Carter. "Excises are not bribes, however, and I will do my duty as I see fit."

These were brave words from a local squire, and Judith gave him a warm smile.

"What about my butler?" said Lady Garvey shrilly. "He killed my butler. With a sword! And what's more, he stole my horse!"

Judith suppressed a wince: the last, indeed, was true.

Constable Carter looked unconvinced. "What possible reason would his grace have to attack your butler or steal your horse, my lady?" He gave Dacian an apologetic look and shook his head at Lady Garvey. "It is far more likely that some vagrant was hiding in your maze, and Faske stupidly confronted him. I will set my men to search the locality, but you can be assured that whoever did the deed is long gone from here by now."

"Quite." Judith directed a steely look at Lady Garvey. "Unless you can think of something that Faske was trying to hide?"

Her ladyship clamped her mouth shut, appearing much as if she had tasted rancid milk.

Constable Carter bowed, and made as if to leave. It seemed they might at last be rid of him. At that moment, however, there came a rattle from the longcase clock.

It was a sharp banging, from deep within its bowels. The whole edifice shivered a little. Everyone turned to stare at it, and it fell quiet once more.

The rapping came again. Judith clenched her hands in her skirts. Marigold, it was clear, was now awake and able-bodied. It was not, however, the right time for her to make an appearance.

"What is that?" Constable Carter was the first to speak, his voice sharp with suspicion.

Judith cleared her throat. "I am not certain..."

The clock rattled again, in a distinctly irritated fashion.

A grim smile of comprehension came over Lady Garvey's face. "Yes," she said pleasantly. "What is that, I wonder? It appears some small creature is stuck in my clock. Arnold, do me the favour of dealing with it, seeing as you are useless for everything else. The key hangs on the side. Whatever you find, please kill it."

Constable Carter glanced from under his brows, but stepped forward willingly enough, perhaps eager to make up for his betrayals. Judith tensed. Even if Marigold might fly from the constable's grasp, she would be breaching the Edicts to appear as a bat in the drawing room. It might raise all sorts of questions from no less than the local parish authority. Or heaven forbid, she might appear in her naked, human form.

The constable strode up to the clock and fumbled for the key.

Judith looked at Dacian with anguish, hoping that Marigold would have enough sense to keep quiet and move fast.

"Wait," said Robert suddenly, from behind her. "I think I might know what is trapped in there."

Judith swung around. "You do? How so?"

Robert gave a discreet, footmanly cough. "I regret to inform you, my lady, that it is *possibly* my pet mouse."

"Your pet *mouse*?" Judith remembered to act with hauteur, even as relief swept through her at Robert's quick thinking. "Are you joking, boy?"

Robert cringed and shuffled forward, holding the household accounts in his arms. "I have domesticated a little black mouse, my lady. She scampered off when we were here yesterday." A rattle came from the clock, and he flinched again. "That might be her. She's a mettlesome one. Shall I look?"

Judith sniffed. "I suppose so. Constable Carter, let my deplorable footman rescue his mouse." She paused. "I hope you know, Robert, that you will be losing your position over this."

"Yes, my lady." Robert put the accounts book on a side table, and glided forward, politely taking the key from Constable Carter.

Lady Garvey glared, impotent. "What is this nonsense, Judith? Preposterous! I will not have a rat in my house. Capture that rodent, Arnold!"

The constable shrugged and stepped back. "I wouldn't want to hurt a pet, my lady. And I believe it is a mouse, not a rat?"

Robert bowed in appreciation. Murmuring quietly to the clock, he turned the key and swung the door open. The constable stood close by, peering with interest over his shoulder.

Judith held her breath.

In which there is a noble sacrifice

What seems like a little lie can sometimes cover a much larger deception.
  - from *Lady Avely's Guide to Lies and Charms*

WHEN ROBERT TURNED AROUND, he had a black mouse resting in the palms of his hands. Its long nose twitched, and two dark eyes peered mournfully round the drawing room. A long pink tail curled around its furry body. It was a convincing Illusion, and Judith let out a sigh of relief.

"Oh dear," said Selina faintly, while Dacian grinned.

"Good God!" shrieked Lady Garvey. "Get it out! At once!"

"Yes," said Judith firmly. "Out the window, please, Robert."

"Certainly," said Robert. He crossed to the window, unlatched it, and carefully tipped Marigold onto the sill. She sat there a moment, and then shuffled away until she had disappeared out of sight. Judith hoped that she was the only one who had caught glimpse of a black, leathery wing.

Constable Carter blinked. "Such a tame creature. Amazing."

Robert shut the window with a quiet click, then retreated to his position by the door, a faint redness in his cheeks. Judith's shoulders drooped with the release of tension. Marigold was safe at last, even if she would have something to say about it later.

Lady Garvey's jaw was tight. She raised her quizzing glass to glare at Robert across the room. "You really must control your servants better, Lady Avely. It wouldn't surprise me if he put the mouse there himself."

Judith heard some note of discord in Lady Garvey's voice and turned to stare at her. Why should that last sentence sound with the tenor of a lie? Judith examined her face closely, and her eyes fixed on the quizzing glass. It flashed like an opaque mirror.

Lady Garvey was myopic; she was short-sighted and could not even see to the other side of the room without it. Even now she was peering at Robert with distaste, as if to properly examine him through the ornate circle.

Yet, when Judith had entered the room, Lady Garvey had been looking down to the driveway without her glass. Just as she had seen Dacian without it, on the drive, a day ago. Moreover, she had seen enough to remark upon his appearance from a distance.

The insight struck Judith like a blow. The quizzing glass was a ruse.

In fact, *Lady Garvey* was a ruse.

Judith's breath caught in her throat. She had been wrong. Harriet had not taken the place of her servant. She had become the mistress of the house.

It was *Lady Garvey* who had died. Harriet, with the help of Mrs Froode and Georgina and her own cunning, had taken her place.

Judith stared at the slashing brows and beaky nose, trying to see past the Illusion. Belatedly, she could see the determined angle of Harriet's shoulders under Lady Garvey's arrogant posture, and her quiet assurance beneath the theatrical haughtiness. The quizzing glass itself probably held the charm.

Oblivious to Judith's consternation, Dacian smirked at Robert conspiratorially. "Just be glad the mouse wasn't in your teapot, Lady Garvey."

"Pfft," said Harriet, superb in her portrayal of an imperious matriarch. She dropped her glass with disgust and stalked over to the clock to slam it shut. "Servants these days are useless. And so are you, Arnold. You couldn't even kill a mouse."

Judith watched the confidence in her step with a new awareness. The walking stick and slow tottering must have been part of the act, like Dacian's hunch. Harriet must retain some natural vigour - perhaps enhanced by the Galenia flower - enough to glide about as Lord Garvey's ghost, or even creep behind Faske with a steel sword in her hand.

Curse it, she had used the very same tactic that Judith had: taking advantage of society's assumptions about older matrons.

Dacian winked and strode over to clap Constable Carter on the back. "I am much obliged for your good sense today, my dear sir. I perceive that we share a similar sense of duty."

The constable gave a short nod in acknowledgment, then turned to usher Selina out the door. He paused at the last moment. "I hope we can let this matter go now, Lady Garvey. May your son rest in peace."

A taut silence met this vain hope, but the constable did not stay to question the tenor of it. Perhaps he felt that he would do well to stay out of squabbles between nobles, for he followed Selina out, their footsteps loud on the wooden stairs.

As soon as the footsteps had faded, Lady Garvey - Harriet - spoke in a low, quivering voice to Dacian. "You will not escape justice so easily, you cur."

Her words broke the tableau. Dacian kept his face placatory and stepped forward. "I will be happy to talk about justice, Lady Garvey. We have come to discuss your housekeeper, and the hold she has over you."

Harriet raised her brows. "Oh? What nonsense is this now?"

"Wait, Dacian," said Judith.

"Mrs Froode," said Dacian. "We know she is not whom she seems to be. And she had a hand in your son's death."

"What?" said Harriet coldly. "*You* killed my son! How dare you talk such balderdash?"

Judith, certain now, with the word 'son', finally stepped forward. "Stop your play-acting, Harriet. I know it is you hiding beneath the Illusion."

Dacian's eyes widened and he fell back a step. "Wait... *She's* Harriet?"

Judith nodded. "She took Lady Garvey's place, not Mrs Froode's."

"Rubbish," said Harriet, slamming her walking stick down. "Utter nonsense!"

Judith continued calmly. "We know you orchestrated Charles' death, and murdered Faske by your own hand."

Harriet's fingers clenched on her stick. "How dare you spout such lies!"

Judith indicated the heavy book that Robert had placed on the table. "These accounts prove that you continue to live in this house, albeit under a different name, for it is your handwriting throughout. It is time to end this charade and renounce your place here."

Harriet eyed the tome. "You are imagining things, Lady Avely. Perhaps your mobcap is tied on too tight. That is Mrs Froode's handwriting in there."

Judith gritted her teeth at the lie. "I'm not leaving until you admit to your part in Charles' death."

There was a hostile silence. Judith and Harriet locked eyes, Harriet's sparking with anger. But their silent battle of wills was interrupted by footsteps on the stairs.

Georgina burst through the door.

Her golden hair was in disarray. Leaves clung to her rose-coloured gown, and the red ribbon above her ear had come undone, trailing over her cheek.

"Grandmama! I just saw Constable Carter leaving with Selina. Why does he not take the duke?" She stared round at the grim faces. "What has happened? Why is his grace still here?"

Judith spoke. "We know this is Harriet, Georgina. The pretence is over."

The girl flushed. "What do you mean?" she faltered. "This is Lady Cordelia Garvey, my grandmother."

It was a lie. And it explained why Judith had not caught Georgina out before, for 'Grandmama' could refer equally to Harriet and Lady Garvey. Only when she gave Harriet the false title did her words ring hollow.

Judith sighed. "Do not deny it. I know you have been helping her, though at least you had no part in Charles' death."

"What?" said Georgina blankly. "It was the duke who killed my father." She turned a fulminating gaze upon Dacian. "How dare you try to shift the blame onto an old woman?"

Dacian folded his arms uncomfortably across his chest. "That old woman used her Illusions to manipulate me into killing Charles."

Georgina went pale. "That's not true." She spun to Harriet. "Tell them, Grandmama."

"No, it is not true," said Harriet harshly. "A Banbury story, by a Banbury man. Do not believe them, Georgy."

Georgina's slender shoulders drooped, and she scowled at the duke once more, her cheeks flushing.

Judith, however, had heard the lie clanging in Harriet's words. She looked from one to the other, realising that Harriet did not want her granddaughter to know the extent of her villainy. She opened her mouth, then shut it again, unable to bring herself to puncture the girl's innocence. It would be a terrible thing to know that your grandmother had killed your own father.

Georgina, emboldened, stalked towards Dacian, youth granting her a foolish bravado. "I suppose that you are after the Galenia flower, your grace? I warn you, I am its guardian. I might not have the Healing talent of my mother, but at least I can safeguard her creation with my own Gift. If you plan to take it with you, you should know that it shall wilt without my help."

Dacian held his ground, but his expression became pitying. "You are a Healor, then? No wonder your grandmother keeps you so secluded, if you are sustaining her life."

"It is my choice!" snapped Georgina. "She is the only family I have left, apart from Uncle Kenneth. Of course, I willingly care for her."

Dacian nodded slowly. "I thought that the Bollophers had relatives in London?"

"No, they do not." A faint crease marked Georgina's brow.

"Enough of this," said Harriet abruptly. "I told you to stay in your room, Georgina. Why are you here?"

"I couldn't let you face them all alone," said Georgina defiantly.

"I thought I locked the door," Harriet snapped.

Georgina shot Judith a look before replying. "Yvette unlatched my window, and I climbed out. She told me that I ought to know what is going on."

Harriet shook her head angrily. "If you want to see what is going on, you should follow Selina Southcott to the constable's house. She is going to provide testimony to clear the duke's name, drat the girl. I would appreciate it if you would go with her, and find out exactly what she intends to claim."

Georgina frowned, looking from one to the other. Judith remained silent, and Dacian, with a raised brow, followed her lead.

"Very well, Grandmama," said Georgina reluctantly. "If you

wish it, and if you feel safe here with these visitors…" She looked suspiciously at Dacian once more, who held up his hands in a gesture of surrender, perhaps to show that he hid no duelling gun upon his person.

Harriet's fingers clenched on her walking stick. "Do not doubt me, my child. I will handle these interlopers. You follow Selina, and report back to me."

Georgina gave a short nod of acquiescence, and backed out of the room, but not before one last admonishing look. She stepped past Robert, who lowered his eyes as she passed.

Only once her light footsteps had died away, did Judith once more look to Harriet.

By the window, 'Lady Garvey' calmly lifted her quizzing glass over her head and set it aside on the table.

"You are correct," she said. "I will not prevaricate any longer. Thank you for not forcing the issue before Georgina."

With the Illusion charm removed, her true face was revealed: plain, unremarkable, with thinning grey hair and pale lips. Judith frowned. Harriet looked much older than her recollection of nine years ago - but perhaps even then she had been augmented by Illusion. And now her papery cheek was marked with red scratches, laid down by Marigold's talons. So it had indeed been her beneath the Illusion of Lord Garvey's ghost and Lord Kenneth by the maze.

There was a triumphant gleam in Harriet's grey eyes, as if she relished finally being her true self before them.

"How did you know me, Judith?" A cool, reserved register had replaced the strident tones of Lady Garvey, and Harriet raised her eyebrows in mild interrogation.

"You saw the duke through the window, without your quizzing glass," replied Judith.

"Ah." Harriet gave a rueful sigh, and threw her walking stick down. "Stupid of me. I was simply surprised to see him waltzing up my driveway just like that. Though his grace has always been rather arrogant."

Dacian spoke bitterly. "Not *your* driveway, if I may be so bold."

"It is mine now," she corrected him. "You are a fool if you think I shall simply renounce it. You may have convinced that silly constable that you are some noble protector, but I know the truth. You were misusing your Gift that night, and the Musor Custos will ensure that you are punished. How full of pride will you be when you lose your power and your memory, your grace? I shall be interested to observe how deep your hubris goes. I am certain that it is bottomless."

Anger stirred in Judith. "What of you, Harriet? *You* misused your Gift. You took my image in vain and sullied it with your vulgar pantomimes, to incite a man to murder. You cannot talk of hubris. Lord Garvey might have been despicable, but it was not for you to decide his death."

"I had to be rid of him." She returned to her armchair, with restrained movements that were somehow more unnerving than the regal air of Lady Garvey. Dacian watched her carefully.

She only sat down with a sigh. "Charles was going to marry that girl and throw me out of the house. Where would I have gone? And what would I do without the Galenia? My lungs would clog up and I'd be in a poor house. You tell me what you would have done, Judith, before you judge me so harshly."

Harriet tilted her head and looked at Judith with an air of mild enquiry, as if she was discussing quite something else than arranging the death of a man.

"And Faske?" asked Dacian. "Why did you kill him? Because he tried to steal the Galenia flower?"

"Oh, yes," said Harriet pleasantly. "He was going behind my back with Kenneth. Judith was so kind as to tell me all about their little Poleney scheme, and so she signed the warrant for his death."

"It wasn't that," interrupted Judith, who could hear the hollowness of the lie. Moreover, she had thought this through, and refused to take the blame. "You could have simply fired Faske and found another butler. You killed him because of your own miscalculation. That night when my companion attacked you, you retreated into the servant's entrance as Kenneth, but the real Lord Garvey was in the house already. Perhaps in the confusion of it all, you let slip your disguise for a moment. Either way, Faske began to guess the truth: that you were not who you claimed to be."

Frown lines marred Harriet's brow, and she sighed. "You are right, I am afraid. Faske had the gall to covertly threaten me, in the greenhouse. I couldn't have him voice his suspicions to Kenneth. And of course, his death by sword was convenient, seeing as the duke was around to take the blame."

Judith felt a quiver of rage, but she tried to appear dispassionate. "What of Lady Garvey? Did you dispose of her too?"

The pale lips pursed regretfully. "Cordelia grew tiresome. She was approaching death anyway, so it was little matter to help her along. I had to intervene and arrange things to my satisfaction, for if she was known to die, then Kenneth would move into Garvey House immediately. She was so cruel to him - and to me as well. You know it yourself, Judith, how she lorded her position over me."

Judith shook her head. "That is no excuse to take a life, or cast your sordid deceptions." She paused. "How were you out in the fields by the conifers, to cast your tricks?"

Harriet smirked, the first sign of cruel mischief showing. "Oh, I wish I could have seen your face! I knew you were going to visit Selina, for you left the window open the evening before, at the inn. My vampiri companion overheard your plans and reported them to me. I simply cast a suitably amorous performance into a charm and sent Georgina to Southcott Hall to watch and wait. If you hadn't walked home that afternoon, she could have said the word when you rolled past in the carriage." The smirk sharpened. "Did you enjoy the show?"

Judith grit her teeth, remembering the glimpse of Georgina that she had seen at Southcott Hall. She had thought the girl was there to visit Selina, but she had been there on Harriet's command. "You shouldn't have involved Georgina in your vile plots, Harriet. Your time here is finished. You must let Kenneth take up his inheritance, and let Georgina out into the world."

"And if I don't do as you say?" Harriet's smile turned cool. "I might be in breach of the old rules, but so is your precious duke. If you report me, he will also find himself under investigation."

A silence fell. Judith stared at Harriet's placid face, angry that she should try to blackmail them. Worse, she had a dawning suspicion that Harriet was right. Revealing her machinations would also bring to light Dacian's slip in control, and his part in Lord Garvey's death.

Dacian folded his arms. "I am afraid that your threat does not hold water, Mrs Bollopher."

"And why is that?" Harriet turned to look at him.

"Because *I* am an agent of the Musor Custos."

His words were calm. Only Judith heard the echo of a lie, and she kept her face impassive even as she admired Dacian's quick wit. Harriet's expression faltered from its benign patience into something like fear, creeping across her face like a cloud.

Dacian continued. "In my exile, an emissary of the Custos approached me to take on some of their duties. I am empowered to charge you with breach of the old rules. Primarily, with using your Gift to harm others and cause death."

Harriet's scrawny throat bobbed. "Is that so?" Her pale hands crept to dig into the side of the armchair.

"Yes, and I am imbued with the power to take you to the

Warren. You well know that I have the strength to carry you there myself if needs be," said Dacian implacably.

The clock ticked in the silence. Harriet's hands dug convulsively into her skirts, her face crumpling, her shoulders bowing. Judith let out a sigh of relief: it seemed they were finally victorious. Yet she should have known better than to trust a villainous Illusor.

In the next moment, the image of a beaten old woman vanished, and in its place, they saw the small circle of a pistol. Harriet held it firmly, pointing at Dacian, even as he had begun to move forward.

"Stay where you are," she said crisply. "Even your hasty Gift is not as fast as a gun, Sargen."

Judith's throat closed in horror, even as she heard Robert gasp behind her. At the window, black wings pummelled against the glass: Marigold, hopeless, outside.

They were all - even Dacian - useless in the face of a pistol.

"Yes," said Harriet smoothly. "You think you are so clever and bold, with your evidence and tricks, but you have nothing to answer a bullet."

Dacian stood very still. As if in a dream, Judith saw a vision of him lying on the drawing room floor, blood seeping from his body, his face blank with death.

"Judith." His voice was like stone. "Robert. Both of you, leave now."

"No," said Robert shakily from the door.

Swallowing, Judith forced her limbs forward with slow steps. Harriet's eyes darted towards her, and the gun trembled a warning.

Judith ignored it and stepped in front of Dacian. "You cannot shoot us both."

"Can I not?" A faint smile pricked Harriet's lips, yet the scratches on her cheek seemed to stand out more starkly. "It would be rather convenient, to tell the truth. I would rid myself of both of you in one blow. Perhaps your footman can line up behind as well. How far can a bullet travel through flesh, I wonder?"

"No," said Judith. "Robert, please leave us." Silence met her plea, thick with tension.

"Judith," hissed Dacian. "Get out of the way. For God's sake."

Then, out of the corner of her eye, Judith caught sight of movement in the oriel curtains.

It was Wooten, his black head protruding from the maroon stripes. He must have somehow slunk inside, in all the comings and goings, perhaps behind Georgina's skirts. Judith dared not focus her vision on him, but hope bloomed suddenly in her heart. Perhaps Wooten could help them.

As she glared into Harriet's cold eyes, Judith could sense him inch out from under the folds of fabric, in his bat form. He began creeping along the cornice of the wall, keeping close to the ground, his wings folded tightly against his body. He had abandoned his purple dressing gown, no doubt reasoning that it would draw attention.

She had to keep Harriet's gaze fully occupied.

"No." Judith said over her shoulder to Dacian, while keeping her eyes locked with Harriet's. "I will not let her shoot you. This way she will have to account for both of our corpses. That will be difficult to explain to Constable Carter."

Harriet let out a huff of amusement. "Constable Carter will know nothing about it. As far as he is concerned, you will both return to London forthwith. I am good at hiding things, you know."

Wooten had reached a bookcase against the wall with remarkable quickness. He vanished behind it. Judith, staring down the barrel of the pistol, was barely aware of it. Her heart was beating in her throat, and she knew that at any moment Harriet would grow bored of talking and pull the trigger.

Dacian stepped closer, coming right up against Judith's back. One arm slipped around her waist, holding her firm. "This is a good way to die, at least - with a woman pressed up against me."

Harriet frowned. Behind her, Wooten appeared at the base of the mantelpiece. From the corner of her eye, Judith saw him begin crawling up the smooth wood, using his clawed wings to haul himself upwards.

She wondered what he intended to do. Then her eyes drifted over the heavy, ugly candelabra that stood at the end of the mantelpiece above the armchair. It was made of brass. It could be fashioned as a weapon. If only Wooten could somehow tip it onto Harriet's arm at the right moment...

Harriet was speaking with soft derision. "You always were a rake, your grace, but I know that you feel more than simple lust for *this* particular woman. It is your stupid passion that allowed me to manipulate you so easily. Fitting that you cling to it even in death."

Judith was only half listening. She had realised Wooten's dilemma at the same time as he reached the crest of the mantelpiece. To grasp the heavy candelabra, he would have to be human. And he had no clothes.

To his credit, Wooten did not hesitate, even as he stood exposed on the edge of the mantelpiece in the drawing room. He shifted into his human form: a slender male, with only a light fur on his chest to cover anything. His expression pained, he clasped his hands over his lower regions and edged towards the candelabra.

Dacian was talking. He must have seen Wooten too, but he kept his eyes fixed on Harriet. "Is that so? How did you guess that I loved her, even then?"

Judith, hearing the truth in his voice, felt her heart jump beneath her breastbone.

Harriet's expression soured. "Everyone knew it, you fool. Except for her, of course."

Wooten reached the candelabra. His face became anguished as he moved his hands to grasp it.

Judith took pity on him. She cleared her throat. "If I have only discovered it now, Harriet, you must allow me one last kiss before I die."

Not waiting for permission, she spun slowly in the circle of Dacian's arm, turning her back on Wooten's nakedness. She raised her face to Dacian's and kissed him, long and lingering. Behind her, she heard Harriet snort in disapproval.

It should have been agonisingly sweet, but Judith's attention was too acutely focused behind her, fearing that any moment Harriet would shoot her in the back, and imagining Wooten wrestling, naked, with the candelabra.

She could feel Dacian's other hand reach to clasp her own, fumbling, while she waited for Wooten to act.

"Enough," grated Harriet. "Face your death now. I will shoot you regardless. Don't think I won't do it. I don't have much time before Georgina comes back."

Judith turned again, rotating slowly. She saw Wooten frozen, holding the candlestick like the Sword of Damocles above Harriet's head. Why was he waiting? Did he hesitate to commit the solecism of hitting a lady on the head with a candelabra? Or was he afraid the gun would fire regardless?

"I'm surprised at you, Harriet," said Dacian suddenly. "Is that nudity on your mantlepiece?"

A few things happened at once.

Wooten's face became horrified. Harriet blinked and almost turned to look. Before she could do so, Wooten heaved the candelabra back and swung. And at the same time, a bank of yew hedge suddenly appeared to Harriet's right. It was flush with red berries, and its sudden appearance was enough to startle her.

Even as this unfolded, Dacian twisted something on Judith's finger. She heard him mutter a single word.

Veho.

Her body began to implode in on itself. The last thing she saw was Wooten forcefully crashing the candelabra down on Harriet's head as she scowled at the yew hedge.

And the last thing Judith heard was the sound of a pistol shot.

Then the room vanished from view entirely, and she was wrenched through space into blackness.

In which a matron rides to the rescue

If only we would all speak the truth.
  - from *Lady Avely's Guide to Lies and Charms*

WHEN SHE OPENED HER EYES, Judith was in a hexagonal stone room with small square windows.

Her body felt as if it had been shaken like a pillowcase in the wind, then neatly refolded. She staggered backwards to lean against the comforting bulk of grey stone, and cursed aloud.

Damn Dacian! The devil take him for such a trick. What if Harriet's bullet had hit him? The world seemed to falter again, and Judith splayed her hands against the cool stone, trying to combat the wave of nausea that swept through her.

Unfortunately, she was not alone. Across the narrow, circular room, a man sat behind a small wooden desk, his mouth open in astonishment. The glow of lamplight showed that he was clad in the scarlet wool uniform of an infantryman, with its smart white crossbelts. His cocked hat held an ostrich feather, indicating a higher rank, perhaps captain. He had a sensitive, long face, with blue eyes, which currently showed white around the edges.

"Who are you?" Belatedly, he struggled to his feet. "Where did you come from, ma'am?"

Judith pushed herself off the wall and stood straight. She was still furious with Dacian, but chose to direct her ire at the man who now faced her.

"I am Lady Judith Avely," she said coldly, "and I have just come from Garvey House in Stokesford. Where am I? I must hasten back immediately."

She crossed to peer out of a narrow window, set deep into thick stone. The full moon showed the flat glimmer of sea outside, a low rumple of hills beyond.

Falmouth, of course. Curse the man.

"You are in Pendennis Castle." She turned back to see the soldier bow and lift a frowning gaze. "Which, I may add, is a military fort. Civilians - especially ladies - are not permitted entrance. I take it you used a Travel charm to arrive here? Where did you obtain such a thing?"

Judith pressed her lips together. She did not want to land Dacian in trouble, nor, for that matter, Lord Triskett. Still, she was glad that she was able to talk freely of the Musing to this man, as it would make things a far sight easier. "I used a very old Travel charm, made scores of years ago. Probably from a time before Pendennis Castle was reinforced." She could imagine the Triskett boys exploring the ruins, and making their own travel-ways there. The fort had only recently been rebuilt, to face the looming threat of Napoleon.

The captain came out from behind his desk. "I think I must see this charm, and determine its provenance, my lady. My name is Captain Drumpellier, by the way."

Carefully, Judith did not hide her hands behind her back, though Dacian's topaz ring was in full view, hanging loose on her left finger. She held the captain's gaze with a raised brow. Intriguingly, a note of untruth had sounded in his last claim.

"I must insist," he said. "This is a military fortification, and I cannot allow unauthorised entrance."

She decided on which card to play for now: a gesture of compliance. "The charm was a gift from the Triskett family."

"Ah." His eyes narrowed.

"We can discuss the matter later. Right now I must return to Garvey House. The Duke of Sargen is there and in danger. He may have been shot."

Her voice quivered on the last word, and it was not an act. A surge of fear jolted her anew as she remembered that final tableau and the sound of the gun firing. She hid her fingers in her skirts and stepped forward. "I must insist that you provide Travel for me to return to Stokesford at once, Captain Drumpellier."

"The Duke of Sargen?" the captain repeated. "The duke who was in exile?"

"Yes, his grace has returned. Please, you must help him." When Drumpellier simply stared, Judith hardened her tone. "He is a peer of the realm, Gifted in Impacting. If you save his life, I am certain you will not regret it."

"Ahem." Drumpellier broke out of his trance, and returned to his desk to rifle through a drawer. "Stokesford, you say? I might have a Travel charm to take us to Somerset, but you will owe me a complete explanation afterwards, do you understand? I will be using a valuable military resource to help you."

"Of course." Hope made Judith breathless. "Anything. Just take me back as soon as possible. He might be losing blood as we speak."

"Ah hah." The captain held up a compass, turning it so it gleamed in the lamplight. "This will take us to Bury Castle, if I remember correctly."

"Will someone see us?" She couldn't bear more explanations.

Captain Drumpellier chuckled. "Only the sheep." Then his expression sobered. "I am afraid that I must accompany you, my lady. This will require us to adopt a rather intimate embrace, so the charm may carry us both."

Judith gestured impatiently; she did not have time for the niceties of decorum. "Whatever is necessary." She was momentarily furious again, that Dacian hadn't done the same so he could come to Falmouth with her. Yet she knew he wouldn't abandon Robert to face Harriet's pistol alone. Nor, for the matter, leave his vampiri companion naked on the mantelpiece.

So it was that Judith arrived at Bury Castle with Captain Drumpellier's arms tightly clasped around her waist. As soon as the disorientating, wavering feeling subsided, she extricated herself. Blinking, she looked around.

She had expected another stone room in a fort, but instead she stood on an open hill, with grass under her feet. The grey ruins of ramparts fell away close by, and beyond that, a group of sheep huddled together, asleep under a heavy sky. Bury Castle, she now remembered, was an ancient hillfort that had long since fallen into the earth.

"How far to Garvey House?" Judith stared out over the empty fields, not knowing which way to start walking.

Captain Drumpellier straightened his coat, putting the compass away. "It is south-east from here, at least an hour's ride."

"An hour's ride! Where are we to find a horse?" Her heart sank. An hour was far too long. Dacian might die alone, before she reached his side. She dared not contemplate the possibility. Thank God Robert was with him; he would help.

The captain turned and began walking briskly. "We will commandeer horses. The benefits of a military jacket, you perceive."

She followed, her slippers rapidly soaking through with dew as they made their way downhill. They crossed a small stream, wetting her skirts, and soon she was icy cold. A village came into view, with thatched roofs, low stone walls, and windows glimmering with candlelight.

Captain Drumpellier knocked authoritatively on the first farmhouse door, and after a short discussion (and bestowal of coins) they were led out to a field which housed a large roan horse sleeping near a trough. A smaller white pony slept companionably next to it.

The farmer set about saddling both mounts, and as soon as the roan was bridled, Judith clambered onto the trough and grasped the pommel. Using the height of the stone ledge, she swung herself into the saddle without delay.

Captain Drumpellier cleared his throat. "I believe that is my horse, my lady."

"It is mine," she replied shortly. "And you will let me have it, or I will inform your superiors that your name is not really Drumpellier."

His eyes widened. Indecision momentarily twisted his features, then he stepped back, jaw tight. "God speed. Rest assured that I will be following close behind." He grimaced wryly at the white pony. "Or as close as I can manage."

Judith garnered directions to Stokesford from the farmer, then guided her roan out of the field and spurred it into a trot.

Following the narrow roads, she pushed the horse into a canter wherever she could, holding the reins loose and leaning forward in encouragement. Wind whipped up her skirts, and chapped her cheeks, but her pounding fear made it irrelevant.

She rode like her mobcap was on fire but it was a long hour before the familiar promenade of Stokesford's main street came into view. Passing the apothecary at a trot, she dug her heels in for the last stretch, her fingers now cold and clenched round the leather.

Leaves swirled around her as she thundered up the ash-lined

drive. Pulling the roan up, she swung herself off and marched to the front door. Thank God, it was unlocked. She pushed her way through, ready to run up the stairs. Then she heard laughter.

It was coming from the back of the house. The timbre of it was familiar and dear. Dacian.

Relief and hope made her heart thud harder. Judith ran, thrusting open the servant's door into a kitchen.

She pulled to a halt, panting. A domestic scene greeted her.

Selina Southcott sat on a stool, smiling, and nursing a tall cup of chocolate. A sliver molinet was set before her, next to what looked suspiciously like a bottle of brandy. Dacian leaned against the stove, also holding a steaming cup and an air of amusement. Marigold, tucked into Dacian's flannel handkerchief, sat against a pepper grinder. Wooten, the bat of the hour, was wrapped up in black silk and perched elegantly on an upside-down teacup, a thimble in his hand.

The heady fragrance of cocoa, spices, and brandy hung in the air, along with a faint metallic smell.

Everyone turned to stare at Judith. She tore off her mobcap, which was damp from the ride, and threw it aside. Then she marched up to Dacian and leaned both her hands against his hard chest.

"How dared you send me away!"

"Judith!" He put his cup down as he pulled her into his other arm. "How...?"

Caught against his chest, tears suddenly rose to her eyes. She brought her own arms to curl around him, and snuffled into his shirt. It was like being in a hot bath after a freezing day, and she sagged with relief against him.

"How dared you send me away!" she repeated. "You could have died!"

"Hardly. I threw myself to the side." Dacian tucked her head under his chin and squeezed her tight. Judith breathed in the smell of him: brandy, cocoa, and smoke. Then Dacian added, "Robert took the bullet for me."

"What?" Judith pulled away in shock. "Where?"

She looked round, and finally saw Robert. He lay on a bench, propped up by pillows and out of view of the door. His legs were covered with blankets, but Judith could see that one side was bulky with bandages. His face was pale, and his hands gripped a cup of chocolate as if it were keeping him upright. Next to him sat Georgina, her face pale and downcast.

Ignoring the girl, Judith flew to his side. "Dear boy, what happened?"

He smiled wanly. "The gun fired to the left, after Wooten's intervention."

Wooten huffed. "And it wouldn't have touched you, if you hadn't foolishly leapt forward like that, throwing yew hedges about."

Dacian came up beside her. "It was just a nick, thank God, but he's lost a bit of blood."

Judith put her hand on Robert's sturdy shoulder, filled with remorse. "I should never have let you come with us."

"I wouldn't have missed it for the world," said Robert staunchly. "Finally got to see Wooten in his true form." He winked at Wooten, who huffed again.

Robert, she realised, was slightly drunk. "How much brandy did you give him?" she asked Dacian with reproof.

"A bit. We used it to wash the wound too. Hurts like the devil, so we dosed him up before we poured it in."

"Oh, goodness," Judith turned back to Robert, tears starting to her eyes. "You poor boy. I'm so sorry."

Robert blinked up at her. "Nothing to fuss about."

Judith shook her head in reproof, then turned to Georgina, who had been listening, head down, hands clenched in her lap.

"And you?" she asked gently. "How much do you know now?"

Georgina looked up with red-rimmed eyes. "I heard it all. I didn't trust you all" - here she gulped - "so I crept back to listen, to save Grandmama if I could. I heard her terrible confessions."

Judith put her hand over the girl's cold ones. "I am so sorry."

Dacian coughed. "Georgina has helped Robert a little, with her Healing Gift."

"Thank you, Georgina," said Judith. "You may still come to Elinor's wedding, if you wish, though perhaps you would prefer to stay here with Mrs Froode for a while."

Georgina, looking rather wan and shocked, merely nodded.

Judith turned back to Robert. "We must fetch a doctor for you, and take you somewhere to recuperate." She dared not mention Cornwall again. "Perhaps back to Sargenet, if it suits you."

"Well," said Robert, "my injury means that I cannot gain useful employment with Lewis anymore." He paused. "Perhaps I shall have to paint landscapes in Cornwall instead."

Judith stared in delight. "Really?"

Robert shrugged. "For a bit. While I'm injured."

"That's wonderful!" Judith cleared her throat. "Well, not wonderful that you were shot, I mean. But I'm so pleased."

Robert grinned up at her, a bit more colour in his cheeks.

"This calls for more brandy." Dacian waved the bottle at Judith. "Want some, my dear?" His eyes were also rather bright. She suspected they had all been partaking liberally, in their triumphant denouement, without her.

"May I simply have chocolate?" She took a stool and perched next to Robert, anxiously surveying his inert form. "What have you done with Harriet?"

Dacian looked a bit shifty and didn't answer immediately. It was left to Marigold to explain. "The duke confined her with his power, then tied her up with the curtain ties. She is upstairs, straining like a sail on the wind, and cursing like a sailor too."

Judith gave Georgina an apologetic glance. "And Mrs Froode?"

"Also tied up." Dacian busied himself pouring out the dregs of chocolate. "She swears she was on our side, but I thought it better to be cautious. Honestly, I am not certain what we should do with the two of them. We cannot hand them over to the good Constable Carter." He handed Judith her cup with a wry expression.

She sipped it gratefully. "I think the solution might present itself sooner than you expect." After that mysterious pronouncement, she turned her attention to Mrs Selina Southcott, who had been quietly observing the discussion, her apple-green mobcap on the table beside her. "And you returned, Mrs Southcott."

Selina nodded, smiling. "I thought I might be of use."

"Hm." The long ride from Bury Castle had given Judith time to think about certain inflections in Selina's tale, and she examined her closely now. "You have something to confess, do you not?"

Selina's eyes widened. "I do?" Her fingers tightened on her cup.

Marigold tilted her head. "It seems as if she does."

Judith nodded. "Mrs Southcott, you are an Impactor, I believe. Furthermore, you were not entirely innocent in the matter of Lord Garvey's death."

A red stain spread through Selina's cheeks. Everyone stared as she guiltily looked down at her chocolate. Then she met Judith's eyes and coughed.

"You are right, Lady Avely. I am indeed Gifted in Impacting."

Judith nodded. "I remember the ease with which you moved the heavy pots in the glasshouse for Harriet, nine years ago. And you used your power again on the night of Garvey's death." She was sure of it, and she wanted Dacian to hear it.

Selina licked her lips. "Yes, it's true. When Lord Garvey had me cornered against the Apollo statue, I considered throwing him aside, even though it would reveal my power. I was uncertain what to do, undecided - then the duke appeared, angry and violent, and fluctuating with the same kind of power I recognised in myself. So I grasped the opportunity."

Dacian braced himself against the wooden table, staring at Selina. "You mean to say it was *your* Impact that threw Garvey aside?"

Selina shrugged. "Perhaps a bit of both. Certainly, I contributed."

Dacian eyed her in astonishment. "*Now* you tell me this?"

Selina had the grace to look ashamed. "I could not let it be known by anyone that I had a part to play in the whole sordid affair - that I was even present, let alone a cause of his lordship's death. My prospects would have vanished, and I would have been tarred with a black brush."

Judith spoke coldly. "The duke's prospects vanished, and he was tarred instead."

Dacian's shoulders sagged. "Nine years of exile, and meanwhile a slip of a girl helped me kill Garvey?"

Selina nibbled on her lip. "I am sorry, your grace."

Dacian sighed. "Well, to tell the truth I am glad of it. His death has weighed on my conscience. Or should I say," he amended, "it bothered me that I allowed my power to kill him, when I did not mean to do so."

Judith interposed. "I hope you are willing to testify on this matter too, Mrs Southcott, should the Musor Custos ever have questions about that night."

Selina gulped. "Yes, indeed." She stood and nervously fiddled with the large iron kettle, filling it with water.

"More brandy?" said Dacian, but Judith could hear a new lightness in his voice. "Come, Judith, let me top up your chocolate. We deserve something to ease our spirits, after these adventures."

She presented the cup to him, and he poured in some of the

rich, sweet alcohol. Judith took a look swallow, and the rush of it warmed her innards. "What a night it has been."

"Yes, how the hell did you find your way back here so quickly?" Dacian demanded, suddenly recalling that particular mystery. "I swear I sent you to Falmouth. Did you land there?"

"I did," said Judith severely. "In Pendennis Castle, where a useful captain assisted my return. He should be here shortly."

Dacian looked around as if to see a captain materialising from the walls. "Why did he not escort you to the door?"

"I took the faster horse," explained Judith, "from near Bury Castle, where we Travelled."

"Travelled?" Dacian's eyes narrowed. "Together?"

"Yes."

"With two charms, I hope."

"One."

Dacian put down the brandy with a clunk, and was at her side in an instant. "No one Travels with you except *me*, do you hear? Did he have the effrontery to put his arms around you?"

"If he did, you are well served," replied Judith. "You shouldn't have sent me to Falmouth in the first place."

"Have pity, Judith," he grumbled. "Better Falmouth than dead."

"Not if *you* were shot." She stood and grabbed his shirt, trying to shake him. It was like trying to shake a stone wall, and she let go again. She rather wanted to throw herself into his arms and declare her affections, but she was aware of their audience. It would be better to wait until they were alone before making declarations of love. She couldn't be certain what might follow. Hopefully some ravishment.

As she stepped away, Dacian grasped her arms instead, and shook her slightly. "What were *you* thinking, moving in front of me like that?" To her astonishment, she felt her own feet lift off the floor. "Don't ever try to take a bullet for me again!"

"You forget your strength, your grace," she said with reproof.

He put her down again with a grin. "I'll forget a lot more than that soon, you infuriating woman."

"That brandy seems to be potent stuff," remarked Marigold. "Maybe I should try some."

Wooten sniffed. "You don't need brandy to make a fool of yourself."

"Says he who exposed his equipment to the drawing room."

"I was being heroic!"

"Ha," muttered Marigold, obviously displeased that she had been relegated to a mere spectator instead of a participant, if there was nudity to be had.

"Where's Yvette?" Robert interposed. Hearing his question, Judith pointedly turned away from Dacian to look at Marigold.

Marigold shrugged. "I don't know. She vanished." Her tone was brittle.

"Probably in the belfry," said Wooten. "Reflecting on her sins. I *told* you not to trust her."

"That's not helpful, Wooten," said Judith. "Yvette was heroic too, you realise. She betrayed her blood companion to rescue Marigold."

"Only after entrapping me," snapped Marigold. "And it is not *rescuing* me to lock me in a clock!"

Judith sighed. "I quite sympathise. It's a bit like being sent to Falmouth."

"It is not!" said Dacian. "I would never lock you in a clock."

"See!" said Marigold. "Even the duke wouldn't do it."

Judith shook her head. "Yvette also told us what Harriet planned to do," she pointed out. "And she led me out of the maze. She has tried to make amends for her complicity."

Marigold folded her arms and looked mutinous. "Clearly she is ashamed enough to keep away."

Judith swept her eyes over the kitchen, wondering if a bat lurked in a high pot or behind a window. "Hm. I wonder."

At that moment, a clatter came from the front of the house. Judith extricated her hand from Dacian's and turned to face the kitchen door. "Quick, Marigold, hide! You too, Wooten!" Judith did not want the captain to find them in breach of the Edicts. There was too much else to explain.

Marigold hopped smartly off the table and vanished over the side, while Wooten sighed lugubriously and allowed himself to be swept into Dacian's pocket. Dacian raised a brow, and Judith merely nodded towards the kitchen door, where the sounds of booted heels rapidly approached.

Sure enough, the harassed countenance of Captain Drumpellier soon presented itself. His red uniform looked a bit more creased than it had an hour ago, and his sensitive brow was marked with a heavy line.

He stared round at the company, until his eyes found Dacian, whereupon he gave a deep bow. "Your grace! Is it indeed the Duke of Sargen?"

Dacian cast an amused glance at Judith, then pulled himself up. "It is indeed I." Then he recalled his grievance. "And I'll thank you not to haul this lady around the countryside; that honour belongs only to me." He folded his arms forbiddingly across his chest and glowered at the newcomer.

Captain Drumpellier seemed unaffected. He gave a grim smile and turned to Judith. "My apologies, my lady. I have since realised that you must be Lady Avely, the new mistress of Castle Lanyon. You will have your work cut out for you there, I'm afraid."

"Oh?" said Judith cautiously.

Drumpellier did not enlighten her; he merely turned back to Dacian. "And I must thank you for leading me to this reprobate." His expression hardened. "Your grace, you are under arrest for the misuse of your Gift, three times resulting in fatality. As a representative of the Musor Custos, I bind you for punishment."

Everyone stared, speechless. For a moment, the only sound in the kitchen was the faint bubbling from the kettle.

The captain lifted a single hand.

Pressure clapped through the room like soundless thunder. For a moment, Judith thought it was Dacian's Gift, then she realised he was raising his arms in defence.

The captain's own Impact lashed out and bound Dacian to stillness.

Dacian's black eyes snapped with anger, but his limbs were now contained by the very same power that he had tried to wield. His handsome face was fixed in a frown of repudiation, his shoulders stiff, while thwarted pressure thrummed in the air.

Captain Drumpellier strode over to the frozen figure of the duke, his own brow tense with effort. "I hereby take you into custody, for the verdict of the Custos." He wrapped a cursory arm around the ducal waist and nodded abruptly to Judith. "Lady Avely, good evening. I hope to see you at Castle Lanyon soon."

Judith drew air back into her lungs. "What? You can't just snatch him away like that! We have evidence!" She turned to Selina. "Tell him how you helped!"

Selina's eyes were wide as she stared at the duke's frozen form. She put her shoulders back and said quietly, "You must know that I contributed to the force that threw Lord Garvey."

Captain Drumpellier raised a brow. "Is that so? Weren't you a young woman at the time?"

"Yes."

"I'm afraid that I don't believe you."

Beside him, Dacian seemed to quiver, even as he was held still by Drumpellier's power.

"You must!" said Judith in outrage. "She is an Impactor, and she was defending herself!"

The captain frowned. "Regardless, the duke's power was the primary cause of death - and it was his third offence. He must be restrained. Or are you suggesting that I restrain you as well, ma'am?" he said to Selina.

Selina's eyes lowered, and there was a long pause. Then she folded her hands and shook her head slowly. Judith's mouth fell open in anger.

Captain Drumpellier gave a small, sharp bow, and pulled a pocket watch out with his other hand. "Good evening," he said. And then, "*Veho*."

"No!" shouted Judith, but it was too late.

Dacian and Drumpellier dissolved before her eyes, even as Dacian's gaze locked with hers in a flash of warning. The space that held him soon showed nothing but an empty stone wall.

"No!" she screamed again, then turned with fury on Selina. "How dare you? He could be stripped of his power, and his memory! You should have pressed the matter!"

Yet it had been Judith who had brought the Musor Custos right to him.

"You think I should run the same risk?" Selina leaned shakily against the stove. "I have three children, Lady Avely! I cannot afford that sort of punishment!"

Judith ground her teeth together, tears rising in her eyes. "He cannot be taken from me. Not now."

Marigold's head popped out from under the table. "We will go after him, and rescue him. Wooten, too, I suppose - he was hiding in the duke's pocket."

"That's a good point," said Robert, from his bench, "Wooten might help him. Have they Travelled back to Pendennis Castle, do you think?"

"I don't know!" Judith's mind was blank with shock. "I suppose it is possible. That was where I found the captain, in a stone room in a tower. It must be a base for the Custos as well as the army." That explained why his name had rung falsely, if he were there under two different guises.

"Well, then," said Marigold. "We follow them. The Custos must surely take evidence before they mete out punishment."

Robert nodded. "We'll get you into the fort, Judith, even if it takes another Illusion to do it. Or," he added, "you could simply use the duke's ring again?"

Judith clutched at her pocket, where she had stowed the topaz ring to keep it safe. Thankfully, she felt the hard circle of it under the fabric. Did she dare Travel after the duke, into the den of the Musor Custos?

Of course she did.

She only hoped that she wouldn't be too late.

To be continued!

in *Lady Avely's Guide to Guile and Peril*

(releasing 2025)

Note from Rosalie

Dear readers,

Thank you so much for continuing the Matronly Misadventures with me. *Lady Avely's Guide to Guile and Peril* will be out in 2025, and yes, I, too, am worried that Judith will not make it to Elinor's wedding on time.

As always, reviews are very much appreciated, and anyone who takes the time to drop a line is a doing their good deed for the week!

If you haven't yet read the Lady Diviner series, featuring Judith's children, now is an ideal time to do so, as *Lady Avely's Guide to Guile and Peril* contains spoilers for books later in that series.

To keep up with my new releases and monthly book gossip, simply join my mailing list at rosalieoaks.com/newsletter and nab your free e-book, *A Pendant for Trouble*.

Much love to my readers. I am so grateful that you take the time to read my books, and I hope you find some comfort and joy in them.

Happy reading,
Rosalie

Thank you to Patrons and Others

So much gratitude to my Patrons who supported me while I wrote this book! You are the best.

Annelise Bauer
Tania Clucas
Julie Margaret Collins
Anna Fridlund
Myra Galland
Ginny Harris
Megan Hodge
Justin Kennedy
Shane Kennedy
Adriana Kosmo
Susan Mason
Charleen McCready
Cortney McInerney
Tamara Ng
Kristin Rafe
Eva Schiffer
Kimberly Shore
Karen Slater
Sarah Swarbrick
Fiona Tewson
Taylor Trenchard
Mary Lee Vacca
Ginny Williams

Much thanks also to my beta readers who helped shape the final manuscript, as well as catching many a typo and inconsistency; my continuity reader, Allen Schroeter, for his keen eye; and my proofreaders, Xenia Tashlitsky and Carmen Rutter-Hedley, who caught the remaining errors. You all helped to ensure this book conducts itself with decent literary propriety!

With love,
Rosalie

Rosalie's Private Tea Parlour

If you'd like to be part of the lovely community that supports my authorly endeavours, please pay a visit to my Private Tea Parlour (otherwise known as Patreon), where you may read my books before anyone else, as well as peruse deleted scenes, short stories, book club posts, and much more.

You even get to read Dacian's letter that he wrote to Judith from Spain!

My wonderful Patrons also gain a secret key to the Lamplighters' Guild Discord community, filled with delightful bookish folk and conversations.

I'd be thrilled to have your support. Pop along to patreon. com/rosalieoaks to have a peep.

Happy tea drinking,

Rosalie

The Lady Jewel Diviner

Diamonds, Death, and Devonshire tea... in a magical Regency England

Miss Elinor Avely's proper upbringing cannot prepare her for the tiny, spinster vampire who crashes into her sitting room and demands to be fed with a sheep.

Elinor already has enough troubles without having to catch ruminants.

First, her gift for divining jewels has landed her in scandal and exiled her from London society.

Second, a nobleman of dubious repute has asked her to find a cache of smuggled jewels, hidden somewhere along the Devon coastline.

Last – and worst – Elinor has been invited to cream tea at the local manor. And while the autocratic and magnificent Earl of Beresford might be there (and perhaps the jewels themselves too), Beresford is the last person Elinor wants to meet over cream tea.

When a dead body is discovered along the cliffs, of course, such delicate considerations become secondary. Fortunately, Elinor now has a small vampiric chaperone – even if said spinster has a habit of appearing stark naked – and together they are ready to risk the hard questions.

Where are the jewels hidden? Who killed the smuggler? And just when *is* the cream tea being served?

The Lady Jewel Diviner is the first book in a cosy mystery series set in Regency England, with generous servings of magic, manners, and romance.

About the Author

Rosalie Oaks writes novels set in a magical Regency England full of manners, mystery, and soothing beverages. As a child, she loved conducting home-made theatre productions with her three younger brothers. Now she directs her characters instead, but like her brothers, they don't always do what she says.

While writing, Rosalie consumes vast quantities of tea and chocolate, and steadfastly ignores the housework.

Further intimate details, such as her favourite books and recipes, can be found in her Private Tea Parlour on Patreon.

Books by Rosalie Oaks

Lady Diviner

A Pendant for Trouble (prequel novella)

The Lady Jewel Diviner (Book 1)

The Moria Pearls (Book 2)

The Sapphire Library (Book 3)

The Golden Flute (Book 4)

The Selkie Scandal (an internovella)

Matronly Misadventures

Lady Avely's Guide to Truth and Magic (Book 1)

Lady Avely's Guide to Lies and Charms (Book 2)

Lady Avely's Guide to Guile and Peril (Book 3) (on pre-order)

rosalieoaks.com